heretic

j.f.r. coates

j.f.r. coates

Text copyright 2021

Cover by Ilya Zyor

www.artstation.com/ilyar

Heretic

978-1-922061-75-1

Print Version

J.F.R. Coates

Queensland, Australia

acknowledgements

I would like to thank my husband Jamie for supporting me while I wrote this book (and Resistance). Without his support, these two books would have taken much longer to complete.

As always, I must also thank my family. When growing up, my parents always encouraged me to keep reading. That love of books has fuelled my desire to create my own stories for many years now.

I must also thank those who support me on Patreon. Your financial support has been most appreciated. Thank you for being there with me throughout this entire process.

And I must also thank you all – my readers. For every review and comment, thank you. They do more to help me than you could ever imagine. I hope you enjoy the conclusion to Rhys's story.

For starats everywhere.

In Essie's name.

We stand up and fight for what we believe in.

J.F.R. Coates

about the author

J.F.R. Coates was born and raised in picturesque Somerset, England, but she moved out to Brisbane, Australia as a teenager. She grew up reading from a young age, starting with Enid Blyton's *The Famous Five* and *Secret Seven*, before finding her calling with J.R.R. Tolkien's *The Hobbit*. Speculative Fiction has gripped her ever since, and now she calls amongst her favourite authors Maggie Furey, Phillip Pullman, and Robin Hobb.

She still lives in Brisbane, where she lives with her husband and – as seems ubiquitous for authors – her two cats.

You can follow her on Bluesky at @jfrcoates.bsky.social, or Facebook at /jfrcoates.

She also has a Patreon, which allows for sneak-previews of what's to come, as well as additional stories that fit in around her novels. All support is always gratefully received. https://www.patreon.com/jfrcoates

J.F.R. Coates

chapter one

The shuttle was quiet. Forty people had boarded at Shanghai, all travelling on to Delhi, but no one was interested in conversation. Thirty-eight humans and two starats sat quietly, with only the occasional rumble of the shuttle engines and click of the toilet door breaking the silence. Some of the passengers read books or watched a video to pass the time, though the flight was not a very long one.

One human had not brought anything to entertain herself during the flight. She had a window seat though, giving her the opportunity to stare down at Terra as the Chinese mountains passed by below. Occasionally, she glanced down to her right hand, where an unfamiliar ring adorned her finger. She smiled. They had not yet decided what surname to keep. She might become Stephanie Griffiths, or he could become Rhys MacArthur.

Stephanie leaned her head against the vibrating wall of the shuttle. She closed her eyes for a moment. Rhys had been so nervous when he had gotten down on his knee for her, but she had said yes without any hesitation. They hadn't had much chance to make any arrangements yet, as her visit in Shanghai had only been a short one. She hadn't even had the opportunity to tell her family. Her parents had certainly welcomed Rhys into the MacArthur clan, especially as Rhys had been deprived of one of his own for several years now. She couldn't wait to see their reaction to the new ring on her finger.

"That's beautiful."

Stephanie smiled at the compliment. The woman sat in the seat next to her had been silent for the whole flight so far, but she had seemingly seen the ring on her finger.

Stephanie opened her eyes and turned to face the woman, but she wasn't there. The seat was empty. She looked up sharply, catching sight of the woman as she made her way into the toilets at the back of the shuttle.

"I'm sorry, I shouldn't have spoken."

The same voice again. Stephanie looked across the row of three seats on her side of the aisle. The aisle seat was taken by a starat, who stared down at its lap.

Stephanie narrowed her eyes and recoiled back in her seat. She turned her head to look forward. Had it really been the starat who had spoken? Why had it spoken to her? How had it? The creature shouldn't have known about what concepts like beauty were. It had a simple mind with simple thoughts, capable of following orders and little else.

The starat didn't say another word. The silent woman who had been sat between them didn't return back to the same seat, leaving a vacant space.

Stephanie's breath quickened. Her eyes kept sliding back across to the starat, despite her best attempts to keep looking forward. Something felt amiss. Her mind raced as thoughts seemed to break through a barrier she had not known to have existed. She slowly looked back across to the starat.

"You think it looks nice?"

The starat squeaked in surprise. It – she – looked over to Stephanie. Her brown eyes were wide as she looked over to the human. Her ears flicked back as she nodded quickly. "I do, yes."

The silence, previously so comfortable, felt slightly awkward. Stephanie tried not to keep looking towards the starat, but something about her seemed odd. There was a light in her eyes, a brightness of intelligence Stephanie had never seen in a starat. She had never really looked before.

"What's your name?" Stephanie asked, the question escaping her mouth before she had chance to consider it.

The starat blinked. "Rina. My name is Rina."

Stephanie held her hand out, reaching across the empty seat between them. "My name is Stephanie."

Rina took hold of Stephanie's hand. She stared up at the human. A smile slowly broke across her furred face. "You've had an understanding."

Stephanie paused. She withdrew her hand and looked down at the starat, who stared at her with earnest, excited eyes. She tried to process what had happened in her thoughts, and how her perception of the starat had changed so drastically. One moment, she had been a creature. Now, she was a person. Stephanie could think of no better word to describe the change. An understanding. She nodded her head. "I have."

"It happens to humans sometimes," Rina said quietly. She looked around the shuttle. No one else appeared to pay any attention to her, or the conversation they were having.

"Why? How?" So many other questions bubbled up in Stephanie's mind, but those seemed the most important.

"I don't know," Rina replied. She shook her head slowly. "No one knows how it happens, but sometimes it just does."

"And you're all like, well, you?" Stephanie asked, gesturing her hand weakly towards the starat.

Rina smiled sadly. "We are. Every last one of us. There are some humans who know and still hate us for it, but most who have an understanding realise how bad we're treated," the starat said. Her voice trembled and she looked down at her clasped hands in her lap. "And then there are some of us who are more than that."

"What do you mean?" Stephanie asked.

Rina opened her mouth to answer, but she was distracted by quick movement in the aisle. The second starat on board the shuttle hurried over to them. Rina slid across to the middle seat in the row to allow the newcomer to take a seat. His eyes blazed with panic and terror.

"Easy, Arnav. She's had an understanding," Rina said quietly, placing her hand on the other starat's wrist.

Arnav pulled back and shook his head. "They've found us," he said, his voice strained and harsh.

Rina's ears pulled back, falling almost flat against her head. "Are you sure?"

Arnav nodded. He said nothing else. He looked down at the floor and trembled.

"What's going on?" Stephanie asked. She looked between the two starats, but neither of them seemed to be able to meet her eye.

Rina's shoulders trembled. When she finally looked up again, there were tears flowing from her eyes. "I'm so sorry," she whispered. "We're all dead. We're going to die."

Stephanie gripped hold of the armrest. She had no answer to that. What could she say to such a declaration? She felt her face pale.

Arnav looked up to her. His fur was still dry, but he looked close to crying too. "The Vatican are chasing us. We thought we could get away, but they've tracked us down."

"I won't let them take you," Stephanie said quickly. "I'm with the military. I have authority. As soon as we land in Delhi, I'll do... I'll do something. We have a few hours to think of something to keep you safe."

Arnav laughed bitterly. "We're not going to be landing. When it comes to starats like us, they don't allow survivors. They certainly won't allow witnesses. They're going to shoot us down from the sky."

"How do you know that?" Stephanie asked.

Arnav held a hand to his furred forehead. "I know things before they happen. Only by a few minutes, but that's enough for the Vatican to want me dead. There are others like us. We have abilities we can't explain. We keep them quiet, but sometimes the church learns about us, and that's a death sentence."

"I'm so sorry," Rina whispered again. She reached out with trembling hands, holding onto Stephanie and Arnav together. "Because of us, everyone here is going to die."

"We should tell them," Stephanie said, starting to rise to her feet.

Arnav jumped across to pull her and Rina down.

The shuttle exploded in a deafening crash. Metal twisted and tore as heat singed over Stephanie's body. She was thrown from her seat, ripped out of the shuttle as it fragmented around her. In her hands, she managed to keep hold of the two starats.

She began to fall. Sky and ground alternated, over and over and over again.

A pitch black sky dotted with faint stars stretched to infinity above. The ground below was icy and cold; white and pale pink. They alternated and spun, gleaming on the inside of a visor.

The shuttle, miraculously intact once again, shone brightly in the sky. The engines fired up. Standing on the open access hatch was a lone albino starat, whose eyes blazed with power and fury.

A single starat fell from the sky, descending towards the surface of Pluto. Bracing himself for impact, Rhys curled himself up into a tight ball. He struck the ground hard, but the rock was softer than it should have been. Darkness gripped fingers of ice into his mind. Memory and dream became one and the same.

***

The starat woke with a jolt.

Rhys's eyes fluttered open. He jerked upright and screamed in pain as his withered arms protested the sudden movement. He wasn't on the shuttle, but nor was he left lying on the surface of Pluto. Instead, he lay on a mattress in a room that looked a cross between a ward and a dormitory. A dozen other beds filled the room he found himself in. There was no one else present.

Aches and pains covered almost every inch of his broken and battered body. He could barely move without triggering another burst of pain, but the starat forced himself to swing his legs over the side of the bed. He had been stripped naked sometime since his fall from the shuttle, but he couldn't see any clothes around him.

Rhys struggled to bring his mind up to date with everything. He knew he had been pushed from the shuttle by Snow. That much was obvious. She, and Amy included, planned to use the terrifying weapon Rhys had uncovered in the labs of Pluto. He had protested that, and Snow had pushed him out of the shuttle, presumably with the intent of killing him. That had clearly not worked, though Rhys was in enough pain that death perhaps couldn't yet be ruled out.

And then there was the dream. He had dreamed about the crash that had claimed Stephanie's life before, but never like that. Never had it seemed so clear to his mind, and there had certainly never been a starat there before. Unlike most dreams, everything seemed crisp and clear to his memory, even as he woke up.

Slowly, Rhys placed his feet on the ground. He hissed in displeasure as spikes of pain ran up his legs, and his hands burned in agony as he braced them against the mattress to push himself upright. He tottered on his feet as he struggled to find his balance. He felt like he had reverted to those first few days of being in this starat body, before he had understood how to balance and walk on his new legs.

Gritting his teeth to fight back the pain, Rhys stumbled forwards, towards a door at the far end of the ward-like room. He'd seen enough of medical bays over the past few months. He didn't want to be around any others.

"Hello?" he called out, hating how his voice trembled in pain.

The door at the far end of the room opened and a starat with tawny fur and dark spots stepped through. The newcomer's fur looked luxuriously soft and thick, especially around his pointed ears.

Rhys's ears flicked. He felt a little shame at his nudity, but he made no effort to hide himself. His body hurt too much to even worry about moving his hands quickly. He looked towards the other starat, who seemed vaguely familiar. Something nagged at the back of his mind, sure that he had seen this starat before.

The starat slowly approached Rhys. His hands were raised. "You shouldn't be standing up yet. Please, get back into bed."

Rhys swayed on his aching feet. He didn't want to lie down again, but nor did he think he could remain upright for much longer. He reluctantly obeyed the starat's request and gently eased himself back onto the bed, sitting on the edge of the mattress with his tail draped over his lap to preserve a little modesty. "Who are you? Where am I?"

The starat perched on the edge of the bed next to Rhys. "This is the starat quarters in the Tombaugh Station on Pluto. I believe you fell from a shuttle as it escaped. I found you on the surface and brought you in."

Rhys nodded slowly. His thoughts gradually caught up with the raid he had led. "I was, yeah. They drained the air."

"Captain Herschel ordered the air drain to deal with the dragon. Once that was recaptured and the raiding force was rebuffed, air was restored. I was lucky that I'd taken refuge in the airlocks," the starat explained. His bright green eyes glanced up, meeting Rhys's gaze. "You were one of the soldiers in the raid?"

Rhys gasped. He knew where he had seen the starat before. "You were who I spoke to in one of the labs. I told you to run. Your companions? Were they safe too?"

The starat flicked an ear. "That was you? Interesting," he said slowly. His piercing gaze dropped away again. "We all made it through alive. No starats were hurt."

Rhys leaned back against the headrest of the bed. He struggled to get comfortable, with his legs and arms aching no matter what position he tried to rest them in. He could barely move his hands without precipitating a spike of pain through his withered muscles. "My name is Captain Rhys Griffiths, formerly of Terra, now of Centaura. I was ordered to lead a raid against Pluto to acquire information. I was… I fell from the shuttle as we were leaving."

The other starat looked over Rhys's body. "Looks like you've been through some shit, Rhys Griffiths. Not all of those injuries were sustained from the fall," he said, before holding a hand to his chest. "But I have been rude and not introduced myself. My name is Elijah. I have no home other than Pluto, unless you count my time imprisoned on Charon."

"You were on Charon?" Rhys asked in surprise. He had a vague memory of being told a starat prisoner had escaped during the raid on the small moon, though he himself had never seen the escapee. He looked over Elijah in surprise. Had he been the escaped prisoner?

Before Rhys could question Elijah on that, the other starat had already asked a question of his own. "What caused those injuries to your hands? The symptoms remind me of Devil's Blood."

Rhys flicked his ears in surprise. He curled his tail, swishing the tip gently. "I think that was what it was called. I was tortured by a cardinal, but I was rescued." He stared down at his withered and damaged arms; little more than bone and sinew now. His fur had been seared away in places, leaving just burned and blistered flesh. "It's not just that, though. I… I don't think you would be able to understand."

Elijah smirked. "Try me." He tapped a finger against his head. "There's a lot more up here than you might realise."

Rhys sighed softly as he tried to work out how to best explain subspace and what it could do. He resisted the urge to rest his hands over his muzzle, instead keeping his arms still and to his sides. "I can manipulate space and reality using subspace," he said slowly, keeping an eye on Elijah's reactions. The other starat didn't even blink. "Unfortunately, if I'm not careful, just trying to move something can cause a lot of pain."

"Sounds like what Kalisha can do."

Rhys tilted his head to the side. He leaned forward slightly. "You know someone else who can do that?"

"It is a fascinating skill. Quite beyond anything I can do, but my talents lie elsewhere," Elijah said with a nod. "I don't think you should walk around yet, but I am sure Kalisha would like to meet you later. She will be finished with work in a couple of hours. That give you plenty of time to rest."

Rhys slumped back against the headboard behind him. He knew what was being expected of him: that he was to lie back and do nothing. He hated the idea, but he knew he didn't have much choice. "Do you have anything to deal with the pain, at least?"

Elijah bowed his head. "I can find something for you, yes. We steal enough from the humans to have enough to go around."

Rhys thumped his tail against the bed. "I was on Centaura for barely a month, and already I'd been able to forget what starats here had to go through."

"You haven't been a starat long. You were never used to our ways," Elijah said with a shrug. He slipped off the bed and started to rummage through a set of drawers between the beds opposite.

Rhys narrowed his eyes and flicked his ear in confusion. "How do you know that?" he asked, surprised that Elijah had known about his human life.

Elijah glanced back and smirked. He tapped one finger against the side of his head. "I remember everything I learn. A couple of months ago, I got my hands on some classified documents mentioning Captain Rhys Griffiths, the starat who had once been a human. Teleporter accident, I deduced, though the report didn't actually state what had happened. I didn't believe it at first, but I thought about it for a couple of days and worked out how it would be possible."

"You worked it out?" Rhys yelped. He tried to stand up again, but quickly desisted as pain lanced through his arms and legs. "How? Is it reversible?"

Elijah straightened his back and looked right at Rhys. "Reversible? No."

Rhys twitched the tip of his tail. He wasn't sure if he would have wanted to reverse his transformation were it possible. His body was broken and painful, but he still didn't know if he wanted to be human again. He didn't know if he wanted to go back.

The other starat offered a couple of small white pills for Rhys to take. The miniscule weight of the tablets burned onto Rhys's palm as he struggled to move his arm up to his muzzle. Swallowing the tablets was easy enough, but the movement from his arms still ached even as he lowered his hands back down to his side. His muscles burned, and his skin felt taut and stretched with every movement, almost like it would tear were he not careful. He could only hope that the small pills would provide some relief to the constant pain.

Rhys took a deep breath. He needed to understand the situation he found himself in. He knew he had been left for dead by Snow, and no matter how far away she was now, there was little he could do to catch up to her. He needed to focus on what was happening in the Sol System. The albino starat planned to turn the Vatican's subspace weapons against Terra. For all the hatred he now harboured towards the humans of Terra, he couldn't allow them all to be killed in such away. The Terran starats, too, would be caught up in the assault, with no chance to protect themselves.

Whatever Amy and Snow had planned, Rhys knew he needed to stop it. Unfortunately for him, he was stuck on Pluto without any allies to help him. His ears flicked. Except for one.

"I need to speak to Captain Herschel," Rhys said.

Elijah wrinkled his muzzle in distaste. "You really have forgotten what it's like to be here. Why would he speak to you? We're just starats to James."

Rhys paused. He wasn't sure how much he wanted to tell Elijah about the truth of the raid on Pluto. He twitched his muzzle, but before he could think of what to say, the door at the far end of the room opened. Three starats curiously poked their heads inside the room; one male and two female. Rhys thought they might have been the other three of the starats he had briefly come across in the middle of the raid. Two had dark fur, almost black. The third, one of the two females, had much lighter fur with a red tint.

Elijah flicked his ears in surprise. "I didn't think you were finished for a few more hours."

The darker furred of the female starats shrugged her shoulders. "James can get fucked. He's been really odd the last few days," she said. Her eyes moved towards Rhys, who quickly pulled the bedsheets up over his lap. "Besides, our surface walker is awake, and he's much more interesting than anything James has to offer."

"You'll like him, Kalisha. He can do what you can do," Elijah said, his eyes flicking towards the female starat who had not spoken.

The red-tinted starat took a step back and blinked. "You can? That's very interesting indeed," she said in a soft whisper. Her voice reminded Rhys of Snow's gentle, ephemeral voice. "Perhaps we can die together when the Vatican learns of us."

"Optimistic as always," the other female starat said, slapping her companion gently on the back. "I'm Alison and this is Mikkel. Pleasure to make your acquaintance."

Rhys kept his eyes on Kalisha, feeling a little unnerved by her proclamation. "I'm Rhys. Rhys Griffiths."

While his name had meant something to Elijah, none of the other three reacted to his introduction. They didn't remember his name from the incident on Ceres. Rhys was almost glad of that. Perhaps he could feel like a true starat amongst them, without the guilt of his human past feeling like a weight around his neck.

Kalisha stepped forward, moving away from her two companions. She approached Rhys's bed. "Perhaps you might be willing to show me some of your talents," she said. She held one hand out, and Rhys noticed then that some of her fur appeared singed around the fingers. Black streaks ran up her wrists. He couldn't smell oil or grime on her.

"I have not had much training in them," Rhys admitted, lowering his eyes away from Kalisha's fierce gaze.

"And I have had no training at all," the russet starat replied. She grinned, showing off every last one of her teeth. "So, what are you waiting for?"

Rhys's hands trembled as he lifted them up, unable to stop the pained shaking. "Pain stops me," he whispered hoarsely. "I overextended myself, and I'm hurting because of it. I... did you see a broken gun turret after the raid?"

"Yeah. It was twisted and partially melted," Mikkel said in awe. The dark-furred starat's green eyes gleamed. "I've never seen anything like it."

Rhys lightly touched a hand to his chest. "That was me. Subspace makes me feel powerful when I'm using those abilities, but there is a heavy price to pay."

Kalisha's muzzle twitched into a smirk. "Then learn not to give in to that temptation," she said. Her right hand extended out, and with the familiar scent of cinnamon, a shirt materialised in her hand. She held the clothing out to Rhys. "Learn to do the small things without penalty, and slowly your power will grow."

"Still creeps me out," Alison added. She wrung her hands and turned slightly to the side. She stuck the tip of her tongue out.

Kalisha turned to look at the other starat. "As it should," she warned. She dropped the shirt on Rhys's bed when he didn't take hold of it. She held her left wrist in her right hand. "These are abilities that will get us killed if the wrong people know about it."

Rhys bowed his head. "There are so many dangers to starats here, but there's more coming. I need to speak to Captain Herschel so I can get a warning sent out to Terra."

Mikkel and Alison both scoffed in laughter.

"Why would James listen to you? He's a creep," Kalisha said. She narrowed her gold-flecked eyes towards Rhys, and her tail swished behind her.

Rhys looked around the small group of starats. He didn't know how to explain the situation, but then he remembered one important detail that he had almost forgotten. The human he knew as General Carson had once been a starat in the Pluto station. "Were any of you here with a starat called Samantha?"

Elijah and Kalisha both shook their heads right away, but the other two nodded eagerly.

"Yes," Mikkel said brightly. His smile then faded. "But she disappeared. We never knew what happened to her. James was acting weirdly then as well, but no one else seemed to be odd."

Rhys's eyes flicked towards Elijah. He then turned back to the other three. "I was once human, but a teleporter accident robbed me of that. The same thing happened to Samantha. She was robbed of her body and given a new one." He paused and looked around the group of starats. Kalisha's eyes flicked to Elijah, who nodded once. "While I became a clone of a starat called Twitch, Samantha became a human: Captain Herschel."

"Wait, she became… she became him?" Alison said, clapping her hands to her mouth.

"She escaped and fled to Centaura. She is now he. General Sam Carson. He organised a raid here, which I led. Our goal was to capture Captain Herschel and leave a decoy in his place," Rhys explained. "General Carson. Samantha. That's why you've noticed Captain Herschel has been acting odd today, because he's no longer here. Samantha is."

A stunned silence followed Rhys's words. Mikkel and Alison both slumped down onto empty beds. Only Kalisha remained standing.

"So, when you say you want to speak to Captain Herschel…" the russet-furred starat said uncertainly.

"I really want to talk to General Carson. Sam. Samantha," Rhys said, struggling to get his thoughts right. He had thought of the general so much as the human Sam Carson, that he still struggled to properly identify him as the female starat he had once been, long before they had first met.

The four other starats all looked towards each other. A brief, silent conversation seemed to pass between them, told only through body gesture and tail flicks. At the end of it all, Elijah nodded his head. "I'll take you."

Rhys grinned and almost slipped out of the bed. A jolt of pain stopped him, and he was glad it did. A moment later he remembered that he still wore nothing beneath the bundled bedsheets. "Uh. Do you have anything for me to wear?"

Mikkel gave Rhys a thumbs up. "You look about my size. I've got something for you. Just hang on a moment."

***

Mikkel's clothes fit perfectly, though he needed some help from Elijah to actually wear them. He didn't have enough movement in his arms to dress himself. Getting his hands through the sleeves of the borrowed shirt proved to be agonising. The painkillers he had been given didn't seem to be doing too much to help ease the pain in his body.

Only Elijah went with Rhys. The other three remained behind, not wanting to get dragged into any orders from the humans they might come across. They were curious to learn more about Samantha, but they were willing to wait for their former companion to come back to them.

The corridors of the space port looked eerily familiar to Rhys. He had walked these corridors before, but then he had carried a rifle in his hands and was a hostile force intent on killing the enemy defenders. Now he walked freely, though nervously. He could still see small amounts of debris that had not been cleaned up, and bullet holes in the walls where shots had been missed.

Hardly any humans walked through the station. Those who did ignored Rhys and Elijah entirely. Rhys wondered how many of the humans he passed had been defending the port; how many Rhys had opened fire on. He curled his tail as he thought about it. Rarely before had he been forced to see an enemy after combat. He had never needed to put a face to the anonymous soldiers in battle.

Elijah walked slowly. He never commented about Rhys's injuries, and while he never offered support, Rhys got the feeling that he was constantly braced to take Rhys's weight should he fall. Rhys never needed that help, for which he was glad. Though his feet ached and his knees protested, he was able to stay upright. He felt weary, but he knew he couldn't sit and rest. There was too much to do; too many dangers lurking over the horizon that needed to be addressed.

Terra had to be warned of the threat coming from Amy and Snow.

A cold shiver passed down Rhys's spine. A chilling thought had suddenly come to his mind. He had been acting under the assumption that General Carson would be able to help him, but Rhys had no assurances that the general wasn't on Amy and Snow's side. Carson had certainly been one of the leading figures in coming up with the Pluto raid. Had he been duped by Amy too, or had he been in on her plans?

That potentially changed everything. Rhys knew he would need to be careful. Any wrong words and he would be entirely at General Carson's mercy. In the Sol System, the human would be able to act however he wanted towards a starat without raising any eyebrows.

Suddenly wondering whether he was walking right into danger, Rhys kept his silence and followed Elijah. One way or another, he was going to learn Carson's motives.

chapter two

Captain Herschel had a small office tucked away close to the centre of the Tombaugh Station, near the laboratories that studied the captive dragon. The office was unoccupied when Elijah cautiously opened the door. A desk filled most of the room, with a few chairs scattered untidily in front of it.

Rhys went to take a seat, but Elijah's hand hooked beneath his shoulder, pulling him back up to his feet. He hissed in pain and tried to break free from the other starat's touch.

"I'm sorry," Elijah said, loosening his grip. "You don't want to sit down."

"Why? Carson won't care," Rhys replied.

"The people he might be with will care," Elijah said simply.

Rhys bowed his head. His feet hurt and he swayed as he tried to find his balance, but he didn't try to sit down again. He had been spoiled on Centaura. Even on Ceres, he had still been able to cling to his privilege of rank long enough not to truly experience starat life in the empire. This was his first true realisation of what such a life might be like. He could not allow himself to get sucked down into that.

"How long do you think he'll be?" Rhys asked quietly. He didn't look up.

Elijah poked his head back outside into the corridor. "He's almost always here," the starat said uncertainly. His tail flicked. He glanced back to Rhys and smiled. "But he's not Herschel, is he? Of course he's going to act a little differently."

"Does that make things difficult?" Rhys asked.

"Just means we might have to go on a walk to find him," Elijah said brightly, before his smile faded a little. He glanced down to Rhys's legs for a moment. "Unless you have an idea where he might be? What's his mission here?"

Rhys flicked his ears. "Preventing development of a subspace weapon. I think," he said, a little of his uncertainty and fear creeping into his voice. Was Carson here to prevent that development, or to further it?

Elijah's expression darkened. "Ah, that. In the labs then. Come on, this way."

"You know about the weapon?" Rhys asked. He winced in pain as he limped after Elijah, whose pace had quickened slightly as they moved away from the small office again.

Elijah gestured for Rhys to be quiet. "I'll tell you what we know later, alright?" he asked, looking back and holding his hand out to offer Rhys some physical support. "The four of us have been doing what we can."

Rhys bit down on the immediate reply. He glanced nervously around, expecting to see some approaching humans, but the two starats were alone. He tucked his tail in close between his legs anyway, unsure if Elijah was afraid of being overheard.

Rhys recognised the laboratories. One of the doors had been recently repaired, fixing the damage he had caused when he had released the dragon. To Rhys's disconcertion, Elijah opened the repaired door and stepped inside the lab. Rhys followed just behind him, though his heart skipped a beat at the familiar scent of the creature.

The dragon was back in its cage, though the powerful six-limbed creature was currently sleeping. Its eyes were closed as it lay on its side, limbs occasionally twitching. Rhys eyed the dragon warily, not yet convinced that the creature really was asleep. He could still feel the ache in his ribs from where the powerful tail had struck him.

"Psst, here," Elijah whispered, drawing Rhys's attention away from the dragon.

Three humans were also in the room, though none of them had even looked in the direction of the starats. Two of the humans, Rhys didn't recognise. Neither were military, so Rhys had to assume they were scientists or researchers at the Tombaugh Station. The third, however, Rhys did know. He knew the man as General Carson, but to everyone else present, he would be Captain Herschel. He looked strange without his thick, bushy beard.

After a touch from Elijah, Rhys stayed back, keeping well away from the three talking humans. He couldn't help but overhear.

"…respiratory failure, but with heavy sedation, it should survive," one of the scientists was saying. Coming in mid-conversation, Rhys struggled to understand what they were discussing, before realising they were talking about the health of the dragon behind them. The creature had suffered in the brief period of being stuck in the artificial vacuum when the air had vented during the raid.

Rhys glanced back towards the dragon and flicked the tip of his tail, tuning out the rest of the conversation. The dragon wasn't the only one who had suffered in those conditions. Emile, the pirate known as the Silver Fox, had given up his life in order to save Rhys. That sacrifice appeared to have been for nothing, as Rhys had been thrown from the shuttle before they had even managed to leave Pluto.

The starat's thoughts darkened. He hated to think what Leandro's reaction might be, losing his love so soon after they had been reunited. Should he ever make it back to Centaura, he would have to face the grey-furred starat's grief and accept blame for the loss of the Silver Fox.

Elijah's elbow nudged against Rhys's chest. He looked up and quickly stepped out of the way as two of the humans approached. Neither of the two researchers seemed to realise the starats were there, as they were engrossed in their own conversation.

Only General Carson remained behind. He had his back to the two starats, palms pressed down on the desk as he looked over some information on the holoscreens. If he knew the starats were there, he didn't address them at all.

"Fuck, this is a mess," the human muttered.

Rhys cleared his throat.

"What else was it?" Carson said, still not looking back.

"It's Rhys. I'm still here. I need your help."

The human finally moved. He turned around, though his eyes initially looked at the wall above Rhys's head. His focus slowly drifted down and his brow furrowed. No recognition was in his eyes. "What is the meaning of this?"

Rhys blinked and took half a step back, confused by the aggression in Carson's voice. Had he made a mistake? Had the switch not been made? He was sure he had seen Herschel on the shuttle before his confrontation with Snow. He touched a hand to his chest. "I'm Rhys. Rhys Griffiths."

"I don't give a fuck what you're called. I'm busy. If you don't have anything worthwhile for me, get out of my sight," the human growled. He started to turn away again. His ear wiggled slightly.

"I…" Rhys spluttered in confusion, unsure what was going on. This had to be the general. "Carson? You know me."

Before the human could turn away entirely, Rhys could see a flicker of confusion in his eye. There was still no recognition there, but the name had certainly precipitated a response.

The movement was too quick for Rhys to respond to. One moment, Carson was at his desk, the next, the human's hands were around Rhys's throat. The starat was lifted off his feet and pressed back against the dragon cage. The creature within started to stir, letting off a slight growl.

Rhys couldn't breathe. His burned hands tried to push back at Carson's arms, but he didn't have the strength to do anything.

The human's eyes blazed with fury and hatred. "I don't know what jumped up plans have gotten into your pathetic little head, but you are nothing to me," Carson snarled. His fingers squeezed a little tighter. "If you dare speak up to me again, I will have you spaced. Get that into your simple head."

Elijah spoke just one word. "Samantha."

Confusion filled Carson's eyes. He stared at Rhys still. Understanding flooded in. His pupils expanded in shock, and then revulsion.

The human released Rhys and staggered back. He stared at his hands, flexing his fingers. "What the fuck happened?"

Rhys dropped down to his knees and wheezed in several deep breaths. His throat felt rough and sore; just another ache to add to the growing malaise of his broken body. "Nice to have you back, General."

Carson slowly dropped down to his haunches, resting his back against the wall behind him. "Are you alright? I'm so sorry for that."

Elijah helped Rhys up to his feet. The two starats moved away from the dragon cage. The creature inside had fallen asleep again, though the tip of its tail lashed around in some kind of dream. "No worse than I was," Rhys spluttered, leaning heavily into Elijah for support.

Carson shook his head. "I can't explain what happened. I looked at you and I saw… nothing. A creature. An animal. How could I even think that?" He held his hands over his mouth. His gaze slowly turned to Elijah. "You know who I am. Who I was."

Elijah nodded. "Rhys told me. I thought your old name would give you an understanding."

"An understanding? Yeah, so that's what that feels like. But how could I think those awful things?" Carson said with a shake of his head.

Elijah shrugged. "I don't know what causes it, but humans are able to look at us without being able to see the truth. It seems like they choose to see us as animals, despite all the evidence. I've theorised that there's some sort of energy projecting this across all humans, but I can think of nothing that would be powerful enough to affect everyone in the system."

"I think Snow can do that sort of thing on a small scale," Rhys said uncertainly. "But for everyone? All humans? It sounds impossible."

"Unfortunately, I can't access all the information. The Vatican keep all subspace knowledge locked away too tight for me to access," Elijah said with a weary sigh. "But I apologise, I am distracting you, Rhys. You wanted to see Carson for a reason."

Rhys's mouth felt dry. He feared bringing up the topic about the subspace weapons with the human, especially as he could still feel what Carson's hands felt like around his throat. If he was truly working for Amy and Snow, then perhaps he might act violently towards him again.

Carson's eyes met Rhys's. "Why are you even here?" the human asked, scratching behind his ear. "You should have left with the others."

"I had a disagreement with Snow," Rhys replied, lowering his eyes. He struggled to remain standing upright, despite Elijah's supporting arm around his shoulders. "How much do you know about the weapons they've been developing here?"

"In truth, little," Carson admitted. He glanced around the laboratory. "Everyone here fears them, and what they're capable of. I know that the Vatican is funding the weapons, and I've heard rumour that they're to be deployed on Centaura soon, but there seems no evidence of transporting anything across to Alpha Centauri. My understanding is that it was researched here, but they already had the components to build on Centaura."

Rhys bit his lip. "I don't think Amy and Snow ever intended to stop production of the weapon. They wanted to know how they worked so they could use them. Their target is Terra."

Carson raised a brow. "Are you sure about this?"

Rhys spread his arms wide. "Why else do you think I'm still here? Snow pushed me out of the shuttle because I learned the truth. I'm only still alive because Elijah found me on the surface."

"Shit," Carson said. He paused for a moment. "Fuck," he elaborated.

"You didn't know about that?" Rhys asked warily.

"Of course I didn't," General Carson said, holding his hands up. He frowned and chewed on his lip. "Look. I'll do what I can to get a warning sent out. I thought I was here to prevent these weapons from ever being developed. If Amy really wants to use this information to destroy Terra, then she needs to be stopped. Starat or not, that is evil."

"What can we do to stop this?" Rhys asked.

Carson rubbed his hand over his mouth. He grimaced. "Your influence will be drastically reduced here. I'm honestly not sure what you could do to make any difference. Best to let me take control. You can trust me, right?"

Rhys hesitated before nodding. "I think so," he said. He wasn't happy about being told he was to sit on the sidelines. That was not what he wanted to do. He needed to do something, or else he would feel the constant anxiety that not enough was being done.

"I'll send a message out to Terra, warning them of this threat. They'll be well defended," Carson said. He reached out to place a hand on Rhys's shoulder. "You though, you need to get some rest. I can tell you're hurt and struggling. I'll get some medical supplies to you."

"Be careful," Elijah warned. The starat's tail curled. "If you're too obvious about helping us, the Vatican will know. They might also be wary about how you were able to learn about a Centauran plot."

"Don't worry, I will be," Carson said. He held his hand out to the starat. "Thank you for coming out to see me. Your intervention has cleared my mind of whatever malaise had taken over it. You've stopped me from descending into a terrible mindset."

Elijah grinned as he took hold of Caron's hand. They touched only for a brief second before Elijah dropped his hand. "It's my pleasure. And should you perhaps want to continue those good feelings, Mikkel and Alison would love to meet you again, even in this new body."

Carson's knuckles whitened as he gripped the frame of the door. "Alison and Mikkel? They're still here? I…" Tears sprung in Carson's eyes, but he quickly wiped them away. "Tell them I would love to see them, should they wish it. I've missed them both so much."

Elijah nodded his head. "I'll let them know. We should make our way back though, before anyone sees us talking," he said, casting a wary eye towards the door, which still remained closed.

"Of course, yes," Carson said quickly. He seemed a little flustered, and he wiped his brow clean of sweat despite the cool, air-conditioned air that circulated slowly through the laboratory. "I'll get you those medical supplies. Anything else you need, too. Just ask me. When I'm not with any other humans, but you knew that already."

"Thank you, General," Rhys said, giving the human a quick, painful salute. "Captain, I suppose I should say here."

Carson smiled weakly. "Captain James Herschel, at your service." He saluted Rhys back. "Be safe, Rhys. This is a dangerous place for starats who step out of line. I'll do my best for you, but I still have my mission here too. It is more than just Amy's orders I'm following."

"I understand," Rhys replied. He felt a little pressure from Elijah, and he started to move towards the door. The human stepped to the side, allowing them both to open the door and go out into the corridors beyond. The door hissed closed behind the starats, and Rhys felt an overwhelming sensation of relief. Carson had believed him and did not appear to have known about Amy's plans. Even the brief moment where Carson had acted like a typical Terran human had left no lasting fears in Rhys. That behaviour, whatever had caused it, was no more.

The starat soon noticed that Elijah wasn't leading Rhys back to the starat quarters. Instead, they walked in the opposite direction, closer to the airlocks on the outskirts of the port station. The windows on the outside of the curved corridor looked over the barren landscape of Pluto. Rhys's eyes were naturally drawn to the sparse rocky ground. Hardly any natural light lit the white and red rocks, despite the thousands of stars visible in the inky black sky.

Somewhere out there, Rhys had fallen from the escaping shuttle. He didn't know how lucky he had been to survive. The lesser gravity of Pluto would have limited his falling speed, but the aches in his body still told him that the impact with the ground had hurt.

Rhys was led into one of the rooms close to the airlocks that opened out onto the barren surface. The small room contained an array of communication gear, all primed to beam out messages to the orbiting moons of Pluto, as well as equipment that could handle the preparation of long-range messages.

"Why are we here?" Rhys asked in confusion. The door slid closed behind him. No humans were present, and nor were any of the port's starats.

Elijah flashed a grin. "To send a message, of course. I'd prefer to have insurance. I'm sure Carson is trustworthy, but I can't guarantee he'll get a message out to the right people. I will. Between his people and mine, perhaps something can be done."

Rhys flicked his ears back. He settled down on one of the available seats, next to Elijah. "And who are the right people?"

Elijah started typing on one of the holoscreens, his fingers moving too quickly for Rhys to keep track of. His eyes flicked back and forth across the screen as he wrote. He typed using a code Rhys couldn't decipher. The other starat didn't answer as he wrote out his message. He didn't say a single word.

The message was sent. From Pluto, it would flit in and out of subspace, using a network of small beacons dotted around the Sol System. The message network was important in regions that got little ship traffic, which were usually used to courier messages from place to place. Even if the message was sent direct to Terra, it would take several hours to make it back to the centre of the system. Over such a distance, messages couldn't be too large, and data loss was still a frustrating problem. The more network beacons that were used, the slower the message would transmit across the system, but the more reliable it became. Most military ships could make the same journey in less time, but Rhys knew they couldn't trust any of those to deliver their messages.

"Sending a message to Terra," Elijah eventually said. His ears flicked back and his tail swished. "Carson will be sending his message to the chancellor, probably. He'll faff and hum about doing something, before deciding this isn't a genuine threat. He might designate one person to verify the warning, if we're lucky. Doesn't hurt by warning them through Carson, but it's probably not going to work.

"That's why we need my message too. There's some starats on Terra who will know what to do with this information. Trust me. If you want to get information and messages around the Sol System, you get a starat to do it, not a human."

"Will they actually be able to do anything?" Rhys asked, curling his tail up against the back of the chair, which had not been designed for a starat to sit comfortably. Between the chair and his aching body, he struggled to get comfortable.

Elijah didn't meet Rhys's eye. "I don't know. I have given them some suggestions, but I can't transmit the full import of the weapon. Not only is there a risk it could be intercepted, but it's too complex to truly put into a message like this. For that, we'd have to actually tell them in person."

"Then we have to go to Terra," Rhys said.

Elijah laughed. "Oh, if only it was that simple. I've been trying to get somewhere ever since I was freed from my cell. I've gotten this far," he said, pointing towards the window, through which Charon could still be seen looming in the sky. The moon never changed its position relative to the larger dwarf planet it orbited. "Starats can send messages to each other easily enough, but there's no way a starat can move around the system without permission from a human."

"Carson can give us that permission."

"Nah," Elijah replied. "You heard him. He may have been a starat once, but now he's almost all human. He wants us to stay still like good little starats and let the humans do all the work."

"He didn't mean it like that," Rhys said, a slight whine coming to his voice in protest of the accusation.

Elijah sighed. "I know he didn't mean it like that. But all humans here, even the ones who have had an understanding, think they're still better than us. They can't help it. It's almost like there's something in the air."

The back of Rhys's neck prickled. His fur stood on end, but he didn't know why. Something Elijah had said disturbed him greatly, but he knew it wasn't the implications about Carson's true thoughts about starats. Then he realised.

"An understanding?" he asked. The words sent another shiver of discomfort down his back. "I'd never heard that phrase before, until a dream I had, just before waking up today."

Elijah perked up an ear. "A dream? What kind of dream?"

Rhys's breath hitched in his throat. His vision darkened around the periphery, and he stared down at the holoscreen in front of him. He could see nothing else but the projected screen. A hand touched against his back, but he barely even reacted to the contact.

"I'm sorry, I shouldn't have asked," Elijah said softly.

Rhys shook his head. "I saw someone die. I've dreamed about her so many times, all years ago now. But never like that. In this dream, she saw a starat as a person, and the starat used that same phrase. Stephanie had an understanding, but I'd never heard that phrase before, not before today."

"I don't think it means anything," Elijah said. His hand slowly stroked down Rhys's back, but his touch was jerky and uncertain.

"How could I know what that was though? Dreams come from memories and experiences," Rhys replied.

"Perhaps you heard it sometime, but didn't think anything of it?" Elijah suggested.

"Might have been," Rhys said uncertainly. He wasn't sure if he believed that was the case, but he couldn't think of any other explanation. Perhaps it was simply a coincidence, and he was thinking too much about it. The thought of the dream disturbed him though. He could still remember every last detail of it. Stephanie had been just how he had remembered her, but she had never, to his knowledge, had any sympathy towards starats. But then, Rhys knew he would have been oblivious to it, had it existed. More likely, it was just a facet of Rhys's own imagination. He didn't understand why Stephanie had come to the forefront of his mind again. Why now? He had learned about the truth of her death weeks ago and not dreamed of her.

Rhys hissed softly to himself. He wiped his eyes gently, making sure not to hurt his blistered hands. He turned his head to look up at Elijah. "I'm sorry, I'm not usually like this. Things are just happening that's…" Rhys paused and sighed. He flicked his ears up. "Why don't you tell me a little something about yourself? Why were you on Charon?"

Elijah's eyes brightened. "I was imprisoned there because I am, or at least, was, an ongoing experiment. A starat two point oh, if you will."

Rhys blinked and stared, his mouth hanging slightly open. That had not been the answer he had expected. "An experiment? How?"

Elijah tapped a finger against his head. "I said I have a lot of information up here, and there's a reason for that. I've got cybernetic implants in my head. They pretty much made me a living computer."

"Why would they do that?" Rhys asked, frowning in confusion. He wouldn't have thought any Terran human would want to make a starat better in any way.

Elijah shrugged. "They're not going to test on a human, are they? Starats are disposable. But if they keep me under observation and see if this works, then they can enhance humans with more powerful brains." The starat's muzzle broke into a wide, devious smile. "Of course, I'm not under observation anymore. I broke out, and they monitored me from right here. Didn't take long for me to erase all their files on me."

Rhys curled his tail up over his lap. He hadn't known such experiments were being run in the empire. He certainly hadn't expected to learn starats were being used as lab rats for new technology, but nor could he say he was surprised.

"They don't know you exist anymore?" Rhys asked. He couldn't imagine what the world must be like for Elijah. He had been reluctant to get his organic arms replaced by cybernetics; so reluctant that he had missed the opportunity on Centaura. Just the thought of having his mind and brain augmented with electronics made Rhys uncomfortable.

Elijah spread his arms wide and smiled. "I'm an undocumented starat," he said brightly, before his smile faded a little. "Though that brings its own problems, as you might realise. Travelling off this rock is pretty much impossible without justification, and I can't get that."

"Sounds like we both need to get away from here," Rhys said quietly. He stared down at his lap, instinctively going to clasp his hands together before reconsidering.

"I've been trying to do that for nearly a month now," Elijah said dully. The other starat sat down on a seat opposite Rhys. "Neither of us are documented starats. We're not meant to be here, according to all the records. Until that changes, we're both stuck here."

Rhys growled beneath his breath. He had to get to Terra. Somehow, he had to warn the humans there of the dangers they could be in. He didn't know how. A plan could be formulated later, but there was nothing he could do on Pluto. He doubted General Carson would be able to get enough attention to the subspace weapons, and it would take too long to keep sending messages to Terra from the farthest reaches of the Sol System.

"It will give you chance to rest and recover," Elijah continued, breaking through Rhys's thoughts.

Rhys lifted a brow. "Rest? I am… well, I was a captain. I've never had the opportunity to do that before. Not for years."

Elijah held out his hand. "Well, now you do. Let's go back to our quarters. No humans to give us orders there, and you can give your body chance to actually recover from your injuries."

Rhys didn't take the offered hand, but he did reluctantly rise to his feet. "I suppose you're right. But I still want to try and leave at the first opportunity."

"Then let us hope some opportunity presents itself."

***

Day and night meant little to Pluto. The dwarf planet was so far out from Sol that the natural light barely changed outside. Deep twilight and total darkness were not much different, especially when the stars were aflame in the sky. They were a constant fixture as they slowly rotated across the sky, with Charon also hanging above the surface. The largest moon of Pluto appeared larger in the sky than

Luna did to Terra. The lights of the prison complex on the moon's surface were visible every time Rhys looked out the window.

There was never any movement on the dwarf planet's surface. Pluto was isolated and barren, though the lights of a lone spaceship did occasionally move against the backdrop of stars. For two days, the injured starat had been forced to lie and rest, giving his body the chance to recover from his fall.

With the help of stronger pain medication delivered by General Carson, Rhys slowly began to feel better. His legs and chest were healing, but little could be done for his arms. Elijah knew of no cure for the Devil's Blood that Cardinal Erik had used on him, and even the damage from his subspace exertions proved stubborn to heal. His hands remained blistered. Every movement of his fingers was painful, even with the medication.

After those two days, Rhys was permitted to leave his bed again. At the insistence of Kalisha, Rhys had not been idle during his recovery. He had been pushed to start practicing his technique with subspace so he could develop his skills and limit the injuries he caused to himself. Kalisha had been sitting in on his practice as much as she could, eager to further her own abilities.

Kalisha had a lot of raw talent, Rhys could tell that much. She knew nothing about subspace though, or why she was able to use her abilities. Rhys struggled to teach her what he knew, but he had barely understood most of Snow's lessons as it was. Together, they were able to stumble forward into the bright white of subspace. With every attempt, Rhys found it that little bit easier to sink into the right mindset to manipulate subspace, and he was beginning to be able to continue his thoughts and movements through realspace at the same time.

For all of his progress in furthering his subspace talents, Rhys was beginning to get restless. He knew Elijah's message would have arrived on Terra, but there had not been any reply. Elijah had warned Rhys not to expect one soon. His unknown contact on Terra would need to wait until conditions were right to reply, even if it was just an acknowledgement that the information had been received.

Snow would have made it back to Centaura by now. Already, she could be furthering her plans to strike out at Terra. The friends Rhys had left behind on Centaura would know he had not returned. Twitch and Leandro would have been waiting for him, and he had failed them. He had abandoned Twitch when the starat had needed him most.

Rhys forced his hand into a fist and growled. A glass of water fractured.

The splintering glass caught Rhys's attention. He loosened his subspace grip and took a deep breath to compose himself.

"You alright?"

Rhys looked up to see Kalisha in the doorway of the starat quarters. No one else was present, with the other starats all running errands throughout the port. Though Elijah wasn't a registered starat in the Tombaugh Station, he still kept himself busy and helped the other starats with their work.

"Yeah, fine," Rhys replied tersely. He didn't want Kalisha to pry into where his thoughts had been going. He was glad when she didn't question him further.

Instead, Kalisha glanced back out to the corridor. "We've picked up a ship on the incoming sensors. Elijah's trying to identify it, but it's nothing like anything we've seen before. Thought you might want to come and take a look."

Rhys's ears perked up. "What kind of ship?"

Kalisha laughed. "That's just the thing, we don't know."

"Huh," Rhys said. He swung his legs out of bed, glad that he had already dressed himself. Though his feet still ached, along with the now-familiar twinge in his left ankle, the pain was much more manageable after a few days of rest. He barely limped anymore, though his arms still felt like they were about to split open. "Isn't there a scanner? The operator should know what kind of ship it is."

"Who do you think operates the scanners?" Kalisha replied with a grin. Her tail swished in amusement as she led Rhys out of the starat quarters. "All across the solar system, starats run the scanners, process communications, and basically run the empire. Without us, Terra stops like that." The starat snapped her fingers for emphasis.

"Then why don't you?" Rhys asked. He struggled to think of how he had perceived the running of the empire when he had been a human. Had he just failed to notice the sheer number of starats in critical locations? Had he truly been that blind?

"Getting every starat to strike at once is not an easy thing to organise, especially if you're trying not to start a slaughter," Kalisha replied. She lowered her voice and stopped speaking entirely as a human passed them, walking in the opposite direction.

"But it's something you're trying?"

"Me? Hah. No," Kalisha laughed. She smirked back to Rhys. "But someone on Terra is. It's hard to organise anything this far out. By Essie, I miss it when I was stationed on Ceres."

"Ceres?" Rhys yelped in surprise. "When were you there?"

"Left about a few years ago. Why?" Kalisha asked. She glanced back to Rhys.

"I was stationed there when all of this happened," Rhys said, gesturing down to his body. He was almost glad that Kalisha had been there before Rhys had arrived at the dwarf planet. She had not seen him as the human he had been. He would not have to admit to her that he would have not recognised her.

"Perhaps I should be glad I left there then," Kalisha said quietly. Her focus moved down to her hands. She traced a finger up one of the dark streaks that ran through her fur. "It's easier to hide my abilities out of the eye of the Vatican. Their eyes are probably still fixed on Ceres after all of your influence."

Rhys's ears drooped, and his tail slipped between his legs. "I didn't mean for any of that to happen."

"I know you didn't, but it would have happened anyway. Any sign of starats getting a little uppity, and the Vatican swings its hammer. Starats like us, well we get the special treatment," Kalisha said, baring her teeth. She slowed her pace to walk alongside Rhys, placing her hand against his back.

"I know all about that already," Rhys said sombrely. Over the last few days, his thoughts had slowly drifted further away from his dream of Stephanie, and there hadn't been any repeats. The pain of her loss, dug back up by Amy's revelations and the dream, had been slowly buried again. That she might have died because of a starat with subspace abilities hurt him deeper.

Kalisha's attention had moved down to Rhys's arms. "You do have more scars than most," she said quietly, seeming to misinterpret just what Rhys had meant.

Rhys tried to push his tail out from between his legs, but the tip remained curled. A shiver trickled down his back as a feeling of apprehension gripped around his heart. His pulse quickened, though he couldn't be sure why. He followed Kalisha into the communications and sensory centre of the station.

Elijah was the only other starat present, as he stood in front of the holoscreens, frowning at the information he saw. No humans were inside the small room.

"This ship is unlike anything I've ever seen before," Elijah said, not looking up as Rhys and Kalisha joined him. Using two fingers he swept some of the information onto a second holoscreen to show Rhys. "It's small, for starters. Less than a quarter the size of any ship I know of. It should be too small to go to subspace safely, but this thing is shrouded in Denitchev radiation. It's been through subspace, and for quite a long journey, I think."

"Is it a threat?" Rhys asked warily. He wasn't sure if General Carson should be notified, or the defences of the station raised.

Elijah shook his head, flicking across a small piece of incoming code from the unknown ship. Rhys blinked at the sequence of letters and numbers.

"It's an identification code," Elijah explained, realising that Rhys had been floundered by the sequence. "The ship is from the Vatican. It's the highest heresy to raise defences to them. The code can't be replicated, either. That's a Vatican ship, but it's not coming from Mars."

Kalisha leaned over Elijah's shoulder to look at the data. She hissed softly. "It's not coming from any known body in the Sol System. There's nothing but empty space out that way."

The uncomfortable prickle made itself known to Rhys's back again. His throat felt dry as he expanded out the map on the holoscreen, which estimated the direction of travel from the unknown vessel. Kalisha was right. There were no bodies in the Sol System where the ship could have come from, but Rhys's attention was cast further afield. The Vatican ship had come from somewhere beyond the system, and that meant Sirius or Alpha Centauri.

An insidious thought had started to trickle into Rhys's mind. He hoped he was wrong. He prayed he was wrong, though he didn't know to whom he prayed. Veritas would never hear his prayers. The map told Rhys one thing. The unknown ship had come from Alpha Centauri. His hands trembled and throbbed with discomfort. He licked his lips, trying to bring some moisture to them. "Does the identification code have a name attached to it?"

Elijah clicked his tongue. "Uh, yes. It does. Cardinal Erik Aurealiusson. Do you know him? Rhys? Are you alright?"

Rhys staggered and slumped back against the wall. His head spun. "I have to go. I have to leave, now."

Kalisha and Elijah shared a quick glance.

"Is everything alright?" Kalisha asked.

Rhys raised his trembling hands. "Cardinal Erik is the one who did this to me. He followed me to Centaura and tried to kill me there. He's followed me again. He's here for me, and you're all in danger because of it."

Elijah set his jaw. His eyes flicked back and forth, almost too rapidly for Rhys to see. The starat then held out a hand. "Come with me. I can keep you safe. Kalisha. See if you can delay the cardinal if possible. Keep him in his ship for a little bit."

"I'll see what I can do," Kalisha replied, her voice terse. She turned her back on Elijah and Rhys as she focused on the holoscreens.

"You should leave me. Pretend you never saw me," Rhys hissed quietly, ignoring the offered hand from Elijah.

The other starat blinked and shook his head. "Not going to happen. We look after our own here. Kalisha, Mikkel, and Alison took me in right away, and now we're doing the same for you. You're one of us, so we will protect you."

"He'll kill you as well," Rhys said quietly.

Elijah flashed a smile. "He'll have to catch us first. You with me?"

Rhys didn't want to take the offered hand. He feared that doing so would drag Elijah and the other starats into a conflict that was not theirs. They couldn't possibly understand the severity of allowing Cardinal Erik to see them aiding him. Against that monster, Rhys knew he had to stand alone. He could not allow himself the luxuries of allies in that fight.

Ignoring the pain in his arms, he took Elijah's hand.

Against all of his best judgement, he accepted the help on offer.

chapter three

Rhys was taken back to the starat quarters.

An announcement reverberated through the small room, coming from the speakers that were ever-present throughout the station. General Carson had given the order for everyone, starat and human, to muster by the airlocks. Rhys knew there was only one reason for that. Cardinal Erik wanted to see everyone. The cardinal would recognise him in a moment.

Elijah didn't make any effort to move back towards the corridors. Instead, he sat on the edge of his bed. He grinned at Rhys. "We just need to stay here for a little while."

"Won't someone come for us? They'll know we're not there," Rhys replied, uncertain that Elijah had properly thought things through.

"Nah. They won't know we're missing, because we're not meant to be here, remember? There's only three starats registered to this station, and they're all out there," Elijah replied, pointing in the vague direction of the airlocks. "So long as Carson doesn't snitch us in, we'll be safe here for the moment. The others will come back and report on what the cardinal has to say, and we can proceed with a plan from there."

"And what if the cardinal comes with them?" Rhys asked, his voice shaking a little. He didn't want to confront Cardinal Erik, not again. Already, the cardinal had tortured him nearly to the point of death and had almost killed Twitch too. What other damage would the cardinal be able to inflict upon him? Rhys longed to be rid of his Vatican shadow, but the cardinal had followed him to Centaura and back. He had proven a difficult shadow to shake.

"I don't think he'll do that," Elijah said calmly. He leaned back and lifted his feet up onto the mattress, resting his hands behind his head.

Rhys began to pace. He didn't sit down like Elijah had. He was too restless to sit still; too nervous to stop thinking about the cardinal who would soon be prowling the corridors of the station. He recalled only too well the feeling of dread and terror the cardinal had inflicted on him when they were together on Ceres, and that had been before Rhys had become a starat.

A new thought started to make its way into the back of Rhys's mind. Something about the cardinal's appearance didn't quite match up to what Rhys knew. His ears flicked down and he frowned. "He doesn't know I'm here. He can't know I'm here."

"What was that?" Elijah asked, his ears perking up.

Rhys stopped pacing. "He can't know I'm here. The *Freedom* will have just got back to Centaura. Even if the cardinal left right after realising I wasn't on board, he couldn't possibly have made it here so quickly. He might have known I was coming to Pluto, but there's no way he can have known I was still here."

A small smirk started to spread across Elijah's muzzle. "I was wondering how long it might take you to figure that one out."

"You knew he couldn't be here for me?" Rhys asked in surprise.

Elijah nodded. "I knew it from the moment you told me who it was. I knew he couldn't be here for you."

Rhys tucked his tail close between his legs. He should have understood that too, but he had allowed his fear to get the better of him. "If he's not going to be looking for me, perhaps I can go and find out what he's doing here. I just can't let him see me."

The other starat raised his brow. "And what do you plan on using that information for?"

"I don't know. If it's worth something, your starat friends on Terra might be able to use it," Rhys said with a shrug of his shoulders. "He might have information with him on what he was doing on Centaura. It couldn't have just been about me. I know he despises me, but that's a long way to go for just one starat."

Elijah rubbed his hands together. "Well then. It just seems like his ship might be unattended. Why don't we go and poke around?"

"Will we be able to get in?" Rhys asked, with a nervous flick of his tail.

"Of course. Starats are given full access everywhere. We're the ones who keep the port running and do the maintenance on the ships. We come and go as we please, so long as we stay beneath the notice of the humans," Elijah replied with a smirk. He rose from the bed and placed his hand on Rhys's shoulder. "What do you say? Are you ready to break into a cardinal's ship?"

Rhys took in a deep breath. He nodded once. "Yeah, let's do it."

***

Cardinal Erik had left his ship in orbit directly above the Tombaugh Station, in between Pluto and the orbiting Charon. The ship was not visible from the surface, but shuttles provided easy access between the two. Rhys would have refused their use anyway, but the small ship in orbit had not responded to a connection request from the station's teleporters. Elijah hadn't been sure whether that meant the cardinal had disabled the teleporters on his ship, or whether the ship simply didn't have any.

Over half an hour had passed by since the cardinal's shuttle had landed, and Rhys had heard nothing of the Vatican man. There had been no more messages over the PA system, and Rhys hadn't seen any ominous sign of red robes sweeping around the corner.

Elijah stood by the shuttle bay, programming one of the small shuttles to connect to the orbiting ship. No one else was around. They hadn't even seen any humans wandering the corridors or heard anyone approaching. Everyone's attention had been taken up by the visiting cardinal.

"This is the most unusual ship I've ever seen," Elijah said, muttering to himself as Rhys kept watch. The starat hissed in frustration. "The security system doesn't seem to make any sense. It's not responding to any request I make. Give me a moment. I'll have it in a minute."

The starat frowned as he worked. His tail gently moved from side to side. His tawny fur was most unlike anything Rhys had seen on every starat he had known. Their fur usually tended towards brown or black, with only Leandro and Snow falling outside of that. One, from age. The other, from albinism. Elijah's spotted fur was something so new that Rhys couldn't help but keep glancing towards him.

Rhys forced his eyes back down the corridor. There was only one direction for someone to come across them, as behind him led just towards the shuttles. All the vessels were accounted for, meaning no one was outside the station but for the skeleton crew on the military ship in orbit above Pluto.

Even though he therefore had no reason to look back, Rhys kept on doing so. The starat intrigued him in a way he hadn't experienced before. His ruined hands clenched into pained fists. His chest felt tight, and he wasn't entirely sure fear was the only emotion he felt. Confusion welled to the surface. This was something Rhys hadn't felt in a very long time. Not since… Stephanie.

Why was everything coming back to her?

"Got it," Elijah crowed in success. He clapped his hands together. "Coming, Rhys?"

Before Rhys had more chance to ponder the direction of his thoughts, he quickly followed Elijah through to the nearest available shuttle. The doors hissed closed behind them, sealing away the port through a small airlock.

The shuttle detached and launched less than a minute later. Rhys couldn't help the flashbacks of his dream starting to bubble to the surface of his mind again. The thought of the shuttle being ripped apart by missile fire plagued his imagination. He tightened his grip on the armrests beside him and ignored the pain in his hands.

"Should only take a couple of minutes," Elijah said, not looking back at Rhys. Instead, the starat busied himself with the onboard computer of the automated vessel. He tapped at the screen a couple of times, before settling down in one of the seats at the front, a couple of rows ahead of Rhys's chosen seat. There was room for a dozen people in the shuttle, with the seats far enough apart to provide room for a human's larger frame. Despite all the extra room, Rhys's tail still felt pinched behind him.

The shuttle barely vibrated in flight. Only the slightest pressure on Rhys's chest even told him that the shuttle was in motion.

Despite the flashes of his dream coming to the forefront of his mind, no missiles ripped through the shuttle. No alarms wailed. The shuttle quickly and quietly departed the surface of Pluto and docked with the mysterious ship that had brought Cardinal Erik to the isolated dwarf planet at the edge of the Sol System.

A pair of green lights lit up, advising the two starats that the shuttle had successfully docked with the ship. Elijah glanced back at Rhys and grinned. "Here we are."

Rhys warily looked towards the shuttle airlock. Even though he knew that the cardinal was on the surface, he had confirmed that before going to the shuttle bays, he was still cautious of any presence that could still remain on the ship.

The airlock doors opened, one at a time, as the starats stepped through. On the other side of the airlock was the bridge of a ship unlike anything Rhys had ever seen before. Everything was jet black and gleamed with a soft light from above. There was a sharp, crisp scent on the air.

The bridge was much smaller than Rhys had seen on any military ship. There was only one console seat, right in the middle of the bridge, in front of the wide screens that were currently switched off. No windows opened onto the empty space beyond the hull.

Rhys slowly stepped forward, away from the airlock doors. His fur raised up. "I've never seen anything quite like this," he said uncertainly. Towards the back of the bridge, he could see a closed door leading to other areas of the ship.

Elijah's smile gleamed brightly, and his eyes were wide. "I know. Nor have I. It's incredible, isn't it?"

"Not the word I would have used," Rhys muttered to himself. He rested his hand on the back door of the bridge, before turning away from it. His eyes quickly scanned over the monochrome interior of the ship. All the usual consoles of a military vessel appeared to have been condensed down into one. This was a ship designed to be piloted by one person and not a crew. Rhys's tail slowly swished back and forth as he watched Elijah approach the centre console.

Elijah ran his hand over the silent and dark terminals. His ears pricked up. "Hey, Rhys. I think I saw a supply drawer over near you. Can you check if there's any connection cables over there? I need one end to be a little square around this big," he said, using his fingers to measure out the size he needed.

Rhys turned to find Elijah had been right. He pulled open a small set of drawers, finding inside a collection of spare parts. He found a set of cables bundled together, and he pulled them out until he found one that matched the description Elijah had given him. Other than the cabling, Rhys sifted through a few small tools and tapes, all useful for running emergency repairs to the electronics inside the ship. Rhys raised a brow. He hadn't expected Cardinal Erik to be a skilled engineer.

"Find anything?" Elijah called out, breaking into Rhys's thoughts.

"Oh, yeah. Here," Rhys replied. He pushed closed the drawer and hurried across to the consoles at the front of the bridge.

Elijah grinned as he took the offered cable. "Perfect," he said. The starat connected one end into a slot on the console, before dropping down into the lone seat. "Now, let's see what this baby has to say."

To Rhys's surprise, the starat reached up to pull down his right ear. He caught sight of a brief flash of silvery metal amongst the thick fur, before Elijah simply pushed the connection port into the socket there.

Rhys took a step back, holding one hand up towards his muzzle. He blinked a few times as Elijah slumped slightly in the seat.

"Wow, she's chatty," Elijah said. His hands gripped the armrests either side of him, then took a deep breath. He lifted one hand up, but he didn't turn his head. The cable was almost pulled taut, preventing him from moving his head much. "There should be a little switch up here somewhere. Should read power diverter, or something along those lines. Can you flick it on for me, please?"

Rhys didn't move. He only stared at the starat with the cable connected to his head.

Elijah slowly turned around. He flicked his ear and grinned bashfully. "Sorry, I should have mentioned this," he said, lightly tapping one clawed finger close to the cable socket in his head. "My designers thought it would be good to allow me to connect to any computerised system, both wirelessly and the old-fashioned way. It led to a few consequences they didn't intend, but I've found it pretty useful. I know exactly where this ship has been."

"And where is that?" Rhys asked, his throat a little dry.

"The switch, please," Elijah said, holding one hand to his head, close to the cable. "She's very talkative. It's a little too much."

"Oh, sorry," Rhys said, quickly looking up to see where Elijah had indicated. He could see a few switches, just about in reach for a human sat in the chair, but a little too far for a starat's shorter limbs. He stretched his arm painfully above his head. He found the correct switch and turned it on.

Almost immediately, Elijah sighed in relief. "That's better, thank you. Slows down how fast she runs. Makes it easier for me to understand everything."

"It's like a voice?" Rhys asked. He didn't know whether to back away or approach. Elijah suddenly appeared drastically different to Rhys. Less starat, and more machine. His tail flicked nervously.

Elijah's muzzle twitched. He faced forwards again, towards the console. "Not a voice, no. More an awareness. Like a thought running through your head that doesn't belong to you. It's hard to explain. I wouldn't expect you to truly understand."

Rhys opened his mouth, then paused. He had been about to agree that he didn't know what that felt like, but then he remembered that was not the case. There had been a time when he had felt a thought, an emotion, run through his head that had certainly not belonged to him. In the park where Rhys had rescued Twitch from Cardinal Erik, he had felt a presence within his mind, helping to fuel the power behind his subspace abilities. Something had touched his mind then. He didn't know how similar that was to Elijah's ability to speak to computers.

Realising that he had fallen silent, Rhys glanced back up towards Elijah. The augmented starat had focused fully on the console in front of him, hands clasped in his lap as he listened to whatever information the computer was telling him.

"What's it saying?" Rhys asked nervously.

"The ship was built at a facility in Gael, on Centaura. It was registered by the Inquisition and appears to be a recent gift to your cardinal," Elijah explained, not looking back again. "There's little information on what the cardinal is planning to do next, but co-ordinates are already prepared for a jump to Mars."

"What do you think that means?" Rhys asked. He slowly crept forward again, placing his hand on the back of the chair. He immediately regretted that decision as pain flared through his forearm.

"It means he's definitely not here for you," Elijah replied. The other starat unclipped himself from the computer, letting the cable hang loosely from the console. He turned to look up to Rhys. "If I had to guess, I would say he's here for an update on this subspace weapon you mentioned, or perhaps to inform someone how it's proceeding on Centaura."

A little relief washed over Rhys's shoulders, but he still felt tense and nervous. The cardinal may not be directly after him, but he feared the reaction he would get should Cardinal Erik know he was present. Rhys would still need to be careful.

"I don't think there's anything else we can learn here now," Rhys said. He slowly turned on his toes, peering towards the back of the small bridge. He longed for something to stand out as unusual, something to tell him just what Cardinal Erik's intentions were, and what the Vatican were planning. Nothing jumped out at him. The jet-black walls all seemed to smooth out into one curved, undulating surface. Only the lights of the various systems and consoles stood out.

"Hold on, there's one more thing I want to check first," Elijah said. He rose to his feet and made his way towards the back of the shuttle. He pushed open the door and stepped out into the narrow corridor beyond.

Rhys hurried after the other starat. Outside the bridge, the corridors were a little brighter. Gone were the ubiquitous black surfaces. Instead, he was faced with pale grey walls, lit by a narrow strip of LEDs along the ceiling. Everything was tight and cramped, without much room between the walls. Even Rhys felt claustrophobic. He could only imagine the space felt even smaller to a human.

There were no stairs down to the lower levels. Instead, there was just a ladder in a hole cut into the floor at the end of the corridor. Elijah quickly scampered down, but Rhys hesitated. He didn't trust his hands to support his weight.

"You alright?" Elijah called up, after realising Rhys was no longer following him.

"I can't make it down there, not with my hands," Rhys replied. He looked down. All he could see below was another corridor, much like the one he was stood in. "You go on and check what you need to see. I'll wait up here for you."

Elijah gave Rhys a quick salute. "Right you are. I'll only be a few minutes."

The starat quickly disappeared from view. Rhys could hear his claws patter away down the corridor below. Rhys didn't know what Elijah hoped to find down there, but Rhys didn't wait by the ladder.

Instead, he moved back into the bridge, hoping to see something he had missed before. His eyes scanned over the ebony fixtures.

Everything seemed so clean. Rhys could tell that the ship was new, as nothing had had the time to scuff and dirty from repeated use. The dark surfaces gleamed bright, barely even touched by the lone operator. Rhys's tail swished from side to side. A ship with a crew of just one person. He could barely even believe such a thing was possible; especially one that was capable of subspace flight. To have enough power to run a Denitchev drive at this size was something Rhys had not believed possible, but the evidence was right there before his eyes.

Rhys took a couple of steps forward, then paused. The floor beneath his feet felt different. He tapped his toes against the floor, feeling around a small area a little larger than the size of a human lying down. The floor felt hollow, like there was nothing beneath it.

Curious, Rhys crouched down and gently rested his hand against the floor. He found a small seam, almost invisible to the eye. The pitch black of the smooth floor kept the seam hidden from view, and Rhys's damaged hands could barely feel it. Without any claws, Rhys knew he had no chance of digging his fingers into the seam to pull up the floor, and nor could he find any handle or latch.

After a few seconds of scrabbling around for grip, Rhys hissed to himself in frustration at the wasted effort. He knew exactly how he could lift the floor.

The starat closed his eyes, still not quite confident that he could access subspace while distracted by his other senses. He slowed his breathing and put all his focus into his sense of smell, still finding that to be his most reliable guide into the eerie white domain of subspace. He sought out the elusive smell of cinnamon to fill his nose.

Rhys reached out slowly. His awareness extended through his arms and into the floor of the bridge. He could sense the floor stretching out around him, as well as the myriad of wires and cables beneath the surface. Then there was the void right in front of him; an empty space where he could sense nothing at all. A dark black pit loomed large, but it did not feel like one of the entities that had so terrified him. This was not a seemingly conscious mind thriving in subspace. This was just a void, an empty space beneath the floor.

Realising he was getting distracted, Rhys focused his mind on the floor beneath him. The seams meant nothing to him now. The ethereal imprints of his hands dug into the floor and lifted, pulling the panel up with a grinding protest of motors. A spark of pain lanced through his elbows, but Rhys gritted his teeth together and ignored the sensation. Pain was something he was rapidly learning to ignore.

A loud crash ripped Rhys out of subspace. He blinked his eyes open to see the panel of the flooring had swung up on its hinges, crashing against the far wall. Rhys grimaced, hoping he hadn't caused any damage to the ship that the cardinal might notice. His eyes then slid down. What had been a dark void in subspace was little more than an enclosed cabin, small and compact inside the tiny ship. Most of the space was taken up by a narrow bed, with drawers and cabinets built into the cut away floorspace either side of the mattress.

Rhys peered down. The cardinal appeared fastidious in his organisation, as the bed barely even looked like it had been slept in. The starat reached down, pulling open one of the drawers at random. He felt an itching at the back of his head, feeling slightly disturbed that he was rummaging through Cardinal Erik's personal belongings.

A pair of syringes rattled as Rhys pulled open one of the drawers, with a couple of vials rolling around beside them. The starat froze. He stared at the vials, both filled with a familiar black liquid. Devil's Blood. The poison that had been used to damage his arms and cripple Twitch's legs. Rhys snatched a vial and pushed the drawer closed.

"Found anything?"

Rhys startled at the sudden voice. He hadn't heard Elijah come back, but as Rhys looked up he could see the other starat stood in the doorway at the back of the bridge.

"I found this," Rhys said, holding up the vial he had taken. His fingers ached just holding the small glass bottle, with the weight making his hand tremble. He was glad when Elijah took the vial from him.

Elijah's eyes darkened. "Devil's Blood. I've never had the chance to get hold of any to analyse. This could be useful. If I know how it works, I might be able to synthesise an antidote. Maybe even a cure."

Rhys's ears flicked. Perhaps there could be hope for restoring his arms and Twitch's legs. He tried not to let his hope grow too much. "Did you find what you were after down there?"

Elijah nodded. He pocketed the small vial of Devil's Blood, then placed his hands on the edge of the raised floor panel, ready to close it once more. "I did, yeah. The miniaturisation tech for the power supply is incredible. I didn't think it was possible to create enough power to run a Denitchev drive in such limited space. I'd love the chance to see how it's all put together, but I don't think the cardinal would appreciate that."

"Not at all," Rhys replied, curling his tail up tight to his legs as he thought of the cardinal's anger at their mere presence on his ship. "We should get back down to the surface."

Elijah returned the floor panel back to its original position, hiding away the cardinal's small cabin. If Rhys had not already known the cabin was there, he wouldn't have been able to see any sign of it at all. He was also glad to see that his subspace pull had not damaged the floor in any way.

The two starats returned to the docked shuttle. They had learned little during their escapade. Cardinal Erik was not on Pluto to track down Rhys. That made Rhys feel a little better about the danger he was in, but it didn't help him understand the cardinal's motives. He got the feeling there was something more going on that he hadn't yet seen.

Rhys's tail swished as he sat back down in the shuttle. His thoughts swirled. He felt like he had an incomplete picture. The Vatican were creating a subspace superweapon, which had something to do with Centaura. He also knew Amy and Snow were trying to gain control of that weapon to turn it against Terra. For a brief moment, Rhys wished he had a brain like Elijah's; augmented and capable of working through all the information and coming up with a coherent answer to his circular thoughts.

"You look troubled." Elijah gently placed his hand on Rhys's shoulder. The other starat took the seat next to Rhys.

"I'm scared and confused," Rhys replied, the words out of his mouth before he could stop them. He hadn't intended to admit his fear.

"We know the cardinal isn't here for you," Elijah said. His arm draped around Rhys's shoulders. "He's going to be here to get an update from Captain Herschel on these subspace weapons. They must be preparing them to attack Centaura."

"Then we need to get to Centaura and warn them," Rhys said, but he already knew that such a thing was pointless. He couldn't even get off Pluto. What chance did he have of getting all the way to Centaura without help?

Elijah's fingers squeezed a little tighter against Rhys's upper arm. "I don't think that will be necessary. Amy and Snow may be targeting Terra, but they'll be focused on stopping the attacks on Centaura first. Let them deal with Centaura. We just need to focus on stopping their work out here."

Rhys curled his tail against the back of his seat. "I suppose you're right there," he said quietly. "But out here we can't even do anything to help protect Terra."

"I sent out a message with all the information we know," Elijah replied, but Rhys got the sense that even the other starat was frustrated with how little he was able to do as well.

"There has to be something more," Rhys grumbled quietly. He knew the problems that presented themselves. Even if they were able to wrest control of a ship, they would face the trouble of being a crew of just starats, unable to dock at any port in the system. The ship they took would be marked as stolen, and no one would even listen to what they had to say. They would be destroyed before they could even open comms. Unless they could gain authorised passage into the central regions of the Sol System, then they were stuck.

The shuttle beeped as it approached the Pluto surface once more. Rhys barely even noticed the touchdown, and it was only when Elijah stood that Rhys realised that they had landed.

Rhys stumbled after Elijah as the airlocks opened. Chilled recycled air rippled over Rhys's fur. The Tombaugh Station was quiet still, with no one present around the shuttle bay. Elijah sealed the airlock doors behind them, before wiping the logs of the excursion to the cardinal's ship. They didn't want the cardinal to know they had made an unauthorised trip.

The tap of claws running towards them caught Rhys's attention. His ears perked up. At the same moment, an oily voice started to speak over the PA system. A voice Rhys never wanted to hear again. Cardinal Erik.

"Rhys Griffiths. Make your way to the captain's office. Now."

Alison skidded around the corner. The starat's shoulder slammed against the wall as she tried to make the turn, but her feet slipped out from beneath her. She gasped and wheezed as she crawled closer.

Elijah scampered forward to offer her a hand to get back up to her feet. She batted him aside and looked to Rhys.

"He has him. He has Mikkel."

chapter four

Rhys knew he had no choice but to go to the captain's office. He didn't know what the cardinal had planned with Mikkel, but he was certain that he was being held as a hostage to force Rhys to turn himself in. The starat knew he couldn't allow someone else to get hurt because they got between himself and Cardinal Erik. There had already been too much pain inflicted when it should have been targeted towards himself.

The voice of the cardinal had come through the speakers twice more, each time sounding more and more angry towards the starat. Rhys knew he was running out of time, but the captain's office was on the opposite side of the station to the shuttle bay. His aching legs couldn't move much faster.

Elijah tried to pull Rhys back, but he kept pushing him away. No matter how many times the other starat's hand grabbed at his shoulder, Elijah was never able to stop Rhys's determined walk, nor break into his frustrated inner monologue.

Alison hurried just behind the two, with Kalisha soon joining them. Despite Rhys's growled demands for them to leave him alone, the three starats refused to go anywhere else. Rhys's patience finally snapped as they neared the captain's office, with the sounds of human voices drifting out into the corridor.

Rhys spun around on his toes and jabbed a finger towards Elijah. "You can't come with me. Leave. Be safe. It's best if you pretend you never even met me," the starat snarled.

Elijah briefly looked back to Alison and Kalisha. When he turned back to face Rhys, he shook his head. "That's not going to happen. We look after our own here, we've told you that already."

Rhys growled again. He clenched his hands tight, feeling the scar tissue on his fingers stretch painfully. "You don't understand what this man will do to you. He will treat you with the same fury as he treats me. I don't want you to get hurt."

"We're not going to just let you get taken," Elijah replied, crossing his arms across his chest.

Rhys glared around at the three starats. Fear was in their eyes, but none of them looked like they were about to turn and flee. Ears struggled not to fold over, and tails twitched with nervous energy. Alison set her jaw and clenched her fists.

"We're staying with you," Alison growled.

Rhys's ears drooped. His anger faded, to be replaced by a sense of dread mixed with quiet relief. The support was good, but he feared what might happen to the starats for showing that support. "Do you have a plan? Because I sure as shit don't."

"If they've only got a couple of guards, I might be able to fight them," Kalisha said. Cinnamon spiced the air as subspace sparks crackled between her claws.

Alison hissed softly. "If we fight them, then we will have to leave. We won't be allowed to stay here."

"I thought that was the whole point?" Kalisha replied, rolling her eyes. "We're either going to get away, or we'll be a nice squishy new housing for all their bullets."

"I'd rather not be the latter," Rhys growled. He tried to tense his fists, only to wince in pain. His ears flattened. "Every second we waste puts Mikkel in more danger. We don't have time to work out something complicated."

Elijah grinned nervously. He tapped his forehead with one clawed finger. "I might have something brewing up here. Just go on, Rhys. We'll be right behind you."

Rhys hated not having a plan. This was what he was meant to be good at. He swished his tail in frustration at the thought, but knew he had no option but to trust Elijah. Another warning came across the PA system, demanding that Rhys make his way to the captain's office. This time, he could also hear the voice of Cardinal Erik bellowing out from the office itself, easily coming across the corridors to him.

Trying to keep his tail out from between his legs, Rhys started to walk again. He feared the reaction he might get from Cardinal Erik, but he couldn't risk Mikkel being hurt because of him. A shiver ran down Rhys's back as he turned a corner to see the captain's office, with two humans standing guard outside it.

Neither of the human guards even turned to look at the starats. They spoke quietly amongst themselves, and only fell silent when Rhys was just a couple of metres from them. They both glanced down and tightened their grip on the firearms in their hands. One silently reached out to open the door between them. The guards didn't block any of the starats as they followed just behind Rhys.

Four humans all squeezed in behind the desk, crowding the small office. The large figure of General Carson was one of the humans. By his side was the familiar red robes of Cardinal Erik, whose wide brimmed hat partially obscured his eyes. The cardinal gripped Mikkel tight in his hands. The starat held his head low, not looking up to the others.

Cardinal Erik grinned savagely as he lifted his head. His eyes burned with fury. "Rhys Griffiths. I knew you'd come."

"Let him go, Cardinal. Your quarrel is with me, not him," Rhys said firmly. He forced his tail to remain behind him, and his ears upright. He doubted the cardinal could properly read starat body language, but he wanted Mikkel to know that he was confident, even if he didn't feel much confidence inside him. The cardinal terrified him, and for good reason.

Cardinal Erik's lip curled up into a sneer. "You don't get to give me orders, animal."

"And you don't get to threaten starats. How many have you hurt in your desire to get your hands on me?" Rhys asked, trying to inject some confidence and bravado into his voice.

Cardinal Erik tightened his grip on Mikkel, with one hand around his throat. "I could exterminate every starat in the empire and it would not be enough of you purged," the human replied, his face reddening in anger. Around him, the three other humans adjusted their weight slightly, shuffling back half a step from the cardinal. General Carson appeared to bite down on his tongue.

"Let him go, and you can have me," Rhys said. He struggled to keep looking forward, hoping that Elijah's plan wouldn't see him in the arms of the cardinal.

"Take it," Cardinal Erik said, snapping his free fingers in the direction of Carson.

"He is one of my starats. You can't just take..." Carson started to protest, but Cardinal Erik cut him off with a glare.

"Is it? I thought you had three starats registered to this port, but I see five here? Care to explain yourself, Sam?"

Carson took a step back. "Sam? That's not... James. Captain James Herschel. You must have me mistaken for someone else."

Cardinal Erik's grin widened, though that never reached his eyes. They remained cold and fixed on Carson's face. "Are you sure about that?"

"Quite sure, Cardinal," Carson said. His ears twitched as he looked down at Rhys, never meeting the eyes of the cardinal. "But it remains that this starat is part of this station's crew. It must just be a glitch in the system."

"You will be well compensated for the inconvenience," Cardinal Erik said, his eyes still fixed on Carson. "But I sure hope you aren't suggesting you would stand between the Vatican and our divine mission to purge out heresy. I am sure Pope Adamantius would not view such thoughts kindly."

Carson immediately shook his head. His hand rested on Rhys's shoulder, but didn't do much to hold the starat in place. "Of course not, Cardinal. I will comply, but I would like it known that I need all these starats to maintain a smooth operation of this station. Their presence might sometimes be considered unsavoury, but there is no doubting their importance to our work."

The cardinal sneered. "They are a disease on humanity. They make us lazy and complacent," he said, turning his attention towards the other two humans in the room. Rhys couldn't see what the other three starats were doing in the doorway, stood behind Carson. The cardinal snapped his fingers again. "Take all five of them."

Carson released Rhys's shoulder and stepped forward, between the starat and the cardinal. "Now hang on a minute. I must protest this," the tall human said.

"Take this one too. I have reason to suspect he is a traitor and a spy," Cardinal Erik said.

"No, you don't understand," Carson said, but he was quickly interrupted by the humans around him. They immediately turned on their captain and commander at the orders of the cardinal. The guards from outside the doors also stepped inside, the two of them taking hold of Carson, while the others herded the starats towards the corridor.

Rhys slowly backed out of the office, his eyes never once leaving Cardinal Erik's blazing eyes. The human didn't release Mikkel as he started to advance, the same hungry grin still spread across his face.

As Rhys moved back, he bumped against another starat, who had not been moving. Rhys glanced back to see Elijah stood over him. He had not moved from where he had been standing, right in the middle of the doorway. "Ready?" the starat asked quietly.

"For what?" Rhys replied.

Rhys got no verbal answer. Instead, he got a slight push to his shoulder, forcing him out into the corridor with Carson, the human guards, and the other starats. Elijah advanced forward a step. He carried something in his hand that glinted in the light. A small glass vial filled with black liquid.

In one fluid movement, Elijah unstoppered the vial before any of the humans could react. He thrust his hand forward, and the viscous black liquid arced through the air.

Cardinal Erik lifted his arm, releasing Mikkel from his grip, but he didn't move quickly enough. The Devil's Blood splashed against his face. He screeched in agony and fell back, clawing at his face with both hands.

A moment of stunned stillness followed. Elijah broke the entrancement with a bellowed yell. "Run!"

Rhys paused only to take Mikkel's hand, ignoring the stinging pain from the pressure of his fingers against the other starat's palm. He pulled him away from the office, pushing past the human guards before they could grab hold of either starat.

Elijah started to run, but Rhys paused again and turned back. For just a couple of seconds, he waited and reached into subspace. Cinnamon overwhelmed him as he reached out, wrenching the office door closed. Sparks flew as the control panel overloaded and fried, locking the cardinal and one of the guards inside. Four humans remained outside the office. Three had guns.

Rhys turned to run. Mikkel had not stopped. He had caught up to the others and turned the corner, already out of sight. Only Kalisha had lingered, and she waited a few paces ahead of him. Behind him, he could hear one of the humans trying to open the office door. Two others began to chase him. He could hear nothing from Carson.

Rhys struggled to catch up to the other starats. He kept his head low, unwilling to present a big target for the pursuing humans, but he didn't know how long he would be able to keep ahead of them.

The starat's chest burned. His legs ached. He stumbled a couple of times as Kalisha's tail disappeared around a corner. For a brief moment, Rhys felt all alone with no protection from the humans.

Rhys turned the corner and almost ran into Kalisha. The other starat had stood her ground alone. Elijah and the others had paused further up the corridor, but they hadn't yet started to run back towards them. Rhys turned to stand by Kalisha's side. He didn't know what the starat's plan was, but he knew it had to be better than aimlessly running until they got caught.

The two humans turned the corner just a few seconds later. Only a couple of metres separated them from the starats, and they had their guns raised. The weapons were aimed right for their heads.

"I've always wanted to do this," one of the humans sneered. He held up his pistol, his finger preparing to squeeze the trigger. "Now just stay nice and still."

Rhys braced himself. He had no weapons, and nor did Kalisha. She didn't need any. She raised her hand. Cinnamon tickled at Rhys's nose.

Both humans fired their weapons at the same time. Light burst and subspace crackled around Rhys. The pistols exploded, sending metal shrapnel out in a wide arc, ripping through the hands of the humans and forcing them to retreat, yelling in pain.

Smoke drifted through the corridor as the shattered remains of the pistols clattered to the floor. Both humans staggered back, clutching at their wounded hands. Blood splattered against the tiles.

"Move!" Kalisha said, turning quickly on her toes.

Rhys didn't need to be told. He followed the starat, sprinting after Elijah and the others. This time there was no sound of pursuit from behind, though an alarm had started to ring out. Rhys curled his ears at the grating sound. It wailed out a warning, with a flashing red light adding to the usual harsh white glare from the ceiling lights.

"Where to?" Alison asked, once Rhys and Kalisha had caught up to them.

"Shuttles, now," Rhys ordered, a touch of old authority coming into his voice. "We can't stay here, and there's a ship we can steal."

Elijah's eyes lit up. "I like this idea," he said with a grin. He nudged Mikkel along. "We can't let them cut us off. We have to hurry."

Rhys glanced back down the corridor. A third human had joined the wounded two. For a brief moment, his eyes locked with those of General Carson. Then the human looked away, focusing on helping the wounded up to their feet. None of the three made any movements to stop the starats from fleeing.

As they ran past the starat quarters, Rhys came to a halt. Only Elijah noticed and stopped with him.

"We can't wait, Rhys," Elijah said quickly, holding out his hand to tug him along.

Rhys fended off Elijah's arm and hurried inside the quarters. There was something he needed to find. His bed was at the far end of the room, but it only took Rhys a few seconds to slide next to the bed and reach beneath it. There he found the space suit he had been wearing when he had been pushed from the shuttle. His hands hurt as he pulled open a couple of the pockets, but inside was what he had been after. A small datastick he had used to copy all the information he had been able to learn about the subspace weapon being developed.

Elijah waited by the door, twitching his tail nervously. His eyes were focused on the corridors outside the small room. He didn't look back to Rhys. "You got what you were after?" he asked.

Rhys held up the datastick. "We might need to convince someone what we know is here," he explained. He was glad to see that no humans had closed in on them yet. His fingers itched by his side. He would have loved a pistol in his hand, though he also knew he would barely be able to hold anything with much more weight than the small datastick.

The other starats had not waited for them. As he had all he needed from the starat quarters, he followed Elijah as they ran for the shuttle bay again. A little guilt crept into the back of Rhys's mind as he ran. There had not been much in the way of personal possessions in the starat quarters, but Rhys was still being responsible again for dragging people away from their homes, from all they had ever known.

Rhys didn't have much more time to be lost to his thoughts. Shouts echoed from ahead, the voices both human and starat.

Elijah swore softly and picked up the pace. Rhys could not keep up. His ankles hurt with every step, and it was all he could do to remain upright. He quickly lagged behind, clutching hold of the datastick in his right hand.

Three humans stood between the starats and the shuttles. The alarm appeared to have caught them by surprise, as none of them were fully prepared. Only one had a weapon on him, and all three were missing parts of their uniform. Had they been under Rhys's command, he would have been bitterly disappointed by their disorganisation. For now, though, it was a situation he might be able to exploit.

Mikkel clutched his arm, hunched over slightly. The other starats had all backed away, with Elijah quickly taking up position at the front of the gathered group.

"What the fuck is going on?" one of the humans asked. All three looked incredulous at the group of starats in front of them.

"Let us through," Rhys called out. He approached the other starats, who parted to allow Rhys to stand at Elijah's side. He struggled to control his breathing, but his heart raced away inside his chest. The injuries he had suffered hadn't helped, but Rhys really needed to do something about the fitness levels he had adopted in his new body.

The one human who had remembered to grab his pistol raised his weapon. Once more, Rhys stared down the wrong end of the gun. Cinnamon filled his nose again.

The pistol fired three quickfire shots. This time the gun didn't backfire, but the bullets did not fly straight. One ricocheted off the air to strike the ceiling, while the other two impacted the walls with a pair of loud cracks.

Kalisha stepped forward, her hand still raised. Her eyes blazed white, and small sparks of golden light swirled around her outstretched hand. "Let us through," she barked, repeating Rhys's earlier command. She had the authority of her subspace powers to lend weight to her words, while Rhys simply had a broken and battered body.

All three humans retreated a couple of steps. "What heresy is this?"

"Do you want to find out?" Kalisha asked, tilting her head to the side.

The humans continued to retreat, clearing a path for the starats to reach the closest shuttle. Elijah quickly moved to prepare the shuttle, tapping away at the computer to open the first of the airlock doors.

Rhys stayed by Kalisha's side. He kept his hands by his hips, but he focused his mind to ready himself to dip into subspace if he was needed. Her golden eyes were narrowed in her focus, and the black streaks that ran up her arms seemed to smoulder with energy.

Two of the three humans turned to flee once the way out was cleared of the starats. Only the one with the pistol remained. His hand shook as he raised his weapon again. "What manner of devil are you?"

Kalisha gnashed her teeth at the human. "I'm the absolute worst of them all," she snarled. She clenched her fingers and the scent of cinnamon poured from her body as she reached into subspace. The gun ripped from the human's hand and reappeared in her own. "I'll be having that, thank you."

The human stared at his empty hands for a moment, then looked up to Kalisha, who now had a much more real and obvious weapon in her hands. His eyes widened, before he turned to flee after the others. Kalisha did not lower the pistol until his footsteps had faded into almost total silence.

"Inside, now," Elijah called out from behind them.

Another voice screeched out from further inside the port. "Stop them!"

Rhys turned to see the airlock doors were opened, and the other three starats were all inside the shuttle. Kalisha hurried inside first, with Rhys following just behind her. The doors hissed closed behind them, sealing them from the spaceport. A small rumble shivered through the shuttle as the engines fired, launching the five starats away from the dwarf planet's surface.

Rhys slumped down in the nearest seat and stared across at Kalisha, who still had the pistol clutched tightly in her hand. "How did you do that?" he asked in awe.

Kalisha raised her brow and flicked one ear back. "I thought you knew about how it's done."

Rhys shook his head. "No, with the gun. I tried that before, but it caused too much pain if I interact with an object someone is already holding."

"Oh," Kalisha said. Her other ear flicked back against her head. "I don't know. I've practised a few times, taking stuff from Alison and Mikkel. I thought it was something anyone with these skills can do."

"I don't think so, no," Rhys said quietly. He stared down at his hands and the ruined, bony, furless fingers. He realised a little blood was trickling from a cut in his palm, and he carefully unclenched his fingers to realise the datastick had pierced his weak flesh. "Shit," he muttered, pocketing the datastick and wiping his hand on his sleeve to stem the flow of blood.

Mikkel cleared his throat. He was the only starat still standing, though he rested his hands on the back of a vacant chair to keep his balance. "Firstly, thank you for getting me out of that man's hands. But, perhaps more importantly, what the hell just happened down there, and where are we going now?"

Rhys exhaled slowly. "I brought this on you. The cardinal was with me on Ceres when I first became a starat, and he's been wanting to capture me ever since, to bring me to justice. He is willing to harm and kill any starat who stands in his way. As for where we're going, we're going to steal his ship and leave Pluto far behind us."

"And go where?" Alison asked nervously.

"We need to go closer to the centre of the system. I want to go to Terra, but there's no one I trust there who will allow us to approach in a stolen ship," Rhys said slowly. He flicked his ears and frowned. "In fact, there's only one person I trust in the whole system who will actually listen to us."

"Who is that?" Mikkel asked. He had to steady himself after the shuttle jolted slightly. For a moment, Rhys feared that the military ship in orbit around Pluto might have locked onto them, but nothing further resulted from the brief destabilisation.

Rhys met the eyes of every starat in the shuttle. "Admiral Garter on Ceres. He's our best hope now."

Before anyone could respond, a loud clang rattled through the shuttle as it connected to Cardinal Erik's ship. The airlock doors slid open, and Elijah quickly hurried through into the bridge of the small ship. Rhys gestured for the other starats to lead through, before he closed the airlock doors behind him.

"We don't have long," Rhys said quickly, addressing the starats.

Elijah had already got to work. He had sat down at the bridge and connected himself up to the ship's computer. His eyes were closed, with his lips moving as he silently muttered along to the voice of the ship.

"Don't have long before what?" Mikkel asked, turning to Rhys. There wasn't any anger in his eyes, but there was fear.

"Before they shoot us down," Rhys said tersely. He approached Elijah and placed his hand on the back of the chair. He didn't know how well Elijah could hear him, but he spoke to the starat anyway. "Don't worry about getting too close to Ceres yet. Just get us out of here and we can reposition later if we need to."

"Understood," Elijah said simply. He barely moved, but the cockpit screens lit up brightly, showing a visual panorama of the view around the ship. Pluto shone brightest below them, with Charon looming close by too. In between them both was the bright dot of the military ship. In the great distance between them, the dot seemed to move slowly, but Rhys knew the ship was likely travelling quickly.

There was one advantage lending itself towards Rhys and his band of starats. At the military ship's current angle, the trajectory of any fired weapons would strike the Tombaugh Station. The captain of the military ship would not risk opening fire yet. They needed to reposition. That gave Elijah around a minute to get the ship under his control and safely navigate a path through subspace.

The engines began to fire up. A deep rumble vibrated through the ship, seeming to be louder and more powerful than anything Rhys had ever felt before. Even standing below deck on his ship had not given such a powerful feeling.

"She's got kick," Rhys said, in slight awe at the power he felt through his feet.

"And she knows it," Elijah said with a grimace. His hand trembled as he reached out for one of the switches in front of him. "Alright. Here goes nothing. Co-ordinates locked on. Hold onto something. This might be rough."

Rhys barely had time to tighten his grip on the back of the chair before the small ship shot forward. The small craft seemed to be much more manoeuvrable than anything Rhys had been in before, with the view of Pluto quickly twisting away.

The engines were powerful. Rhys glanced down at the displays in front of Elijah, marvelling at the acceleration the small ship was capable of. He felt a slight tightening in his chest, but the inertia dampeners were capable of keeping the worst of the pressure at bay.

A small ping sounded through the bridge. Rhys recognised the sound, which repeated every couple of seconds. The military ship protecting Pluto had locked its weapons onto them. The computer flashed up to identify the military ship as the *Rossi*. They were running out of time to reach subspace, but they were still too close to the dwarf planet's gravity well.

"Alright, watch this," Elijah said. He leaned forward and flicked a switch on the dash. Nothing appeared to happen but for a single green light flashing on.

A few seconds passed before Rhys realised the quiet ping hadn't sounded again. "What did you do?"

Elijah grinned. "She seems to have a decent cloaking field that scrambles sensors. No one can lock weapons on us."

"Impressive," Rhys said quietly. He kept watch on the ship's screens, but he could see nothing flash up in warning. The other ship was no longer tracking them. "How did you know this ship could do that?"

Elijah tapped his finger to his forehead. "She told me. She's registered as the *Vigilant*." He hesitated for a moment. A nervous grin spread across his face. He turned his head slightly, pulling taut on the cable connected behind his ear. "I've never flown a ship before. Never even got the chance to drive one of the rovers on the surface. It's exciting."

"Wait? Never?" Rhys yelped. He had half a mind to pull Elijah from the seat, but he managed to restrain himself. He didn't know what effect that might have on the starat's mind, or indeed on the ship, if the starat was pulled abruptly away from the connection between the pair.

Elijah shook his head. "Never. Don't worry though. The ship's good enough to fly herself. I'm just pointing her in the right direction."

Rhys swished his tail nervously. The *Vigilant* appeared to be moving just fine, but Rhys knew from experience that piloting any ship was no easy feat. Elijah shouldn't have been able to switch the engines on without any experience, but he had managed that. Rhys felt oddly comforted by that realisation. If Elijah was capable of switching on the *Vigilant* despite having no experience, then perhaps he could achieve the impossible and fly the ship too.

"Running the co-ordinates for the subspace jump now," Elijah said, his voice sounding as calm as any navigator Rhys had flown with.

"Wait a moment," Rhys said, crouching forward and manually bringing up the navigation systems. He felt a flicker of movement from the starat as he brought up the mostly familiar programs. As he had expected, the systems had a defined limit on the speed it allowed ships to pass through subspace safely. The reason for subspace desertion had never been understood by the empire, but Rhys knew the answer to that now. He also knew how to protect the ship from the mysterious entities. He increased the allowed speed and ignored the automated warnings.

"Are you sure?" Elijah asked warily.

Rhys stepped back from the console. "Absolutely. I can keep us safe, don't worry."

"Alright. Running the calculations now," Elijah said, still sounding a little nervous.

That made two of them, Rhys thought to himself. He glanced up at Elijah, amazed that the starat was taking to this so naturally. The other starat was augmented in ways Rhys had never known about before, but was that really the only explanation behind the starat's talents?

"Jump point in two minutes," Elijah said, breaking into Rhys's thoughts. "Scans show the imperial ship is searching for us, but they can't get a lock on us. No signs of weapons being prepared."

"Good. Hopefully it stays that way, or else we're in a bit of trouble," Rhys replied. He kept his eye on the scanner reports flashing up on a couple of the screens. He could see the pinged flash of light that was the *Rossi*, as well as the celestial bodies of Pluto and Charon. None of the other moons of Pluto flashed up. They were probably on the other side of the dwarf planet.

Rhys moved away from the front of the bridge, leaving Elijah on his own for a moment. The other three starats had sat down together, leaning against the back wall of the bridge, next to the closed door. They huddled together, nervously looking towards the screens at the front of the bridge. Rhys knelt in front of them.

"I'm sorry for dragging you away from your home," Rhys said, bowing his head.

Mikkel laughed. "Are you kidding? I've been looking forward to leaving Pluto for years. This is exciting."

"It wasn't our home," Alison added. She reached out to lift Rhys's chin, making him look into their faces. "It was our prison, just as Charon was to Elijah. We were going to get out of there eventually, or we were going to die there. Now we know there's life for us away from Pluto. We're glad we're free of that place."

A smile slowly twitched onto Rhys's face. His ears perked up. "You are? Well, I'm happy you're here with me. We're going to go into subspace soon, and you might be alarmed at what you see on the screens. I just want to let you know that I'll be keeping us safe."

"What sort of things might we see?" Mikkel asked, a touch of fear returning into his voice.

Rhys shook his head. "I don't know what they are. I don't like them at all, but we need to get to Ceres quickly, before we can be followed," he said, before turning to look at Kalisha. "This might be a skill you can learn too. Would you care to join me?"

Kalisha rose to her feet. She clapped her hands together. "New skills? Sounds like fun," she said brightly. "Just show me the way."

A dull ping echoed through the bridge. Rhys's ears flattened. He knew what that sound meant. The imperial ship had locked onto them again. "Elijah? Status report?" he called out loudly.

"Incoming missile fire. Subspace jump point in five seconds," the starat replied, his voice still remaining perfectly calm despite the situation.

Rhys counted down the seconds. He could only hope the imperial ship was too far away for the missiles to cover the distance in such a time. A second ping sounded. Then a third.

Elijah pushed forward on a lever and the *Vigilant's* engines changed in pitch to a higher whine. The screens changed to white.

The *Vigilant* launched into subspace. They were away.

chapter fiue

The wordless voices screamed at Rhys. He couldn't tune out the anger raging at him from the subspace entities, but he could shield the ship from their menace. For two hours he focused on keeping them away from the ship, never once pausing. He had hoped to teach Kalisha how to shield the *Vigilant* from the entities, but the effort had taken all his concentration and focus. She had watched over him, but he doubted she had managed to learn anything.

The anger projected through subspace was to a level Rhys had never experienced before and hoped to never feel again. There were times he felt his muzzle twisting into a silent snarl, his hands clenching into pained fists, as he mimicked the rage flowing into him.

The starat could get no relief. The anger pulsated through his mind as the shadowy entities swirled around the *Vigiliant*. They did not rest, and so Rhys could not either. Even a moment of weakness could allow them in.

Time no longer had meaning to Rhys. His body shook from the exertion, but he couldn't tell if hours had passed by, or mere seconds. All he could see was the dark entities swirling across the backdrop of subspace. The only scent he could detect was the overwhelming tang of cinnamon. The scent filled his nose and drenched his tongue, infusing his senses with the taste. Voices spoke around him, but those were drowned out by the incoherent rage of the entities.

Everything went black. Terror gripped Rhys, convinced that he had failed. Then he realised that he could no longer hear the anger. The darkness in front of him wasn't a void of nothingness, but it was instead pinpricked with the light of a million stars. Realspace had returned to the console screens.

Rhys swayed. He fell, but not before a pair of waiting arms wrapped around him. He stumbled backwards into Kalisha as she slowly helped him down to sit on the floor. His head spun and his throat was parched. Just another list to the growing ailments he suffered from.

"Are you alright, Rhys?" Kalisha asked. Her head never seemed to stay in the one spot. Rhys struggled to look at her.

"Water, please," Rhys groaned, forcing the words from his dry, burning throat.

A few seconds passed before one of the starats was able to get a bottle of water to Rhys. He didn't question where it had come from. The cardinal would have needed his own supply of food and drink for the long journey from the Alpha Centauri system.

The water did little to soothe Rhys's throat, but he drank all that was on offer for him. One of the starats held the bottle, as his arms felt incapable of moving.

Once he had drank his fill, Rhys closed his eyes and rested his head back against the wall behind him. He took in a few deep breaths as he tried to clear his mind of the ordeal he had gone through. Slowly, Rhys lifted his hands up off the floor. The effort felt almost as demanding as keeping the entities at bay. His arms shook from the movement. He knew pain was going to come later, but for the moment they were entirely numb.

Rhys turned his head. Elijah was still sat at the console. The other starat looked forward onto the screens, which displayed a field of stars without any celestial bodies close by. Three pinpricks of light moved from right to left across the screen, but Rhys's vision blurred too much to tell if the lights were other ships or asteroids.

"Where are we now?" Rhys asked. He coughed, clearing some mucus from his throat, and grimaced in disgust. He tasted blood.

"On approach to Ceres," Elijah replied after a moment of hesitation. He reached up to flick a switch above his head. "I'm broadcasting Cardinal Erik's identification code, so we're not going to be shot down."

"What if they already know we've stolen the ship?" Mikkel asked. The starat moved across Rhys's vision to stand just behind Elijah's seat.

"Impossible," Rhys said. He tried to raise his head, but weariness took hold of him. He squeezed his eyes closed for a moment and took another deep breath. "We travelled faster than any imperial ship can manage. The fastest they can get a message this far from Pluto will be another two hours, at least."

Mikkel clicked his tongue. "Still doesn't change what will happen when we try to disembark."

Rhys tried to sit upright again. This time he managed to lift his head away from the wall, but he couldn't bring himself to stand just yet. His arms felt numbed and deadened, and he could barely even move his fingers. He needed to stand. There was still more that he needed to do.

With Kalisha's help, Rhys was able to stagger up to feet that felt like lead. He leaned heavily on the other starat for support, as each step required a monumental effort. Only Cardinal Erik's sustained torture had left him feeling so weary. Mikkel stood aside to allow Rhys to stand by Elijah's side, with Kalisha still providing support so he didn't fall down.

"Can you send a tightbeam to Admiral Garter? He's the one I need to speak to," Rhys asked, hoping that Elijah was capable of doing so. His plan wasn't reliant on speaking to the admiral before they arrived at Ceres, but it would make things run smoother.

"I'll see what I can do," Elijah replied. He didn't reach towards the console, as most of what the starat could do was done from the mental link he had with the *Vigilant's* computer.

Now that he was standing, Rhys could see a little more across the ship's screens. In the distance, he could see one dot of light that was larger than anything else. Sol wasn't visible on screen, so Rhys knew the dot of light had to be their destination. Ceres. He was back.

A shiver ran down Rhys's tail. Ceres was where this had all begun for him. Had he taken a post anywhere else in the system, then he wouldn't be stood here now, in a stolen ship with four starats. Four other starats, with himself being a fifth amongst their number. Rhys couldn't imagine his life any other way now. Already his human face was beginning to fade into his memory.

"I've got a connection," Elijah said suddenly. The starat sat up sharply in his seat and perked up his ears. "Sending a contact request to a personal communication device registered to Admiral Nigel Garter."

Rhys trembled. He knew Admiral Garter well, and the two had parted on good terms, even considering the circumstances of his departure. This meeting would be different. They were no longer colleagues, with the admiral having been Rhys's direct superior officer. This time, Rhys was a fugitive and a traitor to the empire. By all rights they should be enemies. Admiral Garter would be within his rights to order an attack on the *Vigilant*.

The screens flickered for a moment.

"Fuck," Elijah muttered to himself. He leaned forward and flicked a couple of switches back and forth. "It's hard to maintain a stable connection."

"Some things never change," Rhys replied wryly. In the time since he had left, it appeared Ceres had not progressed with the upgrades the port had hoped for. The communications network across the dwarf planet had been one of the worst in the system.

The screens flickered a second time. This time, an image of Admiral Garter became visible. His eyes were not looking towards the screen, and from the angle of his head, Rhys believed they had connected with a handheld communicator. A moment later, the human started talking.

"Cardina – ah shit."

The image dropped away. Different voices came through the speakers, all muffled and indistinct. A door opened and closed as footsteps sounded. Almost a minute passed before the face of Admiral Garter returned to the *Vigilant's* screens.

"I told Essie I didn't want anyone contacting me directly. It's too dangerous," Admiral Garter said, a touch of anger entering his voice. His brow was furrowed, adding another half dozen lines to his already weathered face. Rhys had never seen such a reaction from the elderly human before.

"Essie?" Elijah asked, turning to look up at Rhys and Kalisha.

A flash of confusion passed over Admiral Garter. His eyes flicked back and forth, before they settled in one spot. His pupils dilated a little. His voice was small and quiet, all anger faded from voice and expression. "I never thought I'd see you again, Captain Griffiths."

"Likewise, Admiral," Rhys replied with a nod of his head. His arm twitched by his side, but he didn't have the energy to bring it up in a salute. "Though I'm not sure I can lay claim to the title of captain anymore."

"I am sure there's many stories to tell, but most importantly, I must ask why you are in a ship broadcasting the personal code of Cardinal Erik Aurealiusson."

"I would feel more comfortable telling you face to face, Admiral. If we can be given safe transit to the surface, then I can tell you everything you need to know," Rhys explained. He looked back for a moment to see the nervous hope in the eyes of Mikkel and Alison.

Admiral Garter ran his hand over his chin. He frowned in thought. "I think it would be a bad idea for you to come to the military port. Hold position for a few minutes. I'll get you clearance to land in the civilian port. There'll be less scrutiny there. I'll be back in contact shortly."

Before Rhys could respond, the screen went dark and showed the display of stars once more. Rhys swished his tail and chewed on his lip. There was a lot the admiral hadn't said, but some tantalising pieces of information had been given. There was a new civilian port on Ceres, for starters. Perhaps things were moving quicker than he had initially thought.

The starats had focused on something else. "Did he really say Essie?" Mikkel asked in awe.

"He can't have done," Alison said, shaking her head. "No one can speak to Essie. He died a long time ago."

"He definitely said Essie," Elijah said slowly. His ears flicked and folded slightly. "Unless it's a codename. A starat, perhaps, starting to organise a way to fight back against humans."

"You think Admiral Garter is involved with the starats you contacted on Terra?" Rhys asked. He wasn't sure if he could believe such a thing. Admiral Garter was certainly sympathetic to starats, Rhys had learned as much in the brief time he had been a starat on Ceres, but to be involved with such an organisation seemed to be a risk too far for someone like the admiral.

"I'm not saying he is," Elijah said slowly, pausing for a moment to gather his thoughts. His hand drifted close to his right ear and the cable that connected him to the ship. "I haven't heard of anyone going by the name Essie, but I'm just saying that it's possible that someone could be using the name to gather support from starats across the empire."

"To us, that name is hope," Kalisha whispered. Her hand gripped a little tighter around Rhys's shoulder. "If someone uses that name, it means they will stand up for starats and never back down. The name is as important to us as Veritas is to humans."

"Then let us hope that this Essie isn't a fraud like Veritas was," Rhys muttered to himself. He then grimaced and pinned his ears back. He glanced to the other starats, who had all widened their eyes and stepped back in shock. "Best not to repeat that anywhere else. I learned a few things on Centaura. Not all of it is safe knowledge around here."

"I won't say a word," Elijah said, holding his hand up. His eyes were bright, and a smirk had come across his face. "But I should like to learn more from you sometime."

Rhys flicked his tail nervously. Had a member of the Vatican heard him, he would already have been dragged away to their vaults below the surface of Mars, erased from existence. He was reluctant to say anything more than might have him branded a heretic, beyond his mere existence as a starat.

Before Rhys could properly consider a response, a small beep sounded from the console. A text message had come through from the admiral, granting them permission to take safe orbit in a designated area around the dwarf planet, and then shuttle down to the surface at the Noveau Ceres port. Rhys was not familiar with the name, and he knew that for all his time on Ceres there had not been a second spaceport on the dwarf planet. He was interested to see what had been built.

Elijah slowly manoeuvred the *Vigilant* closer to Ceres, bringing the ship into a stable orbit. The dwarf planet appeared as little more than a dull grey rock on the screens, with few visible signs of human activity on the surface. The lights that shone up were few and far between, with almost all coming from the various mining operations scattered across the surface.

"Let me do all the talking, please," Rhys said, managing to get his hand on Elijah's shoulder. The contact prickled at his palm. Whereas before he had barely felt anything in his arms, now they felt overly sensitive. Every hair from Elijah's fur felt like a blade digging into his skin.

A clean, crisp female voice spoke through the ship's speakers as they neared the dwarf planet. "Noveau Ceres to *Vigilant*. You have permission to park in the civilian orbital region. Co-ordinates have been sent to your ship. Do you require a shuttle?"

"Negative to the shuttle, Noveau Ceres," Rhys replied, leaning forward to make sure his voice was easily heard. He was glad there was no visual connection to the port.

"A… affirm on that," the human on the other end of the line said. Her brief hesitation remained unquestioned.

Rhys knew exactly why she had hesitated. His voice didn't quite sound human. Sure, he spoke the words as any human would, but there was still that slight lisp to his voice that was present in every single starat. Their mouths just weren't built the right way to sound exactly like a human did.

That the operator didn't question Rhys's voice meant she had probably just accounted for his voice as a distortion across the connection. Or so Rhys hoped. He knew it was possible that there would be an armed guard waiting for them on their arrival to the surface. Rhys could only hope that Admiral Garter's influence was enough.

Over a dozen ships were parked in orbit around Ceres. None were military vessels, but Rhys knew they would have their own area of space to patrol. These were all civilian vessels, with most being contracted to the mining companies that worked on Ceres. There wasn't much tourism on the dwarf planet, so seeing cruise and transport ships in this part of the asteroid belt would be rare indeed. Every single ship looked as large as any Rhys was used to, with the *Vigilant* being truly dwarfed by them all.

Elijah parked the *Vigilant* and switched off the engines. The ship remained in a stable orbit around the dwarf planet, locked into a set speed with the other parked ships to ensure that they never collided. Without the constant thrum of the engines vibrating the ship, everything felt silent to Rhys's ears. His heart skipped a beat as he looked down at Ceres. His life had changed there. He had never expected to see it again, especially not so soon after he had left.

"We should get to the shuttle and prepare to descend," Rhys said. He turned to look around the bridge, still leaning heavily on Kalisha to keep upright. For the first time he was able to get a proper look at what had happened during the flight, while he had been distracted by subspace. Alison and Mikkel had opened the cardinal's bed and had been resting there. Some of the human's belongings had been dispersed around the cabin, but there appeared to be nothing useful amongst them.

Except for one lone vial of Devil's Blood. Rhys's eyes fell on the small glass vial of blackened liquid. He tried to pick it up, but Kalisha kept a firm grip on his shoulders. Seeing his movement, Mikkel scooped up the vial and kept hold of it.

Once Elijah had fully disconnected himself from the *Vigilant*, the five starats made their way to the shuttle. Knowing what their destination was, Rhys felt a little worry beginning to creep into his body. This was a place where he would have no influence. At least on Pluto he knew he had General Carson's presence to fall back on, should the situation get dire. On Ceres, he had only Admiral Garter, and he doubted the human would be able to step in.

On Ceres, Rhys would be a mere starat. Even worse, he would be somewhere without authorisation from any human. Should that be discovered, he dreaded to think what the consequences may be.

Rhys gratefully settled down on the first available seat as the shuttle disengaged from the *Vigilant*. Slowly, the five starats began their descent to the surface. Ceres awaited.

***

The shuttle landed with barely a bump. The journey down to the surface had taken a little longer than Rhys had expected. Elijah, who had been sat by the shuttle console to keep track of the automated progress, had not raised any alarms or concern. The airlock doors had also not opened right away, but even this had not raised any worry from Elijah. Rhys forced himself to maintain the same level of calm, but his foot kept tapping nervously against the floor.

Finally, a green light shone above the airlock, and the inner door hissed open smoothly. No one came in to greet them, for which Rhys was thankful. He still hadn't managed to come up with a believable lie about why five starats and no humans had been present on a Vatican-identifying spaceship, of a design that wasn't recorded on any imperial designations.

Rhys's feet felt a little more stable. His head wasn't spinning so much, and his vision less blurred. He rose out of his seat warily, but he didn't need Kalisha's continued support. He was the first to step into the airlock, though the outer door didn't open until all five starats were behind him and the inner door closed.

When the door finally opened, Rhys stepped out into a strange environment. His first impression was that of cleanliness; of bright, polished walls and clear, sharp air. His second impression leaned more towards thinking the spaceport was cheap and hastily put together. The walls had the look of simple plastic about them, and the ground beneath his feet was the bare rock of Ceres, without anything to cover it.

Two human mechanics were working on the airlock doors to the right. One looked up towards the starats, but quickly looked back down again. No one else was present, but signs had been helpfully tacked onto the walls to provide navigation towards the main hub of the civilian spaceport.

Almost every shuttle bay had construction working taking place; all being undertaken by humans. None looked up at the group of starats, though a couple of disinterested glances were thrown in their direction for a couple of seconds.

The only way out from the shuttle bays was up a couple of steps off the planet surface, onto a cheap, plastic floor that bowed beneath Rhys's weight. It extended down a long, narrow corridor, which eventually led to a larger area that had the look of a permanent building. The spaceport lounge had a dozen desks on the far wall, though only one of them was occupied with staff. The other eleven were all empty, with the ceiling lights switched off across over half the room.

For a moment, Rhys felt lost and confused. He didn't know where to go next, but nor did he want to remain standing still for long, as that would only get them noticed. A starat drawing human attention would not end well. They would be separated and put to work, and then they would never get the chance to speak to Admiral Garter.

Thankfully, Rhys's dilemma was solved by a presence standing in the illuminated doorway to his left. Admiral Garter stood there. The human quickly turned on his heel and walked away, and Rhys knew better than to call out to him. Instead, Rhys just gestured for his companions to follow him, and he slowly walked after his only friend and ally on the dwarf planet.

Rhys never got too close to the admiral, and not once did the human look back to make sure he was still being followed. The two did what they could to make sure neither appeared to be following the other. No one stopped the admiral, and the five starats were left alone with barely a glance in their direction.

The corridors were no longer lined with plastic walls, and there was a proper floor covering the ground. The building had the feel of something more permanent, though the thick pipes hanging from the ceiling to distribute air around the spaceport still appeared cheap.

Finally, the admiral paused. He opened a door to a small room and stepped inside. The door remained open as Rhys approached. He made sure no humans were looking in their direction when he slipped inside, with his companions all hurrying in behind him.

The small room had little in the way of furnishings. Several boxes of tools and building material were stacked in one corner. A large window overlooked the bare terrain of Ceres, with the more familiar sight of the military port visible towards the horizon. A rail track connected the two ports.

Admiral Garter leaned against the window, looking towards the starats. He slowly removed his glasses and wiped them idly on his sleeve. "I never expected to see you again, Captain Griffiths. When I heard you were defecting to the CGP, I thought you would find a safe, comfortable life there. I see perhaps I was wrong."

Rhys couldn't help but laugh nervously. "It's been a bit chaotic," he admitted. He scuffed his foot against the floor and looked out over the desolate landscape beyond the admiral. That empty terrain had been so familiar to him. He had done his best to forget it. "Truth is, Centaura has its own troubles and largely ignores Terra."

"I get the feeling there's a rather large 'but' coming," Admiral Garter said tersely.

Rhys nodded and took a deep breath. There was no point in delaying the news he had to give. "There's a threat to Terra. A very real one, as best I can tell. A rogue group on Centaura seeks the destruction of Terra, and possibly Mars too," he said, fumbling around in his pocket to pull out the datastick. His fingers barely closed around the small component, and he had to let it fall into his palm rather than risk holding it. "I have all the information I was able to get about this new weapon from a computer on Pluto, where it is being developed."

"Pluto? How could the CGP be developing this weapon on Pluto?" Admiral Garter asked in surprise. He gently took the offered datastick from Rhys's shaking hand.

"I believe the Vatican originally started development on it, so it could be used on Centaura first," Rhys said. His ears pinned back as he struggled to sift through his thoughts. He still didn't think he had the full story. "The SFU on Centaura then got their hands on the plans for this weapon and want to use it on Terra."

Admiral Garter looked down at the small datastick. "And how potent is this weapon?"

Rhys tucked his tail close to his legs. "Total annihilation of all life on the planet. If this works as I fear, then not one human or starat will survive."

The human looked sharply up at Rhys. He didn't say anything as he returned his glasses to the bridge of his nose. His eyes then moved to the starats standing just behind Rhys. "You're sure about this?"

"I wish I wasn't," Rhys whispered. He bowed his head. "I don't know when this threat will come, but I don't think it will be long."

Admiral Garter pocketed the datastick. He frowned. "The SFU, you say? The name sounds familiar, though I'm not sure if I can place it just yet," he mused quietly. He tapped his free hand against the window ledge behind him, then looked towards the other starats again. "These starats all from Alpha Centauri as well?"

"Pluto," Elijah said with a smirk. He stepped forward to stand by Rhys's side.

"I thought the SFU were doing good," Rhys explained. He grimaced. "I was betrayed by them when I realised the truth of what they truly planned. I was abandoned on Pluto after we ran a raid on the Tombaugh Station. Elijah took me in."

Admiral Garter raised a bushy white eyebrow. "Stealing starats again?"

"Freeing them," Rhys corrected.

"Of course, yes. My apologies," Admiral Garter said. One hand slipped into his pocket to drop the datastick safely inside. "I trust there is probably a reason why you have come here?"

"You were the only one in the system I could trust to give us safe passage off our ship," Rhys admitted. His eyes were momentarily distracted by some movement on the surface. A large, airtight vehicle was moving away from the military port, travelling on the tracks towards them.

"Your stolen ship? That one you can't claim was freed. I haven't heard from Cardinal Erik in a while, so I assume he's been tracking you?" Admiral Garter asked. From the tone of his voice, he didn't seem to be questioning Rhys. He already knew the answer to that one, so the starat just nodded. Admiral Garter remained quiet for a few more seconds. "I will take precautions to try and prevent the cardinal from finding you here, but I don't expect much to work. The ship's arrival was well-broadcast."

Rhys flicked his tail. "There wasn't much we could do about that. We had to leave Pluto. We had to make sure people close to Terra knew about this threat from the SFU."

Admiral Garter tapped his hands against the window ledge again. "I think you need to run a full briefing with me over at Normandy. There is a lot that needs to be understood."

"Will it be safe for all of us?" Rhys asked, gesturing to the starats stood just behind him.

Admiral Garter sucked in his breath. "No, I don't think so. Probably best if just you came with me."

"I'd like to come too," Elijah said, cutting across Rhys before he could answer. "I'm a quick thinker, and I can fill in any gaps Rhys might have."

Admiral Garter turned to Rhys, who nodded. "Very well," the human said. He rummaged in his pocket again and pulled out a keycard and three small, round yellow tokens. He held them out for Kalisha to take. "These will get you into the new hotel that's being built in this port. I was given a room there for my personal use. The card will let you in. No one will bother you there."

"And what are the tokens for?" Kalisha asked, taking hold of the offered keycard.

"A new security measure," Admiral Garter said. Lines furrowed his brow. "Partly as a result of you, Captain Griffiths. New rulings to control starat movement. Starats on official duty must possess one of these tokens, or else they risk punishment. Word came through from Windsor to enforce that from almost the moment you left for Terra."

Rhys's ears curled down. He growled softly. He knew there would be repercussions for his actions, but he still hated to think of starats being more firmly controlled because of what he had done last time he was on Ceres.

Kalisha distributed the tokens between herself, Mikkel, and Alison. They clutched the small disc of plastic tightly in their hands and didn't speak a word of protest about the system. There was just weary resignation in their eyes.

"Will we find the place easily enough?" Kalisha asked. She never quite managed to look Admiral Garter in the eye, but her head was lifted a little higher than Mikkel's or Alison's.

"The hotel is called The Grey Idol. It's well signposted, you can't miss it. And my room number is on the card," Admiral Garter explained. "Once I understand what the situation is, I can arrange something a little more suitable for you all."

"Most appreciated, Admiral," Rhys said. His arm again tried to salute, but he could barely lift it. "I apologise for dropping in on you quite suddenly like this."

A brief smile brightened the admiral's face. "You continue to make my life interesting, Captain. It's not quite the calm stroll to retirement I had been hoping for."

Rhys grimaced. "This isn't exactly how I thought things might have gone for me, either," he admitted. His ears flicked back. "I wouldn't change anything though. Despite all the shit I've put up with, I'm happier now."

"I am glad to hear that, Captain. I did worry when you disappeared on Terra," the admiral said, holding one hand over his chest. "But we should get back to Normandy. Your friends will be safe in the hotel, you have my word."

Rhys nodded. He turned to face Kalisha. "I'll be back as soon as I can."

Kalisha grinned. "We'll be fine, don't worry. Go and do what you need to do. We'll be waiting in the hotel and seeing what amenities we can use on your friend's credit."

"The room service is substandard and the views boring," Admiral Garter said. His mouth twitched into a brief smile. "There is a reason I still bunk in the *Europa* every night."

Rhys felt a little nervous for the starats. He didn't like leaving them behind, but he knew two of them would be much less conspicuous than all five remaining together. All the same, he couldn't help but keep glancing over his shoulder as they left in opposite directions after leaving the small room. Only once Kalisha's russet tail disappeared around the far corner did he focus fully on where they were going.

Fear and worry began to worm inside Rhys's stomach. There was something about Ceres that set his fur on edge. He didn't like being back on the featureless grey rock, and every glimpse outside the windows reminded him of where he was. This was where everything had changed for him, and the trauma of those first few days had not had the chance to heal.

What worried Rhys even more was the humans who would likely still walk the corridors of Normandy. The last thing he wanted was to run into Captain Favre or Cooper.

With Elijah by his side, Rhys followed Admiral Garter. The human walked a safe distance ahead of the starats, making sure that no onlookers could think that they were in a group together.

Despite the familiar sight of the Ceres horizon, Rhys no longer felt like he belonged. He was an intruder into a place where he had once felt familiar. The only thought that remained consistent from his human life to now was that he longed to get away from Ceres. That much, at least, would never change.

***

The Normandy spaceport had barely changed since Rhys had left. A few more decrepit corridors had been repaired enough to be reopened, but the underground facility still had the feeling of a place that should long ago have been abandoned. Lights flickered on and off. The air filters clicked and hummed loudly. Paint flecks drifted through the air like dust carried on recycled currents. The smell of mould tickled at Rhys's nose.

There were so many familiar faces amongst the crowd of humans. These were people he had worked with over many months as being a resident captain of the port. They had never been a part of his crew, and he had not worked with most closely, but he could still remember the names of many. None of them recognised him; neither as the human they had once worked with, or even as the starat who had caused so much hassle.

If Cooper or Captain Favre were present, then Rhys saw no sign of them. Rhys was glad of that. He doubted either of them would recognise him, but he still had no desire to risk a confrontation with them. Echoes of Admiral Garter's admonishments towards him rung around in his ears. The human had impressed on him not to get angry or to lose his temper with Favre or Baron, the other resident captain at the time. Rhys had to resist the urge to ask Admiral Garter whether Favre and Baron were still present, and if anyone else had been brought in to fill the position he had vacated.

Despite the aching familiarity of the walls he found himself surrounded by, Rhys still did not feel comfortable or settled as he followed the admiral. His feet were capable of navigating the way with ease, but his mind couldn't erase the fear he had felt within the port.

Rhys soon realised where they were going. The briefing room had been the location for a couple of heated conversations with Captain Favre after his teleporter incident. It had been recently refurbished, with repairs being completed on the room just before Rhys's departure. The air circulators were almost perfectly functional, and the walls weren't dirtied with age just yet. Rhys also knew they contained some of the port's more advanced sound proofing systems and secure locks, meaning that any conversation within had the best chance of remaining completely confidential.

Admiral Garter closed the door behind the two starats and secured it. No one with anything less than the admiral's clearance codes would be able to access the briefing room, ensuring privacy during their conversation.

The human took a seat in his usual position, looking back out over the small room. Rhys felt strange as he sat down where he had done so a couple of months earlier. For a moment, he could feel the tight cut of his captain's uniform on his body, as well as the power and confidence his rank had given him. The power had eroded rapidly, but he still maintained the confidence, though it had been forced to change to something new.

Admiral Garter adjusted his glasses, before he rested his hands on the table in front of him. But for a slight grizzled look to some unkempt facial hair, the admiral had not changed since Rhys had last sat in the very same seat.

Rhys tried to mimic the admiral's position, but the table cut into his forearms painfully. He was forced to drop his arms down by his sides.

"If you would then, Captain Griffiths. Tell me everything you know," the admiral prompted.

Rhys took a deep breath. He began to recount his tale.

chapter six

Rhys took a couple of hours to brief Admiral Garter on the severity of the threat coming from Alpha Centauri. He didn't tell the human everything. Rhys was aware that the admiral was a foreign agent, one who could utilise secrets Rhys had learned during his time on Centaura. The starat said nothing of the exact location of Centaura, nor anything of the Stellar Guard's strengths.

Instead, most of Rhys's briefing focused on the Starat Freedom Union and the capabilities of Amy and Snow. They spent some time with the plans Rhys had taken from Pluto, going over the technical readouts of the subspace weapons. Elijah occasionally chipped in with some comments, but he mostly remained quiet and listened to Rhys and Admiral Garter.

Rhys used the briefing as an opportunity to gradually get more information on exactly how the subspace weapon worked. The devices appeared to be little more than standard Denitchev drives, which initially confused him. Then Elijah pointed out the scaling on the weapons. They were larger than anything Rhys had ever seen before.

None of the three were able to determine exactly how severe the threat would be from one such weapon. The readouts Rhys had taken hadn't included estimated damage caused, and even Elijah was unable to work that out with what information they had.

Despite the relatively limited conclusive information, the admiral took the threat as significant. They had no estimated timescale, and they didn't even know the full capabilities of the weapons, but the three agreed that significant action would be needed to protect Terra. The problem was convincing Terra that there was a threat to contain. No one would ever listen to a starat, and the admiral was just one man with no justifiable answers to the question of how he had acquired the information.

Rhys growled softly to himself. His throat was sore, and no amount of lukewarm water from the chiller was enough to sate his thirst. His head spun from all the information he had processed, and his hands had been starting to ache again. The thought of trying to convince Windsor that action needed to be taken filled Rhys with dread.

Admiral Garter had risen to his feet to stretch his legs. There were no windows in the room to look out of, so the admiral had clasped his hands behind his back and stared at the holographic projector, whose flickering display showed a readout of the Denitchev drives being designed for the weapons.

Elijah remained in his seat, next to Rhys, but leaned forward. "May I ask you a question, Admiral?"

The admiral half-turned to look down to the starat. He nodded.

"When you first spoke to us, you mentioned Essie as though he was still alive. What did you mean?" Elijah said. He furrowed his brow, with his ears pinned down to his head.

Admiral Garter fully turned around. He placed his hands on the back of a chair and pursed his lips for a moment. He looked up to meet Rhys in the eyes. "I was contacted about two days after you broke away from Terra. I don't know who they are, but they use the codename Essie."

"Hah, I knew it would be a codename," Elijah said brightly, clapping his hands together. He grinned and flicked his tail. "I think they might be from the same group I send messages to occasionally."

Admiral Garter nodded. He moved his hands from the chair and clasped them together. "I don't know what this group aims to achieve. They seem organised, and I get the impression they've been in hiding for a long time. That they had the courage to reach out to me speaks a lot of their growing confidence."

"Do you know where they're based?" Rhys asked. He tapped a clawless finger against the table and instantly regretted it. Pain shot up through his hand. He managed to disguise the grunt of pain in a cough.

"I believe they're based near London, but I have no closer fix than that," the admiral said with a shake of his head.

"Me neither," Elijah admitted. "I have co-ordinates to send messages to, but those co-ordinates lead to a field in Hampshire. I can only assume there's someone to divert the messages to the true location."

Rhys slowly exhaled in a long, low hiss. "I think we need to contact them again. I feel like they might be our best hope at getting something done."

"I'm not sure I follow your logic, Captain Griffiths," Admiral Garter admitted. He pulled out the chair from beneath the table and sat down again. He kept his hands clasped as his arms rested on the table.

Rhys smirked. "Starats control more than you could possibly imagine, Admiral. We're given access to everything. Every control system, every communications array. Most of this is done without any human supervision. Small acts of rebellion are done every day. A big one takes only a spark."

Admiral Garter looked between the two starats with new wonder in his eyes. "Then why haven't you been able to overthrow us yet?"

Rhys glanced to Elijah, leaving him to answer that one. "Fear, mostly. Should humans realise the magnitude of our strength, they will move swiftly to crush it. The power we have is, mostly, symbolic. Should Windsor or the Vatican realise what they have given us, they will unleash their full fury on us."

The admiral's eyes darkened. "I can see them doing that," he said quietly. He sighed and drummed his fingers against the table. "I don't understand the stubborn refusal most people have of seeing starat intelligence."

"I don't understand it either and I used to believe the same way," Rhys said, grimacing in embarrassment of the human he had been just a few months earlier. He was unable to understand how he had been so blind to them, when now it was obvious.

"That will be the hardest thing to change, but there's no point working on that if Terra is eradicated," Elijah said with a swish of his tail. The starat's eyes flicked between Rhys and the admiral. "Can we get a message sent to Essie and see what action can be taken?"

The admiral checked his wristwatch, then rose to his feet. "I can arrange that. It may have to wait until tomorrow, though. I have already been away from my duties for long enough. Captain Favre will be in my ear about it, I'm sure."

Rhys felt a little uncomfortable about leaving such an important message for so long, but he understood that he had taken up a lot of the admiral's time already. He nodded slowly. "I'll prepare a message to send," he said.

The admiral rummaged through his pockets to pull out a couple more of the yellow tokens. He handed them both to Elijah. "Take these and head back to Noveau Ceres. I'll summon you tomorrow morning. Until then, rest. You look tired, Captain Griffiths."

Elijah took the two tokens and closed his hand around them.

Rhys's fur bristled at the suggestion that he was tired. He knew the admiral was correct, but he still didn't like hearing it so directly. He curled his ears against his head and sighed. "I'll do what I can to relax, Admiral."

"Good. Keep your head low, Captain Griffiths. Not everyone here will have forgotten you just yet," the admiral cautioned. He held his hand out to shake Elijah's, but he hesitated when he got to Rhys. After a second, he placed his hand on Rhys's shoulder. "It is good to see you again."

"Good to see you, too, Admiral," Rhys replied. In lieu of saluting, he nodded his head towards his former superior officer. The conversation had put him back into the mindset of his time on Ceres, and he had to shake his head a couple of times to clear his thoughts as the admiral opened the briefing room doors.

The admiral quickly walked off, leaving the two starats behind. Elijah kept his hand on Rhys's shoulder for a few seconds, giving the human plenty of time to walk away, lest any human realise they had all been talking together. There was no need to be concerned about such a thing, as the corridors outside the briefing room were all deserted.

Out of habit, Rhys almost started walking for the shuttle bay. His feet knew the old paths he used to take through the spaceport, especially with his mind so distracted.

"Do you know this place well?" Elijah asked quietly, leaning in close to Rhys so he could keep his voice as silent as possible.

"Yeah, why?" Rhys asked, curious to know what the other starat had in mind.

"Anywhere high up?"

Rhys flicked his ears in surprise. He frowned for a moment. "There's the observation tower. Why do you want to go up there?"

"There's something I want to work out, and I need somewhere as high as possible," Elijah said slowly. The two starats both glanced up at a human who passed by in the opposite direction, but the human didn't look down at them. She didn't even seem to realise they were there. Rhys curled his tail close. Once he had been that oblivious of starats.

Feeling a little like a ghost amongst his former colleagues, Rhys adjusted his path. The observation tower was one of the few places in the Normandy spaceport that rose above the surface of the dwarf planet. The control tower was one, with the starats' residence being the other. Rhys knew he would need to visit the dome built on the surface, though he couldn't remember the names of any of the local starats who had remained behind. He was sure they wanted to know what had happened to the three of their number he had taken. David, Twitch, and Steph had all come from Ceres, after all. They had left without much warning.

There wasn't a single starat on the way to the observation tower. Only humans walked by. None of them tried to give any orders, though Elijah had the tokens ready should anyone try to divert them. They had to look like they were moving with purpose, already following the commands of another human.

Rhys found the effort exhausting. The constant fear and worry weighed down on his shoulders, and only Elijah's quick footsteps by his side kept him moving. It was a fear no human could hope to understand; the fear that made any starat cower in front of humans, no matter how brave and courageous they normally were away from their masters.

Rhys had never felt that around the humans on Centaura.

***

The observation tower was empty. The glass domed ceiling glinted in the soft light coming from the stars overhead. Rhys stared out across the barren Cerian landscape, which had changed significantly since the last time Rhys had stood in the watchtower. The Noveau Ceres port was being constructed not far away, connected by the lone rail line between them.

Most of the new port had a temporary look to it, though a few permanent buildings were being constructed amongst the prefab materials. The new port added a little variety to the monotony of the Cerian surface, but Rhys couldn't see anything on the bare grey rock that seemed interesting. His eyes were slowly drawn up to the vista of stars above them.

"You know, the last time I was here, I was looking for Aaron on the *Terrestrial Dawn*," Rhys said quietly. He peered up through the glass, unsure if Elijah was even listening to him. He got no vocal reply from the other starat, but he continued speaking anyway. "That was what started everything. One thing happened after the other, and suddenly I was waking up as a starat."

Rhys sighed softly. So much had changed in such a short amount of time, yet Rhys could still see himself fitting back into his old life. He could slip into his captain's uniform again and return to his old duties, finding himself familiar with the routine and structure that entailed. But for one, crucial detail. He stared down at his withered, partially furred hands. No one would treat him with respect. That much had been made abundantly clear the last time he had been on Ceres.

Rhys stumbled back a couple of paces as a sudden feeling of vertigo overwhelmed him. He closed his eyes and lowered his head, reaching out for a handrail to regain his balance. He flicked his ears and winced as the pressure on his palms sent waves up pain rippling up through his arms. Nausea welled up in his throat, and he swallowed hard to force it down again.

Rhys glanced across at Elijah. The other starat stared across the bare landscape. His eyes flicked back and forth, but otherwise he barely moved at all.

"Did you find what you were looking for?" Rhys asked, cautiously approaching the other starat.

Elijah's ears flicked up, before he turned his head. "Sort of," he said with a grimace. "I thought it was just being underground, but I couldn't pick up any wireless signals down there. Turns out the place is just shit in general."

Rhys laughed. "I could have told you that," he said brightly, before pausing. His ears curled forward. "You can pick up wireless signals in your head?"

Elijah grinned. His bright green eyes shone, reflecting the starlight. "Amongst other things. I can't broadcast, but I can intercept and understand wireless signals, yes. Here though, everything feels muffled and old."

"Nothing's been upgraded since the port was built," Rhys muttered darkly. That had always been a source of frustration when he had been stationed on the dwarf planet. "If something isn't broken, it's breaking."

"And it's all French?" Elijah asked.

"Yeah. The old Union built the port, before they merged into the growing empire," Rhys explained. He flicked his ears back. He was wary to believe anything his knowledge of history told him, given what he had learned about the Vatican. How much of the history he had believed to be fact was actually untrue?

"But why are they still naming the new port in French? Tradition?" Elijah asked. His hand traced along the handrail on the edge of the circular room, peering out through the glass towards Noveau Ceres.

"Pretty much, yeah," Rhys said. He stood by Elijah's side, but didn't rest his hands on the railing. He bumped his elbow against Elijah's and smirked. "Though I thought you knew everything in that cyber head of yours."

Elijah stuck his tongue out. "I remember everything, but I don't know everything," he said, matching Rhys's smile. "I still need to learn something, just as you do. I'm just faster and better at it."

"Your head must be a very strange place," Rhys said quietly. He stared out at the shuttle train as it slowly left Noveau Ceres, making its way across the barren surface to connect the two ports.

"I feel like everyone else must have a very quiet head," Elijah replied. His hand slowly moved to touch against Rhys's. "I wish I could remember what I was like before I was this, but that seems to be the only thing I'm not able to recall."

Rhys had tensed from the light touch, partly in pain, but also in part because he hadn't expected it. His mouth opened slightly, though he didn't know what words were about to come out. Before he had chance to speak, they were distracted by the sound of approaching footsteps, accompanied by the familiar click of claws.

He turned to see an unfamiliar starat standing at the top of the stairs. Her eyes widened. "Twitch! I thought that was you!"

Before Rhys could react, the starat had sprinted across the observation tower and embraced him tightly. Her arms squeezed around his sides, mercifully leaving his arms alone. "We've all missed you so much."

"I'm not Twitch," Rhys said quickly, managing to take a step back and extricate himself from the tight embrace. He held a trembling hand to his chest. "I'm Rhys. Rhys Griffiths."

The starat blinked and took a step back of her own. "Oh," she said quietly, scuffing her foot against the floor. Then she gasped and held her hands to her mouth. "Oh! You're the one who…"

"I'm the one in the teleporter incident, yes. I was human," Rhys explained. A little weight was taken off his shoulders; weight he hadn't even been aware of carrying. Starats at Ceres recognised him. That meant Cardinal Erik hadn't taken out his wrath on the starats at the port.

The starat's eyes flicked up to Elijah, and then back to Rhys. "And Twitch? Is he here? David and Steph?"

Rhys shook his head. "No, sorry. They're safe on Centaura," he said, not wanting to bring any worry about Twitch's injuries. He had to have faith that Twitch had been able to recover.

The starat clapped her hands together. "Centaura?" she yelped with joy. She grinned widely and pulled Rhys into another hug. "They got away from here, that's amazing. Have you… have you come back for us?"

Rhys wished he could bring better news, but he had to shake his head again. "I'm sorry, I'm not. But we are here for an important reason. Perhaps you might be able to help us."

The starat nodded eagerly. "I can do that, sure. Perhaps you'd like to come down to our quarters? There will be lots of starats who would like to hear how Twitch and the others are doing."

Rhys glanced to Elijah. Admiral Garter had instructed him to return to Noveau Ceres and stay out of the way, but he couldn't see much harm in doing this. He wouldn't stay there for long; only for enough time to get some more information, and to inform the starats what had happened to their former companions.

Elijah shrugged his shoulders. "Let's go say hi, shall we?"

The Cerian starat beamed brightly. She hopped from foot to foot, seeming to buzz with the same energy that filled Twitch. "This will be such a lovely surprise for everyone," she squeaked in excitement.

Rhys felt a slight twinge of worry. He remembered the reception he had gotten from the starats last time. Though around half had been positive about his introduction, there had been a lot of scepticism. A few had been outright hostile. He could only hope that the intervening time, and his actions in them, would bring about a more positive reception.

As the starat started to walk away, moving back towards the stairs, she halted and spun around on the spot. She gasped and lightly slapped at her forehead. "My name. I don't think we were introduced last time you were here. I'm Skye."

"It's lovely to meet you, Skye," Rhys said, bowing his head towards her. "If you lead the way, we'll follow just behind." He let the other starat bound ahead a few steps before he started walking, keeping close to Elijah. He leaned his head in close to the augmented starat. "Are you sure this is going to be a good idea?"

"Yeah, why not?" Elijah said, speaking quietly so the starat ahead wouldn't be able to hear the conversation. "Would be good to get a starat's perspective on everything. I'm sure the admiral is good, but he won't get the same view a starat does."

"I suppose you're right," Rhys replied. He flicked his tail back and forth as he started to descend the curving stairs. "They might even know a bit more about this mysterious group of yours on Terra."

Elijah smiled, perking his ears up. "Exactly. Plus, I doubt even the admiral will know where we are. He won't mind if we're wandering around, so long as we keep the tokens."

"At least Favre and Cooper won't be where we're going," Rhys muttered to himself. They were the last people he wanted to see on Ceres, and he was thankful he hadn't run into either of them yet. He hoped to keep things that way.

Once more, Rhys descended into the labyrinthine corridors of the Normandy spaceport. He felt like he vanished into the shadows the moment he went below ground. Human eyes slid right off him, and there were no starats around but for the two he walked with. That would change soon.

***

The starats' residence had not changed at all. The large warehouse rose above the Cerian surface, protected by the airtight dome. Skye led the way towards the closed doors. She had barely been able to contain her excitement on the walk through the port, only falling silent and still when they approached a human.

Several dozen starats were gathered inside the warehouse. A few looked up as they entered, though none seemed particularly interested. Most of the starats were sat down or lying on the beds that lined the room, in groups of around half a dozen. That changed when one of the nearest starats raised their head and looked right towards Rhys.

The starat's eyes widened. "Oh shit. He's back."

Rhys raised his hands quickly towards the light-furred starat who had noticed him. "I'm not Twitch. I'm Rhys. Rhys Griffiths. I don't know if you remember me."

The starat slipped off her bed and approached him. She breathed in deeply. "You're the one who was human?" she asked, though Rhys was sure she already knew the answer. A small crowd was starting to gather behind her. "Why have you come back?"

Rhys looked around the group of starats. He recognised some faces, though he knew no names. He lifted his voice so that he could be heard by everyone, even those starats who had not come close. "I came before you a few months ago, scared and confused. Insecure in my body." He paused and laughed. "I'm still scared and confused, but I'm no longer insecure. I have been through hell as a starat, but I have seen good places and the potential for a better future for all of us. For all of you."

"Where? How?" one of the starats shouted out, from towards the back of the gathered crowd.

"I took three starats from you when I was last here. Twitch, David, and Steph all came with me. I foolishly thought they could work on my ship while I remained captain," Rhys explained, slowly moving his eyes around the starats, making sure not to drop his gaze. "That did not last long, but they stayed with me when I fled to Alpha Centauri. They are there now, safe, I hope."

"Alpha Centauri?" a starat gasped. The whisper spread through the crowd, rippling through as more and more realised just what Rhys had said.

Rhys held up a hand to forestall the inevitable questions he knew would come. "I'm not here to take more starats to Alpha Centauri. Truth is, I am here by accident," he said. His tail curled as he saw the disappointment spreading through the starats. "There is a threat coming; one that will obliterate the lives of billions, human and starat alike. I am here to stop that from happening, but to do so, I need some help."

"Can't do it yourself?" one of the starats scoffed. Rhys thought he recognised the voice as one of the starats who had spoken out against him at his first visit to the starat quarters. "I thought humans were meant to be good at that."

Rhys flinched. His hands trembled as he slowly clenched his fingers up into a fist. He struggled to keep the anger from his voice, but he couldn't quite manage it. "I have suffered as a starat. I have lived through hell for months. I understand that you have lived through that hell for years, for your entire lives, but do not speak to me as though I am still just an uncaring human," he snarled. He held up his hands, showing his withered muscles and declawed fingers. "When I first came here, that was a fair accusation. Now, it is not."

Elijah cleared his throat and stepped forward. "We travelled from Pluto in a stolen Vatican ship. We came here, as starats, to ask for help."

"What kind of help?" Skye asked. She had moved amongst the other starats, standing at the front of the crowd to face Rhys.

"Information, mostly," Rhys said. His anger slowly drained out of him, and he struggled to relax his fingers. They felt stiff. He could barely move them. His head spun and he winced from the effort of uncurling his fists. "I understand Admiral Garter has been in communication with someone codenamed Essie. I need to know any information about this starat, and where they might be located."

One starat raised his hand. "I was the one who transcribed that first message from Essie. I..." The starat hesitated for a moment, his eyes flicking across to one of his companions. "We didn't send the admiral the message straight away. We didn't believe it. Everyone here has all read the message, and each one between the human and Essie since. We may have left out a couple of things for the human."

Rhys flicked his tail and twitched his muzzle. He understood why the starats would be hesitant to trust the admiral. He had always shown a soft touch towards starats, but he was still human. "Is it possible to see the original message?"

"Yeah, come with me," the starat said.

Before Rhys could move more than a couple of steps, the starat who had dissented raised his voice again. "Why are we trusting him? For all we know he's just lying to us again. He comes back here, speaking of vague threats and warnings."

Rhys took a deep breath. He looked around the group of starats, which now numbered every single one who had been present in the warehouse. He had the rapt attention of all present. "There is a group on Centaura, of starats, who believe that everyone in the Empire is unable to be saved. These starats would destroy Terra without remorse. I need to warn Terra and prevent this from happening."

"Fuck them. What has Terra ever done for us?" a starat shouted. A few more agreed with her.

"You don't understand," Rhys said, raising his hands. "Human and starat would be extinguished without mercy. Terra, the entire planet, will be pulled into subspace and destroyed. Starats would be killed as well as humans."

A hush fell across the starats. "Is that even possible?" one of them asked.

Rhys extended his right hand. He took a deep breath and closed his eyes for a moment and reached down into subspace, getting that familiar scent across his nose. The starats around him all blazed brightly against the white backdrop of subspace. Their mere presence burned at his fur, making him tremble and take a step backwards.

Before he could reconsider, he reached out and pulled at some clothes that had been discarded across the nearest bed. His fingers burned from the movement, but by the time he opened his eyes, the clothes were draped over his wrists.

"What the fuck?" the nearest starat to him gasped. Several took a few steps back.

Rhys swayed. Dark spots flickered over his vision. His knuckles cracked as he moved his hands. "There's a lot I learned on Centaura," he said, his voice sounding breathless even to his own ears. "Most of all, I learned about the lies upon which the empire is built. I know I'm asking a lot of you, but please trust me. If those starats get their way, then every life in this system is at risk."

The starat who had spoken most against Rhys bowed his head. He scuffed a foot against the dusty concrete floor. "Very well."

Rhys slowly made his way through the group of starats, feeling a little unsteady on his feet. He tossed the clothes back onto the bed he had pulled them from and followed the starat who had the information he needed. Elijah followed just behind him, though Skye remained with the others. Rhys could hear her excitedly talking amongst her companions.

At the far end of the warehouse was a small kitchen built against the back wall. A few beds were close enough to the kitchen that they almost touched the storage cupboards. The starat led Rhys towards the bed at the very end of the row on the left of the warehouse. At the foot of the bed was a small trunk, which the starat opened and rummaged through.

The starat pulled out a thick ream of paper and handed it over to Rhys. There were at least fifty pages. The weight was almost too much for Rhys's hands, but he was just about able to grip hold of the paper.

"This is every message we've had between the human and Essie," the starat explained. He flicked his ears back. "Were we wrong to hold back what was really being said?"

"I don't know the answer to that yet," Rhys replied with a shake of the head. He didn't start reading. "What's your name?"

"Remi."

"Well, Remi. Thank you for letting me see these. May I take them with me for now?" Rhys asked. He wanted the chance to read through the documents, with enough time to make notes and observations. Sitting in a warehouse with starats all around him didn't seem like the best environment.

"Of course, that's fine," Remi said quickly. He closed the trunk again and perched on the edge of the bed. "I can print off another copy easily enough."

Rhys flicked through a couple of the pages, but nothing immediately jumped out at him as being of particular interest. "Thank you," he said again. The words on the page started to blur, and Rhys was forced to squint. A wave of dizziness started to overwhelm him, and he slowly slumped down to sit on the side of the closest bed, opposite Remi.

"Are you alright, Rhys?" Elijah asked, sitting down by his side. His hand rested on Rhys's shoulder.

Rhys took a few deep breaths and closed his eyes. His head still felt like it was spinning, even with his eyes seeing nothing but darkness. "Yeah, just a little tired, I think," he said. He could hear the weakness in his voice. Every word sounded like it was spoken from across the room, vague and distant to his ears.

Elijah's hand didn't leave Rhys's shoulder. "Is there a science lab around here somewhere? One that doesn't have humans in for extended periods of time," the augmented starat asked.

Rhys curled his ears down, unsure if the question was being asked to him. He struggled to think of any.

"Yeah, there is," Remi replied. His voice trembled slightly. "Why do you need one?"

"There's a few things I need to know as well," Elijah said tersely. His fingers squeezed gently onto Rhys's shoulder. "The quicker the better, I fear."

"I'll see what I can do to get you access," Remi said. A second hand brushed against Rhys's knee, this time coming from opposite him. "Is he alright?"

"I'm fine," Rhys mumbled to himself, but he still kept his eyes closed and head bowed. A strange weakness had come across him, and he barely felt like he had the energy to move any part of his body, but most of all his arms. "Just a little tired."

"We have spare beds here, if you'd like to stay," Remi offered.

Elijah's hand tightened on Rhys's shoulder. "I appreciate the offer, but we have companions who will be worried for us if we don't make it back. The admiral has given us his room at the hotel at Noveau Ceres."

"If you're sure," Remi said uncertainly. His hand moved away from Rhys's knee.

"I'm telling you, I'm fine," Rhys said. He forced his eyes open and looked up to Remi. The starat didn't have a solid outline. His body swam and waved through the air, blurred around the edges. Nausea welled up within Rhys's body as the world spun uneasily around him.

"I'm fine, I think," Rhys repeated, but now he was suddenly less sure. His eyes watered as he struggled to focus on something – anything – as all started to fade into one dark blur.

He was briefly aware of Elijah speaking, but the words didn't make it through to his ears. He slumped to the side, resting against Elijah's body. His eyes fluttered closed again. All fell into darkness.

chapter seuen

"Lieutenant Scott, report immediately to security. I repeat, Lieutenant Scott, report immediately to security."

"Damn," Edgar Scott muttered. He grimaced and rose to his feet. He had hoped they would have longer than that. "We'd better hurry. Rhys, come on. You first."

The injured starat refused to move. Despite all the pain and suffering the starat had gone through, he did not approach the teleporter room. Instead, he stared down the corridor, towards where the sounds of pursuit echoed from. "Twitch first, please." He hesitated as someone shouted from not too far away. "They're here. Go through, Twitch. Please."

"Not before you," the second starat said. Twitch reached out tentatively, trying to reach out for Rhys, but the captain pushed back.

"You first, please," Rhys begged. Tears sprung to his eyes, though Edgar couldn't be sure whether it was fear or pain that drove the moisture from his captain's eyes. Rhys Griffiths had never showed such desperate emotion before. "Please. You have to go first. I need to be…" The starat's voice descended to a volume Edgar couldn't hear, though Twitch nodded.

"Just make sure you follow, alright?"

"I'll be right behind you, I promise," Rhys said. He looked up, briefly meeting Edgar's eyes.

Twitch finally moved towards the teleporter. The starat pulled the pod door closed. With a final flash of his smile, he was gone. Disappeared in a burst of bright light. Safe on the Star Hub.

The teleporter needed a few moments to reset itself and prepare the pod for Rhys. Edgar used that time to usher the wounded starat inside the small room and close the door behind them. The sounds of shouting were getting too close to be comfortable. Edgar wasn't sure if they had time for two more uses of the teleporter. He loosened the pistol holstered by his hip, before wedging a chair beneath the door handle.

"Hurry, Captain."

Rhys hesitated by the teleporter pod. He muttered something beneath his breath, too quietly for Edgar to hear. The human simply unholstered his pistol. Footsteps were sounding from close by. They were only moments away.

The door thudded hard. Someone hammered on the other side. Only then did Rhys finally close the pod door. Edgar raised his pistol and aimed towards the door, ready to open fire. "Go, Rhys! Go!"

The hinges gave way and the door shattered open. The chair was kicked aside as four humans faced Edgar. Three were airport security, while the fourth was a Vatican official in pale green robes.

Edgar got three shots away. Two found their marks. One guard died immediately, though the other was just wounded. Pain flared through Edgar's body as they returned fire. His shoulder and thigh burned with an intense fire, and he staggered back.

Edgar's head turned. Rhys was still in the pod. If he didn't do something, then the guards would catch up to Rhys anyway. His thoughts raced, while everything else processed so slowly. There would be more guards. There would always be more. He couldn't stop them coming, but he could give Rhys time.

Each teleporter was specifically configured to pair with another. It would take them half an hour to recalibrate a second pod to connect to the same part of the Star Hub as this one. Edgar knew what he had to do. He raised his pistol again, but he didn't aim for the guards. He aimed for the pod.

Rhys vanished in a burst of white light. Edgar fired his pistol at the same moment.

When the light faded, there was no sign of the starat. He had safely made it to the Star Hub. Bullet holes shattered the pod window. Red lights flashed as an alarm flared. The pod couldn't be used now. There were other ways up to the Star Hub, but none close to Rhys's location.

Edgar grimaced as he turned to face his fate. His shoulder burned in agony, but he pushed that pain to the back of his mind. His hand trembled as he squeezed his grip onto his pistol. "Which one of you bastards is next?"

Neither of the surviving guards spoke. Instead, they stepped to the side to allow the Vatican official to speak. The priest held a weapon in his hand, a modified pistol with a crucifix emblazoned along the side of the barrel.

"You, is it?" Edgar asked. He struggled to hold his pistol up. He was losing blood from his shoulder wound, and his arm was beginning to feel numb.

The priest seemed to show no concern for Edgar's weapon. "Lieutenant Scott. You have been found guilty of heresy towards the Vatican of Mars. By the authority of Father Jon Svensson, given unto me by Pope Adamantius, I hereby sentence you to death."

"So be it," Edgar said. His fingers tensed around the trigger of his pistol.

The priest was quicker. Edgar never felt the pain as everything cut to black.

***

Rhys jerked upright. Pain flared through his arms. For a wild moment, he thought that he had been shot in the shoulder. Thoughts slowly trickled down into his mind as he realised where he was, and even who he was. He stared down at his trembling hands. Small patches of fur still covered them. He wasn't human again.

Scott's death had gone ungrieved for so long. His death had come at a frantic time for Rhys, and he had barely had an opportunity to stay still for long enough to think about the sacrifice of his former navigator and, briefly, first officer. He bowed his head and squeezed his eyes closed. "I'm sorry, Scott."

"Who is Scott?"

Rhys glanced up. He hadn't realised he wasn't alone. For the first time, he got the opportunity to take in his surroundings. He was lying on a comfortable bed, which was in the middle of a large hotel room. Kalisha was sat on a chair across the room, looking out over the windows. There wasn't a great view, just the inside of a translucent dome and the barren surface of Ceres. Weak sunlight bathed the rock in light.

"A human who died to keep me safe," Rhys said simply. He frowned as he looked around the large room. No one else was present but for Kalisha. He had never seen the room before, but he knew where he was. This was the hotel room Admiral Garter had given the starats for their stay on Ceres. He had no memory of getting there. The last he could remember was being in the starats' quarters, talking with Elijah and Remi. Then there had been the dream of Scott, and he had woken up in the bed.

"How are you feeling?" Kalisha asked. She rose from her chair, only to sit at the foot of Rhys's bed.

Rhys wasn't sure how to best answer that question. His heart still thudded in his chest, disturbed from the dream he had woken from. His arms were aching as they usually did, and there was a sharp pain in his neck he couldn't account for. "Alright, I think. What happened to me?"

Kalisha curled her tail up over her lap. "Elijah thinks it was the Devil's Blood. It's getting worse and will continue to do so every time you use subspace."

"But I had something to stop that. My ship's doctor had an antidote," Rhys said. He stared down at his hands and tried moving his fingers, but he found even that small movement was beyond him without significant pain.

"Elijah doesn't think that was enough," Kalisha said with a shake of her head. She idly played with the tip of her tail. "He thinks the poison was just held at bay, but now it's starting to attack you again."

"Where is he now?" Rhys asked. None of the other starats were present. There was no one but Kalisha, and Rhys couldn't even smell any of the other three. None of them had been present for a few hours at least. His breath caught in his throat as he thought back to the agony he had been in when the Devil's Blood had been running rampant through his body; when Edgar Scott had sacrificed his life so Rhys could escape Terra.

"He's taken Alison and Mikkel to the labs. They're having to go when the humans aren't there, but Elijah is running tests on the Devil's Blood sample he got on the *Vigilant*," Kalisha explained. Her eyes flicked back towards the windows. "I'm worried about what might happen if they're caught there."

Rhys bit his lip. He didn't like the thought of Elijah risking himself with Alison and Mikkel. Especially not for him. He feared what might happen should the Devil's Blood continue to ravage his body, but nor did he want any of the starats to risk themselves on his behalf. He knew he would need to speak to Elijah about it when he returned.

Struggling against the pain, Rhys swung his legs out of bed. He still felt a little vertigo at the movement, but a few deep breaths helped to clear his spinning, blurred vision. He didn't want to collapse a second time. Once he could see clearly again, the starat glanced around the room. Everything looked neat and organised, like it had barely been used at all.

"There were some documents," Rhys said hesitantly, looking for the stack of papers Remi had given him.

Kalisha hopped up off the bed. She pulled open one of the drawers at the desk in the corner of the room and took out the papers inside. She placed them down on the bed in front of Rhys, ignoring his outstretched hands. "We haven't looked at them yet. Thought you might want to read them first."

Rhys was glad Kalisha had ignored his waiting hands. Even the act of turning a single page sent a spike of pain through his fingers. All the pages together would have been too heavy for him.

"Did I miss anything else while I was asleep?" Rhys asked. He kept his eyes down on the first page of the transcript, though nothing appeared particularly interesting right away. His ears remained perked up to listen to Kalisha.

"Your human friend had some antidote, which Elijah was able to give you," Kalisha said, her voice slow and quiet. "He said it might hold the infection back for a little bit."

Rhys understood then why his neck hurt so much. He carefully lifted a hand up to press against the side of his neck. A small plaster had been stuck to his fur, protecting the small wound from the injection of the antidote. His eyes flicked up. "Anything else?"

Kalisha shook her head. "You were asleep all night. We didn't want to disturb you. Elijah thought it was best that you rest and sleep off the illness. He said that you would be stubborn and try to work through it if you were awake." She stuck her tongue out and paused, giving Rhys the chance to groan and look away. "Your admiral friend wished you a quick recovery, but otherwise no one has tried to contact us. No one seems to have followed us from Pluto."

"He will come after me," Rhys said with a shake of his head. He looked up to Kalisha and tried to keep the fear from his eyes and voice, though he wasn't sure how well he succeeded.

Kalisha's muzzle flicked into a nervous smile. "I don't doubt that. He seemed quite the nasty piece of work."

Rhys laughed bitterly. "That doesn't even come close." He held up his hands and struggled to keep them still, but his elbows trembled from the exertion. "He tortured me for over a week, just to see me in pain. He would gladly do that to all starats if he could."

"Then we had better make sure he doesn't find us," Kalisha said. She reached out with one hand and pulled a chair towards her through subspace.

Rhys wrinkled his nose at the cinnamon scent that accompanied the quiet fizzle of subspace manipulation. He wished hiding away from Cardinal Erik was so easy, but he knew they had hardly been quiet about their arrival. The *Vigilant* still orbited above Ceres, and they had used a Vatican code to gain access to the dwarf planet. Their trail would not be difficult to follow.

Unfortunately, Ceres was also the safest place for them at the moment. Until they were able to decode where the mysterious starat who went by Essie was located, they had nowhere to turn to. Admiral Garter was the only other person Rhys could trust.

That was why Rhys was reading through messages sent to the admiral without his permission. Worse still, they were the original messages, while the admiral had only received edited versions. Rhys's ears pinned down as he started to read. His heart quickened and he felt a little nausea building in his throat. He would never before have considered going behind the admiral's back like this.

Even so, Rhys read on. He needed to know what was going on, and he needed to know who he could trust. If this mysterious Essie could help him, then he would need to find out where they were.

The transcripts were all translations from the original coded messages. At a quick glance, Rhys couldn't determine the cipher that had been used to decode the messages. Kalisha had been unable to work out the method used either, as she had only rarely worked in communications on Pluto.

As Rhys read, he began to slowly get a bigger picture of what was happening on Terra. A growing union of starats had been building on the streets of London. Rhys had stared at that information several times, almost refusing to believe it. How could a group of starats go unnoticed in the middle of the largest city in the empire?

Most of the messages to the admiral had been requests for assistance in moving starats around the system. None of Admiral Garter's replies were included in the documents, but judging from the one side of the conversation Rhys could read, the admiral had been assisting in some way. He had been facilitating the movement of starats throughout the Sol System, directing them to a rendezvous point in the very centre of London. The proximity to Windsor seemed to be a deliberate point that Essie's organisation was making. They called themselves Essie's Heresy.

Kalisha didn't interrupt Rhys as he read. She remained quiet and practiced some of her subspace skills. But for the occasional smell of cinnamon, Rhys wasn't distracted at all. For a couple of hours, he took the opportunity to read and learn about Essie's Heresy. From what he could understand, they were not active yet, like Amy's Starat Freedom Union. They were merely gathering numbers and freeing starats from their lives of slavery but were not yet at a stage where they could attempt to act against the Terran government.

Rhys didn't yet know what assistance he could offer Essie's Heresy, nor what they could do for him, but he knew he needed to get in contact with them. Essie would be able to spread the message through the system about the subspace weapons. He would need to get Admiral Garter's permission to send an urgent message to Terra.

A door opened and closed. Rhys glanced up quickly. Kalisha rose to her feet and peered around the corner to see who had come in. Her tail relaxed and she moved out of sight to greet them. Rhys struggled to follow her. His legs were a little unsteady and weak. He threw his arm out for balance, only to hiss in pain as his palm pressed against the wall.

Elijah had returned, with Alison and Mikkel just behind him. The augmented starat slumped down at the dining table. He grimaced as he looked up to Rhys and shook his head. "I can't work it out," he muttered. He tapped his claws against the table and stared at the wall opposite.

"No luck then?" Rhys asked. He sat down opposite Elijah.

Kalisha moved into the kitchen and filled a kettle with water, while both Mikkel and Alison took a seat of their own.

"Some, I suppose. But not enough," Elijah said with a growl. "I was able to identify all of the ingredients in the Devil's Blood, but for one. I've never seen anything like it before, and it reacts unlike any other material. I'm sure that's what is infecting you, but until I know what it is, there's nothing I can do."

"Why now, though? Why has it been so long before getting worse?" Rhys asked. He didn't expect an answer as he stared down at his hands. He couldn't even rest them on the table without hurting them.

Elijah clicked his tongue. "Subspace, it has to be. You exhausted yourself keeping us safe on the way from Pluto. That did something, I know it. Might be best if you didn't use your subspace abilities until we know for sure."

Rhys's ears curled down. "Are you suggesting I limit myself more? I can barely hold anything with my hands," Rhys protested. He shook his head and tried to tense his fingers. He knew he didn't have the fine control over subspace that Snow, or even Kalisha, had. Any ability was still better than relying solely on his broken body. "Without subspace I can't do anything."

"This thing is wasting your body away from the inside," Elijah warned. He reached across the table and placed his hand close to Rhys. "I don't know how quickly this might spread through you. Please. Take things safe and limit what you do. If you start getting tired or weak again, let me know."

Rhys sighed and bowed his head. He knew Elijah was speaking the truth, but he didn't like the thought of it. Should Cardinal Erik follow them to Ceres, then Rhys would be totally defenceless against the cardinal. He was glad he had starats around who could help him, but Rhys didn't want to put them into danger.

Alison and Mikkel excitedly told Kalisha about what they had seen through the port. Rhys was amused at their excitement, especially at something he found so mundane and ordinary. Ceres was the complete opposite of interesting for him, and he hated the fact that he was back.

To starats who had been stuck on Pluto for years, though, it must have seemed exciting. Of course, Kalisha would have been aware of everything, having been stationed on Ceres before she was moved out to Pluto.

Kalisha prepared coffee for everyone. She placed cups down on the table in front of the starats, though Rhys wasn't quite sure how to drink his. He just remained quiet and distracted himself with his thoughts. The companionable chatter around him reminded him of sitting amongst the starats he had taken to Centaura. Rhys had often sat quietly amongst them, letting Twitch lead the conversation in his exuberant style. Leandro would also always have something interesting to say; some incredible story of experiences few humans could hope to witness.

Rhys missed them terribly. He hoped they were all safe.

Letting the conversation happen around him, Rhys curled down his ears and lost himself to thought. He needed a plan. First, he needed to get a message to Terra. Then he would need to act. He returned his attention back to the transcripts, just in case there was something else he had missed.

***

Rhys had been summoned back to Normandy to meet with Admiral Garter. Elijah had gone with him, while the other three starats had all remained back in the hotel. Kalisha was disappointed not to come, but Elijah had argued that it was better for fewer starats to run the corridors of Ceres, just in case they were sent on any errands. Better to remain safe, if a little bored, in the hotel.

The admiral hadn't given a reason for the summoning when he had sent a message through to Rhys. Assuming schedules hadn't changed in the time Rhys had been away, the admiral wished to see them just after the morning briefing with the resident captains.

Voices could still be heard inside the briefing room when Rhys and Elijah arrived. They didn't go inside, not wanting to interfere in the confidential meeting. The door was open, so nothing confidential was discussed. With the door open, Rhys recognised most of the voices. He could hear the admiral speaking, with occasional comments coming from Captain Favre and Captain Baron. A fourth person also spoke occasionally, but Rhys didn't recognise him, not until Admiral Garter addressed him as Captain Uwele. That was the man who had been intended to take Rhys's position as captain of the *Harvester*.

Rhys briefly wondered which ship Uwele had taken, after Rhys had fled the system with the *Harvester* and most of its crew.

A few humans walked past the waiting starats. A couple looked towards them, though most didn't even seem to see Rhys and Elijah. Rhys felt a little like a ghost, patrolling the corridors where once he had been someone important. Now he was ignored entirely.

The meeting inside the briefing room finally concluded. Rhys had not been able to make out much from what had been said, with the voices slightly distorted around the corner and muffled by the constant drone of the air circulators. Only occasional words had come to his ears. He had spent so long as a captain on Ceres that being left out of briefings was an unexpected punch to the gut. He had no right to sit at the briefing table with the admiral, not anymore, but some part of his mind still tried to convince him that he should have been in there.

Captain Favre was the first to come out from the briefing room. He didn't even look down at Rhys. His brow was set into a familiar frown, and his hair looked to have greyed a little since Rhys had last seen the Cerian captain. The Cerian swept away, out of sight even before Captain Baron and Captain Uwele came out. The two humans were in deep conversation with each other.

Rhys had never met Captain Uwele before. He had been Aaron's first officer before his friend's defection to Alpha Centauri, but Rhys had never been introduced to Uwele in their brief encounters. Rhys had braced himself to dislike Uwele. The man had been lined up to steal his ship from him. That was not the impression Rhys got.

Captain Uwele's face was lined, but the wrinkles were those of laughter and smiling. He gestured emphatically in his conversation with Captain Baron, and his amber eyes briefly looked down towards Rhys as they walked by. No hatred or disgust came across the human's face. There was even a brief smile there.

Rhys flicked his ears in confusion, then turned to enter the briefing room. Admiral Garter wasn't the only one still inside.

Giles Cooper, once Rhys's first officer, thrust his hand into Rhys's chest as he prowled towards the starat. "Move," the human snarled, pushing Rhys to the side and slamming the starat against the frame of the door.

Rhys bit back on the immediate response that came to his lips. He contented himself with glaring at Cooper's back as the human stalked away. Elijah had quickly jumped to the side and avoided the lieutenant's swinging hand.

Relieved that his former first officer had not done more to him, Rhys turned away from Cooper's retreating back. If Admiral Garter had noticed the exchange, then he did not comment on it. He silently waved the two starats inside the briefing room and didn't say a word until the doors had closed behind them.

"I trust you are feeling better, Captain Griffiths?" the admiral asked. He switched off the projector that had been displaying some charts and maps of the nearby regions of the system.

"For now, at least, Admiral," Rhys replied. The twitchiness in his arms was getting worse, and moments of disorientation still threatened to throw him off balance. He quickly took a seat, not wanting to risk another bout of vertigo.

"It is my understanding you wish to go to Terra," Admiral Garter said. He turned to face Rhys, still standing up with his hands clasped behind his back.

Rhys's eyes flicked up to Elijah. He could only assume the augmented starat had mentioned something to the admiral, as he couldn't recall saying that in their previous meeting. "I think that would be for the best," Rhys said after a moment of pause. "There's nothing I can do here. On Terra, I might be able to do something."

"You want to find this Essie, don't you?" Admiral Garter asked gruffly. He sounded like he already knew the answer.

Rhys nodded once. "I do, yes. I trust that you will do all you can to raise awareness of this threat, Admiral, but I feel restless here. I can do more on Terra than I could ever do here."

Admiral Garter raised an eyebrow. "You were an incredible captain, and I have no doubt that you are as skilled a starat as you were a human, but I don't understand what you expect you can do on Terra that you can't do here."

Rhys spread his arms wide, making sure not to brush his hands against the table. "I don't know yet. But I have to do something."

Admiral Garter began to pace back and forth. "You do understand that if I were to help you in any way, that would be construed as treason. Even what I have already done will be viewed poorly," the admiral said, after a brief pause to gather his thoughts.

"Anytime you have spoken to me since I've been a starat has been treason," Rhys replied. He watched the admiral as the human paced. "The only way to avoid that is to remove those who enforce those rules."

The admiral paused. He looked down at Rhys and frowned, sending more wrinkles across his lined forehead. "I don't like that thought at all. But I respect that it may be necessary. I will do what I can without actively interfering, as I have told Essie many times. I can arrange transport for you, but I will do no more than that."

"I appreciate that, Admiral," Rhys said with a nod of his head. His tail twitched behind him as he tried to get comfortable in the chair, which was not designed for a starat's tail. "I just ask that, should it come to a fight, I would see you on my side, rather than as my enemy."

Admiral Garter's face darkened. His eyes narrowed and his lips tightened. "I refuse to answer that. I would remind you that I am still an admiral for the Terran Empire, and that I have pledged my service to the emperor, as you once did."

"You..." Rhys said, but he was interrupted by a raised hand from the admiral. That, combined with the fury in the human's eyes, told Rhys that he was better served keeping his mouth shut. A squeeze on his shoulder from Elijah added to that.

The admiral cleared his throat. Some of the anger seemed to fade from his eyes, though his jaw was still firmly set. "You went through circumstances I did not, and will never, go through. Your disloyalty to Emperor Neicwyk is understandable to me. That does not mean I share those beliefs. My loyalty is still to the empire. I will offer my assistance to improve life for starats, but that does not include fighting against the empire. Am I quite clear?"

Suitably chastised, Rhys bowed his head. "I understand, Admiral. My apologies."

"Should this be your course, then know that I will not follow you," the admiral said softly. "I will not stop you taking this path, but it is not mine to walk."

Rhys let out a slow breath. He struggled to find the right words. He knew that he had taken the admiral's support for granted, and that he had believed the human was more committed to the injustices Rhys saw. That was not true. The admiral was still a part of the empire and seemed content in that decision.

Rhys's ears curled low. He resisted the urge to drum his fingers against the table. "I assume this wasn't the reason you call me here, though?"

Admiral Garter finally took a seat. He clasped his hands in front of him, resting them on the table. "I received a message from Captain Herschel on Pluto. He was enquiring about you. I am unsure how to respond."

Elijah's hand pinched against Rhys's shoulder again. "This might be a trap," the augmented starat warned. "We don't know if the cardinal is still there."

"There was no mention of the cardinal in Captain Herschel's message," Admiral Garter said uncertainly. He unclasped his hands and spread them. "I assume you have no grudges against the captain, and that you expected he might contact you?"

Rhys nodded. He didn't want to mention anything about the true identity of the captain. He didn't trust the admiral enough to inform him that Captain Herschel was actually Sam Carson, a former starat and now general in the Centauran military. He doubted that would go down too well. Admiral Garter would still be obligated to inform his superiors of the spy in their midst.

"Pass on my regards to Captain Herschel, and let him know I am safe and well," Rhys said, ignoring the pressure from Elijah on his shoulder. He was glad to hear that Carson had not been taken prisoner by Cardinal Erik. Rhys hadn't had much chance to think much about what could have happened on Pluto since his departure. He suppressed a shiver at the thought of the cardinal.

"I'll have a message sent out shortly," the admiral said. He leaned back in his chair, and for a moment he looked old and weary to Rhys's eyes. The human clasped his hands together and looked up to the ceiling. "Ever since I announced my retirement, everything has been one stressful time after another, and almost all of it has had something to do with you, Captain Griffiths."

Rhys pinned his ears back. He wasn't sure if the admiral was accusing him of causing the chaos, or just acknowledging that he was a bystander in it all. He hoped the latter was true, as a nervous grin came across his muzzle. "Just trying to keep things interesting for you."

Admiral Garter laughed bitterly. "Interesting? That's one way to put it, Captain. I fear my heart cannot take much more of this excitement."

Rhys breathed a quiet sigh of relief. "One way or another, Admiral, I'll be out of your way soon. Hopefully that will calm everything down for you."

The human shook his head. "Somehow I doubt that. I fear you have started something which can no longer be stopped." He paused and looked down at Rhys. "You should have taken the promotion to admiral when I offered it."

Rhys twitched his nose. "Then no one would have warned you about the subspace weapons. You'd have watched as Terra was consumed."

Admiral Garter had no answer for that. He just sat silently, his face frozen in terse thought. Only his chest and shoulders moved in time with his slow, regular breathing. For a dozen seconds he sat like that, completely still. Finally, he blinked and shook his head, snapping out of his reverie. "Do what you need to do, Captain Griffiths. Stop this threat however you can. I will contact you when I have arranged your transport to Terra."

"I will do my best, Admiral," Rhys said, rising to his feet. He recognised the implicated dismissal in the human's voice and understood that the conversation was over. There was nothing more for either of them to say. Rhys knew he couldn't push the admiral for further support. He got the feeling he had already strained the limits of their working relationship. Should they meet again after this, Rhys knew he would need to tread carefully. He might not get the same civil response.

With Elijah's hand on his shoulder, Rhys turned and left the admiral behind. His tail curled close to his legs. He could only hope he had been right to say what he had said. Unease prickled through him. Conflict was coming, whether he wanted it or not. He wished he knew which side he truly stood on. A threat was coming from a rogue faction on Centaura, and Rhys knew he had to save Terra. He also knew that Terra would never accept help from someone like him.

A brief thought crossed Rhys's mind. For a moment he was tempted to forget it all and flee to somewhere safe. His conscience would never allow that. He had to keep on fighting until the end.

That end felt like it was too close.

chapter eight

"Do you ever get the feeling that something awful is about to happen?"

Rhys glanced up. Kalisha was stood in her usual spot by the windows, staring out across the barren surface of Ceres. The starat's russet tail swished idly as her eyes flicked back and forth, tracking some movement that Rhys couldn't see.

"Almost every day," Rhys replied. He approached the windows and looked out, but he couldn't see anything out of the ordinary. A shuttle descended to the surface at Normandy, smoothly docking at the shuttle bay. A prickle ran down Rhys's tail as he watched the structured movement.

Nearly a full day had passed since Admiral Garter had promised to provide transport to Terra, but there had been no further communication from the human. Rhys had started to grow nervous about the delay, hoping that he hadn't managed to talk the admiral out of providing assistance.

"There's something different about this," Kalisha said slowly. She rested her hand against the window. "It's like something's crawling through my fur."

"You sure you've showered?" Mikkel called out. He was sprawled across the only bed in the room, resting with his hands behind his head.

Kalisha flicked her hand back. Rhys saw a blur pass through his vision. He turned his head in time to see an alarm clock flick from the bedside cabinet to smack against Mikkel's torso.

Mikkel yelped in surprise and pain, curling up and holding his hands to his belly. "Deserved that," he muttered. He rubbed at his belly and winced, before knocking the alarm clock away from his body. "But seriously. Everyone gets bad feelings like that. It's nothing to worry about, I'm sure."

"No one else has powers like me," Kalisha retorted. She turned away from the window and glared at the starat on the bed. "This is different."

"Rhys has them," Mikkel pointed out.

Kalisha turned on her toes to glare towards Rhys. "You said you feel like something bad is about to happen, right?"

Rhys shrugged his shoulders. "I have pretty much since I became a starat. It's just been one never-ending stream of shit things following on from each other," he admitted with a wry grin. "Getting hard to keep my head above it all."

Kalisha scoffed and shook her head. "This is real. This is serious," she said with a growl. Pushing Rhys aside, she stalked towards the table and snatched up one of the yellow tokens Admiral Garter had provided them. "I'm going to have a look around and see if I can talk to Skye again. She might know what's going on."

"Then I'm coming with you," Rhys said, hurrying after Kalisha before she could leave without him. His fingers closed around one of the tokens, and the weight of the small disc of plastic felt like a boulder of molten rock against his palm.

"Taking it seriously now, are you?" Kalisha growled. She didn't look back.

"Elijah said not to go out alone," Rhys replied. The augmented starat had gone back to the laboratory, taking Alison with him. They had been gone several hours already.

"If you're not going to slow me down, then come along," Kalisha said. She opened the room door and hesitated. She looked back towards the bed. Mikkel had barely moved at all. "If Elijah and Alison are back before us, let them know where we've gone."

Mikkel's ear flicked up. "But you haven't told me where you're going."

"Normandy. Where else is there on this wretched rock?" Kalisha replied. She prowled out of the hotel room without a second glance back to the other starat. Rhys hurried after her.

The sense of unease at the back of Rhys's mind slowly increased as they made their way through the corridors of the civilian port. Nothing seemed out of place. Construction continued to go on around them, but Rhys could almost understand the worry Kalisha radiated in her hunched posture and nervous, jerky movements. It was almost like an unpleasant smell on the air.

The train between Noveau Ceres and Normandy was full, forcing Rhys and Kalisha to remain on their feet as they passed between the airlocks of the two ports. Dozens of whispered conversations filled the ground-locked shuttle as it trundled across the surface. Rhys tried to ignore the conversations, but he soon found himself distracted by one word which got repeated by almost every human present.

Cardinal.

Rhys felt like his whole body had been dipped in ice. He trembled as shivers wracked through his body, and for a moment he thought he was about to collapse again. His vision swam as he leaned into Kalisha for support. "I think we've made a big mistake," he whispered quietly, making sure to speak softly enough that none of the surrounding humans could hear him, though he doubted any would be paying attention to them.

"Why?" Kalisha replied, just as quietly. Her eyes narrowed as she looked towards the airlock door at the front of the train. The vehicle shuddered a few times as it began to brake, slowing down as it approached the Normandy end of the tracks.

"They're all talking about a cardinal. Who do we know who is trying to find me?" Rhys hissed. His eyes frantically looked around the small shuttle. There was no way out at the moment. On the other side of the airlocks was nothing but the airless vacuum of Ceres. In a way, that seemed almost preferable to falling into the grasp of Cardinal Erik.

Kalisha didn't move her head. She continued to look towards the front airlock doors. "He's not going to be waiting for us. He doesn't know we're on the train," she said after a few seconds. She rocked back on her feet as the forces of deceleration pushed against the occupants of the shuttle.

"Are you sure about that?" Rhys asked warily. He looked around. No one appeared to be listening to them. Kalisha did not reply.

The shuttle slowed to a complete halt, a brief judder and clang of metal against metal signalling the end of the journey. A few more shudders and metallic bangs echoed through the shuttle as the airlocks connected, before the doors hissed open with a quiet efficiency rarely seen at Normandy.

There was no cardinal on the other side of the door. No one was waiting for them. The humans started to filter out through the doors, with some bumping past Rhys and Kalisha with no regard for the starats at all. They had already passed through a security check at the Noveau Ceres side of the transfer, so there was unhindered access to the Normandy shuttle bays from the airlock.

Rhys and Kalisha were the last to leave the shuttle. The air in the port had the same unpleasant smell to it. Rhys wrinkled his nose as he followed Kalisha out into the narrow, dark corridor that wrapped around the shuttle bays.

One familiar face lurked amongst the crowd of humans as they left. Even worse, that familiar human had stopped and turned around. Giles Cooper stared directly at Rhys. There was no look of recognition in the eyes of his former first officer, but there was interest. He didn't look right through the starat, as most other humans seemed to do.

Rhys glanced back. There wasn't anywhere to go behind him; only a long corridor that terminated a few dozen metres away. The only way out was through the airlocks, but none of the shuttles were prepared for departure. His eyes flicked back towards Cooper, who had started to advance on him.

The human's eyes narrowed. His face reddened in a way Rhys recognised. Any brief thought that Cooper had experienced one of those understandings the other starats talked about was quickly discounted. Cooper strode with anger and purpose, not confusion about some strange new thoughts and perspectives.

"You're the one he's looking for, aren't you?" the human spat. One big, meaty arm lashed out and grabbed Rhys by the collar before he could move away.

"Who is looking for me?" Rhys growled. He tried to push Cooper away, but he had no strength in his arms. The human's grip was too strong. He couldn't twist away.

Cooper cuffed Rhys across the face. "Don't talk back to me. You can save your words for the cardinal."

The human turned around, dragging Rhys with him, but his progress out of the shuttle bay was blocked. Kalisha stood between him and the door, her hands raised in defiance. Beyond her, the corridor had cleared of the others who had been on the train.

Cooper laughed. "Stand aside."

Kalisha shook her head. Her mouth was pressed closed, with her eyes wide. Her russet tail was held rigidly behind her legs as though she was forcing it not to curl close to her body. "I'm not letting you take him."

Rhys couldn't see Cooper's expression from his position, but he could hear the sneer on his words. "You're just another uppity rat to take to the cardinal."

Kalisha's brow raised. "We'll see about that," she said, lifting her right hand.

Cinnamon filled the air as Kalisha's eyes blazed white and gold. Heat crackled around Rhys's face, but Cooper's step did not falter. The human reached for Kalisha with his free hand, but before he could grab her, a deafening screech caught his attention. He looked to the left at the same time as Rhys.

The starat managed to peer around Cooper's body to see the inner door of the nearest airlock rip from its housing. The door flung across the corridor and smashed into the human's side. His grip briefly tightened on Rhys's collar, before loosening.

Rhys quickly rolled away, hissing in pain as the corner of the door bashed against his thigh. A red light began to flash in warning, but that too was ripped away from the wall in an explosion of sparks.

Cooper crashed to the floor, pinned by the heavy weight of the airlock door. His face reddened as he tried to lift it. He managed to move the thick metal a little, but not enough to free himself.

Rhys trembled as he rose to his feet. He bared his teeth at the human beneath him and snarled. "You have a lot of fucking nerve to treat me like that, Giles."

"What did you say?" the human snapped. He grunted as he tried to move the door. He didn't seem concerned at all about how it had gotten to pin him. Rhys knew Cooper's mind sometimes worked slowly. He was ruthless when it came to executing a well-thought-out plan, but he was single-minded when it came to his anger and frustrations.

Rhys stood over Cooper's head. The temptation to kick the human rose, but Rhys managed to suppress it. "Giles Cooper, former first officer to Emile Salazar. You have a lot of fucking nerve to attack me after Emile's love of starats."

Cooper's face twisted into a savage snarl. He spat up at Rhys, but missed. "I turned the Silver Fox in because of his fucking love of starats. Literally. He soiled himself with beasts like you and I couldn't take it anymore."

Rhys crouched down next to Cooper. He ignored the pain in his hands to grab hold of the human's cheek, forcing Cooper's eyes to meet his own. "The Silver Fox died to save my life. Even knowing who I am, who I had been, and knowing that you had been my first officer. Even with all of that, after years of imprisonment, he gave his life for mine."

"Your first officer?" Cooper growled. His brow furrowed and his face reddened. "I would never…"

Rhys tapped a hand against his chest. "Captain Griffiths. You should be rotting in a cell for what you did to me. Enjoy your freedom while it lasts."

The starat didn't give Cooper chance to respond. He whipped around, catching the human across the face with his tail. He hurried after Kalisha, who had retreated a few paces to watch with a wary eye. She showed no sign of pain or exhaustion after ripping the airlock door out. A single red light flashed above the outer door, which remained closed and kept the atmosphere inside the port. Soon, there would be someone to investigate the damage that threatened to compromise the safety of the port, and Rhys had no desire to still be around for that.

"Was that your sense of danger?" Rhys asked, hurrying alongside Kalisha into the corridors of Normandy. The crowds from the train had quickly dispersed, filtering through the underground corridors that ran like a spiderweb beneath the surface of Ceres. Only Cooper had stopped, with no one else even looking towards the starats.

Kalisha shuddered. "No. There's still something else. He mentioned a cardinal looking for you, didn't he?"

Rhys flicked his tail. "Yeah, he did. Can only mean one person," he said. He got the feeling he might have made a mistake in coming along with Kalisha. Back in the hotel he had been safe, but in the corridors of Normandy he was exposed to Cardinal Erik. He had only just escaped the Martian on Pluto. He couldn't count on being so lucky a second time.

The creeping sense of unease and the thought of being watched prickled at the back of Rhys's neck. He glanced up to see the security cameras by the ceiling, recording everything that happened within the port. Usually, Rhys didn't worry about them at all, but he got the uncomfortable sensation that Cardinal Erik was looking at him through them.

Kalisha appeared to be following her nose. She paused at almost every intersection, jumping out the way of humans, and lifted her nose in the air. She took several deep breaths before making her decision on which way to go.

"Where are you even going?" Rhys asked her, after the sixth pause. He knew they were close to the base of the control tower, which was one of the few buildings that rose above the surface of Ceres. He couldn't imagine what might be there that would have any interest to Kalisha.

"You can't smell it?" Kalisha asked, glancing back to Rhys. Her ears curled down.

Rhys realised he hadn't been paying attention to his senses. He had assumed Kalisha was following a scent in subspace that was too faint for him to detect, but he realised that was not the case. The scent was in realspace. A faint smell of starats permeated the entire spaceport. The air filters weren't strong enough to entirely remove the scent. This was different. A lot of starats had come through these corridors recently, and all at once.

"What happened to them all?" Rhys asked, his voice quavering a little. Now that he was aware of the smell on the air, he couldn't believe he had missed it.

"I don't know, and that's what I'm scared of," Kalisha replied. Her ears flicked up and down repeatedly, never fully settling in one place. Her nose twitched several times. "This cardinal has to be connected."

"He always seems to be," Rhys replied. He peered ahead through the flickering lights. The scent of the starats was growing stronger with almost every step he took. They were close. He glanced across to Kalisha. "You should go back."

Kalisha stopped. She stared at Rhys. Her tail arched up and quivered at the tip. "Not a fucking chance."

"You don't know this man. He's dangerous. He could kill you," Rhys growled, turning on his toes to glare at the other starat. "Go back to where it's safe. Let me deal with him."

Kalisha scoffed. She barged past Rhys, continuing after the starat scent. "Not happening, Rhys. You don't get to stand against him by yourself." The starat didn't even look back at Rhys to make sure he was still following after her. "If he threatens one of us, he threatens all of us. We stand together or not at all."

Rhys reached out, almost grabbing hold of Kalisha's hand before thinking better of it. "He will kill you," he hissed. He struggled to keep up with her pace. "I won't let anyone else die for me."

"For you?" Kalisha growled. Once more she stopped and spun around. She glared at Rhys and jabbed a finger towards his chest. "I'm not doing this for you. I'm doing this for them. I lived here. These starats were my family and my friends. Don't think everything is about you all the time."

"I..." Rhys bowed his head. "I'm sorry. I just don't want you to get hurt."

Kalisha placed her hand on Rhys's shoulder. There was still anger in the furrow of her brow and the set of her ears, but her eyes were soft. "I'm a strong girl, Rhys. I'm not going to let him hurt me if I can help it."

Rhys took a deep breath. He stepped away from Kalisha and her arm dropped away. His tail tucked close between his legs as he looked beyond her. The stairs that wound up towards the control room were just across the corridor, but that was not where the trail of starats led. Instead, that went a bit further beyond. Rhys knew the gym was one of the few rooms further that way. He struggled to think why the starats would be taken there, before he remembered the size of the gymnasium. There would be enough room there to house all the local starats, with room to spare. Other than the dome on the surface, the gymnasium was probably the largest single room in the Normandy port.

Rhys set his jaw. He winced as his fingers tightened into a loose fist. "Let's go get the bastard then."

"Together," Kalisha said.

"Together," Rhys replied. He twitched his tail and followed Kalisha as she started to move again. All seemed eerily quiet and still, in a part of the port that was usually amongst the busiest. The control tower was one of the most critical areas of the port. There was usually a steady stream of humans traversing the spiral staircase that led above ground.

Rhys exchanged a quick glance with Kalisha. If there was a plan between them, then Rhys was unaware of what it might be. He could think of nothing. He just wanted to put himself between Cardinal Erik and the starats of the port. Despite Kalisha's assurances that she would be happy to get in the cardinal's way, Rhys knew that she would only end up making a pointless sacrifice. The cardinal was here for him. The only way to get the human to leave would be for Rhys to go with him.

Rhys flicked his ears and tried to remember what he could about the Michon Fitness Centre ahead. The gym facilities had only recently been reopened after repairs. Rhys had never had the opportunity to use the gym, as a crack in the inner walls had risked an environment breach. Repairs had taken a long time. Inside, Rhys knew there were three rooms. One small room contained the athletic equipment: the cardio and muscle building machines. The second room was much larger. That was the gymnasium, which doubled as a parade hall where small scope training routines could be practiced. The third was the locker room and showers.

The silence was soon broken. The closer the two starats got to the gym complex, the more noises that reached Rhys's ears. Talking, mostly. Voices were raised, with one speaking loudest of all. Cardinal Erik was definitely there. Captain Favre was a second human present. If Admiral Garter was there, then he remained silent.

As Rhys approached the end of the narrow corridor, towards the closed doors of the fitness centre, he could tell that the parade hall had a new purpose. Every starat in the port had been taken there. Cardinal Erik's loud voice was still indistinct enough that Rhys couldn't clearly make out what the human said, but Rhys could hear the anger and rage in that shaking voice.

Kalisha put her hand on the door to the fitness centre. The door slid open with a quiet hiss, sounding much more modern and maintained than the rest of the port. Beyond the sliding door was a small foyer, which then opened out to the three other rooms in the centre. No one occupied the desk that was tucked neatly into one corner.

Cardinal Erik's voice was easier to hear now, with one fewer wall and door to muffle his words. Rhys couldn't tell if he spoke to the starats, or any humans in the room. The cardinal roared about a heretical plot that was doomed to fail. Nothing could take down the Vatican, and any starat who tried would be foolish in addition to being tormented for an eternity in the bowels of Olympus Mons, let alone the inevitable descent to Hell that would surely follow.

Rhys gritted his teeth together. He hesitated for a moment. He didn't want to just barge right in there and confront the cardinal. He had to know what was going on in the main hall.

Kalisha pushed open the door and ran inside.

Rhys swore beneath his breath and hurried after her. The large hall felt cavernous to Rhys. The distant ceiling was mostly new metal, which gleamed brightly in the ever-present flickering of the lights. The hardwood floor made his claws click with every step as he caught up to Kalisha.

The starats had all been corralled into the middle of the room. They were not physically restrained in any way, though a ring of humans towards the edges of the room did have rifles raised, aimed towards the starats. Cardinal Erik had paused mid-stride as he paced around the ring of starats. A gaggle of humans on the far side of the room included Captains Favre, Baron, and Uwele. There was no sign of Admiral Garter.

Cardinal Erik's lip curled as he turned to the newcomers. "Impressive. You came willingly. Perhaps you are learning where your place truly is, beast?" A blistering red rash ran up the side of the cardinal's face, almost sealing over one eye.

"Let them go," Rhys growled. He met the cardinal in the eye, keeping his back straight to lift himself up every last centimetre possible.

The cardinal sneered. "You are in no position to bargain with me," he said. He snapped his fingers, and half of the armed guards turned their rifles towards Rhys and Kalisha.

Rhys tapped a hand to his chest, clenching his jaw to stop any expression of pain reach his face. "It's me you're after, not them."

Whispers spread through the humans on the far side of the room. None of them quite reached Rhys's ears, but he knew that they were discussing. Him. A starat who dared to speak back to a human, especially one with as much importance as a cardinal of the Vatican.

Cardinal Erik turned his back on the other starats. Kalisha took a step to the side, partially obscuring Rhys from the cardinal. "Am I not?" the human growled. He stepped forward. His crimson robes billowed around his body with every step. The slight scent of cinnamon filled the air.

Doubt trickled through Rhys's spine. His tail quivered. Had he misunderstood the cardinal's purpose? He took half a step backwards, before stopping. Kalisha hadn't moved back with him. He didn't want her to be isolated against the cardinal.

The cardinal stopped halfway between the other starats and Rhys. He lifted his voice to a bellow. "Let it be known that I am here for each and every one of your filthy, animalistic excuses of a soul," he yelled. His arms lifted, and he looked up towards the ceiling. "You will all be judged by Jesus and Veritas. They will speak through my lips and pass their verdict unto you all. No starat will be safe from my ire, and nor will any human who bears sympathetic thoughts onto these animals who would pretend to be human."

"We are not human!"

A lone voice spoke out against the cardinal. It came from the middle of the starats, clustered in the centre of the room. Rhys recognised her voice as the starat he had met up the observation tower. Skye pushed her way to the front of the group. She beat her hand over her chest. "Look at us," she snarled. For the moment, the humans, and indeed all the other starats, had been stunned into brief silence. "We are not human. We are better than that."

Cardinal Erik was the first to regain his composure. He slowly turned to face Skye, who did not quail or flinch in the face of the cardinal. "Heretic," the human hissed, his icy voice cutting through the scared silence. "You will pay for your untrue and slanderous words."

"She's right," Kalisha barked out. She lifted her hands up, and the scent of cinnamon grew even stronger. "We are better than you. We do not kill those who are different to us. But we will stand up to those who seek to crush us. We serve you no longer."

Rhys quickly scanned the room, assessing their odds. Twenty guards were present, to just over fifty starats. All those humans had rifles, while none of the starats were armed with anything more than tooth or claw. Then there were the captains and other humans on the far side of the room. Rhys couldn't tell whether they were armed, but he expected them to be. The starats had the numbers, but there was no way they could win the fight without taking heavy losses.

Skye raised her fist in the air. "For Essie!"

Everything happened at once. The lights switched off with an audible clunk and the burst of cinnamon. A roar of starats screaming in anger filled the room, and claws clicked against the hardwood floor. Gunfire erupted. The flash of the guns was the only thing to light the room. A staccato motion of silhouettes danced in a surreal display of beauty and violence. Screams of pain echoed. Most were human. Some were starat.

Shadows moved in front of Rhys, but he couldn't tell whether they were friend or foe. In the darkness, he couldn't see. He tried to avoid everyone. Without a weapon, he was useless. He couldn't punch. His subspace skills weren't quick enough to survive the rapid pace of a fight.

Bursts of bright white light exploded. The air fizzled and crackled with heat as Kalisha moved. The starat moved quickly. In the brief flashes of light, Rhys could see she had one hand raised to fend off any attacks, while the other whipped to the side as she controlled her subspace skills. Humans yelled in pain and fear in response to her motions, but Rhys could not see the end result of her abilities. In the intense flashes of light, her fur looked to be snow white.

A human fell into Rhys. The starat quickly spun to the side. Before the human could react, Rhys kicked out hard with his right foot. His claws raked down the human's belly, cutting through his uniform with ease. The guards had not been expecting a fight. The human wore no combat armour, or else Rhys would never have felt hot blood against his foot as he stumbled back.

Another body fell against Rhys. This one starat. Rhys jumped forward and spun around, almost slipping as his blood-stained foot slid over the hardwood floor. Subspace crackled at his fingertips, but without a target for the energy, it just burned at his hands.

Fumbling in the dark, Rhys tried to find the human he had downed. He almost tripped over the human's legs. The fallen guard didn't move. More by luck than anything else, Rhys managed to find the human's rifle. The weapon was almost too heavy for Rhys to lift. He hissed in pain as he tensed his fingers around the rifle and held it up.

Feeling more confident with a rifle in hand, even if he could barely move it, Rhys relaxed a little. He slowed his breathing and drew in his focus. Even in the darkness, human and starat were easy enough to distinguish. Humans were tall; starats were not.

The muzzle of Rhys's rifle lit up several times as he opened fire. Two humans fell in the darkness with barely a sound. His fingers burned in agony with every movement, with every pull of the trigger. His arms and shoulders screamed in distress from the weight. His breath grew heavy as he struggled to bite back on the hiss of pain that built in the back of his throat. His tail thrashed uneasily.

The cadence of battle seemed to be changing around him. Fewer human voices called out. The burst of gunfire was less ordered. Muzzle flashes sparked from lower to the floor. Skye yelled in anger.

A knife touched to Rhys's throat. A strong arm gripped around his waist and pulled him roughly back.

Rhys tried to elbow the human who had hold of him, but the contact felt weak and ineffective. The human didn't even flinch in pain.

"I've got you now," Cardinal Erik hissed in his ear. The human pulled Rhys back abruptly. "I will deal with the heresy you have spread here later. First I deal with you."

With another rough pull, the cardinal forced Rhys back a few steps. The starat struggled to twist the rifle around in his hands, hoping to get a shot off on the human. His grip failed. The weapon fell to the floor.

The cardinal dragged Rhys through the darkness. He tried to cry out, but the cardinal's hand around the starat's chest moved up to clamp down on his muzzle. Rhys bit the hand. Blood dripped onto his tongue. The cardinal howled in pain and wrenched his hand free from Rhys's teeth. A clenched fist then struck Rhys's muzzle through the dark.

"Filthy animal," the cardinal hissed. Rhys was satisfied to hear the pain in the human's voice, but the coppery taste on his tongue was an unfortunate price to pay. Not all of that blood was the cardinal's. The knife to his throat didn't move away.

The doors opened behind them. For a moment, a spear of light lit up part of the hall. Bodies, human and starat alike, scattered across the hardwood floor. Most on the floor were human.

With a quiet hiss from the doors that was barely heard over the shouting inside, the view was sealed away again. Rhys was alone with the cardinal.

Cardinal Erik pushed Rhys in the back to get him to move. With the knife staying still at his neck, Rhys stumbled forward. He knew he could try to struggle, but the cardinal had him at too much of a disadvantage. Anything he tried to do would be quickly crushed, with the knife likely slid across his throat. Any attempt to kick out, or even try dipping into subspace, would be too slow or ineffective.

The only chance Rhys had was to hope someone had seen the cardinal take him; for someone to catch up and rescue him. The cardinal seemed to realise that too. He pushed Rhys at a rapid pace, almost too fast for the starat to cope with. They passed no one, not even a human. The cardinal snarled softly to himself, muttering about the lax security in the port.

Rhys had to wonder the same thing. His ears pinned down. Where was Admiral Garter in all of his? There should have been many more humans present. Dozens more active guards and security teams, as well as the engineers, mechanics, and other non-combat roles that should have been buzzing around the port.

Footsteps occasionally echoed somewhere ahead. Rhys thought he could even hear the quiet click of starat claws, but he could see no one. The cardinal's snarl got ever louder and fiercer, until they finally reached the shuttle docks. One attendant remained there; a pale-faced young man who looked barely old enough to have graduated from the academies.

"Cardinal, sir?" the attendant said, stepping out from behind his desk and saluting the human. "Is there anything I can do for you?"

"Where is everyone?" the cardinal growled, though most of the venom had faded from his voice.

"Uh, I'm not sure, Cardinal, sir," the attendant replied. His hand remained by his brow, continuing his salute of the religious leader. "The admiral declared an emergency situation to the north. He might have taken everyone up there?"

The cardinal's hand tensed slightly, pressing the knife a little firmer against Rhys's throat. The starat tried not to move at all, barely even breathing lest he slice his throat open on the sharp blade. There was still a chance to escape. He wouldn't allow himself to be tortured by the cardinal again, but he could still see some hope of getting away. Ending his life on the cardinal's blade wasn't yet something he was ready to consider.

"Get a shuttle to my ship and raise the alarm with the admiral. A situation has arisen in the fitness centre that needs his immediate response," the cardinal growled. He pushed Rhys forward, towards the nearest closed airlock.

The attendant shuffled to the side, away from his desk. His arm finally lowered from his salute, hesitantly. "The admiral first, Cardinal, sir?"

"No, you buffoon," Cardinal Erik snarled, some of his anger returning in a flash. "The shuttle first."

"Right, yes. Sorry, Cardinal, sir," the attendant said, flustered as he returned behind the desk. His eyes frantically scoured over the computer readouts in front of him. "Uh, the *Vigilant*, right?"

"Yes," the cardinal snapped. "I want a shuttle prepared ten seconds ago."

The attendant ran his hand through his short hair. "I, uh. There's a maintenance worker on your ship's hull, Cardinal, sir," he said, speaking quickly as though he could lessen the impact of the news with the pace of his words. "There's only one docking point on your ship. I can't send you up until the worker's shuttle is recalled."

"Then recall it," the cardinal said, his voice dropping to a deep growl.

The attendant's face bleached white. "But, Cardinal, sir, that will mean…"

"Do it, now, or I shall judge you as harshly as this beast," the cardinal snarled, pressing the blade a little closer to Rhys's throat.

"I, yes, of course, Cardinal, sir," the attendant stammered. His hand shook as he pressed a few buttons, before a green light lit up above the closest airlock. "Shuttle has been recalled. You are… you are free to enter shuttle 1A. It will launch in seventy-five seconds."

"Veritas keep you," Cardinal Erik said. He shoved Rhys in the back to push him towards the airlock doors as they slid open. The cardinal didn't follow immediately. He stopped to look towards the attendant. "Remember. Admiral Garter. Fitness centre. See to it now."

"I will, Cardinal, sir. Veritas keep you."

Cardinal Erik shoved Rhys forward again, through the airlock doors and into the shuttle beyond. The airlock hissed closed behind them and sealed with a dull clank. "Sit," the cardinal barked, pushing Rhys in the back again.

Rhys stumbled forward, but he didn't sit. He turned to face the cardinal. His eyes flicked over the human, wondering what advantages he might be able to gain over him. His hands had been declawed, but his feet had not. Perhaps if he could kick out at the cardinal, he would be able to gain the advantage. Rhys's eyes fell on the knife, still held out threateningly. The blade was already covered in blood, though that all belonged to the cardinal from Rhys's bite.

Rhys's eyes dropped. This was not his moment to escape either. He sunk down into a seat, trying to ignore the cardinal's savage grin.

The shuttle launched just as the attendant said it would. Rhys's stomach lurched with the movement, which wasn't fully countered by the inertia dampeners. The starat kept his mouth shut and ears low. His mind raced, but he couldn't manage to put enough coherent thoughts together to come up with an escape plan. He wasn't able to defeat the cardinal physically; at least, not when the cardinal was armed with that knife. There had to be another way to escape, but Rhys would only have a short time to do so. Once they reached Mars, for Rhys was sure that was where he was being taken, then he would have limited opportunities.

Only a few minutes passed before the shuttle connected to the *Vigilant*. The airlocks sealed together, and the green lights shone brightly through the shuttle as a safe environment was confirmed beyond the closed doors. Cardinal Erik grabbed Rhys roughly by the collar and half-dragged the starat through to his ship.

The cardinal's nose wrinkled. "You and your beasts ruined a good ship with your stench," the human muttered. He tossed Rhys to the floor. "Computer, status report."

No answer came from the ship. The cardinal's face reddened as he waited for a few seconds. "Computer!" he barked. His eyes flicked down to Rhys, and he waved the tip of the knife in the starat's direction. "If I find you have damaged my ship with your stench, then I will ensure that every starat in the system will pay for your crimes."

"You'll have to catch us first," Rhys spat. He stared to rise to his feet, but he hesitated when he saw the cardinal had pulled a pistol out from his robes.

"If you move any further, then I will shoot you," the cardinal warned. The pistol was armed and ready to fire, Rhys could tell that. "If your heretical, impure filth even attempts to use the holy gifts against me, then I will obliterate you."

Rhys lowered himself back down to the floor. He bared his teeth in a snarl. "Why not just kill me?"

Cardinal Erik turned his back, but Rhys could tell he was still alert to his movements. The cardinal flicked some switches on the dashboard, and the engines began to power on. "I will kill you, beast. But first you must know your sins."

Rhys bared his teeth but remained silent. There was no argument to be had with Cardinal Erik. No way he could change the human's mind or convince him that he was wrong about starats. Whatever understanding some humans seemed to go through, Rhys knew that Cardinal Erik would never go through one.

The cardinal fired up the engines a little higher and went through the navigation systems on board the *Vigilant*. He worked quickly and efficiently, not looking back to Rhys once. He tapped the screens. "No one on the hull. Lying prick."

The *Vigilant* started to drift away from Ceres. Rhys knew the ship would need to get into position before making the jump towards Mars. At that time of year, Mars and Ceres would not be close to each other. They weren't quite on opposite sides of Sol, but the dwarf planet and the Vatican capital were rarely further apart. That did give Rhys a little more time to come up with some way to escape the cardinal, but at the moment he couldn't see how. He was almost resigned to landing on the red planet.

The cardinal turned from the ship's controls. He grabbed hold of Rhys's collar again and dragged the starat out of the small bridge, out through the door at the back. The starat was then thrown down the ladder without any care for any injuries he might suffer.

Rhys winced as he struck the floor at the bottom of the ladder, feeling his ankle twinge from the impact. He barely had chance to lift his head before the cardinal dropped down beside him. Heavy boots almost crushed Rhys's fingers, but the starat moved them out of the way in time.

The lower level of the *Vigilant* was mostly taken up with a narrow corridor, the wall of which was covered in packs of supplies. Food, water, and backup air cannisters were all secured in place with a myriad of straps and ties, with a medical box taking up some room at the far end. Two doors opened on the opposite wall, leading back underneath the bridge. Ladders also led further down to a second lower level. Through the floor, Rhys could feel the rumble of the ship's engines.

Rhys was thrown into the second of the small rooms beneath the bridge. The room was little more than a small grey-walled box, barely long enough for a human to lie in. There were no furnishings of any sort to adorn the sparse room.

Barely before Rhys could even tuck his tail inside, the door hissed closed and a lock clicked shut. A series of small gaps at the top of the door prevented him from being fully sealed inside the little box, but Rhys could already tell there would be no breaking out. A small glass window gave him a limited view out into the corridor. He hissed towards the cardinal, who just glared at Rhys from outside.

"Beast," the cardinal growled, before turning away.

Rhys tried to keep his eyes on the cardinal as long as possible, but even in the tight confines of the below-deck, the red-robed human was quickly out of sight. The starat could hear his boots against the metal struts of the ladder, before the door to the bridge closed.

Rhys slumped back against the wall. His slid down until he was sitting, tail tucked out of the way. His head thumped against the metallic surface. He didn't know what was happening on the surface. The starat attack had caught him completely by surprise, as it had caught the humans unawares. Had the starats really been planning something like that, or had it been a spur of the moment thing? He doubted he would ever learn the answers to that now.

The engines began to whine and rumble. Though Rhys couldn't feel it, he knew the ship had to be moving with purpose now, rather than just gently drifting away from Ceres. Mars had to be the only destination. The cardinal had already let Rhys slip away on three occasions now: on Terra, Centaura, and Pluto. This fourth time, Rhys knew the cardinal would take no risks at all.

Amongst the rattle and hum of the engine, claws quietly tapped against metal. Rhys's ears perked up. His claws hadn't been touching anything. The noise hadn't come from him.

Furred ears poked up in the small window. A head followed. Elijah grinned down at Rhys. "Thought I'd find you here," the augmented starat said quietly.

Rhys blinked. He stared up at Elijah with his mouth open, expecting the vision to fade into reality. The other starat didn't go anywhere.

"So, I can't get you off the ship now," Elijah continued, not seeming to worry that Rhys hadn't said anything yet. "And nor can I get you out of here without His Holiness up there realising something was wrong. This is a lock I can't break without a physical key. I've hacked the security camera to loop for a few minutes so I could come talk to you, but that won't last for long."

Rhys shook his head and squeezed his eyes shut. Elijah was still there when he opened them again. "Alright," he said softly. If the other starat was still visible, then perhaps he was real. His tail flicked. Elijah had to be the worker who was meant to be on the hull. A smile slowly broke across his face. "What's your plan then?"

"I've got to let him take you onto Mars, I'm sorry," Elijah said. His ears curled down on themselves, and Rhys could hear his foot scuff against the floor. "Too difficult to take him down otherwise, and we're not getting this stolen ship to another port."

Rhys sucked in his breath. "So what, we let him take me down there?"

Elijah nodded slowly. "Yeah. But don't worry. I'll be tracking you at every opportunity. The moment I can get you out of there, I will."

Rhys curled his tail. "Doesn't sound like much of a plan. How will you stay safe on Mars? Or even getting off the ship?"

Elijah grinned and tapped the side of his head. "I'm working it all out up here. Don't worry, Rhys. I'll keep you safe." The starat glanced up towards the ladder. "I'd better get back into hiding. Just wanted to let you know that you're in safe hands still. You can trust me. I'll get you out."

"I'll try to remember that," Rhys said quietly. He leaned back and tried to think confident thoughts, but the moment Elijah vanished again, he could feel the darkness starting to close in around his mind. He didn't share Elijah's optimism or confidence.

Those who went to Mars as an enemy of the church never emerged again. Beneath the dizzying heights of Olympus Mons was a graveyard of humans and starats who had dared to defy the Vatican. Rhys wasn't even sure his heresies were enough to be afforded a position of tainted honour. The church wouldn't hold him up as an example of what happens to those who dared defy them with great acts of heresy. He would be forgotten.

Despite Elijah's presence close by, hope started to fade.

chapter nine

Rhys was bound tightly. Cardinal Erik was taking no risks with allowing him to escape this time. His hands were tied, roughly and painfully, behind his back. His legs were partially bound, allowing him only a slow, shuffling gait as he was dragged forward by the cardinal. They had passed from the *Vigilant* into the shuttle, which had taken them both down to the surface of Mars in complete silence. Not a single word had been exchanged between Rhys and his captor since he had been thrown into the small cell on board the *Vigilant*.

Even when the shuttle doors had opened, and Cardinal Erik had exchanged some terse words with the attendant in the shuttle bay, Rhys was treated like he was not present. The starat was dragged out into a gleaming building that was the exact opposite of everything in Normandy. Bright open spaces stretched out nearly as far as Rhys could see, with a transparent glass ceiling overhead allowing the weak sunlight from Sol to stream through. Thin wispy clouds drifted overhead, not quite obscuring the pale blue sky.

Rhys wasn't permitted the chance to look around. The cardinal walked behind him, one hand on the starat's back to keep him moving. The starat almost stumbled a few times, the chains around his ankles preventing him from moving his feet quickly enough to keep up with the pace demanded of him by Cardinal Erik.

There were no starats in the spaceport. Every single face Rhys saw was human, and most wore the robes of the priesthood. Even those who didn't wear robes had some insignia on them that indicated they were a part of the church. Most wore a crucifix around their neck, while some others wore the crown of roses popularised by Veritas.

Most of Martian architecture had been stylised into a classical Terran appeal, drawing inspiration on pre-space age designs and the aesthetic of the original surge of support for the Vatican. Masonry inspired buildings were common outside the spaceport, though few buildings had any real stone to them. Sweeping domes and reaching spires dominated the skyline, but nothing more so than the natural feature that lifted the horizon to the north of the city.

Rhys knew now where he was. This was the city of Romulus, built in the shadow of Olympus Mons. The starat couldn't help but be awed by the sight of the mountain, whose peak was so high that it couldn't even be seen from the base. The scale of the mountain was impossible to Rhys, and his mind kept trying to tell him that the shape of the northern horizon was completely unnatural. A full half of the horizon was taken by the mountain slopes, rising into eternity.

A gentle gust of wind rippled through Rhys's fur, coming from the north. His fur prickled. A light scent of cinnamon teased at his nose. There was an unpleasant feel about the air that Rhys had not felt the last time he had been on Mars, long before his transformation. Hostility bore into the back of his head, and not all of it came from the humans. He felt as though the very planet itself despised him.

Though transport options were available, Cardinal Erik remained on foot as they began to walk the streets of Romulus. Red dust swirled through between the buildings, blown in from the mountain that loomed high over everything, dominating almost every glance to the north. For almost an hour, Rhys walked ahead of the cardinal, following the rough pushes on his back and shoulders to guide him. They walked towards the great mountain.

For the most part, Rhys was completely ignored. He felt like a ghost in front of Cardinal Erik. Most of the humans they walked by nodded their head in respect to the cardinal and didn't react to Rhys's presence. Those who did merely narrowed their eyes and looked away, sometimes with a silent sneer on their lips or a gestured cross over their forehead.

On the outskirts of the city centre was one of the largest buildings Rhys could see in Romulus. A cathedral, built in the classical style of Terra, loomed over the buildings around it. The cathedral appeared to be made of genuine stone.

Cardinal Erik pushed Rhys towards the cathedral. The massive oak wood doors were thrown open at their approach, with two green-robed priests stepping out of the cool darkness inside to greet the cardinal. Again, Rhys was completely ignored, but for Cardinal Erik's fierce grip on the back of his collar to prevent him from making a foolish attempt at freedom. Both priests were young and fresh-faced. They were also the first humans Rhys had seen who did not wear a mask of fear as they looked towards Cardinal Erik.

Both priests bowed towards the cardinal. "Welcome home, your grace," one said. His long, blonde hair had been tied back in a ponytail that almost reached halfway down his back.

The second priest had darker skin and short black hair. His hands were clasped together as he straightened his back. "His Holiness sent a message through, expecting your imminent return," he said. His voice was soft and musical, lilting in an accent Rhys couldn't place. "He has requested your presence as soon as you can manage."

Cardinal Erik's fingers tightened briefly around the back of Rhys's neck. "I shall go to him immediately," he said gruffly. He pushed Rhys forward. "Ensure that this heretic is taken to the cells. I want it under constant guard. It has already proven slippery. It has been known to besmirch the holy gifts."

The blonde-haired priest took hold of Rhys. His eyes narrowed in the brief instant he looked down to the starat. "I shall ensure it is done, your grace," the priest said.

"Thank you, Father Helvigson," the cardinal said. "Father Johnson, if you could accompany me. I would like to hear of any news I may have missed."

Father Helvigson gripped around the back of Rhys's neck, much like the cardinal had. The human was a big man, with powerful shoulders and a significant height difference over Rhys. The starat knew that he was not going to be able to break free from the human's grip. He was led inside, into a dark foyer and through the main inner doors. Cardinal Erik and the other priest did not follow.

The inside was not what Rhys had expected. There were no rows of pews, nor was there an altar. The outside of the building was consistent with a cathedral or church, but inside reminded Rhys more of a classical library. Rows upon rows of tall bookshelves reached all the way to the arched ceiling. Books – real books of actual paper – filled the shelves.

Humans, priests and otherwise, sat and studied in small alcoves between the towering bookshelves. They all did so with pen and paper, without any sign of electronic technology to assist them. But for the lights overhead, Rhys couldn't see any device powered by electricity. Stained-glass windows threw sparkling reflections of all colours across the room, depicting scenes of Veritas and the betrayal he suffered. Rhys struggled to keep his lip from curling up. A lie. All a lie. He almost shouted that out. It wasn't like he could get into worse trouble. If he uttered a great enough heresy then perhaps he would be killed on the spot, rather than having to suffer the vaults beneath the city. He did not have the courage to do so.

Father Helvigson led Rhys through the library quickly. At the back of the cavernous room was a small door that led through to a flight of stairs leading below the ground. Two humans stood guard either side of the doorway, with two more at the top of the stairs. The stonework aesthetic of the cathedral continued as Rhys descended, struggling to make each step properly with the bonds around his legs.

At the bottom of the stairs was another large room used for study. Father Helvigson barged Rhys in the back, pushing the starat towards a second set of doors, also guarded. All carried weapons Rhys was not familiar with. They appeared to be a more advanced model than anything the Terran military carried. Beyond the doors was a long corridor with white walls. No more stone, no more ancient aesthetic. This was all clean and purposeful. A cold breeze tugged at Rhys's fur, coming from small vents at the ceiling which helped to circulate the air. Cinnamon drifted around Rhys's nose, making the starat feel like he was constantly on the verge of sneezing.

Father Helvigson kept his silence as Rhys was led through one corridor and down another. They descended a few more levels. Each floor looked much the same to Rhys. He caught brief glances at signs giving directions, but the places listed on them didn't give Rhys much information about where he was being taken. None of the doors they passed had informative signs either. Some had a number above the doorframe, but that was all. A shiver went down Rhys's back when he realised they were probably all cells.

Rhys had long known about the extent of the prisons below Olympus Mons, but he had never thought he would end up in them. He flicked his ears. There wasn't as much security as he had expected. He could only see an occasional patrol of guards, always walking around in pairs.

The priest stopped Rhys in front of an elevator. When the doors opened, Rhys was pushed inside. The human followed just behind. There were only two buttons on the inside of the elevator. 'Up' or 'Down'. The priest pressed the button to go down, and once the doors were closed behind them, the elevator lurched into movement.

Rhys opened his mouth to speak. He looked up at the human, but the priest was staring at the closed doors. The starat closed his mouth again. There was nothing to be gained from talking. The priest would either ignore him or strike him.

The elevator rumbled to a halt. The doors hissed open, and Rhys finally got to see the security system for the cells beneath Olympus Mons. The floors above were nothing: holding cells for petty criminals and minor heretics. He swallowed nervously. These were the true prisons for the real enemies of the church.

Father Helvigson pushed Rhys out of the elevator. A narrow corridor stretched out in front of them. Passage down the corridor was impossible. A lattice of red lasers created a grid from floor to ceiling. Even a few metres from the lasers, Rhys could feel the heat of them prickling his fur. A quiet sizzle reached his ears.

Directly to the starat's right was a panel of glass, allowing vision into a side room. Rhys could see no way of accessing the room, but there were three guards inside, waiting for identification from the priest. Father Helvigson held up an electronic tag, which was scanned through the glass by one of the guards.

"Reason for entry?" the guard barked. His voice emanated out through the speakers located either side of the window.

"Prisoner deposit on behalf of Cardinal Erik Aurealiusson," the priest said. His hand did not leave the back of Rhys's neck.

The guard's eyes glanced down to Rhys for a moment. The starat bared his teeth. "Alright. Stay there," the guard said, gesturing to one of his companions behind him.

The second guard moved further back in the small room, towards a pod tucked into one corner. Rhys's eyes widened as he recognised a teleport pod. Sure enough, a flash of bright light followed just after the guard closed the door, leaving an empty pod behind. A few seconds later, the same guard stepped out from a doorway on the other side of the red lasers.

In a synchronised routine, the guard inside the isolated room and the guard beyond the red lasers tapped an identification card against a scanner. The scanners beeped, and the lasers shut off with a quiet click. The priest pushed Rhys forward, but didn't follow himself. The guard took hold of Rhys.

"We'll escort him to cell 1763," the guard behind the glass said. "Inform Cardinal Aurealiusson that he is welcome to interrogate his prisoner any time."

The priest touched a hand to his chest and bowed his head. "I'll be sure to pass on the message. Veritas keep you all."

The lasers clicked back on with a hiss and crack of heated air. Rhys yelped and pulled his tail away, almost caught in the crossfire of the reforming lattice. None of the humans even looked towards him.

Rhys cautiously looked further down the corridor. But for the now-closed door that led into the teleporter, he could see nothing of particular interest. The walls were all smooth and white, with harsh lighting shining down from the ceiling. There was no cover, nowhere to hide should Rhys seek to escape this way.

The guard dragged Rhys along. He grew tired of being pulled everywhere. His feet ached, and his arms were starting to feel numb from being held behind his back the entire time. All he could do was grit his teeth and accept it, though he longed to get back at these humans somehow. The priests, the guards, everyone in the Vatican deserved some punishment. A low growl built in Rhys's throat. A backhand from the guard silenced him.

The corridor ended in another elevator. The doors could only be opened from a swipe of the guard's identification card. Inside the elevator, Rhys could see that there were many more options for floors. There was no simple up or down. There were twenty options. A cold shiver ran all the way down his tail. Twenty further levels beneath the crushing weight of Olympus Mons. Rhys felt like every ton of rock was weighing down on his shoulders, but he still didn't try to get away from the guard. There was no point to that. He could see no way to escape, nor a way for Elijah to follow down and break him out. His tail drooped. His chances for escape had surely all dried up.

The elevator dropped down for what felt like minutes before it reached level seventeen, a long way below the surface. The corridors still looked the same. Four branched away from the elevator in different directions. All were white walls and harsh lights, perfectly smooth. After a short while, the corridor opened out into a massive warehouse-like cavern. Rows upon rows of spherical blocks rose from the floor, all shining white like marble. A disc of thick metal covered the front of most spheres, though some had a black doorway unblocked by the metallic sheets. Those that were closed were done so with a dozen different locks and bars. There were no windows to see inside, but Rhys could hear the occasional bang of a fist flung against the inside of the doors, or the anguished scream of a starat.

Each sphere had a number engraved above the door, whether open or closed. One of the open spheres was Rhys's cell, with the number 1763 imprinted over the door. Inside, he could see an empty black cube of a room, contrasting with the spherical exterior. There were no furnishings of any kind, except for a small metallic grill he could only assume was meant to serve the function of a toilet. One single light in the corner provided weak illumination for the room.

Rhys was thrown into the cell. He stumbled and fell, rolling a couple of times across the tiled floor. He hit the far wall just in time to see the guard pushing closed the door. Metal slammed a few seconds later, and Rhys could just about hear the beep of an automatic lock switching on. Deadbolts thudded into place. A few seconds later, the lone light switched off to plunge Rhys into complete darkness.

"Well, fuck," Rhys whispered to the darkness. He forced himself up onto his knees. The guard hadn't even freed him from his bonds.

Rhys closed his eyes, though the movement made no difference to what he could see. After-images of light lingered, but slowly started to fade. Not even a crack of light from around the door pierced into the new darkness he found himself in.

Of course, Rhys knew he wasn't powerless, even in his bleak situation. He had skills that few prisoners below Olympus Mons possessed. First things first, Rhys knew he needed to escape his bonds.

Slowing his breath, Rhys reached his mind out towards subspace. The cinnamon scent permanently tickling his nose gave him an easy trail to follow. He found subspace easily.

Terror and panic filled his mind. A scream was torn from his throat. He was not alone in subspace. Black tendrils extended towards him. The towering monstrosity of an entity loomed close by.

With a terrified yell, Rhys wrenched his arms apart. A combination of subspace and a surge of adrenaline fuelled strength through his withered arms. Rhys ripped apart the bonds that held his wrists together. The darkness of the entity was replaced by the darkness of realspace.

Rhys's hands trembled as he sunk to the floor, curling up in a ball. He held his arms over his head, fending off an attacker that wasn't there. His eyes were open, but that didn't make any difference to what he saw. The innumerable eyes of the entity stared right through him, shredding apart his thoughts. He cowered in fear, unsure if realspace could save him from the terrifying being.

Slowly, Rhys's thoughts returned to his mind. His whole body trembled, and something wet clung to the sides of his muzzle. Using his tongue, he found that his face was bleeding from something, though he couldn't recall anything that had struck him.

There had been emotion radiating out from subspace. Anger had filled Rhys. Fury. Rage. It had not just been terror. That had come from him. The rest had come from the empty void itself.

But the void hadn't been empty. The entity hadn't been a vague imprint of darkness on the endless white. There was only one word that Rhys could use to describe what he had felt. Consciousness.

Rhys curled into a tighter ball. There was something alive there, just over the boundary of reality, from realspace into subspace. Nothing Cardinal Erik had ever said had filled Rhys with so much dread.

****

Rhys didn't know how long he lay curled in a ball. His whole body trembled as he tried to recover from the sheer terror of the entity lurking in subspace. After a while, he had managed to reach down and slowly fumble with the bonds around his legs, freeing himself completely. Not that he had far to move around.

The entity's presence had cut off his only means of escape. He couldn't open the door without dipping into subspace, but nor was he able to fend off the entity's anger and rage for long enough to do what needed to be done. He didn't want to think about what would happen should the long tendrils of the entity come into contact with him. Snow had never mentioned what the consequences for that could be, but these were beings who could rip apart entire ships. He had no desire to find out what they could do to a fragile starat body.

Rhys slowly sat upright and found a wall to lean back on. No matter where he moved his eyes, he couldn't see anything. Nothing changed in the darkness. Even holding his hands directly in front of his face made no difference.

Tentatively, Rhys patted his fingers around his face. The skin on his hands felt blistered and sore. The warm moisture of blood on his face actually soothed the pain a little. Despite probing around for some cuts on his face, Rhys couldn't find any open wounds. He didn't know where the blood had come from. Without any light, he had no way to find out.

Rhys tried to control his breathing. His heart still raced in his chest. Fear and despair threatened to overwhelm him, but Rhys knew he had to control himself. If he failed to do so, then he would likely die in his cell. Light would never shine on his fur again. If he stayed in the darkness for long enough, would he even notice dying? He would pass from one lightless void into another.

Minutes trickled by. Rhys tried counting the seconds. There was nothing else to do, and at least that allowed him some way of knowing how much time was passing by. He expected Cardinal Erik to come and gloat once he had finished his meeting with the pope. By the time Rhys reached the tens of thousands of seconds, he stumbled and lost track of how far he had counted. He was still alone. No sounds reached him from outside the cell.

Rhys began to wonder if he had died after all. He could feel the floor beneath him, and the wall behind him. He could feel the touch of his hands on his face; hear the beat of his heart and the rise and fall of his chest as he breathed. But that was all. The world beyond his cell no longer existed.

Already, Rhys struggled to keep his thoughts in order. Fantasy and reality began to meld into one. The quiet noise of his breathing became the roar of a ship's engine. The thump of his heart became the rattle of gunfire against the hull. Voices whispered in his ear. They spoke in his own voice. The voice he had once had. His human voice.

Rhys's eyes snapped open. The darkness pressed in close. A roar built deep in his throat. He projected the yell so loudly it echoed around his cell, chasing away the phantoms and sensory hallucinations that had been plaguing him. Silence remained.

"What do you want from me, Erik?" Rhys snarled. He looked up, as though there was a camera the cardinal could look through to see him. He knew there wasn't one, but just thinking that he might not be so completely alone helped soothe his mind. Even if it would only be the cardinal watching him. "Why am I here?"

There was no answer.

***

Time had passed. Rhys knew that much for certain. Mere hours could have passed by, or it could have been days. All he knew was that his stomach complained with hunger, and that he had suffered every last minute – however many there had been – without any change in his imprisonment.

Rhys had tried pacing, but he didn't have enough space to feel satisfied with the act. The walls felt too close. His only company was his thoughts, but without any stimulation to his senses, they threatened to run away into fantasy. He struggled to contain them.

Sitting still with his head against the wall, Rhys kept his eyes closed and tried to imagine what might be going on outside his cell. His thoughts quickly turned to Twitch. He hoped the starat was safe and well on Centaura. All of the starats he had left behind. So long as Amy and Snow weren't causing too many problems there, then Rhys imagined that Centaura had to be the safest place to be. They had a wise head in Leandro to look after them.

Rhys found his thoughts constantly switching towards Elijah. He wondered what the augmented starat was doing. Was Elijah still trying to get in? Had he been captured too? Rhys doubted he would ever know the answers to that. Voices whispered in Rhys's ear again, but this time they were not his own. Elijah's voice spoke. The other starat was soft, calm, and gentle. The individual words never quite reached Rhys's understanding, but he didn't need that. Just the low murmur of a voice that was not his own felt soothing.

Rhys felt himself smiling. His eyes were closed as he slowly lay down. The frantic pace of his heart and breathing had slowed. Calmness spread through his thoughts, despite his dire situation. He reached up with one arm, cupping his hand around a face that was not there.

"Elijah…?"

Rhys's heart started to pace faster again. His thoughts swirled, but not over his isolation. He furrowed his brow. There were thoughts threatening to push to the front of his mind that had not been present since Stephanie, the human who had once pledged to spend the rest of her life with him. She had been taken from him, and Rhys had never found his heart and mind opening to another.

The starat's ears flicked back. He couldn't be having those thoughts now. Not when he was locked away, never to see another face again.

A deafening screech suddenly wailed through Rhys's ears. He yelled in pain and curled up, holding his hands over his ears. That did little to ease the agony.

The screech increased in pitch and volume. It came from everywhere at once, surrounding Rhys in the grating sound. It was everything awful at once. Worse than claws scraped across metal. Nothing Rhys could do alleviated the pain or the discomfort.

As suddenly as it had come, the noise switched off. Rhys breathed deeply. He panted, feeling tears in his eyes and tasting fresh blood on his tongue. His body shook as he slowly uncurled himself and looked up.

A familiar voice filled the cell. Cardinal Erik's laughter came from all around Rhys, enveloping him in the unpleasant sound. "Enjoying yourself, animal? Almost a pity I can't see you, but I can't take any chances this time. You will suffer, and you will do so alone. But don't worry, you will still have my voice to remind you of every sin you have committed, of every black mark on your soul that must be cleansed."

"Fuck you," Rhys snarled, but he didn't know if the cardinal could even hear him. The cardinal continued as though he had not.

"But first, a confession. Should there be any remnant of the mind of Rhys Griffiths remaining, then I speak directly to you," the cardinal said, losing any trace of the anger and rage. He sounded sombre and contrite, and that was enough to make Rhys blink and lean back. "I beg your forgiveness, Rhys Griffiths, for I have wronged you deeply."

"What the fuck," Rhys breathed. He lightly touched his clawless fingers to his cheek and ignored the spark of pain in his hands. Injuries the cardinal had caused him. He suspected the cardinal played mind games with him, but he could not be sure why.

"I had the opportunity to save your immortal soul long before you fell into corruption and darkness. I should have taken that chance," the cardinal continued. He paused for a moment, and a touch of the malice came back into his voice. "I issued the order to shoot down a shuttle carrying heretics of the vilest sort. When investigating those lives sacrificed on the shuttle, I came across your name."

A cold shiver passed down Rhys's spine and tail. His throat, already dry and bloody, felt parched.

"When Stephanie MacArthur died by my orders, I could have taken that opportunity to save your soul too. I did not take that opportunity, and I pray every day to Veritas to beg for his forgiveness," the cardinal said. "Because of my inaction that day, you fell into corruption and darkness."

Rhys choked back a sob. "You're the one who killed her?" he gasped. Tears came to his cheeks, wetting his filthy fur. Rage slowly built up within him like wildfire, but there was nowhere to direct that ire, no target for aim for. His anger rose into his throat and he let out an anguished scream.

Only silence met his anger. Rhys knew that would not be the last he would hear from the cardinal. He might be safe from being physically tortured this time, but already the cardinal had already ripped open his heart anew. There was no way to ignore the cardinal. Without any other sense to distract him, those words echoed through his mind long after silence had fallen.

Cardinal Erik had killed Stephanie.

Rhys curled up and covered his face with his arm. He had done so much to forget about Stephanie, to move on from the pain that her death had caused him, but now he knew who to blame. Cardinal Erik had ruined his life long before the incident on Ceres.

Anger guided Rhys's mind. He dreamed up scenarios where he could take revenge on the cardinal. Visceral and bloody, they helped to direct his rage, but they also began to fuel his hopelessness. They would never come true, and that tempered Rhys's enthusiasm for his violent dreams.

Rhys's thoughts slowly slipped back towards Elijah. Just thinking about the starat calmed and soothed him, just like he had once felt around Stephanie. Elijah was his only real chance of escape. He had to believe that Elijah had what it took to break through the impenetrable defences of Olympus Mons. If he couldn't, then Rhys knew that he would slip away into an even greater darkness than the one he found himself in.

Flickers of white crackled around Rhys's eyes. His nose wrinkled at the scent of cinnamon. Before he even realised what had happened, Rhys stared into the innumerable eyes of the entity. Subspace howled around him as black became white, which became black again as the entity loomed in his vision.

"Please don't hurt me," Rhys gasped. His eyes widened as he looked up to the towering monstrosity. Tendrils of darkness whirled around him, all seeming to emanate from one central point. Nothing stayed the same for more than a few seconds at a time.

Rhys tried to relax his mind to return to the safe darkness of his cell, but he couldn't. Darkness spun around him, but it was only the entity. He glanced back. He was surrounded. He stood in a bubble of whiteness, contained entirely by the reaching tendrils of shimmering darkness.

Anger simmered through the void. The sheer strength of the fury wasn't as intense as last time, but Rhys still quailed back from the endless eyes that emerged from the entity's dark form. Other emotions bubbled under the surface. Fear, curiosity, and confusion all welled into Rhys's mind, though he was sure that most of those did not come from him. The strongest of all was grief. That one did mirror Rhys's thoughts.

"What are you?" Rhys whispered.

The entity pulsed. Light rippled through the formless void in colours Rhys had never experienced before. The tendrils shimmered and reformed in new patterns, never quite getting close enough to touch Rhys. Excitement radiated through the starat's body.

"Are you alive?" Rhys asked. He squinted his eyes and looked up, trying to find some boundary of entity to subspace. He could see none. Everything was the entity. Everything was also subspace. They were one and the same, yet somehow different.

The entity retreated into itself at the question, despite staying the same size. It seemed to shrink and become darker, but Rhys could still see no edge to the darkness. He was reminded of a storm cloud, always swelling and changing, but always seeming to occupy the same part of the sky. Instead of lightning, shimmering tendrils of darkness stretched out and withdrew.

Confusion. Helplessness. Regret.

Rhys furrowed his brow. "No. Not alive. A… a simulation? A reflection?"

Contentment shimmered. The entity lightened slightly.

Rhys's eyes drifted further up. "A reflection, but of what?" he asked, speaking mostly to himself, but feeling the entity's confusion welling within him again. He felt like he was drifting, floating through the small bubble of white subspace amidst the terrifying entity. His ears flicked as he caught sight of something that didn't belong.

The entity was a constant whirling shimmer of movement, like ink poured into a puddle of water. It never stopped moving or changing form. All but for one thing. A sliver of obsidian remained still and consistent through the chaos, right in the heart of the entity. The obsidian seemed to come from nowhere. It remained dull and dark, never shimmering or changing colour like the rest of the amorphous cloud around it.

"Is that…? A spear? A hook?" Rhys asked, murmuring to himself still. The entity darkened into hues of red. Anger returned. Pain followed.

Rhys reached up. The moment he did so, fire burned through his fingers and raced up his arms. Agony beyond which he had ever felt raged through him. His screams fell dull and quiet within subspace, before his mind ripped himself back into the darkness of reality. The pain did not diminish.

Screams ripped themselves through Rhys's throat. He could taste blood just from the volume of his voice. His hands and arms felt like they had been immersed in molten lava, yet also frozen to the exposed cold of space.

Alone in the darkness of his cell, Rhys writhed in pain, desperate for some relief. All around him, the innumerable eyes of the entity gazed down at him. They did not stop watching. They never blinked. Within them was all the anger and hatred Rhys felt, tinged with a never-ending pain.

Buried deep beneath all of that was another emotion. A new one. There was hope.

That was the last thing Rhys saw in the darkness before a different void claimed him. His mind slipped into unconsciousness, allowing the starat to be free of pain for a short while.

The eyes never looked away.

chapter ten

Rhys woke to a voice. Cardinal Erik spoke again. The words didn't make any sense, as though the cardinal was speaking a different language. A few minutes later, Rhys realised that was exactly the case. The cardinal wasn't speaking English. Instead, it sounded like he was reciting a prayer of some sort in Latin.

Other than the chanted prayer, the cardinal's voice did not reference Rhys at all. The starat was free to slowly rise to his knees, groaning softly. His ears pinned down as he struggled to move without exasperating the pain in his arms. He had been asleep at least twice since his encounter with the entity that had sent pain spiking through his body again.

Rhys couldn't be sure how much time had passed. The pain and exhaustion in his body could have meant he had slept for a few days or had just been a few hours. The only regular occurrence had been the arrival of food. The first time Rhys had heard the soft whirring he had been scared, unsure what might be happening. Then his nose had picked up the scent of food. A small bowl of simple gruel had been provided for him, which Rhys had quickly devoured. He had still been hungry after each meal, but it had been enough to keep him alive. For what end, Rhys was not yet sure. He did not know what might happen should he refuse to eat, but he hadn't yet fallen into such despair that he would starve himself with food close by.

Three times now, Rhys had been fed. Three times also he had heard Cardinal Erik's voice to fill the darkness with noise. As he always did, Rhys tried to ignore the cardinal's words. When the human's voice was the only thing to distract his senses, that had proven difficult.

Elijah and Twitch had taken up most of Rhys's thoughts. He used their faces to hold the darkness at bay. He imagined Twitch's laughter. The starat's wonder at exploring an alien planet. The contagious joy. Tears mixed with laughter as Rhys remembered Twitch's expectation that Terra must smell like strawberries. He hoped Twitch hadn't been too disappointed by the reality.

And then there was Elijah. Rhys still felt that aching tightness in his chest whenever he thought about the augmented starat. More than anyone else, Elijah had been able to give Rhys the assurances of protection and care, even in the short time they had known each other. In Elijah, Rhys saw someone who was capable of anything. Except, perhaps, breaking into Olympus Mons. Rhys didn't think less of Elijah for that. No one was capable of that.

With Cardinal Erik's chanting voice in the back of his mind, Rhys felt himself drifting and wandering once more. Right into the cinnamon embrace of subspace.

Rhys knew what he would see even before he opened his eyes. Clarity settled in his mind. The words of Cardinal Erik still echoed in his thoughts, a lingering trickle of realspace reaching his mind. He knew exactly what the entity was.

"You're the voice of Veritas."

Rhys cringed back from the sudden explosion of emotion that blasted into him. Apoplectic rage filled every molecule of his body, and the entity swirled with malicious intent all around him. Rhys drowned in the anger.

"No…" he gasped, his chest heaving for air, despite the airless void of subspace he floated in. "You're what they think is the voice of Veritas."

The anger sucked away. Sorrow and acceptance replaced it. Iridescent colours beyond the usual spectrum swirled through the entity.

Rhys flicked his tail. Understanding continued to flood through him, as though it was being filtered through an outside source. "Veritas died. They heard your voice."

Acceptance and sorrow continued to whirl around Rhys. The emotions fed into his mind. Melancholy shame swept through him.

"They heard you and thought you were Veritas. Their beliefs fed into you, and you reflected that back out to them," Rhys said slowly. He twitched his nose as a got a fresh burst of cinnamon. The entity's tendrils were close now. He could feel their icy heat prickling at his fur. The obsidian spear sucked in light. "The tomb of Veritas. They built it and it trapped you."

Rhys frowned. He knew that he couldn't reach for the spear. The entity surrounded it. If he were to reach the obsidian, then he would need to approach it from realspace. He would need to go to the most sacred location in the empire. Sorrow filled him. There was more.

"It wasn't just that…" Rhys said hesitantly. He shivered. He wasn't having a conversation with the entity, but he was able to understand things that were well beyond his experience. There was no way he could know how the early Vatican had been able to develop Veritas as a saviour for humanity, but he knew that every word that came from his mouth was true. He looked into the many thousand eyes of the entity. "You reflected the thoughts of those priests back into the minds of people. Not just those on Mars. Everyone. The whole system."

Understanding and shame simmered, with an undercurrent of anger. Whispers filled the silence. An echoed cacophony of a hundred thousand voices. Rhys had never heard the words before, but a shiver ran down his spine anyway. He recognised the message. It was the foundation of everything the empire had been built on.

"All glory to the Emperor. Worship His Holiness, the messenger of Veritas. Reject the inhuman."

Rhys struggled to breathe. He had lived all his human life with that voiceless message in his mind. Every decision he had ever made had been to further one or all of those commands. To give glory to the empire. To believe in the message of Veritas. To reject and demean the inhuman. The starats. Every person in the Sol System had this thought going through their head, human and starat alike.

That was what an understanding was. It was listening to those words and rejecting them. Rhys had done so when he had looked into Twitch's eyes and seen a person there, not a beast.

"You project that thought across the system, but you're trapped by the tomb," Rhys said. His voice trembled as he looked up to the spear of obsidian. "If I were to free you, then that thought would leave people's minds."

No answer came from the entity. Rhys knew it couldn't provide one. It could project emotions and reflect thoughts. If there was a conscious mind behind it, then it was something on a level beyond anything Rhys could comprehend. Rhys didn't need confirmation. He knew that his guess was correct. If the entity was freed from whatever trapped it within Olympus Mons, then the thought projected through every mind would end. Not everyone would choose to accept the new reality presented to them. Some would cling to the old ideals. That was something Rhys couldn't help.

The starat looked up at the entity again. He felt insignificant compared to the billowing cloud of subspace energy. He wasn't surprised the Vatican considered this to be akin to their god. "If you help me escape, then I can help free you."

Still no answer came from the entity. Rhys couldn't be sure it even understood him. There was just a soft pulsing of content emotion radiating through subspace.

Rhys took a deep breath, filling his nose with the cinnamon heat of the entity. He felt like he should make some pledge or promise to the entity, but he also knew that it would be a futile act to do so. Instead, he just closed his eyes and allowed himself to slip back into realspace. He grimaced as heat washed over his body, but instead of pain, the warmth infused him with strength.

When he opened his eyes again, he could see nothing. Darkness pressed around his head once more. That would not last.

Rhys slowly rose to his feet. His body trembled, in part from the effort, but also from the overwhelming heat he felt building up inside him. Something fluid trickled down his arm. He couldn't tell whether it was sweat or blood. It might have been both.

Reaching out with one hand, Rhys found the wall to his little cell. He paced around, keeping one hand on the wall and leaving a trail of moisture behind him. His fingers felt drenched in something. Any pain he might have suffered from his arms had been blocked.

The walls were perfectly smooth. Rhys had worked that out from his time inside the dark. But he also knew there were two small vertical cracks in the wall, almost imperceptible to the touch. That was the door and his only way of escape. The door was impossible to open from the inside, but Rhys had learned a lot about the impossible.

After finding the door, Rhys braced his hands against the smooth surface. He took a deep breath, summoning the powerful energy that coursed through his veins.

The heat of the entity filled him. He didn't even need to slip his mind back into subspace to feel the power welling up into his hands. His skin burned. Blood dripped from his nose.

Summoning everything he could muster, Rhys pushed hard. The door buckled against his touch. Heat scorched through his hands as he pushed against the door a second time.

The whole mountain moved.

The floor shook beneath Rhys's feet, but he kept his focus into one last thrust of power against the door. Metal screeched and twisted, before the door blew apart and scattered outwards with a deafening crash.

There was only darkness outside. Heat faded from Rhys's body as he staggered out of his cell, still feeling the mountain moving. A deep, primordial roar filled the prison as the ground shifted. Rhys had never experienced an earthquake before, but he imagined this must be what one felt like. A tremor of fear passed down into his tail. He didn't know whether he had caused that, or if it had somehow been the entity. He wasn't sure he wanted to know the answer.

Rhys turned his head, trying to find something amongst the continued darkness. The last time he had been outside his cell, this area had been flooded with light, but now there was nothing. His breath hitched in his throat. Was he blind? He turned his head to the right.

A pinprick of light shone in the distance. Rhys hissed in pain and drew his arms up over his head, feeling then like he had been blinded after all. The pale green light stabbed into his eyes, piercing all the way through to burn at the inside of his head. Squeezing his eyes closed, Rhys slowly crept towards the light. He couldn't hear much around him. Some hands banged against the inside of doors. His tail drooped.

"I'll come back for you," Rhys called out, knowing that those in the hundreds of other cells would not be able to hear him. He wanted to free everyone from inside the prison, but he could not do so. Not this time.

Rhys carefully opened his eyes again, shielding them behind his hand. The dark silhouette of his arms blocked out most of the light, but what little remained still hurt his eyes. They watered, but he forced himself to keep them open. He had spent so long in the darkness that any light hurt him.

Staggering forwards, Rhys went in what he hoped was the right direction towards the elevator. He just followed the light, finding his eyes starting to get a little more accustomed to the unfamiliar glow. He didn't lower his arm.

Without the heat of the entity filling his body, Rhys began to shiver. Pain returned to his hands, more intense than anything before. He could see something occasionally dripping from his fingers, passing over the dim light ahead. Instead of cinnamon, copper filled his nose. Blood. Nausea threatened to build up inside his stomach, but he gritted his teeth and forced it down.

The light slowly got larger, though not brighter as the darkness closed in around him into a narrower corridor. Rhys was slowly able to lower his arm as he got closer. He squinted up at it, blinking away lingering tears that still blurred his vision. An emergency exit light, with an arrow pointing directly ahead. He was going the right way.

A second, identical light shone in the distance. Ignoring the pain in his body, Rhys forced himself to keep staggering forward. If he stopped, he didn't think he would be able to start again. He needed to keep moving at all costs.

Rhys's eyes flicked up. In the darkness he couldn't see the ceiling, except for in the tiny radius of light the emergency exit sign created. All the other lights were off. Every single one of them. His tail curled and flicked. The earthquake must have knocked out power to the prison. Even the backup systems had been affected. That couldn't be any ordinary incident.

The second emergency exit light was at the elevator. The metal doors were closed, but Rhys knew there was no point in trying to summon the elevator to him. Not only was the power down, but he didn't have an identification card to activate the elevators. Unless he could find another way up, then he would still be trapped in the darkness.

Sickly green light radiated around a small circle. The emergency sign gave no indication that there was another way up, like a staircase. Rhys's memory told him the walls were all smooth and white, though they appeared to glow green in the light. Black smudges trailed behind his fingers as he ran them over the wall, searching for any ridges or bumps that gave away the presence of a door. He found nothing. Even returning into the darkness, the walls remained perfectly smooth.

Rhys hissed softly beneath his breath. He hadn't come so far to just give up again. He turned his attention back to the elevator doors. Placing his hands on the cool metal, doing his best to ignore the black smears his fingers left, he began to pull them apart.

Some lingering strength from the entity remained in his arms. The metal screeched and crunched, buckling in places as the mechanisms holding the doors in place broke. The doors slammed open, sending an echoing bang through the corridors behind the starat.

Rhys panted and fell back onto his haunches. Cool air rippled over his fur, blowing down from the empty shaft in front of him. The elevator cart wasn't present, though Rhys could just about make out the heavy cables in the middle of the open space. They gleamed softly in the pale green light.

"Fuck," the starat whispered. His head pounded with a rapidly intensifying headache. His arms burned with pain, all the way from the tips of his fingers to his shoulders. He couldn't decide whether he was too hot or too cold. He shivered, but he could also feel sweat on his brow.

There was no way Rhys could take the elevator shaft, though he hadn't known what he had expected he could have done. Even if the cart had been there, he wouldn't have been able to go anywhere. Without power, there was nothing he could do.

A door screeched open, somewhere high above Rhys. His head snapped up and he peered into the dark shaft. He couldn't see anything beyond the small circle of green light. He narrowed his eyes and squinted. Almost too high to see, a faint white glow lit up a small part of the elevator shaft. A shadow moved across it. The cables swayed and metal clanked.

Rhys rose to unsteady feet. He lifted his hands, though the movement made him whimper in pain. Someone was coming down. He stepped back a few paces, disappearing into the darkness, away from the shaft and beyond the emergency sign.

Soft grunts and clicks came from the open shaft. Rhys curled his ears. He thought he could only hear one person. One shuffling movement as someone climbed down the cables.

A piercing white light shone out from the empty shaft. Rhys flung his hands up again to protect his eyes. The cover of darkness was stripped away from him.

"Oh, shit," a familiar voice whispered. Rhys had heard the voice all through his isolation, but not from the speakers.

"Elijah?"

The light flicked away. The cables creaked, and a dark shadow jumped out from the void. Claws clicked on the floor. A silhouette darkened beyond the ring of green light, before a starat stepped through. Elijah hurried across, pulling Rhys into a gentle hug.

Rhys rested his head on Elijah's shoulder, leaning into the embrace. He didn't move his arms, as any contact against the other starat burned at his fur. Elijah lightly kissed his cheek. Rhys didn't recoil.

"You did come for me," Rhys whispered. He tried blinking the fresh tears away.

"Told you I would," Elijah replied. He took a step back from Rhys. "Didn't expect an earthquake though. Why do I get the feeling you had something to do with it?"

Rhys curled his tail around his legs. "I think I did. I can't be sure."

"Well you can tell me all about it when we're off planet," Elijah said. He held out his hand, resting it on Rhys's shoulder. "I don't know how long the power will be out. We'd better hurry."

"We can't go off planet yet," Rhys whispered. In the total silence of the darkness, his voice seemed to carry a long way. "There's something I need to do first."

Elijah's ears curled. "Are you serious? If we stay here, you'll be captured again. We don't have a choice."

Rhys shook his head. "No. We need to. We have to go up, all the way up. I have to go to the Tomb of Veritas."

Elijah's hands rested on Rhys's cheeks. He pressed his forehead against Rhys's. "You've been down here for six days. I don't think you're thinking right. We have to leave."

"No," Rhys growled. He pulled back from Elijah and lifted his hands. Doubt flickered in the back of his mind. Had he imagined everything that had happened inside his cell? He quickly discounted the idea. Tearing down the cell door was proof enough of that. "I'm not wrong. Please. Trust me."

Through the darkness, Rhys could see Elijah hesitate. He couldn't see the other starat's eyes, but he knew Elijah was appraising him. With a slump of his shoulders, Elijah relented. "Alright. I think I can get us up there. How are your hands?"

"Fucked," Rhys replied. He tried curling his fingers, but only his thumbs moved. All other fingers felt completely numbed.

Elijah hissed quietly. "That makes things more difficult." He glanced down to his wrist. A holoscreen lit up brightly, making Rhys shield his eyes again. "This way."

Rhys followed Elijah away from the elevator, down one of the other three corridors. They didn't make it as far as another of the cavernous warehouses. But for the torch Elijah carried, there was only one other source of light to see by. Another green sign hung down from the ceiling a little further ahead. In the gentle illumination cast by the sign, Rhys could see a gap in the wall.

Elijah shone his torch through the gap, which led through to a fire escape. A concrete staircase curved in both directions, descending to unknown depths and rising even higher. The door swung loosely on its hinges. An electronic panel on the inside of the doorway sparked.

"Someone else has been here," Elijah said warily. He leaned forward, into the stairwell. "Did you hear anyone?"

Rhys shook his head. He strained his ears, but he couldn't hear the sound of footsteps. "Nothing, no."

Elijah hissed softly. "Stay alert then," he said, before slowly creeping forward, approaching the stairs. He began to climb, with Rhys staying just a couple of steps behind.

The eerie silence oppressed Rhys's senses. But for the sound of their footsteps, nothing reached his ears. Even the air was still and silent.

Hot and cold burned within Rhys's body. His legs ached as he forced them up onto each stair. Built for humans, he had to lift his legs a little higher than comfortable with each step. He quickly found himself struggling for breath. "Does this go all the way to the top?" he gasped, hoping for Elijah to slow a little.

"To the summit?" Elijah asked. He glanced back and slowed his pace slightly. "No, that's over twenty kilometres above us. We'll need to get some transport."

"Transport sounds good," Rhys said, nodding to himself. He squeezed his eyes closed for a moment and almost tripped on the stairs. The light from Elijah's torch curved around him. Every scrap of energy he had absorbed from the entity had drained from his body. The heat remained, lingering mostly in his arms, but the rest of his body was icy cold.

"Shit," Elijah muttered. He stopped and crouched down, rummaging through a small pack he carried by his side. He pulled out a small adrenaline shot and injected it into the side of Rhys's neck.

Almost immediately, Rhys felt the effects of the adrenaline flowing through him. He took a deep, rasping breath as energy surged through him, his senses becoming more alert in the darkness. "Fuck," he whispered. "Where did you get that?"

"I haven't been idle," Elijah said, flashing a smile towards Rhys. "Priests are easy to steal from when you say you're running courier jobs."

Rhys raised his brow. He took a couple of trembling steps forward, not wanting to waste the adrenaline by standing idly. "Get anything useful?"

"Few medical supplies. Also some things that might help work out what poison is in that Devil's Blood," Elijah said, warily taking a couple of steps further up. "You think you'll be alright now?"

"For a little bit," Rhys replied with a grimace. He looked up. Never-ending darkness stretched up into infinity. He couldn't wait until he could see something beyond darkness again. Six days, Elijah had said. Rhys could believe that. His time in the cell seemed like no time at all, yet also an eternity.

Taking a deep breath, Rhys started to move with speed again. His muscles ached, and the pain in his arms had not diminished, but his body had energy to move. He would suffer for it later, but that was something to worry about in the future. The staircase climbed ever on. A closed door came and went every now and then, each with a number to indicate which floor they were at. The numbers counted down.

Footsteps pounded from somewhere below. Rhys didn't look down to see where they came from, or if any light gave them away. A voice screamed. The other voice Rhys had heard in his cell, only this time there were no speakers between him and the cardinal.

"I know you're there, beast. I can smell you!"

Rhys didn't need to say anything to Elijah, and he remained silent in turn. The cardinal knew where they were, but they had a head start on him. They picked up the pace. Rhys moved as quickly as his legs could manage. If he was captured by the cardinal again, then there would be no further escapes. The cardinal would make sure of it this time. He would be killed without hesitation.

Rhys's heart raced. Adrenaline from the shot, and from the cardinal's presence, forced him onwards. They had started at level seventeen; seventeen levels of prisons below the surface of Romulus. Rhys's eyes glanced up at the door as they hurried past. Ten. Still so many stairs left to climb.

Even with the adrenaline burning through his system, pain still distracted Rhys. There were no painkillers in Elijah's pack. Rhys gritted his teeth. He had endured pain before. He could endure it again, especially if it meant staying away from Cardinal Erik.

The human chased after them. Only one set of footsteps echoed through the concrete shaft. The cardinal was alone. For a brief moment, Rhys thought about pausing and confronting the cardinal, ending this constant chase once and for all. He pinned his ears down and quickly suppressed such thoughts. That would only give the cardinal the opportunity to overpower them. Sometimes fleeing was the best option.

Rhys struggled to breathe as they finally reached the top of the stairs. Level one was the last door, and the highest the stairwell climbed. Elijah kicked open the door, while Rhys paused to glance down the stairs. He could see torchlight two levels below them, barely a minute behind. The cardinal had stopped yelling. Even from such a distance, Rhys could hear the human's wheezing pants.

Rhys knew where he was. They had come out in the corridor between the elevators, though that was also just as dark as the rest of the facility. Even the grid of lasers had been shut down. Elijah's torchlight swung through the corridor, glinting off the glass window at the far end, where the guards were holed away. Torchlight from within their small room shone back out, but the only way Rhys had seen in or out was through the teleporters, which would be offline without any power.

Rhys hoped no one had been using them.

"Hurry," Elijah whispered.

Rhys didn't need to be told. He ran after Elijah, only glancing back briefly to see the elevator doors had been ripped open. His eyes flicked back to the augmented starat. He hadn't realised Elijah was that strong.

The two starats ran down the corridor. Rhys warily eyed the dark walls, aware that if power returned, then they would be caught in the middle of a laser lattice. There wouldn't be any way to survive that.

A fist slammed against the inside of the glass window. A bright beam of light shone directly in Rhys's eyes. He hissed in pain and shielded his face with his arm, staggering to the side and bumping his shoulder against the wall as he tried to walk straight.

"Rhys, move!" Elijah called out.

Rhys blinked and looked up. Electricity began to hum through the walls. Lights were beginning to flicker on again. He was still standing amongst the laser emitters. Pushing himself away from the wall, Rhys dived forwards, wincing as his hands struck the floor. He rolled across the ground and tucked his tail in, looking back in time to see the piercing bright light of red lasers arcing across the corridor.

Rhys threw his hand out and forced his fingers closed. Without even thinking, he reached out with subspace and ripped a scanner out of the wall on the far side of the lasers. Sparks showered across the corridor just as the door opened at the far end. Cardinal Erik stood illuminated in the intensifying light coming from the fire escape.

The heat from the lasers singed Rhys's feet, but he was on the right side of the defences. The cardinal was not, and if Rhys's understanding was right, he had no way through the lasers. Without a scanner to swipe his access card, the cardinal couldn't switch off the lasers, no matter what the guards in their little booth tried to do.

"Get back here, beast," Cardinal Erik spat. He stalked down the corridor, seemingly not yet noticing the broken scanner. He lifted his voice to a bellow. "Shut off those lasers."

Rhys scrambled up to his feet. He didn't want to wait around and test his theory. He turned on his toes and fled after Elijah, who had already started to push the elevator doors closed. The whir of electricity and activity filled Rhys's ears, as though the power outage had somehow muffled his hearing. Movement from upstairs pounded through the ceiling.

"Quickly," Elijah hissed, holding open the door to the elevator.

A frustrated howl chased after Rhys. The starat turned in time to see Cardinal Erik stood on the far side of the lasers; the human's face illuminated to appear even redder than usual. The scarring from the Devil's Blood made it look like his face oozed blood. A snarl was etched onto the cardinal's mouth. Rhys raised his hand in farewell and smirked as the elevator doors closed.

"We're not done yet," Elijah grunted. The other starat had jumped up to hang from a bar on the top of the elevator. He slapped his palm against the metallic roof a couple of times, pushing up the panelling.

The elevator lurched and began to rise. Elijah pulled himself up through the gap in the ceiling, before reaching down to take hold of Rhys's hands. Rhys hissed in pain as he was lifted into the air. The full weight of his body seemed to be centred right on his arms. His legs flailed in mid-air for a moment, before Elijah was able to hoist him up and out of the elevator.

Elijah quickly returned the panel into place, while Rhys warily looked up the elevator shaft. The dark metallic shaft felt tight and constrictive, without much room above the upper doors for the two starats.

Rhys crouched down low as the elevator shuddered to a halt. He could hear the doors opening below and humans standing beyond. Clipped voices shouted and argued.

Elijah had not been idle. He tapped on Rhys's shoulder, holding a small metallic grate in one hand. A narrow crawlspace had been opened, leading out from the elevator shaft. Keeping as quiet as possible, Rhys slipped into the claustrophobic space. He had to lean on his arms as he crawled, almost hissing in pain at the pressure on his wrists and elbows.

The way ahead was dark, but the shadows did not worry Rhys. He was more afraid of light shining on them and revealing their position. He glanced back a couple of times to see the dark shadow of Elijah just behind him. The other starat had returned the grill in place, obscuring their passage. If the humans in the elevator were smart enough, then it wouldn't take them long to realise where they had gone. For now, their lights didn't pierce into the darkness.

"Left up ahead," Elijah whispered.

Rhys flicked his tail and nodded. He could barely see anything, even with Elijah's torch lighting up the way ahead. He could see a fork in the crawl space; one to the right and the other to the left. Rhys didn't hesitate. He followed Elijah's instructions and tried not to think about what they were slowly crawling over. Were they in the walls, or were they making their way over a room filled with Vatican guards? Every time a claw tapped against the metallic pipe, Rhys cringed and strained his ears for any noise from below. None came.

Elijah tapped on Rhys's foot. "Wait. Just here."

The other starat tapped his claws against the underside of the crawlspace. He hooked his fingers beneath a panel between them both and carefully lifted it up. Light shone from below. After checking the room was clear, Elijah jumped down.

Rhys struggled to turn around in the tight confines of the crawlspace. Instead, he just slowly edged back until he found the gap, then slipped down to hold onto the edge. His strength failed him. With a quick yelp, he fell and struck the floor hard. His legs buckled from the impact, sending jarring pain through his body.

Elijah helped Rhys back up to his feet, but the pain still lingered in Rhys's hands and legs. They were in a public bathroom. Half a dozen stalls lined one wall, while the other had several sinks and mirrors. The door to the right was closed. Rhys took a step back on the tiled floor, a little confused by their presence there.

Rhys didn't worry about that for long. His eyes tracked across to the opposite wall, and he caught sight of his reflection in the mirrors. He looked bedraggled and weak in a way he had never appeared before. He had a gaunt look to his face and body, while smears of blood covered his fur. His muzzle was almost completely red, while his arms were a patchwork mess of blistered skin where the fur had shed.

"I look like shit," Rhys muttered to himself. He glanced warily towards the door. "No one is going to come in, are they?"

"Nah. Bathrooms are closed for maintenance," Elijah replied, a grin coming to his muzzle. Rhys could see the other starat in the mirror reflections, opening one of the stalls behind him.

Rhys's eyes flicked back to himself. He struggled to turn on one of the taps and lightly run a hand through the cool stream of water. He hissed in pain, but slowly started to dab the water over his fur, trying to wash out some of the worst bloodstains. He succeeded mostly in just wetting his fur rather than cleaning it, Rhys soon sighed and gave up.

"Here. You should put this on," Elijah said. He held some red fabric in his arms. Gold thread ran through the crimson folds.

Rhys's eyes widened. "You have to be shitting me," he said. His throat felt dry as he recognised what Elijah carried. "You want us to dress up as priests? Do you have any idea what they'll do to us when they capture us?"

"If they do," Elijah said, still with that same confident grin. Rhys was put in the mind of Twitch with his sparkling eyes and brash confidence, even when he knew nothing of what he was talking about. Elijah was different though. He always seemed to know exactly what he was doing. Rhys knew very few people like that.

"We're worse than dead if they see us in these," Rhys said. He didn't take the robe from Elijah. Apprehension welled within him. He felt dirty even looking at the robes.

"Then it's a good job they won't see us," Elijah said. He unfolded one of the robes, which came complete with a hood and a dark mesh of fabric across the face. The starat's tail wagged. "There's a subsect of priests who take vows of silence and obscurity as some sort of penance thing. When they go about their business in public, they are required to wear robes like these so they can't be seen."

Rhys blinked and flicked his ears up. "Wait, so you're saying…"

Elijah's grin widened. "We put these on, and we'll look like a couple of short priests. Our faces will be hidden. The robes are long enough to cover our feet. So long as our hands and tails remain covered, no one will know the difference."

"That might actually work then," Rhys said reluctantly. He still wasn't keen on the idea of wearing Vatican robes. Even as a human, he had been aware of the sacrilege of pretending to be a member of the clergy. As a starat, that punishment would be so much worse. However, it did give them a way to move through Romulus without being questioned. "Will this get us up to the tomb?"

Elijah pinned his ears back. He rummaged through the small pack of supplies he carried with him and pulled out a passcard. "This probably will, but I still don't like the idea. I had everything prepared to leave right away."

"I need to go up there," Rhys said grimly. He took the robes from Elijah and grimaced from the weight. Most of the blood on his fur was dry and didn't mark the robes. At least if he got blood on them, the stains would be barely visible against the crimson colouring. The starat frowned as he looked down at the robes. "How did you even get these?"

"I've been planning this for a couple of days now. I had everything put in place for a nice easy escape," Elijah said, shrugging his shoulders. He slipped into a second set of robes, which completely obscured his body. His face was not visible behind the black mesh in the hood. "Not everything went perfectly, but I knew we'd make it here, so I made sure the bathroom would be closed off and these robes would be here for us. Did you need any help with yours?"

Rhys couldn't help but cringe back from the sight of a robed priest reaching out for him, even though he knew it was Elijah behind the faceless hood. He shuddered and curled his tail in close as he shook his head. "I've got this," he said. Taking a deep breath, Rhys put his head through the bottom of the robes and let the clothing ripple down around him. The fabric felt heavy against his fur, and even once he got the hood in place, his vision was obscured and blurred through the mesh.

Elijah was right. As Rhys looked at the mirror, he could see no evidence of a starat standing in the reflection. The sleeves of the robe could pull back and expose his hands, but held naturally, they were covered by the excessive folds of fabric. His feet were likewise completely covered by the trailing length of the robe. Rhys could only hope it would be a good enough disguise to allow them to enter the most holy of places on Mars.

"Alright. I think I know how we can get up there," Elijah said quietly. He slipped his small pack into his sleeve, hiding it from view. He gestured towards the door. "You follow me out there and don't say anything, alright? Remember, we're meant to be silent monks. Don't answer any questions. Just let me handle it."

Rhys took a deep breath and nodded. "Got it. After you then."

Elijah slowly opened the door and looked outside. He nudged aside the closed sign in front of the door and stepped out. Rhys followed just behind and tried not to think of what they were about to do. He checked one last time that his hood was securely in place. He was probably the one starat the Vatican wanted most out of any in the system. He should have been fleeing as fast as he possibly could. Instead, he was delving deeper into the heartland of Olympus Mons.

Rhys could only hope he knew what he was doing.

chapter eleven

No one even looked at Rhys and Elijah for more than a couple of seconds. The robes and the black mesh over the hood completely anonymised the two starats, even as they walked through Romulus. Rhys didn't question where Elijah was going. He trusted that the other starat would find some way to reach the summit of the awe-inspiring mountain that rose from the outskirts of the city.

An occasional gesture was made in their direction. That was usually a kiss of a rosary or a sign of the cross, but that was all the interaction they got. No one spoke a word to them. Everyone moved out of their way. If any lingering glances were cast towards them afterwards, then Rhys didn't see them. No one called out to them, querying their diminutive height. For all the priests could have known, they were just two short humans undergoing penance for serious sins.

That didn't stop Rhys's constant fear. He struggled to stop himself trembling, and his breath hitched in his throat every time he thought someone looked in his direction. He was deep into enemy territory, and he was only going to get deeper.

There were no shuttle services that went up to the top of the mountain, which surprised Rhys. He had expected something of the like, as that was the quickest way to travel to such a height. Instead, there was a train service that crawled up the slopes of Olympus Mons. Only the clergy and approved guests were permitted to make the journey towards the summit, though there were also monasteries and chapels on the endless slopes. Rhys and Elijah were waved through the checkpoint at the entry to the station without anyone requesting to see their faces.

One worker at the checkpoint did ask Elijah a couple of questions, but they were phrased so that he could answer with a nod or shake of his head. He was also asked to provide a passcard, which he was able to do without revealing his hand. The guards let them through without any complaint.

The station consisted of one small building, with an open-air single platform. Sunshades provided places for passengers to sit while they waited for the next train, though the platform was currently completely empty, except for one human dressed in formal blue uniform. He wore clothing more alike those the guards at the checkpoint had worn, rather than Vatican robes.

A mag-train waited at the platform. The sleek white train was curved and shapely, designed in many of the ways that spacecraft couldn't be. Those that needed to go beyond atmosphere needed to be built in a way that wouldn't break apart in zero gravity, which led to the blocky, uninspiring shapes of many of the crafts. Mag-trains were designed for speed through atmosphere. The sharp, pointed nose of the train and the rounded carriages looked fast, even when the train was stationary.

The guard called out to Rhys and Elijah. Rhys initially tensed, before he realised the human was simply calling them over to give them access to one of the carriages.

"Just through here, brothers. The carriage will be yours," the guard said, holding a hand to the rosary dangling from his neck. "We're waiting on a couple more passengers, but we expect to still leave on schedule. Not even an earthquake will slow us down." He flashed a bright smile, which lingered on his face for more time than was comfortable.

Elijah nodded as he walked past the guard. He stepped inside the train, with Rhys just behind. The guard turned away and left them both alone, knowing there wouldn't be a conversation coming from the hooded pair.

The inside of the train was opulent and rich. Red silk curtains were draped across the windows, while the seats were all padded and cushioned. Sets of four seats surrounded tables, upon which were menus and glasses for fully catered services. Beneath his hood, Rhys flicked his ears and frowned. He didn't expect the journey up to the summit of the mountain to be a long one, but everything he saw told him to expect a few hours on the train.

As the guard had promised, the carriage was completely empty. Rhys couldn't even smell any humans close by. The carriage instead smelled clean. Disinfectant and polish were the biggest scents in his nose, other than the lingering coppery tang of blood that he had been unable to wash away.

Rhys glanced out onto the platform as he took a seat opposite Elijah. He then tensed and tapped Elijah's arm, warning the other starat. A familiar face had just come onto the platform. Flanked by three other priests, Cardinal Erik stalked along the length of the train to exchange some words with the guard outside.

Rhys couldn't see Elijah's face. If the other starat was feeling as Rhys was, then his ears would be curled down and tense. He forced himself to remain sitting, with his hidden eyes constantly on the cardinal outside. Through the dark mesh, he couldn't see clearly enough to get a good view of the cardinal's lips, and his voice wasn't loud enough to come through into the train.

The guard pointed towards the carriages, and Cardinal Erik prowled closer. The human's lips still moved in a constant mutter. His face was its usual shade of deep red as his anger clearly boiled close to the surface. The three priests with him stayed a few paces behind.

Cardinal Erik walked directly past the window next to which Rhys was sat. Though Rhys kept his eyes on the cardinal, the human didn't even look towards him. The four priests got on at the next carriage. Only then did Rhys slowly exhale, unaware until then that he had even been holding his breath.

An alarm chimed through the train. The doors to the carriages all closed at once, hissing shut before quietly clicking as they locked. Almost immediately, a gentle whine filled the train as the mag-engines activated. An automated voice came through the speakers.

"Welcome to the Romulus to New Basilica mag-train route. This is an express service, and there will be no set menu provided for this journey. Should you wish refreshments, then please notify one of our crew," the voice droned, not quite managing the inflections of a human or starat voice. "The train will not be leaving any pressurized zones on the ascent, but should oxygen be required, masks are available from the cabin above your heads."

Rhys glanced up. He could see the red crosses on the overhang, out of reach while he was sitting down. He felt a little more secure in the knowledge that there would be oxygen provided, given the great height the mag-train would be ascending to.

"Our estimated journey time will be one hour. We hope you have a pleasant journey to New Basilica," the automated voice continued, before switching off with a quiet beep.

Rhys looked across to Elijah, who remained quiet and still beneath his robes, playing the part of the taciturn priest well. Rhys tried to match that. His tail flicked nervously, trapped between his robes and the seat. He didn't like the idea of sharing a mag-train with Cardinal Erik for a whole hour. So much could still go wrong.

The train slowly accelerated out of the station. Buildings flashed by. The engines were almost silent, and the ride very smooth with barely a bump. Only once the train made it out from the city confines did it begin to ascend the side of the mountain. The lower regions of Olympus Mons were covered in thin, wispy fields of grass. No trees grew on the mountain itself, though Rhys could see some small forests on the plains that stretched away from the mountain and city.

The terraformed nature of the planet was most evident close to Olympus Mons and the largest cities of Romulus and Remus. Away from the central seat of the Vatican's power was much less developed. The air was still breathable, and the temperature tolerable around the equator, but there was little life. Grasses imported from Terra had stretched across some regions, but most of the planet had been left untouched from its lifeless past. Without soil to grow in, there could be no vegetation.

Centaura had been alien to Rhys, but Mars was still just as dangerous a place to live. Outside the cities, chances of survival were minimal. None of that harsh landscape was visible from the train. Rhys could only see what the Vatican wanted to show off, and that was a planet of vibrant life. Forests surrounded the city, and the mountain itself was green with endless fields.

Slowly, the slope of the mountain began to increase. For the most part, the mag-train spiralled up the mountain, taking the long way up the never-ending peak. Though Rhys craned his neck to look, he couldn't see any sign of the top of the mountain, or the great cathedral he knew to be up there.

The silence was oppressive. Rhys longed to talk to Elijah, to discuss the plan of action for what was going to happen once they reached the summit. He kept his tongue. Though there were no staff present in their carriage, Rhys knew that someone could come through to them at any moment. Their success depended on remaining silent and undiscovered for as long as possible.

The city disappeared below the slope of the mountain. Even long before the mag-train reached the summit, Rhys could no longer see any ground that was not part of the mountain slope. The horizon loomed close as the land dropped away. Rhys had never seen anything quite like it before.

Elijah barely moved. He sat with his head against the rest behind him, his long sleeves draped across the table. Even the rise and fall of his chest was minimal, almost as though he was asleep. Rhys wished he felt safe enough to sleep, but even with his exhaustion looming over him, he knew he would not be able to close his eyes long enough.

No one came to disturb the two starats. Even as the mag-train began to slow down towards the summit of the mountain, they remained by themselves. Rhys felt a little shiver when he first caught sight of the great stone cathedral that spread out across the summit. The cathedral looked truly ancient, as it was a perfect replica of the old Vatican City on Terra, only grander: larger. The surrounding landscape was verdant green, almost impossibly so. The grass was so bright Rhys's eyes hurt from looking at it.

The mag-train pulled into a station a short distance away from the grand cathedral. The platform itself was outside, nestled beside a visitor and information centre. Half a dozen guards stood at the station, all wearing ceremonial yellow and blue baggy clothing. These were the Swiss Guard, and they looked like they had stepped out of a history book. Rhys stared at them through the window of the train for a few moments. If the guards were there to project an aura of menace, then they had failed dismally. Rhys almost laughed before he managed to stop himself.

The station buildings hid the cathedral from view. Unlike the cathedral, the station was constructed out of more modern materials. Glass gleamed in the sunlight, which was weaker than it was on Terra or Ceres, but still strong enough to light the mountaintop.

Without any prompting from Rhys, Elijah rose to his feet just before the train came to a complete stop. Rhys was quick to follow, though he didn't want to get off the train right away. He wanted to give Cardinal Erik the chance to leave first, but Elijah headed right towards the doors as they hissed open. A cold blast of air rushed into the train.

Two of the comically dressed guards were stood just outside the doors. They both carried a modified halberd, with a blaster rifle set just above the wickedly sharp blade. The halberds were carried upright, with the butt of the spear placed against the platform. The slight skip of Rhys's heart quietened as he realised that they were not acting aggressively.

"Welcome to the Basilica," one of the guards drawled in what was clearly the start of a well-practiced speech. "Where were you looking to go today? We have…"

The other guard smacked the butt of his halberd against the speaker's ankle. "Apologies for him, my brothers. He forgets to ask yes or no questions to the silenced. Do you require a guide today?"

Elijah shook his head as he stepped down off the train.

Both guards took a step back. The first speaker had reddened entirely. "My apologies, brothers. We won't stop you."

Elijah bowed his head as the two guards swivelled to the side, giving the starats a free path towards the station building. Automatic glass doors led through to a large lobby inside.

Rhys shivered as he followed Elijah off the train. He hesitated as he heard a commotion further down the platform. Glancing in that direction, he could see Cardinal Erik pushing past the two guards at his door, stalking away without a word to the blustering men. One of the other priests following the cardinal called out an apology, but none of them stopped.

The cardinal passed through a different door, but Rhys could see him in the lobby. No one dared to approach Cardinal Erik, and even before Rhys reached the automatic doors, the cardinal had disappeared from view on the other side of the lobby.

Icy cold air chilled at Rhys even through his thick robes. He suppressed a shiver as he looked up. Through the dark mesh in front of his face, he could just about see the slight shimmer in the air that made up the protective dome around the Olympus Mons summit. In normal circumstances, the peak would be wholly unsuitable for life, both in terms of sheer cold and a dangerously thin atmosphere. The dome allowed for the air to be pressurized beyond natural levels, as well as helping to mitigate the fatal chill.

Inside the station lobby was entirely different. The air inside was heated, so much so that Rhys was quickly brought to a sweat. More of the brightly coloured guards were stationed all around the lobby. Rhys didn't know if there were more of them up on the summit than down below, or if they were just easier to see. He tried not to look at them too much.

The lobby itself was brightly lit, with much of that coming from the natural light of Sol. The ceiling was entirely made of glass, giving a perfect view of the weak blue sky. Sol was almost directly overhead. The marble floor shone in the sunlight, throwing up harsh glares that distracted Rhys even through the dark mesh of his hood. He curled his tail close to his legs, making sure that it didn't press out the back of his robes. That was what he tried to convince himself, at least. The fear of being discovered also tucked his tail down.

There was an information desk that took up much of the wall opposite to the station, but Elijah didn't go there. They needed to look like they belonged, and that meant confident, purposeful strides towards a particular destination. Rhys could only hope that Elijah knew what that destination was. He had never been to the summit of Olympus Mons before; he doubted many starats ever had.

Elijah walked towards one of the three corridors that led out of the main lobby. The high, expansive glass ceiling was replaced with one that was lower, with regular square panels of polyester material housing light fittings and occasional information signs. The floor beneath Rhys's feet was marbled tiles. He struggled to keep his claws retracted, lest they click on the rigid surface.

One tile caught Rhys's attention. It was cracked, looking like the site of an impact from above. The starat's eyes flicked up. Only bare ceiling above, without any obvious evidence of a fixture having existed there. He frowned, the lingering sense of confusion remaining with him.

A prickling sensation crawled over Rhys's fur. The scent of cinnamon constantly tickled at the back of his nose. The entire building was filled with it. The summit of Olympus Mons was definitely a weak point between subspace and realspace, the two almost bleeding into each other. He shivered and forced himself to actively block the temptation to sink into subspace. He felt like he could do it easily here, but he was not yet ready for that.

Many doors opened off the corridor, but none were places of worship. Some rooms appeared to be conference rooms and educational facilities. Others seemed to lead through towards places of residence – permanent or temporary – for the priests on the mountaintop. Elijah ignored them all.

Dozens of priests and guardsmen swept past the two starats. The usual indifference was shown to them, but for the occasional clutching of a rosary or signed cross. Instead of hostility on the faces of the religious humans, there was just blank anonymity. That would certainly change if either of the starats disrobed, but for the moment, their disguises were working.

A chill cold wind blew down the corridor. Rhys gritted his teeth as he suppressed a shiver. The cold snap vanished a moment later. They were close to doors leading outside. That was where they needed to go.

The two starats rounded a corner to see automatic glass doors just a few paces away, leading out onto a circular stone courtyard. The sides of the circular colonnades were made from stone pillars in the design of the ancient structures on Terra, with the towering basilica itself directly opposite. Beyond the domed roof of the basilica, Rhys could see the summit of the mountain looming a short distance above.

The door opened for the starats. They stepped out into the biting cold once more. A howling gale blew across the mountain, robbing Rhys of his senses for a moment. A quiet gasp escaped his lips before he could slam his mouth closed again. He glanced around to see that no one had heard him. He could barely hear his own thoughts in the roaring wind.

To the left was a second stone building, looming high over everything but the basilica. Tall spires rose up from the cathedral, also built with traditional stone materials, and in an ancient style. Bright green grass and bushes filled much of the middle of the courtyard, all pristine and perfect. A stone obelisk rose from the exact centre of the courtyard, rising to a pointed peak almost as tall as the basilica dome. Two dozen guards patrolled around the courtyard in groups of four. They all carried halberds, and their faces were red from the cold.

The doors of both the cathedral and basilica were wide open. A red-robed human stood at the doors of the basilica. Even from a distance, Rhys recognised Cardinal Erik. Two of his green-robed priests were still with him, but Rhys couldn't see the third.

Rhys walked by Elijah's side, towards the basilica and the cardinal. Though Rhys had never been to the summit before, he knew from his old school days the rough layout of the place. The Tomb of Veritas was behind the basilica. Unfortunately, he didn't know what sort of access two silenced priests would have towards the most sacred of places. Three guards stood at either side of the basilica, standing across the narrow pathways in the shadows of the great stone building.

As they got closer to the basilica, Elijah turned to the right, towards the ring of columns that surrounded the courtyard. Rhys could feel some of the bushes brushing against his robes. Up close, he could see the leaves were plastic and fake. The grass was likewise artificial. The tip of his tail flicked. He wondered if even the stone of the cathedral and basilica was real, or if that too was fake.

The stonework of the columns seemed real enough. The overarching structure provided a little shelter from the howling gale, but not much. The cold wind cut through Rhys's robes with ease. He didn't know how the patrolling guards were able to tolerate it, and their faces and hands were completely exposed to the crippling chill.

The ring of columns connected to the sides of the basilica, just behind the stairs leading up to the cavernous doorway. They provided a different route towards the basilica, but the columns didn't allow the starats to move behind the guards that blocked the way to the tomb.

Stone benches lined the inside of the boundary colonnades. Half looked back into the courtyard, while half looked out towards the mountainside as it fell away from the summit. There appeared to be two horizons. One, close up, where the land fell away dramatically. The second was an immense distance away, where the far side of the great caldera rose. The distant cliffs were almost invisible, rising to a height that was impossible to judge.

Everything outside the colonnades was bright green; too bright to be truly natural. None of the natural red of Mars was visible.

Elijah patted one of the stone benches that looked out from the courtyard. He took a seat, making sure his robes still draped down over his feet. Rhys took a seat next to the other starat, wincing as he settled too much of his weight down on the base of his tail.

"We wait here for a little bit," Elijah muttered, his words almost lost to the wind.

"How will we get past the guards?" Rhys asked, keeping his voice just as quiet. He glanced around. None of the humans had followed close to them. Their patrol remained on the other side of the columns.

Elijah looked out over the sloping side of the mountain. But for the wind and the quiet sound of the guards' patrolling feet, there was no sound around the plateau. No animal life was visible around the mountain peak.

The starat remained quiet for long enough that Rhys was sure Elijah couldn't have heard him over the wind. "We wait for something to distract them," Elijah said eventually. He didn't turn his head, instead just gazing down the side of the mountain.

Rhys followed Elijah's gaze. He could not see the bottom of the great caldera, nor the base of the far cliffs.

"Like what?" Rhys asked. He turned his head away from the endless slopes, his stomach churning at the sight. He looked back across the courtyard. He could barely see anything, as the hood blocked most of his peripheral vision, and even what he could see was partially obscured by the black mesh in front of his eyes.

"Who do you think the cardinal is here to see?" Elijah asked, slowly turning his head to look towards Rhys. "There's not many who would have his ear up here."

Rhys bit his lip and stared down the mountainside. He wasn't sure about who would have the ear of the cardinal, but he knew that there would only be one person who Cardinal Erik would turn to. He would go all the way to the very top, not just of the mountain, but of the Vatican of Mars itself. He would go to Pope Adamantius.

They didn't have long to wait. A bell clamoured atop the basilica, catching the attention of everyone in the courtyard. The two starats looked back to see what was going on, while many of the guards moved from their stations and patrol routes to stand in an honour guard at the bottom of the basilica's steps. Cardinal Erik came down the stairs and turned around, genuflecting down onto one knee.

Rhys tore his eyes away from the basilica steps. The guards closest to them; stationed at the path around to the tomb, had also moved towards the honour guard. Elijah had already risen to his feet and had silently started to stalk around the colonnade, keeping himself low so the bushes close to the columns provided a little cover. Rhys hurried after him, hissing quietly to himself and cursing that he had wasted a few precious seconds looking towards the humans.

No one shouted out or seemed to notice their quick movement. The passage around the side of the basilica was free. On one side of the path was the stone walls of the towering building, while the other was lined by more plastic hedges. The ground sloped steadily upwards, halving the relative height of the rear of the basilica compared to the grand church's front.

The ground continued to rise beyond the church up towards the summit of Olympus Mons and the highest point on the planet. There was nowhere else in the Sol System that was further from the surface of the celestial body. They stood over twenty kilometres above the surface of Mars, and before the most holy of places in all the three settled systems.

The tomb was cut into the tallest segment of rock, like a dark cave right at the peak of the mountain. Before it was a golden plaque dedicated to Veritas. Static electricity clawed at Rhys's fur as they cautiously approached. Rhys kept one ear open for the sounds of pursuit, but the tolling bell atop the basilica and the howling wind meant he could barely hear anything else.

Rhys placed his hand on the golden plaque. He hissed in pain from the contact and squeezed his eyes closed. The scent of another starat filled the air, overwhelming even the intoxicating smell of cinnamon. He opened his eyes to see the dark shadow of a starat standing amongst them. The starat spat on the plaque.

Rhys blinked. The ghostly starat dispersed on the wind.

"Are you alright?" Elijah called out, turning around and holding his hand out to Rhys.

Rhys shook his head to clear his vision. "Yeah, fine," he muttered. He didn't know what he had just seen. Voices still echoed inside his head, some belonging to starats and others to humans. The mantra of the entity tickled at his mind, almost loud enough to be heard.

"Do we need to go inside?" Elijah asked. He stood halfway between the plaque and the entrance to the tomb itself.

"I think we do, yeah," Rhys replied. His head felt light as he took a couple of steps closer to Elijah. His vision spun as dizziness threatened to overwhelm him. He was sure it wasn't the altitude. Elijah suffered none of the same effects, and Olympus Mons was one of the most secure places for atmospheric protection. The Vatican would take no risks with the pope residing at the top of the great mountain.

Rhys stepped into the shadows of the tomb. Almost instantly, the chill of the mountain faded. He couldn't feel moving air from any heaters, but there was a strange warmth emanating up from deeper within the cave. Chiselled steps led down to a second chamber below.

Feeling almost like he was in a dream, Rhys lifted his hood away from his head as he placed his feet on the top step. Every breath he took felt saturated in cinnamon. The air was filled with static electricity, puffing up his fur and sending small sparks of energy through his fingers. The rock beneath his feet felt spongy and soft.

Harsh electrical lighting kept the chamber from darkness, mixing horrifically with the natural aesthetic of the rest of the cave. Everything had been clearly carved by hand. The walls were all rough, and the floor was only smooth from the repeated wearing of thousands of feet over many years.

The stairs curved around and down, doubling back on itself until it opened into a second chamber, where there were no electrical lights. Rhys could barely breathe as he placed his foot down on the roughly hewn floor, feeling almost like he might sink straight through. The ornate, golden tomb of Veritas filled much of the room. A statue of the human stood above the sarcophagus, wearing a crown of obsidian roses on his head. Obsidian spines, each the size of Rhys's entire body, rose out of the sides of the golden tomb. To Rhys, they looked like a claw trying to grasp its way out from the sarcophagus. Upon each of the eleven spikes was written one of the trials Veritas had gone through in his martyred life.

Rhys slowly walked around the tomb in awe. There was just enough room for someone to circumnavigate the small chamber without touching the obsidian spikes that reached out from the golden casket within. The lid of the sarcophagus was sealed closed. Rhys wondered what was inside, and if that was the reason why he had felt so compelled to come to the mountaintop.

Three small vents in the ceiling, each little more than a crack in the rock, allowed light to spill through from the chamber above. The three shafts of light fell on the forehead, heart, and clasped hands of the golden statue.

A voice echoed down from above. Rhys froze and glanced up. No shadows played on the stairs.

"…matters are clearly very serious," the voice said. He spoke with a soft tone, calming and gentle. Rhys knew exactly who that voice belonged to. He had heard it broadcast across the system often enough, beseeching messages of hope and unification amongst humanity, to believe the message of Veritas and the sacrifice he had made. That was the voice of Pope Adamantius.

The voice that responded to Pope Adamantius was the opposite in almost every way; oily and dirty, spoken a little too quickly and loudly to be considered gentle. "And with all due respect, your excellency, I do not believe you are taking it seriously enough," Cardinal Erik growled.

Pope Adamantius chuckled jovially, as though he had just heard a pleasant joke. "My dear Erik. This is just a starat you are talking about. What harm could come of it?"

"It has proven it is more than just a mere starat. There might be some semblance of human intelligence left inside it, and that proves a danger to us," Cardinal Erik growled.

Before Pope Adamantius replied, Elijah pulled at Rhys's shoulder and leaned in close. He lifted his hood. "You better find what you were here for," the starat whispered, barely loud enough for Rhys to hear.

Rhys nodded and swallowed, trying to get some moisture in his dry throat. He struggled to ignore the conversation happening just above him, knowing full well that they were talking about him. His tail flicked. Some part of him longed to go up there, to confront the cardinal for the many sins the human had committed against him. He wanted to get revenge for Stephanie's death, but the logical side of him wanted to finish what he had started, to escape Mars as quickly as possible.

There had to be something about the tomb that had called him here. He could smell subspace on the air. It infused everything inside the small chamber. Reality felt thin, like any wrong step could carry him through to the endless white void of subspace.

"I need it!" Cardinal Erik roared, distracting Rhys from his frantic search.

"Control your anger, Cardinal," Pope Adamantius replied calmly. "Your passion for catching this heretic is noble, but you must not let it distract you from what is important."

"You are asking me to abandon it, to let it roam freely," the cardinal spluttered.

Rhys's ears flicked. He had missed something important. There had been twelve trials of Veritas, but only eleven surrounded the sarcophagus. There was room for a twelfth spike, but where one should have been, there was only a broken stump.

"We know it is still in Romulus. It will not be allowed to escape. We will capture it and keep it for your disposal."

Rhys trembled. He placed his hands on the nearest obsidian spike, running his fingers over the smooth surface. Something about them was familiar. He was sure they had something to do with why he was there.

"No," Cardinal Erik said sharply, bitterly. "It has escaped me three times now. It's too dangerous to keep alive. When you see it, kill it without mercy or rights. Its soul is already lost and can never join Veritas."

"Very well," Pope Adamantius replied. His voice echoed slightly through the cracks in the stone.

Rhys looked across the obsidian spikes. His eyes widened as they moved to the empty gap where the twelfth should be. The severed stump was perfectly smooth, while the air shimmered around it. The spike hadn't been cut away. It had disappeared into subspace.

"Fuck," Rhys whispered. He darted around to the other side of the tomb, around the back of the statue. The air shimmered and changed. He could see the rip through realspace now, a shimmering disk of golden light with flecks of white and black radiating through. Black ichor dripped from the obsidian spike.

Elijah followed Rhys around. He grabbed hold of Rhys's shoulder. "Wait a moment," he whispered. He pulled his pack out through his sleeve and rummaged through his supplies until he found a small glass vial. He gently unstoppered the vial and crouched down, carefully scooping up some of the black ichor. The thick gunk smelled familiar to Rhys, but he couldn't place it. He cringed in pain at the loose memories, but nothing solid came to mind.

Above them, the voices had turned to gentle, melodic chanting in a language Rhys was not familiar with. He guessed it might be ancient Latin, but he couldn't be sure. He had never learned any of the divine language at school and had certainly not had a need for it since moving into the military.

Elijah nodded and stepped back. He secreted the vial away in his robes again and gave Rhys the space he needed to work.

Rhys wished he knew exactly what he needed to do. The obsidian spike was important. He had seen it in subspace, keeping the entity trapped over Olympus Mons. Was it really that simple? Did he just need to pull the obsidian back into realspace and the entity would be free? Rhys curled his tail and took a deep breath. He might as well try.

Reaching into subspace was easy. What was less so was the burst of agony that ripped through his arms as the entity roared close all around him. Rhys twitched and took half a shuffling step backwards, bumping against the rocky wall. His senses slipped in and out of realspace as he struggled to maintain control with the shrieking pressure of the entity enveloping him. His jaw trembled as he struggled to contain a scream of pain.

Within the swirling inky clouds of the entity, Rhys found what he was searching for. The remaining half of the obsidian spike was buried deep within the heart of the entity.

Realspace and subspace flickered back and forth as Rhys struggled to reach for it. His fingers closed around the broken spire. Flesh blistered and burned from the exertion. The Voice of Veritas pounded in his ears.

He could no longer contain his pain.

An agonised scream burst from his mouth, no matter how hard he tried to bite it back. The chanting above immediately ceased. Rhys squeezed his eyes closed and focused on the obsidian spire, knowing that he needed to finish his work. The entity swirled around him, the black tendrils briefly emerging in realspace before dissolving to nothing.

Rhys got both hands around the spike. His flesh blistered. The obsidian moved in his hands. He gritted his teeth and trembled. His arms burned. His stolen robes were charred around the hem of the sleeves and continued to smoulder.

Footsteps charged down the narrow stairs. Two men in red robes, one with a more elaborate golden trim, burst into view. Cardinal Erik's face was apoplectic with rage. "You!"

"Why are you in our sacred temple?" Pope Adamantius asked, his voice still calm despite his narrowed eyes and furrowed brow. He spoke like a disappointed father admonishing a naughty child.

Rhys bared his teeth. His voice trembled from pain. "Fuck you both," he spat. He then wrenched the obsidian spike towards him, whilst also pushing at the endless monolith of the entity, forcing it away from the ripped hole in realspace. Heat rose from his arms. Searing pain burned through his shoulders and up into his mind. White light encroached on the corners of his vision.

Bright light flashed as the remainder of the obsidian spike burst back into realspace. A fraction of a second stretched out into an eternity as Rhys slowly looked up to the two humans on the other side of the tomb. They were frozen, along with the rest of time and reality. Rhys stood alone, his thoughts racing even as his body refused to act.

A low roar built up in the back of Rhys's mind. Pain and anguish were within that loud clamouring, but also relief and the sense of total freedom. The rip in realspace snapped closed, cracking like an elastic band. Time was restored as a frightening shockwave of subspace energy blasted out from the tomb. Rhys's mind burned.

Senses were obliterated as Rhys was thrown back against the rock wall. He was briefly aware that the same had happened to the two humans, but then all went dark, and he knew no more.

chapter twelve

Vague sensations flashed through Rhys's mind. He thought he was being carried, but he couldn't be sure. His senses weren't working correctly. His vision was blurred whenever he forced his eyes open, and his touch was unreliable. His body burned. He knew that much. Pain flared through every nerve and there was nothing he could do to soothe it. A tinnitus so loud that he could hear nothing else roared through his head.

Sometimes, Rhys thought he heard a voice talking to him, but that might just have been an extension of the tinnitus. He certainly didn't understand the words, if they even existed. The occasional flashes of light made no sense. He closed his eyes for a moment and the cold, mountaintop cathedral turned into the backseat of a car, which then turned into the arms of a starat as he was carried again.

A single thought seemed to take hours to process. Words didn't string together in his mind. There was only emotion, and that emotion was agony. Forces buffeted at his body, which only served to further fuel the pain. He wanted to scream, but his body still didn't want to move at all. His eyes closed and opened again.

He was on a spaceship, lying on something soft. The pain had not receded, but his thoughts had cleared slightly. His senses had stabilised enough to smell the presence of another starat close by, recognising the scent of Elijah.

"Where are we?" Rhys mumbled, his voice slurred and weak.

"We're on the *Vigilant*," Elijah replied, from somewhere above and behind Rhys.

Slowly, Rhys realised he was lying in the small cabin in the floor of the *Vigilant's* bridge. The scent of human slowly crept into his nose, but it was an old smell. The cardinal was not with them. He tried to piece together what had happened on Mars, but nothing after he had freed the entity made sense.

"What happened? How did we get away?" Rhys asked. He tried to sit up, but almost screamed in pain as he moved his arms even slightly. He squeezed his eyes closed and breathed heavily as he tried to outlast the pain and resist the growing nausea.

"I carried you out," Elijah said, still out of view. He wouldn't be able to leave his seat, piloting the ship by himself. "Whatever you did, it knocked out pretty much everyone. They just... crumpled. I've never seen anything like it."

"Dead?" Rhys gasped.

"No, I don't think so. Some were starting to wake up again. Just, dazed and confused," Elijah explained. The other starat's voice was shaky and nervous. "You shouldn't worry about that now. I'll tell you all about it when we get somewhere safe, alright? You just sleep and recover."

Rhys tried to argue, but it was a losing battle. He could already feel exhaustion claiming him again. Not even the pain could keep him awake. He closed his eyes and slipped into darkness.

***

When Rhys opened his eyes again, he was somewhere new, yet painfully familiar. The ceiling above had been the first thing he had ever looked at with the eyes of a starat. He squinted. The crack on the ceiling was in the same place he remembered. He was in the exact same bed where he had first realised his life had been irrevocably changed.

This time, Rhys was not alone when he woke up. He rolled his head to the side to see Elijah sat beside his bed. The other starat immediately smiled.

"Good morning," Elijah said brightly. He leaned forward. "How do you feel?"

"I feel..." Rhys hesitated, uncertain. Ghosts of pain still echoed through his body, and his mind felt groggy and slow. He lifted himself up on his hands and winced in pain, before realising the pain had never actually come. He shifted back to lean against the headboard and stared down at his hands. Short fur covered his arms in a way they hadn't done ever since he had been first captured by Cardinal Erik. Muscle and fat coated his bones again, though still not enough to look properly healthy. He tensed his fingers and found the movement fluid and easy. "I feel fine. How do I feel fine?"

Elijah's tail flicked as he reached out to take Rhys's hands in his own. "Then it worked."

Rhys stared at his hands in wonder. He could feel Elijah touching him, and there was no pain. Tears came to his eyes. "You did this? How?"

Elijah grinned a little wider. "That black stuff in the tomb. That was the missing ingredient in the Devil's Blood. That was why I couldn't reverse engineer a cure. Once I had that, I was able to work it out. I fixed the damage. You had some muscle regrowth too, but you won't have all of your strength back yet. Couldn't do too much about the fur, but it will keep growing."

"How… how long was I out for?" Rhys asked. He shivered and stared at his hands some more. The damage had been almost completely fixed. Only his absent claws remained unhealed.

"Five days. I didn't want to wake you up too early," Elijah replied. His fingers gently rubbed over Rhys's hands.

Rhys pulled his hands back. He almost jumped out of bed. "Five days? Are they… is someone coming after us? They have to know, right?"

Elijah grabbed hold of Rhys's hands again. He shook his head. "No. No one has come after us. Mars has bigger problems to deal with right now. Admiral Garter will give you a full briefing when I say you're fit enough to go and see him."

Rhys nodded. His heart quickened, despite being assured there was no danger. He took a deep breath to compose himself. "You got me out. Thank you for that."

"I wasn't just going to leave you there," Elijah said, sticking the tip of his tongue out. His eyes were bright as he smiled. "Whatever you did up there, it didn't touch me. Might have been my augments. Without replicating the same incident again, I can't test my theories."

Rhys grimaced. "I don't want to go back. You can find someone else to test that theory," he said, shuddering at the mere thought of returning to Olympus Mons. If he never saw another Vatican robe again, he would be happy.

"Well how about we look at getting you some proper food, and then you can go and meet up with the admiral again," Elijah suggested, helping Rhys get out of the bed. "I know he's been looking forward to see you awake again."

Rhys felt a little unsteady on his feet, but there wasn't any of the usual pain or discomfort that he had been quickly growing used to. Instead, it was just the weakness of being off his feet for five days, lying unconscious in a hospital bed. For almost a week before that he had been relatively idle too. All of the gradual work he had been making on improving his fitness on Centaura had likely been undone.

"Do I have time for a shower first?" Rhys asked, running his hand through his chest fur. He could feel the dirt and blood still in his fur, with plenty of matted knots across his chest. His heart beat quickly beneath his hand.

"Of course, yeah. There's one just through there," Elijah said, stepping to the side to allow Rhys passage through to the adjacent facilities, at the far end of the drab medical bay.

Rhys hurried into the bathrooms, his fur itching a little, though he didn't think all of that was physical. He could feel Elijah staring at him as he retreated. It was only when he actually stepped into the shower that he realised he hadn't needed to remove any clothes, as he was already naked. And he had been the entire time. His ears curled down as he began to soak himself in the shower, the water as hot as he could tolerate.

The starat scrubbed through his fur, able to go back to the very first lessons he had gotten from Twitch. For so long since, he hadn't been able to properly clean himself thanks to the pain in his hands and arms. He scrubbed himself with soap, trying to tease out the worst of the knots in his fur, wishing his claws had also been restored. Tears of joy and relief were shed, mixing in with the dirty water that poured from his fur.

When Rhys was satisfied, he shook himself and stepped out of the shower, his fur already beginning to puff up from the moisture. He grabbed a towel and started the long process of patting himself dry. He stared at his reflection in the mirror as he did so. The eyes that stared back had grown to become familiar to him, to the extent that he could no longer reliably say exactly what colour eyes he had once possessed. He knew they had been blue: that had been what he had filled out on every form. But hadn't there been flecks of green amongst the blue? Or had they been brownish?

The human that had been Rhys was never coming back. Rhys didn't miss him. He liked the new version of himself. He just hoped he would be able to properly enjoy life in a way that had been denied to him ever since he had become a starat. New opportunities had opened in front of him. He just had to traverse the darkness immediately before his feet to get there. At least there was one shining light by his side.

Three towels later, Rhys felt like he was suitably dry. He wrapped a fourth towel around his waist and returned into the medical bay. Elijah was still there, sat on the end of one of the many beds. He rose to his feet as soon as Rhys closed the door behind him.

"Feel better?" Elijah asked.

"Much better, yeah," Rhys said. He brushed his hand over his arm, feeling the short and prickly fur that was regrowing. "I feel almost whole again. It's amazing."

"I'm sorry I couldn't fix your claws," Elijah said, lowering his head slightly. "Perhaps when we have more time, I might be able to find a way."

Rhys leaned into Elijah. "It's fine. Don't worry about it. I'm grateful for what you've already done. You have no idea how much of a difference it is," he said, before a sudden urge came over him. He kissed the starat.

Elijah took a step backwards in surprise, holding Rhys at arm's length. His mouth hung upon, with one ear folded down in confusion.

Rhys stepped back too. He hissed quietly and looked away. "I'm sorry, I shouldn't have done that."

Elijah's hand cupped at Rhys's chin, lifting his head up again. "No, no. It's fine. I just... you caught me by surprise." He grinned bashfully. "I don't think anyone has ever kissed me like that. Not since my augments, at least."

"I haven't, not for a very long time," Rhys replied. He shivered and tried to look away again, but Elijah's hand kept his head still. His ears folded down, still thinking he had overstepped his bounds. He was so out of practice of this sort of thing. "Was I too forward?"

Elijah answered by pulling Rhys into a second kiss. This time, the two starats lingered together as Elijah's arms slowly slipped around Rhys's back. The muzzles were a strange thing to get used to in a kiss, but otherwise Rhys found the act to be so completely natural and normal. Emotions he hadn't felt for many years started to bubble to the surface again. They felt right. He felt almost like a teenager in love again.

Elijah broke the kiss. He grinned. His ears curled inwards slightly, and a pink blush was visible beneath his fur. "We should go and get you some food before we get too distracted," he said, kissing Rhys's cheek quickly, before stepping back. "Better get you some clothes too."

Rhys grinned bashfully and nodded. He scampered back towards his bed and found some clothes draped over the end. He didn't recognise them, but they looked like they would fit. It wasn't like he had many clothes of his own; they were all still on Centaura, in the small house he had been looking forward to moving in to. A little house next door to Twitch. He wondered what Twitch would make of Elijah.

Before Rhys could go too far down that train of thought, he got himself dressed and followed Elijah out of the medical bay. The port was silent. There was no one present. No human or starat walked the underground corridors of Normandy. A shiver ran down Rhys's tail. He had barely even thought about the battle that had broken out when Cardinal Erik got his hands on him. The admiral had survived, but who else had done so?

As he walked, Rhys couldn't stop rubbing his arms with his hands. He revelled in the sensation of touch without pain. His fingertips still felt a little tender without the claws there, but he could tolerate their absence. He could feel that his arms were still lacking in strength, but they were no longer frail and skeletal. He had not expected any cure. He wiped away tears of relief and joy.

Elijah broke through Rhys's musings as they reached the canteen. Unlike the rest of the port, it was not completely deserted. One russet red starat sat at one of the tables, with her back to the door. Her ears perked up as the door opened, but she didn't look around.

"So you're still alive," Kalisha said. Still without looking back, she tapped her hand against one of the vacant seats. Three meals were on the table: two untouched and still steaming. "Come and eat. I just finished cooking them."

The smell of fried fish tantalised Rhys's nose. His time on Ceres had rarely allowed him to have such rarities as fish, though he knew the starats at the port had occasionally gotten their hands on a stolen shipment from Terra.

"What happened here?" Rhys asked, taking a seat opposite Kalisha. She had a bandage wrapped around her hand, but otherwise seemed completely uninjured.

The russet starat shrugged her shoulders. "We kicked their asses. Had hoped to stick that cardinal through, but he got out with you before we could stop him."

Rhys tentatively gripped the provided fork, before tightening his grip around the cutlery. The pain had been such a constant that he had almost forgotten what it had felt like. He had gotten hardly any time to enjoy a starat body without the constant crippling agony. He felt like he had been reborn a second time.

Kalisha chewed a mouthful of fish and watched Rhys. "Your friend the admiral showed up. I don't think he was sure what side to take, but he rounded up all the humans." A slow smile broke across her face, and she jabbed her fork in Rhys's direction. "You got a good human there. He fought for us."

"What happened to them? The humans?" Rhys asked, flicking an ear back.

"Some are still here," Kalisha replied. She looked down at her food. "The ones with the admiral are maintaining the port, making it all seem operational and keeping any awkward questions at bay. All the others were locked up in the cells."

Rhys shuddered. He had never been down to the cells beneath the port, but he could imagine they were not in a good condition. "And the other starats? Mikkel and Alison?"

"We lost a few in the battle, but Mikkel and Alison weren't involved," Kalisha said. She looked up and made contact with Rhys's eyes. "They've gone to Terra to meet up with this Essie figurehead. I could have gone with them, but I thought you needed someone to look after you."

Rhys quickly looked away from Kalisha. He ate slowly, not wanting to overexert his body after so long with minimal food. The fried fish and bed of vegetables and rice tasted delicious, much better than anything he had eaten during his first stay on Ceres.

"Do you know what the admiral's plan is?" Rhys asked. He kept trying to run through what the admiral might have been thinking, but he couldn't justify Admiral Garter's actions in relation to their last conversation.

"Plan?" Kalisha laughed. "I don't think he had one of those. He's been waiting for you while he tries to keep the emperor's eyes elsewhere. Then all this shit went down on Mars, so there's been distractions everywhere."

"What exactly happened?" Rhys asked. He glanced to Elijah, who had settled beside him and was happily eating his meal without a word.

Kalisha raised her brow. "I thought you were there. You should be telling me."

Rhys shook his head and sighed. "I know what I did. Or at least, I think I do. But I don't know what happened after that."

"Chaos," Kalisha said simply. She prodded her fork around her plate for a few seconds, while Rhys waited in silence for her to continue. "It seemed like a switch was flipped. Suddenly the control the Vatican have had over the empire was gone. Even here, people began to question why they should listen to Adamantius. I've heard news stories of protests beginning to swell in the streets on Terra. Most of the military still seems to be defending the Vatican and the emperor, but cracks are starting to appear."

"And small cracks like Ceres have been left unattended," Rhys said quietly. His head buzzed. He had suspected he was striking a decisive blow against the Vatican, but he hadn't realised just how quickly that would start to play out. "This is it. This is what Centaura has been waiting for."

Kalisha tapped her fork against the plate. "You mean the group of maniacal starats who are intent on destroying Terra?" she asked wryly. "Those people?"

"No, no. The Centauran government. The good ones," Rhys said quickly, waving his hand to the side. "We still need to worry about the SFU. Still need to stop them, but Centaura needs to know what is going on here."

"I'm sure they've got their own spies who can take the information back," Kalisha said. She returned to her food. "They don't need us. We've got our own shit to fix."

Rhys also returned to his meal, but his thoughts continued to race. The Terran Empire was beginning to crumble already. The military forces at the command of the emperor were still massive, but for the moment those forces were turning inwards and taking shots at itself. That gave Centaura the perfect opportunity to move in.

Rhys's tail flicked as conflict warred within him. He knew that the empire was corrupt and had committed atrocities, especially against starats. If the emperor or pope were able to regain control, then those atrocities would continue. That being said, it was still his home and where he came from. His gut twisted at the thought of giving Centaura such an opening, especially if it perhaps opened the door for people like Amy and Snow to commit even worse acts of terror.

Kalisha reached across the table for the saltshaker. Rhys started to move for it to pass it across, but before he could get it, the shaker vanished and reappeared in Kalisha's hand.

Rhys wrinkled his nose and frowned. "I didn't smell that."

Kalisha flicked her ears as she ground some salt out onto her fish. "Smell it? Oh, right. The cinnamon stuff? I don't think it's an actual physical scent, but... what do you mean, didn't smell it?"

"I mean I didn't smell it at all, like I usually do," Rhys replied, holding his hand to his nose. The familiar burst of cinnamon had not followed. He reached out towards the pepper and closed his eyes, trying to sink down into subspace. There was nothing in his eyes but the darkness behind his eyelids. No trace of cinnamon to follow, no burst of white emptiness consuming his senses.

Rhys opened his eyes and gasped. "I can't."

"It's possible you overexerted yourself on Mars," Elijah said, speaking around half a mouthful of fish and rice. He covered his mouth with a hand and swallowed. "Sorry. You could have done too much. Burned the ability out of you."

"Is that possible?" Kalisha asked, looking between the two starats.

Elijah shrugged. "No idea. I've never been able to sense this subspace stuff. You might as well be talking Ancient Greek when you're talking about it."

Kalisha scoffed. "I'm sure you can read that anyway."

"Nah, no translations are left. They were too heretical for some fragile-minded pope a few centuries ago," Elijah said with scorn and a shrug. His words barely reached Rhys's ears.

Rhys dropped his hand down to the table. His fingers trembled, though not in pain this time. Subspace scared him; terrified him, even. But he had grown to rely on those mysterious powers, and now they had been robbed of him, he felt vulnerable. At least he had strength back in his arms. He would not have been capable of anything without that.

The rest of the meal passed by in silence. Kalisha didn't appear to want more information about the events on Mars, and Rhys was distracted by his own thoughts about what he needed to do next. Elijah had remained quiet throughout it all, and he was the first to finish his food. Even then, he just leaned back in his chair and rested with his hands behind his head.

Conversation had just started up again by the time Kalisha and Rhys had finished, discussing plans to go and meet the admiral. Those discussions were not needed, as the human himself came into the canteen. His face was pinched and dark circles ringed around his eyes.

"It's good to see you again, Captain Griffiths," the admiral said. He helped himself to a coffee from the empty kitchen, before taking a seat a couple of chairs away from Kalisha.

"I hear you have been busy here, Admiral," Rhys replied. He leaned forward in his seat, partially from requirement to keep his tail from pinching against the back. He rested his forearms on the table.

"I fear I may not be an admiral anymore," Admiral Garter replied. He held his cup of coffee in both hands. The steam from the hot drink rose and fogged his glasses. "It is surely only a matter of time before the chancellor realises what has happened here. No messages have gotten out yet, and I know I can trust my crew, but someone from outside will want to speak to Captain Favre soon."

"You fought for starats," Rhys said. The more he thought about it, the less likely it seemed. "I thought you said you would stand by the empire. That was where your loyalties still lay."

Admiral Garter slowly lowered his cup. "I did say that," he said quietly. His hands shook so much that some coffee spilled, but the human didn't react to that, even as it splashed over his fingers. "But when the moment came to act on that loyalty, I couldn't. I sided with the starats even before I knew the cardinal had taken you prisoner."

"Do you know of any others in the forces who have turned against the emperor?" Rhys asked, hoping to press the admiral into making a decision on his next act. If a large percentage of the Terran forces had shown signs of defecting, then there might be no need to send for help from Centaura.

The admiral shook his head. "None that I know of. I've kept an ear out across messages all through the system, but it appears I may have been the only one."

Rhys hissed quietly to himself, sucking in his breath. "Damn. If it's going to be starats against humans, and those humans have the full force of the military, then there's not going to be much we can do."

"And that's not counting the Denitchev bombs," Kalisha added. She picked at her teeth with a claw. "Don't forget those too."

"I was trying not to think too hard about those," the admiral muttered. He put down his cup and rubbed his forehead with a hand, only then seeming to realise about the spilled coffee on his skin. He wiped his fingers on his shirt. "I thought that's why I helped all those starats to get to Terra. Aren't they going to stop that?"

"Not without help they're not," Kalisha said. She laughed without humour. "Do you really think a bunch of starats is going to be able to fix all of this? It's chaos out there. Nothing is going to get done."

"We need outside help," Rhys said, looking around the small group. Three starats and one human. His words felt treasonous, but then he had already done so much against the empire. His words would have appalled him as a human, but now they just felt necessary. "We need someone to go to Centaura."

"They have their own spies," Kalisha said with a sigh. "Why not just let them work it out for themselves?"

"Too slow, and we can't rely on them to act," Rhys said quickly, shaking his head. He clicked his tongue and frowned. "We need someone to tell them what's happened."

"Who will go?" Elijah asked, speaking for the first time since the admiral had arrived.

Rhys sucked in his breath. "I would go, but…"

"You are needed here to stop the Denitchev bombs," Admiral Garter said slowly. He frowned. "It has to be me. I'm the one with a ship. I have a crew who will follow me. If I stay here for too long, then I'll be branded a traitor. You three can go unnoticed for longer."

"I had been thinking to ask you, Admiral," Rhys said, glad that Admiral Garter had been the one to suggest the idea first. "I can record a message for you to take, so that they can have some assurance that what you tell them is true."

"Just so long as they don't shoot me down before I have the chance to explain myself," Admiral Garter said wryly. He drained half of his cup of coffee in one go.

"They didn't shoot me down," Rhys said, spreading his hands wide and shrugging. "I have no reason to doubt they would extend you the same courtesy."

The admiral grunted and stared into his half-empty cup. "You are at the centre of all of this, Rhys," the human said. The shadow of a smile came to his weary face. "I trust that you are leading us to a better world for human and starat."

Rhys leaned back, stunned. "I'm not leading anyone or anything. Everything I have done has been just so I can survive."

Kalisha growled quietly. "And a starat trying to survive in this world is seen as a rebellion. Perhaps humans will be surprised when we actually get around to rebelling for real."

"I don't doubt it," Admiral Garter said quietly. He swirled his coffee around his cup, before finishing the last of it. Rhys could still see the steam rising from the cup. The coffee had not been cold. Immediately, the admiral rose to his feet to get a fresh brew.

"And what do we do?" Elijah asked. He rested his hand on the table, brushing against Rhys's.

Rhys moved his hand to cover Elijah's. "We go to Terra and fix this shit."

Kalisha raised her brow, but she didn't comment on the contact between the other two starats. She shrugged her shoulders. "Well, I wasn't planning on doing anything else and someone sensible has to look after you two. Might as well topple an empire while I'm at it."

"How do we get there?" Elijah asked. He tapped his clawed fingers against the table. "I don't think we should use the *Vigilant*. It's been stolen twice from the Vatican now. It's going to be a little too obvious."

"I can get you there," Admiral Garter said. He had a fresh cup of coffee in his hands. He added a sachet of sugar to that one. "I can get you on a civilian ship from Noveau Ceres. As soon as you're gone, I can ensure the prisoners below will get freed, then leave for the CGP."

"How soon can you have that ready?" Rhys asked. He twitched his tail, excited to be leaving as soon as possible. His last visit to Terra had not been an enjoyable one. He wasn't sure how well this next visit would go.

"There are twice daily flights from Ceres to the Star Hub. I can arrange passage from there down to Cardiff. London will be locked down too much, especially for travellers from Ceres. We have about three hours before the next ship leaves the port," Admiral Garter explained. He cradled his fresh coffee in one hand. "That should give us more than enough time to prepare a message, don't you think?"

"Plenty, yes," Rhys replied. He shivered. Cardiff, more than anywhere else, was his home. He had not had a chance to return there for a couple of years. He wondered what had come of the house he had there. London would have been more convenient to travel directly towards, but he understood the admiral's reservations. "We shouldn't delay. There's a lot to get done."

"Would you want to record in the control tower?" Admiral Garter suggested.

Rhys nodded. "That works for me," he said, before turning to Elijah. "Can you make sure everything is ready? I don't know what we have to take, but we'll want whatever supplies you can get hold of."

"The armoury is yours to raid," Admiral Garter said, a touch of steel coming to his voice. "I doubt any of us will be allowed back here should we fail. Should we win, it's just salvage and spoils of war. Take all you can carry. I'll ensure you have military clearance on your flight so you can transport some weapons. Veritas knows Essie might need some."

Elijah grinned and gave the admiral a quick salute. "Aye sir, I was hoping you'd say something like that." He leaned into Rhys for a moment. "I'll take Kalisha with me and meet you when we're ready to leave."

Kalisha bared her teeth as she made her way to the door. "Ah, this is going to be so much fun."

***

The other two starats went their separate way, leaving Rhys alone with Admiral Garter. The two had spent so much time together on Ceres, over a period of several years. So many conversations had been spoken, both about work and more social matters. Now though, Rhys didn't know what to say. So much had changed between them, not least Rhys's species. Their viewpoints had changed and parted so drastically, yet they were still fighting for the same side. The opposite side to where they had started. They walked towards the control tower in a silence that wasn't quite companionable, but not quite awkward either.

Admiral Garter broke the silence first. "Is the CGP really better than the empire?"

Rhys sucked his breath in. "Yes, I think so," he said, speaking slowly. The admiral paused by the base of the stairwell leading up to the control room above the surface of the dwarf planet. Rhys stopped with him. "They're better for starats, for starters. Much better. We're truly equal there."

"And for humans?" Admiral Garter asked. He looked down at Rhys as he took his glasses from his nose and wiped them on his sleeve.

"I wasn't there for long. I can't speak for everyone, but the humans I met there seemed happier. Like they had fewer things to worry about," Rhys said, pinning his ears back slightly. "They didn't have to be scared about the Vatican for starters."

"Hmm," the admiral grunted. He didn't say anything else, but he started to climb the stairs with one hand on the cracked and discoloured metal bannister. Rhys followed just behind the human, his tail curled close to his legs.

"Do you regret what you did, Admiral?" Rhys asked, nervous about what the answer might be.

Admiral Garter didn't stop or turn back. His shoulders did slump slightly. "No. I did at first, but the decision has been easier on my mind these last few days. I feel like your arguments have merit. I am simply an old man set in his ways. Change is difficult for me to handle."

"I promise you it is worth it," Rhys said, looking up with a little more hope. The light of Sol illuminated the stairwell, shining down from the windows at the top. They gave a good view of the entire spaceport, as well as the burgeoning civilian port being built alongside the ancient site of Normandy.

Rhys only had a brief moment to look out over the barren dwarf planet before Admiral Garter unlocked the control room with a swipe of his passcard. The door beeped and opened, and they both stepped through into the circular room. A skeleton crew of humans manned the stations around the room. Rhys recognised one of the faces; he had served with her before his promotion to first officer, but he couldn't recall her name. The other faces were all unfamiliar to him.

Those humans not actively working stood to attention as the admiral entered. He waved them down. "I need you all to prepare the port for imminent closure. I also need the *Europa* primed and ready for departure."

"Sir?" one of the humans asked, saluting the admiral. She looked uncertainly towards one of the other humans, who lifted his headset and shrugged. "Has there been an update from Terra we missed?"

"No, Ms Liu. Nothing has come from Terra. We've had an update from Centaura," Admiral Garter said. Everyone in the room snapped to attention at that, even those who had been distracted by their screens. The admiral gestured to Rhys. "I'm sure you all remember Captain Griffiths. He has given us an important task. One that might seem dangerous. Treasonous, even. That would probably be a fair assessment of what must be done, but it is important nonetheless."

"We're going to Alpha Centauri, sir?" Liu asked. Her eyes flicked down to Rhys for a moment, and then back up to the admiral.

"We have a message to deliver, which Captain Griffiths needs to record," the admiral explained. He waved his hand towards one of the humans at the communications setup. "If you could get that prepared, Fox."

"Aye, sir," the human said, turning back to his equipment for a moment.

Rhys stood nervously in the middle of the room as the admiral moved away to quietly discuss something with Liu. He looked around at all the humans, nervous for any hostile reactions. A few curious glances were thrown in his direction, but nothing he could see spoke of hostility at all. He knew the admiral had always been sympathetic towards starats. Had that same kindness extended to his crew?

Fox hurried across the room with recording equipment, which he started to set up on a table in the middle of the room. "If you could just stand over there, Captain Griffiths," he said, pointing to a spot a couple of paces away. The human made no comment on the starat nature of the person he spoke to.

Rhys flicked his tail. "I don't know if I can still lay claim to that title," he said, stepping across to the point Fox had indicated.

"If Admiral Garter still calls you a captain, then that's good enough for me," Fox replied, giving a quick smile as he set up the holographic recorder. His smile wavered. "I thought all the shit that happened to you was crazy, if you don't mind me saying. How you were treated. It was awful."

Rhys laughed. "What you saw here was far from the worst of it," he said with a shake of his head. "It's been a shit time all around, but what we're doing here, what the admiral is doing, is going to put an end to it. I hope, at least."

"Well then, we'd better get this message recorded," Fox said. He tapped his hand on the top of the recorder. "This is ready when you are. Just give me the signal and I'll get it recording."

Rhys took a deep breath to compose himself. Words raced through his head as he struggled to think about what he should say. He knew he needed to keep things short and concise, and trust that Admiral Garter would be able to provide additional context and information as requested. A message like this was not the best way of delivering such important news, but short of travelling back to Centaura himself, there was nothing more he could do.

Rhys nodded his head and clasped his hands together behind his back. "Alright. I'm ready."

A quiet hush spread around the room. Everyone, even Admiral Garter turned towards Rhys as he mentally prepared himself for the speech. The little audience put a bit more pressure on him. Fox gave him a thumbs up to inform him the recorder was active. He straightened his shoulders.

"I don't know who will get this message. Fleet-Admiral Bosler. Major-General Ulrich. President Shawn. To whoever Admiral Garter finds, I beg that you listen to me. Terra stands on the cusp of annihilation, with multiple sources threatening everyone here. One comes from Centaura, from within your own. There is a plot by Amy Jennings to destroy the planet, obliterating the lives of billions. There is an opportunity to stop her here, but I cannot do it alone.

"Terra will not listen to me. Terra has its own problems that are more important than the words of a lone starat, if they were even likely to listen to me. I knew of only one person I could trust to send to you, and that is Admiral Garter. He is one of my closest allies. You have my word, for all that counts, that he means you no harm. He will explain the situation here in greater detail than I can through this message. He will answer your questions.

"There is a chance here to stop Amy's madness. But it is more than that. There is also a chance to stop this war and bring peace between Terra and Alpha Centauri, and I believe it can be done without a long, drawn out conflict. Neither system wants that. But for this to happen, I need your help. Please, send your fleet to Terra. I will lay down the foundations, and I await your arrival."

At a nod of his head, Rhys informed Fox to stop the recording. The starat slumped forward and rested his hands on the table, breathing deeply. His tail curled up at the tip, while his ears flattened to his head. "I hope that is enough."

"Will it really come to that?" someone asked. Rhys didn't look up to see who had spoken.

"Some sort of conflict is inevitable," Rhys admitted. He spoke down to the table, before looking up. "If everything goes to plan for me, then Centaura will be here to sweep up the pieces. It will be little more than a formal surrender from Terra."

"We can only hope so," Admiral Garter said. He clapped his hands together. "How long until we can get the port prepared for shutdown?"

"Half an hour, Admiral," came the quick response.

"Good," Admiral Garter said. He turned to face Rhys again. "That gives us half an hour for you to tell me everything you think I should know, Captain. Every detail about Centaura, and everything you know that is happening here."

Rhys grimaced. That was a lot to get through in such a short space of time. His mind raced as he worked out where to begin, before realising that he was already wasting their preciously limited time. He had to sum up everything that had happened since his departure from

Terra, and also give Admiral Garter enough information to pass on to Centaura. "Alright, so here goes…"

chapter thirteen

Rhys kept thinking of new things he should have told Admiral Garter. He had left the human behind ten minutes earlier with a handshake and a promise that each would do all they could to make things work. The starat could only hope that he had been clear and concise enough in what he had shared with the admiral. Admiral Garter had the datastick with all the information of Amy's weapon, as well as most of the information Rhys had been able to uncover since. The developing situation on Mars was probably the most important, as the discontent spreading there would likely soon start reaching other parts of the system. That was the weakness Centaura needed to be prepared to exploit.

Rhys had to try his best to forget all about Centaura now. Even if Admiral Garter was successful at getting the Stellar Guard to deploy immediately to Terra, it would be almost two weeks before they would arrive in the system. For those two weeks, Rhys needed to find a way to stop Amy's plan. He had no leads. No clues that could guide him towards stopping them.

Instead of feeling overwhelmed by what needed to be done, Rhys just kept telling himself that he needed to take the first step, and then work out the second from there. That first step meant getting to Terra. Once there, he could gain a better understanding of what options would be available to him.

The starat waited for Elijah and Kalisha to meet him. He stood by the shuttle train that ran across the surface between Normandy and Noveau Ceres. An electronic board above the airlock doors signalled fifteen minutes before the next shuttle departed for Noveau Ceres. From there, they had almost an hour before the ship departed Ceres for Terra. There was still one more shuttle they could catch after the next, should Elijah and Kalisha be late. Rhys paced nervously. He didn't want to delay any more than necessary.

Time slowly ticked by, before the tap of claws on the floor reached Rhys's ears. Only minutes remained until the shuttle departed, but Kalisha and Elijah had arrived. Both had a heavy bag filled with supplies plundered from the armoury. Elijah handed Rhys a pistol and a holster belt.

"Everything prepared?" Rhys asked, securing the belt around his waist and checking the quality of the pistol. He wasn't sure he could trust too much coming from the Ceres armoury, but he was pleasantly surprised. The pistol was one of the newer models. Though slightly oversized for his starat hands, it felt comfortable in his grip. The tentative squeeze of his fingers grew stronger as he tested the limits of his healed hands.

"All good to go," Elijah replied. He tapped at the pack he carried. "Got some food and plenty of medical supplies. Kalisha's got the weapons, ammunition, and some communicators. We don't have much, but it should help Essie and his heresy."

"We'd better get moving then," Rhys said. He opened the airlock doors and stepped through into the automated shuttle beyond. There was no one inside. Few people remained in Normandy. All of those not in the cells below would be with Admiral Garter, and they would be going up to the *Europa* once they finished shutting down the port and arranging for the release of the prisoners after they left.

The airlock doors hissed shut behind the three starats. A timer screen counted down the time to departure at the front of the empty shuttle. With the pick of the seats available to them, Rhys settled down near the back, remaining by the doors. Kalisha approached the front of the shuttle and browsed through some of the information screens provided about the civilian port. Elijah sat by Rhys's side.

Elijah draped his tail over his lap. "So that thing earlier, in the medical bay. Was that serious?"

Rhys rocked back in his seat as the shuttle started to move. He could feel his cheeks warming as he sought out Elijah's hand. "It is if you want it to be."

"Don't humans usually take each other out to dinner, someplace nice? Something like that?" Elijah asked uncertainly. His fingers squeezed that little bit tighter around Rhys's hand.

"I don't think we'll get much chance to do anything like that for a while," Rhys said with a laugh. He leaned into Elijah's shoulder as the train began to reach its top speed as it hurtled between the two ports. "How about we save that for when this is all over?"

"Just means we have to get through this together," Elijah said, tightening his grip further.

Kalisha knelt in the row of chairs in front of them, placing her arms on the back. She bared her teeth. "And I'm expendable in all of this, I'm sure," she said, sticking her tongue out. "Just fucking kiss already and get it over with."

Rhys obliged. He kissed Elijah softly on the lips. He grinned and kept his muzzle close to Elijah's. "We'll all get through this, I promise. I'm not going to stop fighting until we win."

"And if we lose?" Kalisha asked. She still bared her teeth in a savage smile.

Rhys shrugged. "If we lose, then none of us will be around to worry about it. We're going right into the heart of the empire now. If they're gearing up for a war, then we'll be in the middle of the action. It's going to be dangerous. We'll need to be careful."

"You're the military genius here. How do we do it?" Kalisha asked, swishing her tail high as she kept watching the other two.

Rhys sighed softly and leaned back in his seat. His tail was pinched and cramped awfully behind him, but there wasn't anywhere else for it to go. "Our first priority will be getting in contact with Essie. He's going to know the most about starat movement in the area and may have information that could be useful to us in finding out exactly how Amy will be releasing these Denitchev bombs."

"Ok, but they're in London. We're going to Cardiff. How do we get between them?" Kalisha pressed. She picked at some loose thread on her chair with a claw.

Rhys grinned widely. "I have contacts and resources in Cardiff. We won't be short of options, don't worry."

"They won't be expecting a human?" Elijah asked. His hand slipped behind Rhys's back to rest against his waist.

Rhys waved his hand. "That won't be an issue, no. I'll get us to London with no problems."

"I can only hope you're right," Kalisha muttered, before she slipped down to sit properly in her seat. The shuttle was already beginning to slow again. The distance between the two ports was almost negligible. Had they been on Terra or somewhere with an atmosphere, there likely wouldn't have been a need for a train or shuttle to pass between them.

Rhys could only agree with Kalisha. He hoped he was right as well, or else he would be risking the lives of his two companions, and the lives of everyone who lived on Terra. Should Terra fall, then those on Mars and the many other assorted planets, moons, and desolate rocks through the system would also fall. They could not fail.

Getting off Ceres was relatively easy. Once the train arrived at Noveau Ceres, Rhys led the other two starats through the clean, sterile corridors of the civilian port. Every wall still had the same plastic feel to them, looking a little too tacky and cheap to truly be permanent. Rhys could only hope that they were intended to be temporary, at least. He would hate to think of what the port might look like after a few years of Ceres' harsh vacuum environment to weather and decay the walls.

Shuttles were ready to carry the last of the passengers up to the civilian ship that would be taking the journey to Terra. A few humans lingered around the port, showing none of the tension and isolation Rhys had felt across the divide in Normandy. Passengers and staff were easy to differentiate. All staff wore uniform with the logo of three blue stars with a red streak passing through them. They also had the usual bright smiles and overly-friendly attitude that was common for interplanetary civilian flight. Rhys always assumed that had something to do with putting passengers at ease when they were nervous about flying through the vacuum of space.

Rhys's eyes flicked up towards the numerous shuttle bays, finding the number Admiral Garter had told him to seek out. There weren't many possibilities, and most of the bays were devoid of activity. Only three flights were scheduled to depart for the remainder of the day. One to Luna, and two to the Star Hub.

One human with the nametag Jennifer tensed slightly as the three starats approached her. "Passage to the Star Hub?" Her perfect smile faltered.

"Admiral Garter arranged seats for us," Rhys said, stepping a pace ahead of the other starats.

"Yes, that's right," Jennifer said. Her brow furrowed, and she opened her mouth to speak again. She hesitated. "Yes. Right. We'd better get you on the shuttle." The human moved away, towards the airlock doors and her colleagues at the small desk beside it.

Kalisha leaned forward. "Anyone else found that to be a little weird?" she whispered.

Rhys flicked his tail and nodded. He took a couple of steps after the human. "Yeah. Think we might get a bit of that." The confusion was better than the outright hostility he had been used to. He could only hope that meant things were moving in the right direction.

The humans conferred quietly amongst themselves for a moment, before Jennifer returned to the starats, her exaggerated smile back in place. "Sorry for that. Just had to clear something up. You're of course welcome on board. The admiral confirmed three seats with military clearance. This shuttle will be departing shortly, though the *Wandering Freebird* won't be departing for another forty-five minutes. You're welcome to go up now, or you may wait for a later shuttle."

"I think we'd prefer to go up as soon as possible," Rhys said. Not only was he eager to be off Ceres just to put the dwarf planet behind him, but he also didn't want to run the risk of anyone like Cooper or Captain Favre getting free and coming across to the civilian port. The further from the likes of them he was, the better he would feel.

Jennifer stepped to the side and opened the airlock doors. "Then welcome to the *Wandering Freebird*. I hope you enjoy your flight with Starlight Travels."

Rhys moved through the airlock into the shuttle. Half a dozen humans were scattered through the shuttle, which had a capacity for at least fifty. All of the humans were absorbed in their own activities. Four were reading the news on holoscreens, while the other two had their eyes closed with earbuds in their ears. Rhys could hear the faint sound of music as he walked past one of them. None of the humans reacted to the presence of the starats, even as they sat down close to the front of the shuttle.

Once again, Rhys was leaving Ceres behind him. He wondered if this time, it would be for good. There were so many memories on the dwarf planet. Most of them, Rhys wanted to forget. It had been an unhappy time there, even before his transformation into a starat. But had he not accepted the stationing there, his life would never have been changed so drastically. He was thankful for Ceres, but he never again wanted to see the barren rock again.

As the shuttle began to rise a few minutes later, Rhys switched on the holoscreen in the back of the seat in front of him. He watched the cameras show Ceres receding into the dark sky.

****

Rhys had seen few ships with the grand splendour of the *Wandering Freebird*. Only the *Olympus* came to mind. That was the last place he had been human, and his memories of the ship were somewhat fuzzy and unclear. Scale in his memory was indistinct, as though he was trying to apply a starat filter to memories that had been made as a human. So many of his older memories suffered with the same confusion.

He had no such trouble with the *Wandering Freebird*. The ship was huge, no matter which way Rhys looked at it. Cavernous, spacious halls opened out, with holoscreens simulating windows and providing a view of the surrounding starscape. Rhys remained on the side of the ship that didn't look towards Ceres as they waited for the scheduled departure.

The three starats had all been given a passcard on their arrival to the *Wandering Freebird*, which was used to give them access to the restaurants and other services the ship provided. There were entire levels of the ship devoted to passenger cabins, but those were of no interest to Rhys. They were for the passengers who had been on the full cruise to the Jovian moons.

Military clearance had given all three starats complimentary service. There had been a few more odd looks given towards them as they ordered food and drink, but those had mainly been quickly suppressed. Rhys curled his tail close to his leg as he waited for his food to come out. He thought he understood what was happening. For so long, the people of the Sol System had been listening to the wordless command from the entity above Olympus Mons. Their thoughts and beliefs had been shaped by that whisper. Now it had been silenced. They no longer saw starats as something to be feared and hated. The confusion was their memories of doing so, and the realisations that they no longer had reason for that behaviour. Almost every human they saw was going through an understanding.

By the time their food arrived, the ship's engines had begun to fire up, carrying the ponderous craft away from orbit around the dwarf planet. The flight time was scheduled to take just under six hours before they would enter Terran orbit. The atmosphere through the expansive canteen was one of nervousness. The mood wasn't helped by the news reports playing from the many holoscreens. Small uprisings had been recorded in some of the more distant outposts in the system, and communications with Sirius had been cut off entirely. Murmurs of heresy and blasphemy had been heard even in the streets of Terra.

Rhys kept his focus closer to himself. With his ears perked up, he could still listen to the news reports while his eyes swept around the hall. Every single passenger he could see was human. Their eyes were almost exclusively on the holoscreens, except for those who had their own personal devices to browse.

There were starats amongst the crew of the *Wandering Freebird*. Rhys caught sight of them occasionally, though they were never in the more public-facing areas. He only saw a flash of dark fur, or the whip of a tail disappearing around a corner. It was too soon for those starats to be treated like they were on Centaura. He knew that would be impossible. These starats were still slaves of the empire.

As Rhys slowly ate, an idea began to form in the back of his mind. Chaos was brewing through the empire. He had been responsible for that. There was more that he could do to further fan those flames.

"Something on your mind?" Elijah asked, cutting into Rhys's thoughts.

Realising he had a smirk on his muzzle, he quickly looked up at the starat opposite him. He leaned forward and kept his voice low, though the volume from the holoscreens was loud enough to drown out most conversation. "Yeah. Just thinking what we can do for the starats on this ship."

Kalisha flicked an ear. "We still need to get to Terra first. Then we can start thinking about the rebellions."

"Of course, yeah. But we can still speak to them, let them know what's going on. If we can disrupt what we can, that might help us out in the future," Rhys explained. He curled his tail around a chair leg as a couple of humans walked past, but neither showed any signs that they were listening in on the conversation. "It wouldn't hurt to just talk to them. They might know something more about Essie."

Elijah shrugged and leaned back. "Can't hurt to at least have a conversation."

"So long as we don't start giving them ideas to take over the ship right away," Kalisha warned. She glanced up towards the holoscreens, and her eyes widened. "Hey, isn't that your friend who took you to Mars?"

Rhys didn't even need to look, but he lifted his eyes anyway. The voice that boomed through the holoscreens sent shivers down his spine. His fur crawled. Cardinal Erik had survived the attack on Olympus Mons, though the scarring across his face had gotten worse. His bitter voice carried a tone of forced care.

"Be assured that the Vatican is doing everything it can to see humanity through this troubled time. Pockets of terrorists have sprung up through the system, likely a result of CGP interference. Our vigilance remains unwavering. We will strike at these heretics and keep the people of Terra safe."

Rhys pinned his ears down and covered them with his hands, but the sound of a reporter asking the cardinal a question still cut through. "And in this new role, what do you expect to achieve?"

"As the first Grand Inquisitor of Terra, I will be working with Pope Adamantius's authority, in conjunction with Emperor Neicwyk, to root out and eliminate any threat of heresy," the cardinal replied, a hint of his usual sneer coming back to his voice. "The people of Terra need not fear my eye, lest they have something to hide. May Veritas keep you all."

Rhys still stared anywhere but the holoscreens. His appetite, already diminished from having eaten so recently, had faded entirely. The thought of eating more utterly nauseated him. "He's going to be at Windsor, isn't he?"

Kalisha, who had kept her eyes on the holoscreens, nodded. "Yeah, it seems that way. Just means that next time you're going to have to make sure you finish the job."

Rhys stared at the red-furred starat. His tail flicked and curled tighter around the chair leg. "Kill him, you mean? Fuck, I wish. But I can't let revenge distract me."

"You're going to have to face him, I think," Kalisha replied. She picked at her teeth with a claw. "We're going to London. He's going to be in Windsor. Not far between them, is there?"

"I'm not going to seek him out," Rhys said, placing his hands on the table. He resisted the urge to clench them into fists.

"But he's going to seek you out, the moment he knows where you are," Kalisha replied. She grabbed hold of Rhys's hand in hers. "You're a symbol to him, as much as he is to you. He is the face of your hurt and pain. To him, you are the symbol of the heresy spreading through this system. You will face him again."

Rhys twisted his muzzle into a grimace. "You make it sound like fate. Destiny."

Kalisha snorted in laughter and shook her head. "No such thing. Fate is whatever we make it, but some things are always going to be inevitable. You are opposing forces, and he might feel that killing you will bring an end to this rebellion."

"I haven't even got anything to do with what's already happening on Terra," Rhys growled.

"Not directly, no. But Erik doesn't know that," Elijah said, smiling. He took hold of Rhys's other hand. "But in some ways, you have. This has all been building for a long time, I'm sure. Essie has been quietly working for years. But when you became a starat, you kicked things into motion. Mars only sent that into overdrive. You didn't start this, but you're sure as hell going to end it."

Rhys tightened his grip around both hands. He lowered his head. "I never asked for any of this."

"You did, though," Elijah replied. "The first time you stood up to a human in this body, you did just that. You refused to be treated how humans have always treated starats. You wanted to be equal still. That act was only ever going to lead to this."

"I didn't think that was going to lead to the empire falling apart," Rhys muttered. He sighed. The contact from the two starats felt nice, especially as the touch didn't send pain flaring through his arms anymore.

Kalisha bared her teeth. "And yet here we are. Watching humanity collapse in front of our eyes. I never thought it would be so beautiful."

Rhys's ears flicked. He glanced up to the holoscreens. The news report had moved on from Cardinal Erik. Instead, there was a report about a series of protests sweeping through Australia. The spaceports at Sydney and Brisbane were both closed. Military forces had been dispatched to quell and disperse the protests. Things were beginning to escalate quickly. Nothing was mentioned of the Denitchev bombs, or any additional threat beyond the rebellions.

"At this rate, we'll be lucky to get down to Cardiff," Elijah muttered, his thoughts clearly leaning in the same direction.

Rhys pulled his hands away from the other two starats. He slowly rose to his feet and swivelled his ears away from the holoscreens, trying to diminish the voices coming from the speakers. "I should go and find some of the starat staff and see what I can learn."

"I'll come with you," Elijah said, also pushing his chair back and standing up.

"I'm going to stay right here and finish your food," Kalisha said, leaning back in her seat and lifting her feet up onto the one Rhys had just vacated. "And listen to the news. Might be something else important they say."

Rhys bit his lip. He wasn't sure about splitting up, but then he looked around the hall. No one was paying any attention to the three starats. There was no threat onboard the *Wandering Freebird*. He nodded his head. "Alright. Keep an ear out, just in case."

"Uh huh, sure," Kalisha replied. She looked up to the other two starats and grinned. "Don't get lost in one of the bedrooms now."

Rhys rolled his eyes. There was no answer he could give to dignify that comment, he had learned that much from Twitch. He pulled Elijah away from the table, leaving Kalisha giggling to herself.

Almost one hundred tables filled the hall, with a large balcony looking out over the area. Several different restaurants lined the walls, each providing a different type of food for the passengers to choose from. The only way in and out of the hall was from the balcony level, with several open doorways leading through to other regions of the ship. Staff bustled in and out of service doors, though all were human.

"Where did you have in mind?" Elijah asked. He peered towards a visitor desk, which was littered with information on the services the ship provided, as well as tourist information on Ceres and Terra. The Ceres choices were significantly less than what was offered on Terra, which had many millions of places to visit. On the ship, there was an observation deck, gymnasiums, sports facilities, as well as entertainment areas.

Rhys flicked his tail. He couldn't imagine starats would typically be prominent in any of those places. He imagined they would likely only be involved in cleaning and maintenance, with the strict instructions to remain out of sight of the passengers. Unfortunately, so much of the ship would be out of bounds for passengers. His military clearance gave him some perks, but not the right to go anywhere he pleased.

"I think we just need to look until we find one," Rhys replied. He doubted the starats would be gathered in any one location on the ship. He just had to keep wandering until he came across another.

Elijah's ears perked up. He tilted his head to the right and half-closed his eyes. "There's one radioing in, saying he's going towards the observation deck."

Rhys blinked a couple of times, then curled his ears down. "Keep forgetting you can do stuff like that. But then, with the stuff I can do… could do, it's not that weird, is it?"

Elijah idly scratched his cheek. "I guess it is a little weird," he admitted, a slight blush coming to his ears. His eyes flicked around, finding the directional signs on the wall. He started to move towards the stairs that led away from the balcony level, higher up the ship towards the observation deck.

A human bumped against Elijah. The tall man in a business suit spun around on the spot. "Oh, sorry," he said, before glancing down at the starat. He held a hand up, mouth open, momentarily frozen in position. He blinked. "Uh, yeah. Sorry."

The human turned again and hurried down the stairs, his well-shined shoes clattering with every step against the faux wood floor. Elijah cocked one of his ears up as he watched the human retreat, before laughing quietly to himself. The starat held his hand out for Rhys to take. "Shall we?"

***

Despite Elijah's assurances that there would be starats at the observation deck, Rhys could only see humans when they arrived. The deck had been built to resemble an ocean-bound ship. The floors were wooden, and there was a handheld railing that lined the deck. All around the deck stretched the endless darkness of space, with the stars shining brightly in all directions.

The view took Rhys's breath away. He knew he wasn't standing on top of the ship with nothing between him and the vacuum of space. No one could survive such a thing. However, the *Wandering Freebird's* holographic projectors were so perfect, that he felt like he was. The glimmering arc of the galaxy filled Rhys with both awe and dread.

Realising he was standing still, Rhys took a couple of steps forward. Sound seemed deadened on the observation deck, with hushed whispers coming from the dozen humans scattered around the mystical room. Rhys's eyes immediately sought out Alpha Centauri. From such a distance, he couldn't make out the different stars of that system. It appeared as just a single star to his eyes. He wasn't sure if it was his imagination, but he was sure the star was a little brighter than normal.

"It's beautiful," Elijah said. His hand took hold of Rhys's as he craned his neck to look up at the expanse of stars. A giddy grin had spread across his muzzle. "I think I could name most of them too."

"I know the two important ones, and a few others," Rhys replied, curling his ears in as he leaned next to Elijah. A gentle breeze blew through the observation deck, likely caused by fans situated behind the holographic field. The movement of air chilled him. He pointed up to Alpha Centauri, then swung his hand around to find Sirius. They were both two of the brighter stars in the uninterrupted sky.

"Two stars touched by humans and starats. I wonder how many more of them in the future," Elijah said, whispering quietly. "Someday there might be someone who gets to see them all."

"Not in our lifetimes," Rhys replied. His ears curled. Stephanie had always said that. She had wanted to be the one to do so. She had never left the Sol system.

Though the display above him was just a projection, Rhys couldn't help but feel awed at the sight. He wondered what such a life must be like, hopping between the countless stars. His toe claws extended, pressing against the ship's deck. As much as he adored travelling between the different planets within the Sol System, he would prefer to remain closer to home than the endless stars. He was not sure that type of life was for him.

"There," Elijah said, drawing Rhys's attention down from the stars. The other starat pointed to something much closer. A starat had come out from another stairwell that led down from the deck. He scampered between humans and crouched down by the handrailing. He flipped down a pair of goggles that fit poorly over his face and reached out through the field of stars, pulling close a bag of tools.

Rhys hurried across the deck, easily avoiding the awestruck humans as they looked up, and crouched down beside the other starat. "Hey, do you mind if we talk?"

"Give me a moment," the other starat said, clearly tightening something with a wrench on the other side of the holographic projection. The starat grunted, before leaning back. He tapped the side of his goggles and looked to the side. His tail flicked. "You're not staff."

Rhys shook his head. "No. Is there somewhere we can talk with a little privacy?"

The starat pulled his ears back. "I'm already behind on maintenance. They'll have my hide if I'm delayed too much." He spoke with a lightly mainland European accent, though Rhys couldn't quite place just which region.

"Any urgent maintenance?" Rhys asked, not wishing to get in the way of any important work on the ship.

"Just superficial stuff," the starat admitted. He thumbed towards the field of stars nearby. "Some of these were starting to work loose. Might have had a black hole swallowing up the stars if it got any worse."

"There aren't any black holes near there," Elijah said with a frown.

The other starat groaned softly as he lifted his goggles up. "I mean it would have broken, not an actual black hole. You guys got names? I'm Phillipe. Or just Phil, if you're prefer."

"This is Elijah, and I'm Rhys Griffiths," Rhys said, tapping his hand on his chest.

Phil's eyes went wide. "Wait, the Rhys Griffiths?"

Rhys pinned his ears back. "I didn't realise I'd become a 'the', but yeah. I guess so."

"Well, shit. I guess I've got five minutes. Just give me a moment to finish this," Phil said quietly. He slipped his goggles back on and crawled forward, fiddling around with something on the other side of the holographic displays. Rhys was tempted to lean forward over the handrails to see what was being done, but he didn't want to ruin the illusion of the majestic field of stars.

Rhys didn't have to wait too long. Just a minute later, Phil rose to his feet and tucked his tools away into his bag. The starat twitched with nervous energy as he gestured for Rhys and Elijah to follow him back below the observation deck. Phil did not lead them into the passenger areas, instead slipping through a door labelled staff only.

Phil led the starats down a narrow stairwell, lacking any of the extravagant decorations that the passenger-facing parts of the ship possessed. Instead of ornate light fixtures and incredible pieces of artwork on the walls, with elegant, sweeping patterns, Rhys was faced with the sight of dull, straight corridors with flickering lights. The walls were bare and grey.

The rumble of the ship's engines was noticeable outside the passenger areas. They were quiet, but a constant humming at the base of Rhys's hearing. He flicked his ears in annoyance at the constant sound.

"This way," Phil said, leading down to the left, away from the rumble of activity from the passengers to the right. His tail swished as he walked, showing off his interest and curiosity. He pushed open a door and slipped inside.

Rhys followed just behind. Beyond the door was a small room cramped with shelving, filled mostly with cleaning equipment but also stacks of towels and bedding tucked in one corner. Phil pushed some towels aside to make some room to put down his toolbox. He then turned around to face Rhys and Elijah as the door closed behind them. His eyes gleamed in the weak light coming from the lone fixture swinging above their heads. "So, Rhys Griffiths. What did you come to say?"

"How many starats are there working on this ship?" Rhys asked. He leaned against the shelves, with Elijah staying close to him. Phil was dressed almost exactly the same as the starats working on Ceres, in dark blue overalls smudged with dirt and grime, ripped in places. He struggled not to wrinkle his nose at the odour of oil.

"Fifteen of us, all up," Phil said with a shrug. "We're mostly doing all the menial jobs. Cleaning, simple maintenance, that sort of thing. All the stuff the humans can't be assed to do."

Rhys furrowed his brow. His ears flicked down as he rubbed his chin. Fifteen starats wouldn't be enough to do what needed to be done. "How many starats do you think you could get in contact with when we dock at the Star Hub?"

Phil tilted his head slightly to the right. "Thousands. There's over a thousand working on the Hub, and then all the starats working on the docked ships? Tens of thousands. It might take up to an hour or two, but I could get in contact with all of them if I wanted to. Why?"

Rhys grinned. Those numbers were much better. "Because I need a message to spread. I need all starats across the system to do something for me."

"And what would that be?" Phil asked. The starat's eyes widened further, and he gripped tightly around the spanner still in his grasp.

"I want you all to stop. Stop working. Stop listening to human orders. When the command comes, I want starats to stop being the slaves of humans," Rhys said, a low growl coming to his voice. "I want humans to realise how much they relied on starats for everything."

A savage grin came to Phil's muzzle. "Yes," he hissed, a fury coming to his eyes.

"I don't want starats to attack humans," Rhys said, feeling the warning may have been necessary. "I just want them to stop working. Gather together for safety if they must, but they can't attack humans. Give them the chance to accept their new reality."

Phil shrugged. He tapped the spanner against his other hand. "Fair. But if they jump me, I'm hitting back. What will the signal be?"

"A call on public frequencies. A call from Essie," Rhys replied. He flicked his tail. He didn't know if he would have the opportunity to make such a transmission from Terra. He would need to find a way.

Phil saluted with his spanner. "I'll spread the word and keep an ear out."

"Much appreciated, thank you," Rhys said. He was pleased that Phil seemed so eager to carry out the idea, if slightly disturbed with the way the other starat handled the spanner. He could easily see the metal tool being brought down on a human's head. "I don't know when the call will be sent out. It might be a couple of days. It might be a couple of weeks. There's things I need to do on the surface first."

"Every starat in the system will know of this in two days, you have my word," Phil said with a grin.

"That's good," Rhys said. He felt a small shiver going down his back. He knew the starats who stopped work would all be in danger of retaliation. Not all humans were becoming more understanding of starats. Some would continue to resist and treat starats as inferior slaves. Rhys could only hope that there wouldn't be any lives lost, but he knew that was a naïve dream. There wasn't any way to avoid death; he could only minimise it as best he could.

"I should get back to work though," Phil said, cutting through Rhys's thoughts. He grinned bashfully and picked up his toolbox again, dropping the spanner inside. "Can't send out a message if the boss puts me in isolation for not finishing my duties."

"Of course, yes," Rhys said, stepping to the side and allowing Phil access to the door. He glanced up at Elijah for a moment, before back to the other starat. "I assume you'll need to take us back to the civilian areas?"

Phil laughed. "Nah. I think you can make your way out. Human staff won't look too hard at you. Just go out here and to the right. Follow the noise. You'll be fine." The starat pushed open the door and stepped back out into the corridor, glancing left and right. "I'll keep an ear out for Essie's call. Good luck, Rhys Griffiths."

"To you too," Rhys said, lifting his hand in farewell to the other starat. The door closed again, and Rhys glanced up to Elijah. "Do you think that was a good idea?"

"Good idea or not, there's no stopping it now," Elijah replied, his ears folded downwards in thought. "We're on this path, and it's too late to get off. We have one chance to make this all work."

"Then we'd better make fucking sure it works," Rhys growled. He clenched his fists and took a deep breath, trying to clear his mind. "Let's go back to Kalisha. There's nothing more we can do until we reach Terra."

"Lead the way, then," Elijah said, pushing the door back open for Rhys.

Rhys struggled not to think about the *Wandering Freebird's* wine list. He craved something to drink, just to take the edge off his nerves. He couldn't give into that temptation. This was a time when he needed to be able to fully focus. He was going into a warzone. Terra just didn't know it yet.

chapter fourteen

The shuttle roared and vibrated as it descended towards Terra. Unlike the shuttle from Ceres, this was packed to capacity. Not a single seat was left available. All but three seats were taken by humans. No starats travelled from the Star Hub to Cardiff but for Rhys, Elijah, and Kalisha. Transition through the Star Hub had been quick and simple. Their military passes had allowed them to skip most of the queues, transferring without hassle to the next available shuttle down to the surface. No uncomfortable questions had been asked of them, and nor did anyone search their packs of ammunition and weapons.

Chatter was mostly muted. Focus lingered on the many news channels, with all of the humans staring at their personal tablets and holoprojectors. Thankfully for Rhys, they were all silent as they listened with earphones, but he could still occasionally see the flash of Cardinal Erik's face appear on the screens. His fur crawled every time. The last place he wanted to go was closer to that particular human, but once the shuttle landed, they would be less than three hundred kilometres from each other. That distance was going to keep shrinking.

A tightness in Rhys's chest slowly grew as he watched the holoscreens on the chair in front of him. He tracked the distance of the shuttle as it roared from the Star Hub over Antarctica, towards Europe. It had been years since the last time he had been home. He didn't even know what to expect when he got there.

The shuttle finally landed in the sprawling airport to the west of Cardiff. The glimmering spires of the city weren't visible from the ground, but Rhys had been watching the external cameras as the shuttle had made its final approach. The city hadn't changed too much. A few new buildings had gone up close to the centre, but that was all.

Rhys led his two companions through the mazy interior of the airport. Though he had not been to Cardiff in years, and he now wore an entirely new body to his last visit, his feet still knew the way. He didn't hesitate once, only pausing to give humans priority on making their way through the airport.

Summer wasn't too far away, but the early morning air was still crisp and cool as Rhys stepped outside. The sun had barely breached the horizon. Rhys had managed to get a couple of hours of sleep on the *Wandering Freebird*, but he didn't feel well rested. His body clock didn't know what time it was, and his sleep schedule had been heavily disrupted. He looked forward to the chance to rest and recover, but that time was still a way off.

A local train service departed from a station just to the south of the airport. There was no option to reach London from the local network, but that wasn't the destination he had in mind. Instead, he caught the train to the nearby town of Barry. Elijah and Kalisha had spent most of their time staring wide-eyed at everything around the airport. Rhys pinned his ears down. He wondered if Kalisha had ever been outside in an oxygen environment, and if Elijah had done so before Mars.

Memories trickled through Rhys's mind as he sat and watched the landscape pass by as the train rattled along. So much was achingly familiar to him, having travelled the same route to and from the academy almost every day. That had been a different life, when his eyes had been a little higher up and his only fur had been his occasionally unshaven chin. But for his perspective, nothing had changed out of the train windows.

Rhys was glad that the journey in the train had been a short one. He didn't have time to brood long before the train slowed at Barry Station. With a quiet gesture from Rhys, he encouraged Kalisha and Elijah to follow just behind him.

The small train station consisted of just two platforms, though there were tracks bypassing the station that led to and from the nearby docks. The magtrain slid away almost silently, leaving the three starats alone on the platform. No one else had disembarked with them.

"This place feels quieter than I thought Terra would be," Kalisha said, her voice hushed as she looked up the hill. Trees lined a nearby road, which was almost empty of traffic. The morning commute wouldn't have started yet for most residents of the town.

"Wait until you see the cities," Rhys replied. He couldn't see any humans close by, except for the occasional car which drove on the nearest road. There weren't even any pedestrians. His tail curled close to his legs as he started to walk.

Kalisha reached out to take a handful of leaves as they walked beneath a pair of overhanging trees. She turned the leaves over in her hands, then lifted them to her muzzle to sniff at them. She grinned widely, clutching the greenery in her hands. "This is beautiful."

"This used to be my walk from work," Rhys said, leading the two starats towards the centre of town. It was only a few minutes away, even on foot. Rows of low buildings lined the streets, crammed in close together. A mixture of ancient stonework and modern glass and brick contrasted greatly with each other. The starat ran his hand on the grey stone that overhung the footpath. Awe came to his voice and the familiar chills ran down his spine. "Some of these buildings have been standing for hundreds of years."

Kalisha snorted. "Normandy felt like it was all that old."

"Some of the oldest ports probably are," Rhys said quietly. A low hill rose to his right, with a road angling away from the town centre meandering towards the summit. The starat's feet turned out of instinct as he took the new road. "There's one building up here that's even older than that, though."

"Do we have time for that?" Elijah asked. He remained by Rhys's side on the narrow sidewalk, with Kalisha following just behind.

Rhys smirked. "Don't worry. I'm not taking us on any diversions."

The road felt a little steeper than Rhys remembered. His thighs and calves burned from the exertion of climbing the steep hill. On either side of the road were dozens of narrow, terraced houses. All looked much the same as the ones on either side. Most of the front gardens were little more than concrete and weeds, with just the occasional flowerpot to liven things up.

Close to the summit of the hill, the row of terraced houses was broken on the opposite side of the road with a small park. Within the park was a small stone wall. Rhys pointed to the ancient rocks. "That's Barry Castle. Apparently, it's over a thousand years old." The starat glanced back to his two companions. Elijah peered across with interest, but Kalisha did not share their enthusiasm.

"More like Barry Wall," the russet starat scoffed. She flicked her tail. "It's not very impressive, is it?"

"I used to play in that park every morning," Rhys said, his ears and tail drooping. He sighed and turned away from the castle, instead looking towards the equally familiar house directly opposite the ancient ruin.

Like all the houses around it, the small home was built from traditional brick and mortar. The tiny front garden was slightly overgrown, with a car parked on the driveway; a tarpaulin draped over the vehicle. The windows were dark, with curtains drawn across them all. Nothing about the house had changed since the last time Rhys had set eyes on it.

"Whose house is this?" Kalisha asked. She approached the garden fence and placed her hand on it, peering over into the weed-infested garden. She wrinkled her nose. "Not a good gardener, clearly."

"It's mine," Rhys replied. His mouth twitched into a slight smile as he looked to the upper storey. His bedroom overlooked the castle opposite. He hadn't slept in that bed for over three years. Before his transformation, he had only slept in his ship or in a spaceport cabin after his last visit home.

"Is that why we're here?" Elijah asked, nodding his head towards the covered car.

Rhys grinned. "Absolutely. Thought we could go to London in style. But first, we need to get inside. Wait here for a moment, will you?"

Instead of going towards his house, Rhys pushed open the front gate to the house next to his. He breathed quickly as he approached the front door, then quickly rung the doorbell before he could back out of the idea. Meeting with people he had known as a human had not always ended well for him.

The door opened a couple of seconds later. A dark-skinned human woman, dressed neatly in a business suit, stood in the doorway. After a moment of confusion, she looked down to see Rhys standing at her door. "Oh. Can I... can I help you?" There was no recognition in Ruth's deep brown eyes.

Rhys didn't let himself hesitate. "Hi," he said, trying to keep his voice loud enough to hear. He pulled his ears back. "I'm here to do some maintenance on the house next door. Unfortunately, I don't have a key to get in, but I was informed by my boss that you would have a spare for emergencies?"

"Rhys's place? Yeah, he gave me one just in case," Ruth said hesitantly. She took half a step back and reached for something behind the door. Metal jangled. "I haven't heard from him in months. Not since all those lies they told about him."

"Lies?" Rhys asked, flicking his ears.

Ruth held out a single key for Rhys to take. "That he betrayed Terra. I knew Rhys for years. He'd never do that."

"I'm sure he had his reasons," Rhys replied, managing to hide his smile.

The human frowned. "I feel like I should know you," Ruth said warily. She leaned on her door and stared down at the starat. "I've never spoken to a starat like this before though, so…"

"Everything's changing," Rhys said simply. That much he knew to be completely true. He took a couple of steps back, holding up the key in his fingers. "Thank you for this. I'll return it when I'm done."

"Sure," Ruth said. She started to close the door, but she opened it again before Rhys reached the gate. She stepped out onto the welcome mat. "Do you know Rhys? Is he coming back?"

Rhys hesitated. His hand was on the gate. He could pull it open and ignore the human, but he'd still have to walk past her again to reach his own front door. He turned around. "He'll be back. You just may not recognise who he is now."

"Is that a good or a bad thing?" Ruth asked. She kept one hand on the handle of her front door.

Rhys didn't yet know how to answer that. He smiled at the human and spread his hands wide. "I guess we'll find out."

Ruth had nothing more to say to that. She stepped back inside her home, a confused frown still furrowing her brow. The front door closed, and Rhys could hear conversation happening from inside.

Rhys slipped around into the front garden of his home. He held the gate open for Elijah and Kalisha behind him, then let it swing shut.

The metal hinges of the gate screeched with rust. The key fit in the lock of the front door perfectly, and the door swung open a moment later. Dust filled Rhys's nose. He wrinkled his muzzle to try and get away from the scent.

"Bit dirty, isn't it?" Kalisha mumbled to herself.

Rhys lowered his ears as he stepped inside. He could feel the dust in the carpet beneath his bare feet. "I hired a cleaner to maintain the place. I guess they stopped showing up when Ceres happened."

Despite the dust and dirt, nothing appeared to have changed. Rhys hadn't been too sure what to expect. His house could have been ransacked and repossessed the moment he had been declared a traitor to the empire, but he couldn't see any evidence of that. Nothing had been touched at all.

"What are we here for?" Elijah asked. He ran his fingers over the small coffee table by the inside of the door, wrinkling his nose at the thick layer of dust that clung to his fur. "Just the keys to your car?"

"There's a couple of other things," Rhys mumbled quietly. A narrow corridor right ahead led through to the kitchen and the dining area, while a door to his left opened into the lounge room. Stairs went up to the two bedrooms and a bathroom. There wasn't much to the home, but it was all he had ever needed. More than that, even. The house had been purchased with two in mind.

As memories threatened to flood back through him, Rhys placed his hand on the wooden bannister leading up the stairs. He flicked his tail and placed his foot on the bottom stair. He wondered if coming here had been a mistake. The weight of the house seemed to fall on his shoulders, with every mote of dust in the air carrying the memories of the life he had once lived within these walls.

"Are you alright, Rhys?" Elijah asked. Rhys could hear him moving close behind him, but the expected contact didn't come.

Rhys shuddered and straightened his shoulders. He didn't look back. "Yeah. Just give me a moment upstairs, alright? Feel free to have a look around. Just don't breathe in too much."

"We'll be right down here," Kalisha said.

Rhys hurried up the stairs, almost tripping as he did so. The stairs were a little taller than he was used to. Or, more correctly, his legs were shorter than his muscle-memory had accounted for. The bannister was raised that little bit higher. The light switches were above his head now, instead of just beneath his shoulder.

The lights flickered on after a moment, illuminating the narrow landing. Three doors were all closed. Rhys turned around to the right, pushing open the door that led through to the main bedroom. The carpet felt grimy beneath his feet, and when he sat down on his bed, a plume of dust erupted up to coat around him.

Rhys sneezed loudly, then started to cough until the dust settled again. The room was familiar to him, despite the years since he had last been home. There was not much in the room, but for the bed and two small cabinets either side. A walk-in wardrobe took up one wall, hidden behind full-length mirrored doors. Rhys stared at his reflection for a few moments. The new familiarity looked distinctly out of place amongst the old. His new body seemed wrong in the setting where he had lived as a human.

With a sigh, Rhys turned away from the mirror. There was no going back to his old self. He wasn't even sure he wanted that. He just wanted a place where he felt at home again. His hands fumbled with the drawer of his bedside cabinet. The wood had swollen slightly, and he needed to tug hard to get the drawer to open.

He reached in for his car keys and was about to close the drawer again when he hesitated. The glint of light against metal caught his attention. A piece of jewellery was in the drawer as well. A gold ring with a crimson gemstone. A noise halfway between a laugh and a sob came to his throat. That would have been Stephanie's wedding ring.

His fingers closed around the ring. He dropped it into his pocket. Perhaps one day he could give the ring to Elijah instead. Rhys rubbed his eyes and forced those thoughts aside. That was getting a little too presumptive.

Rising from the bed, Rhys slipped around to the other side of the room and pushed open the glass doors of the wardrobe. He crouched down and fumbled around in the dark beneath all the clothes that would no longer fit him. Beneath a pile of folded shirts on the floor was a small safebox. Rhys quickly keyed in the code, and the door swung open. Inside was a wallet and a secondary cash card. He pinned his ears back. The Centauran government had been successful in transferring all his money in his main bank to a new one on Centaura. It would have been useful to have that on Terra still. He grimaced and checked how much money his backup card had. Less than a tenth of his main funds, but it would do until he was able to work out where his future lay.

Pocketing his wallet, Rhys glanced around his bedroom. He knew he couldn't linger. He needed to get to London quickly, but a small part of him just wanted to stay right where he was. Though he felt out of place now, he could grow comfortable in his old surroundings again.

Rhys switched the light off behind him and closed the door. He could come home when he had saved Terra. Only then could he relax.

***

The drive to London was a long one, but simple. One of the major motorways crossing Britannia linked Cardiff directly to the capital city. Rhys had struggled at first. Unlike the cars on Centaura, Terran vehicles weren't automated. He hadn't driven anything since his transformation, and Rhys had taken a long time to get into a position he was comfortable in. His tail pinched against the chair, and he struggled to adjust his seat so he could reach the pedals and see over the dashboard. Once he got started, he quickly found his rhythm.

The roads were busy, but no one paid much attention to the starat driving. He was just another car on the road, driving between Cardiff and London. Rhys knew from experience that most drivers did their best to ignore all others on the road – until one driver did something to annoy another. So long as he blended in then no one would even look towards him.

Stopping only to recharge the car's batteries – which had depleted significantly after several years of disuse – and for some food, the three starats made their way east across the Britannia countryside. The motorway avoided most of the big cities that dotted the terrain, bypassing around them in great loops.

A little under four hours after leaving Rhys's home in Barry, they arrived in the outskirts of London. Most of the inner city was traffic-free, so Rhys found a place to park the car before switching to foot. Towering spires of glass and metal rose from the banks of the Thames, mixed with some of the historic buildings of London that had survived through the centuries.

Tens of thousands of humans walked the streets of the city, with the only vehicles permitted through the narrow, winding streets being the public transport services. Rhys wasn't sure exactly where to go.

Elijah had memorised the co-ordinates of the rendezvous point Essie had given Admiral Garter, but Rhys couldn't be certain just which part of the city that related to.

Amongst the crowds of humans, Rhys spotted the occasional starat. He didn't approach them. There were no quiet places of London to have a quick conversation to pass on the message of rebellion. Watching eyes and listening ears lined every street. Cameras were present on most street corners, giving an almost total coverage of the city's population. There was no sign of the rebellions and unrest that were starting to spring up in other corners of the planet.

Not all the humans were workers in the city. Some were tourists, excitedly wandering between the landmarks in large groups. Other humans were priests. Hundreds of robed Vatican officials stalked the streets, sweeping through the crowds with no obvious pattern in mind. Rhys struggled to just keep walking whenever a priest came close. A few eyes were turned towards the starats, but no one attempted to stop them. Rhys had made sure his pistol was covered by his clothes. Elijah and Kalisha likewise made sure the weapons and ammunition they carried were not visible. They had to blend in completely with the crowds.

The priests weren't the only dangers. Despite the crowds of tourists, every monument and landmark was guarded by a troop of armed soldiers. Other soldiers patrolled the streets, all clearly armed with rifles. Most humans gave the soldiers a wide berth, but some tourists did try to approach the guards for a picture. They were all forcefully rebuffed with barked shouts and commands.

A loud bell tolled through the city. Eleven times the bell chimed. Only the tourists looked up to gasp with delight at the sound. Most humans ignored it entirely. Behind Rhys, Elijah and Kalisha huddled close, seemingly put off by the loud noises and constant activity all around them.

Big Ben chimed. The clock was all that remained of the historic seat of power in Britannia. The ancient stone building that had once sprawled beneath the towered clock had been replaced by a shining office block, with a small museum to the old building at its base. The clock, once a centrepiece of the city, now appeared more as an afterthought clinging to the side of a glass structure where it clearly did not belong. Rhys flicked his tail as he looked up to the clockface. He knew how that felt.

A tour guide beneath the clock tried to tell an uncaring audience that Big Ben was the bell that was no longer present. The clock was something else. No one listened. Rhys understood that feeling too.

Elijah's co-ordinates led them across the river, using one of the many bridges that spanned the dirty waters of the Thames. A handful of boats traversed the river, mostly private yachts being taken out from the marinas further upriver towards the ocean.

The beating heart of the empire was the northern banks of the Thames in London. The southern banks were not so impressively built up, with fewer towers reaching for the grey, cloudy skies. One magnificent structure still remained across the river. The Waterloo Public Transport Hub dominated the southern bank. Built mostly in stone and marble to achieve a classical appearance, the building loomed large over everything around it.

The building was also exactly where Elijah's co-ordinates led them. Rhys flicked his ears in confusion as he looked towards the wide glass doors at the front of the building. The Hub was one of the busiest in London. From there, all public transport across Britannia was managed. Most magtrains across the island had some connection to the Hub, with all of London's buses also coming from this central location. It was not the place to hide a secret starat resistance.

"Are you sure this is right?" Rhys asked. He stood with his hands on his hips, grimacing as he watched a group of a dozen humans walk into the Waterloo Hub. A cool breeze blew across from the river, chilling the air despite the approaching summer.

"Yeah," Elijah said, though he didn't sound too certain. His voice wavered. "It's right there. Those are the co-ordinates."

Rhys bit down on his lip and hissed softly. "I guess we have a look inside then. Anything you remember about the co-ordinates that hinted at what we need to find?"

"Nothing, no," Elijah said with a slight growl. "I thought it might have been a disused old building. I didn't even think to check what might be at the co-ordinates."

"We'll find it, don't worry," Rhys said, leaning into Elijah's side and squeezing his hand around the other starat's.

Kalisha scoffed quietly, but she didn't say anything. She just peered across the narrow road towards the Hub. Her tail had curled close to her leg, and her hands kept moving down towards her hip, where her pistol had been secreted beneath her shirt.

Together, the three starats crossed over towards the transport hub. The automatic doors slid open for them, with a blast of warm air drifting out of the massive main lobby inside. Hundreds of bright screens hung from the ceiling, all providing information on the myriad of train and bus services planned to arrive and depart from the station. Directions were given to the various areas, with close to a hundred train and bus platforms to choose from.

Rhys was almost overwhelmed with all the information. He couldn't stop moving though, or else the many humans passing through would bump into him. Priests and guards were inside Waterloo as well, not just commuters and passengers. Rhys lowered his head and kept searching, though he didn't even know what to be looking for.

Most of the wall to the right of the main entrance was made of glass, providing easy visual access through to the magtrain platforms. There were two dozen platforms in total, half of which were currently occupied with long distance services across the island. All of the local London transport departed from further down the building, exclusively serviced by an elaborate network of buses. None of it stood out to Rhys. All of it appeared to function exactly how a station should function: a hub for magtrains and buses to depart from.

Almost half an hour passed. Rhys began to feel disheartened. No humans looked towards them, and they saw no starats. Nothing gave away that Waterloo was allegedly a rendezvous point for a starat resistance.

Rhys slumped down on a bench and watched the humans walk by. With his back to the platforms, Rhys looked directly across at a brick wall. In places, archways had been sealed up with concrete, which hadn't been properly blended to the rest of the wall. Elijah sat by his side, while Kalisha paced back and forth nearby.

"I'm sorry," Elijah said. His hand sought out Rhys's. "I should have found out more first. I thought it would be easy to find."

"It's not your fault," Rhys replied. He furrowed his brow and rested his chin on his other hand. His attention was caught by some graffiti scrawled onto the concrete patches in the wall opposite. "I should have done so too."

"I'm meant to be the one with the plan though," Elijah said, tapping the side of his head. "Or else what's the point of all this?"

"Hey, it's not like…" Rhys said, before he trailed off into silence. Amongst the graffiti was a blue letter S. He had seen one like it moments earlier. He rose to his feet and looked over to the concrete arch to the left. Another S, barely visible amongst the scrawled street art. On the one before that, an E. He couldn't see the next arch to the right from where he was standing, but he pointed in that direction and called out to Kalisha, who was closer. "Is there an I on that concrete arch?"

Kalisha lifted her hand and gave a thumbs up. "Yup."

Rhys's fur lifted. He shivered and flicked his tail. That couldn't be a coincidence. He grinned back at Elijah. "I think I've found it." He held out his hand to the other starat and pulled him up to his feet. Together, they ran down the packed concourse, passing the arch with the blue I. The next arch had a blue E. Essie. The graffiti in the arches spelled out the name of the first starat. The name of the starat who had taken his name to lead a resistance. They were here.

Underneath the final E was a small arrow, pointing further to the right. The next archway was recessed a few metres, with the concrete wall covered in shadow. A faded information sign was pinned to the brickwork just beside the archway. *London Underground* was still visible in chipped lettering.

"Psst, here," Kalisha hissed. She had retreated into the shadows of the alcove, which had no direct light shining nearby. Even as the middle of the day approached, this one corner was shrouded in deep shadows. The starat prodded with her foot towards the bottom of the concrete wall. Her toes passed through a small gap Rhys hadn't seen. The hole looked just about large enough for a starat to squeeze through, but not a human.

"No one's looking. Go through," Rhys whispered. He and Elijah swept their eyes around the concourse. None of the humans had any time for the three starats standing in the shadows. Not even the occasional priest or guard looked towards them.

Claws briefly scuffed at concrete and brick behind Rhys. He didn't look back, instead keeping his eyes on the concourse. He didn't want any human to see them and get suspicious. He shrank back any time he thought a human was about to move their head in his direction.

They always looked away again; distracted by a timetable or notification on a tablet or holowatch.

Elijah was the next to push his pack of supplies through the gap and then slide through himself. He huffed and wheezed as he breathed in, claws scratching against the concrete. Rhys's eyes and ears took in everything they could. His head turned from side to side, cautiously looking out for any humans approaching as he took a couple of paces back into the shadows.

Confident that there was no one nearby, he dropped down to his belly and slipped through the narrow hole in the concrete feet first. Almost immediately, he felt the claustrophobia of concrete pressing around his body, snagging on his clothes as he wriggled his way through. Footsteps on the concourse sounded dangerously close by, seeming to echo through the walls.

Rhys almost squeaked in surprise when he felt hands closing around his ankles. While his hands pushed at the smooth floor in front of him, he felt himself get pulled through the gap until he passed through into almost complete darkness.

Sounds from the main concourse were muffled into silence. But for the small hole at the bottom of the wall, there was no light in the darkness beyond. Rhys couldn't see anything. Beneath his feet was a tiled floor, feeling partially cracked in places.

"Anyone got a light on them?" Rhys asked, squinting into the darkness. He didn't dare move, unsure what was hiding in the black void. His heart hammered in his chest. After his last time stuck in total darkness, he wasn't keen to repeat the experience.

A moment later, the screen of a tablet lit up, providing some illumination on Elijah's face, and also the darkness surrounding the starat. He switched on the front-facing torch, and a bright beam of light extended out into the sealed-off tunnel.

Rhys was glad he hadn't moved anywhere. Just a couple of paces away, stairs descended below ground. The floor was cracked and dusty, but footprints were visible in the dirt. They were all the footprints of starats. Some appeared fairly fresh. If there was any lingering doubt that they were in the wrong place, those concerns were chased away from Rhys's mind.

Elijah took the lead. With the light in his hands, he slowly made his way down the dark tunnel one step at a time. The sounds from the station slowly faded away, and before the starats even reached the bottom of the stairs, Rhys could see or hear nothing from above. All they had was the echo of their footsteps sounded from below.

The air was cool against Rhys's fur, but it wasn't still or musty. Something still circulated the air below ground. Faint scents of at least a dozen starats lingered.

The stairs never seemed to end. Struts hung down from the ceiling every few metres, where once there would have been information signs. Broken shards of metal had been kicked to the sides of the stairs. Light fixtures were empty. Graffiti scrawled the walls, but much of the paint had faded into almost nothing.

"What was this place?" Kalisha whispered. She walked a couple of paces behind Rhys.

"The Underground," Rhys replied. He ran his fingers against the wall to his left. "A network of train lines below the surface. It's not been used in about a century."

Elijah flicked his ears. "What better place to run a secret organisation?"

"Somewhere that doesn't stink of dust and grime," Rhys muttered. The dark stairs put him in the mind of Ceres; a crumbling corridor deep below the surface. He had to admit, the Underground had its advantages. If the tunnels had been maintained, then there was the possibility of hundreds of access points across the city, all abandoned or blocked over. It gave the perfect opportunity to move around the city unseen.

The light shone on the distant floor at last. A narrow path had been cleared through dirt and debris. Chipped remains of broken tiles and brick had been piled up in a way that looked random at first. When Elijah's beam of light swept across the cavernous room at the bottom of the stairs, Rhys realised that they were anything but. The piles of debris had been stacked in strategic positions of cover.

Rhys placed his hand on Elijah's shoulder as the other starat placed his foot down on the floor, moving off the stairs. He focused his ears, perking them up completely. The silence wasn't as oppressive as he first thought. There were people breathing in the darkness.

Before Rhys could say anything, a bright light shone right in his eyes. He shielded his face with his hand. Guns clicked in the darkness.

One lone voice called out. "Not one step further."

Kalisha hissed softly. "I think we found them."

chapter fifteen

Over a dozen starats circled around the base of the stairs, emerging from the darkness. All of them carried rifles. They wore dark clothes to better blend into the oppressive shadows. The one who had called out stepped ahead of the others. His fur was almost as black as the darkness around him. All Rhys could clearly see of him was the shine of his eyes, reflecting Elijah's torchlight.

"What's your business here?" the starat barked out.

"We're here to speak to Essie," Rhys replied. He kept his hands raised, resisting the temptation to reach for the pistol at his hip. He could only hope that Elijah and Kalisha were both aware enough to do the same.

The starat leader approached another pace. His teeth were bared. "We were expecting no more today. Where did you come from?"

"We came from Ceres. Admiral Garter gave us the co-ordinates of how to find you," Rhys explained. His eyes flicked around the darkness, counting how many starats were present. He could see fifteen, but he thought he could hear the scuff of claws against concrete deeper into the black.

"Ceres, is it? We had a large group come from there a few days ago. Why were you not with them?" the starat leader asked. His rifle lowered slightly.

"I ran into trouble on Mars," Rhys said, a grimace coming to his muzzle.

Elijah placed his hand on Rhys's shoulder. "If starats from Ceres came through here, then speak to Mikkel and Alison amongst them. They can vouch for us. They were our companions from Pluto."

"Pluto?" the starat whistled. He lowered his rifle, though the weapons of his companions remained raised. "You're well-travelled for starats. Sounds like you've got some good stories to tell."

"Just a few," Rhys said. His tail swished a little freer as he relaxed slightly. The leader had lowered his weapon. He doubted any of the other starats would fire without the black-furred starat's permission. "We have some information that Essie will want to know. About some dangers and opportunities."

The starat holstered his rifle at his back and raised a dark brow. "Are you the starat from Pluto who sent warning of those Denitchev bombs?"

"That was me," Elijah said brightly. "But Rhys was the one who knows all about them."

"Rhys, was it? Perhaps you should come through to meet Essie then. She will be interested to hear what you have to say," the starat said, flicking his muzzle and gesturing for his companions to lower their weapons. He then held his hand out for Rhys to shake. "I'm Alistair, captain of the Waterloo Defenders."

Elijah and Kalisha both introduced themselves to Alistair, while the starats surrounding them obeyed their captain and holstered their weapons. Tension melted away from the air. Rhys always felt better when there wasn't a gun aimed at his face.

Alistair organised his starats. He called out to another, who Rhys guessed to be his second in command, and organised some patrols in his absence. The commander then selected six starats to travel with him, deeper into the Underground. They would be the escort for the three newcomers. Rhys couldn't help but notice that Alistair had chosen six of the largest starats present. He was sure that wasn't a coincidence.

Within five minutes, they were all ready to move again. Most of the starats would remain behind, guarding the entrance from Waterloo. The others would descend further into the labyrinth beneath the city, deeper into the clinging darkness.

All the starats carried torches with them. If any of the old lighting systems were still functional, none were in use. The floor was mostly smooth tile, leading onto concrete as they moved onto the old platforms. The cool air chilled Rhys's fur, and the darkness felt oppressive any time he looked out the narrow beams of light.

The sweeping light fell upon cracked concrete walls, damp with moisture dripping from the ceiling. Faded and scratched paint still lingered on the platform, with a faded brown stripe running parallel to a sudden drop to the tracks. Dull metal gleamed in the light down the drop, which appeared like a trench amongst the concrete.

One by one, the starats all dropped onto the tracks. But for the deteriorated metal beams embedded in the floor, the way underfoot was smooth. Torchlight shone on the walls. What looked like graffiti had been scrawled over the faded paint. Rhys realised that they were directions and maps. His ears flicked as he approached the nearest crude map. He ran his hand over the drawing, which showed just a small section of the vast labyrinth of the Underground network.

"Where are we going?" Rhys asked, turning around to see most of the starats had already started to move towards one end of the platform. A circular tunnel loomed over the tracks, leading into deeper darkness away from the station. Underground, Rhys couldn't tell which direction that was. The rough map indicated six different tunnels leading away from Waterloo.

"Green Park," Alistair replied. He took the lead of the small group of starats. Two of the guards approached Rhys, but he started moving before they could get to him. He had no desire to get separated from the group. The Underground was a maze. If he got lost without a light, he would be stuck below ground with no way of knowing just how far from an exit he was.

Once again, Rhys was in the dark below the surface. Memories of Mars threatened to overwhelm him, but when his mind returned to that horrible place, he forced himself to focus on the beams of light ahead. The sounds of footsteps all around comforted him. He was not alone this time. Even so, Rhys lingered as close to Elijah as he could, gripping onto the other starat's hand. Elijah squeezed back, but he didn't say anything.

Rhys didn't know how long they walked, or how far they travelled. The tunnel twisted and turned, but it remained mostly level. They passed by two other stations without stopping. The platforms rose high beside them, with the open area beyond seeming almost more oppressive than the tunnels themselves. The sound of their footsteps echoed through the darkness, as did every quiet word spoken.

At the third station, Alistair called a halt to their walk. Rhys wasn't sure if they had been walking for about five minutes or an hour. Stuck in the total darkness with no references of natural light, Rhys would not have been surprised with either. Torchlight swept across the walls of the station. Faded signs revealed they were at Piccadilly.

Alistair clambered up onto the platform. He helped a few other starats up, including Rhys and Elijah.

The Piccadilly platform looked almost identical to the one at Waterloo. The concrete platform was narrow and painted with faded lines of brown. Some tiles still clung to the wall, but most had fallen into piles of powdered dust on the cracked floor. The air was cold, though a slight breeze still rippled at Rhys's fur. No sound came from outside the station. Rhys felt like he had been transported to another world and wasn't just below one of the largest cities in the empire.

The station felt like its own maze. Beyond the platform, stairs and corridors seemed to branch off into a myriad of different paths. Directions had been painted onto the walls, providing a helpful guide in the total darkness.

Alistair didn't need the directions. He walked quickly and without hesitation, leading his small group up a flight of stairs. Torchlight shone on lingering evidence of life beneath the streets of London. Discarded scraps of food packaging had scattered amongst the rubble, along with dropped tools and torches. Three of the starats stooped to pick up some of the tools, slipping them into their backpacks. They muttered quietly amongst themselves, disapproval in their tone.

The stairs led onto a wide, circular concourse. More stairs led further up, though Rhys could see no natural light shining down. Nothing was visible unless torchlight shone upon it. Alistair led the group around the concourse, until he went down towards a different platform. Everything all looked the same to Rhys. For all he knew, they had come up the stairs, and gone back down the same ones to reach the exact same platform. Even the signs on the platform looked identical, but the faded paint stripe on the platform was blue instead of brown.

The starats dropped down onto the disused tracks once more and began their trek through the darkness. Torchlight swept ahead. Faint sounds echoed back that were not their own footsteps and voices. The scent of starats was strong on the air. This tunnel was different to the first.

"What's down here?" Rhys asked, calling ahead to Alistair.

The lead starat didn't turn back. His torchlight continued to shine ahead. "Heretics and resisters, Rhys. Starats from all parts of the empire, gathered together for one cause."

"To fight back," Kalisha growled. She walked a couple of paces ahead of Rhys and Elijah. Her russet fur shone brightly whenever a beam of light brushed over her.

"Not yet, we haven't," Alistair said. He glanced back, his black fur blending in almost perfectly to the darkness around him. Even as light shone over his face, he still looked like little more than a silhouette; a void in the darkness. "We haven't had the numbers or the opportunity. But now? Now I think we just might."

Light flickered in the distance. The starats finished rounding a corner to see the next station illuminated brightly. Shadows moved across the light. The chittering voices of starats echoed down the tunnel.

"What is this place?" Elijah whispered. His hand squeezed a little tighter around Rhys's.

Alistair spun on his toes, continuing to walk backwards. He spread his arms wide and grinned. "Welcome to Green Park."

A new voice called out from the light, breaking apart from the rumble of voices beyond. "Alistair? Is that you? We weren't expecting you back for hours."

The starat commander turned again and waved his hand. Two armed guards stepped out of the shadows to the sides of the tunnel. Both were dark furred like Alistair. "We picked up some more newcomers in Waterloo. They need to speak to Essie urgently. They've got important information from Pluto and Ceres."

"This to do with that weapon?" one of the guards grunted. He stepped to the side, keeping a clear passage for Alistair.

"So they tell me," Alistair replied. He paused for a moment. "Do you know where she is?"

"Last I heard, she was on the Jubilee north platform," the guard replied. "You need us to escort them?"

"Nah, I've got it. Omar has Waterloo defended," Alistair replied. He gestured for his companions to follow him, then stepped forward into the light.

The tracks were still empty, but the platform was a cacophony of noise and activity. Hundreds of starats crowded onto the platform, with crude shelters of wood and canvas crammed onto the narrow shelf of concrete. Few starats reacted to the arrival of the newcomers, and those that did called out in greeting and waved a hand.

The smell of cooking fish got stronger as Rhys followed Alistair. A large grill had been squeezed in close to the edge of the platform. A queue of starats lined up by it, plates held at the ready. Two starats stood at the grill, tending to the cooking food. A third starat bellowed out. "Food is cooked! Come and get it! Freshly stolen!"

Though Rhys was tempted by the prospect of food, he kept following Alistair. There was a large crowd of starats around the grill already, and he didn't want to delay meeting with Essie. With a regretful glance back to the grill, he hauled himself up onto the crowded platform and towards the stairs leading up to the concourses.

The Underground station looked to be in as much disrepair as the previous two. Cracks ran through the faded walls, with little remaining of the original décor. The lights on the ceiling were kept lit by strips of wiring taped to the concrete. A power generator hummed close by, though Rhys couldn't tell what was fuelling it. In contrast to the other stations, this was brightly lit and crowded. It was also very noisy. Even the stairs were not free from rough shelters. Only a narrow passage in the middle of the stairwell was kept free, and even that had wires and cabling criss-crossing over the stairs.

Rhys had never seen so many starats all in one place before. Not even on Centaura had there been a gathering of just starats without a single human present. "This is incredible," he whispered. He could barely hear his own voice over the noise, but he could feel the squeeze of Elijah's fingers in response.

There was a small concourse at the top of the stairwell, which was just as crowded as the platform below. Further stairs led up to the surface, but Rhys could see those were blocked off by thick walls of concrete, just like they had been at Waterloo. An interchange passage led through to a second small concourse, which had several more stairwells leading down to further platforms. Alistair led the way to the Jubilee platform.

Fewer starats and shelters lined the stairs down to the Jubilee platform. The air smelled different, and not as much noise drifted up. Echoed voices melded together and bounced off the concrete walls.

One in particular, slightly garbled by the echoes, made Rhys's ears flick. His throat tightened and his heart hammered quickly, though he couldn't be sure why.

The voice was human. "Who…" Rhys started to ask, before realising his mouth was completely dry. He licked his lips and swallowed, before trying again. "Who is that? The human?"

The dark shadow of Alistair grinned. "That's Essie. Come on. She's wonderful. The only human I've ever liked."

Rhys's head buzzed. Fragmented thoughts filled his mind. Vertigo threatened to spill him over and tumble down the stairs, but Elijah's hand squeezed tight around his. He remained upright, but only just. His feet felt like they had been filled with lead, but he still didn't know why. Something about the human voice filled him with terror.

The Jubilee platform was used as storage. Hundreds of crates were stacked up against the wall, rising almost all the way to the sloping ceiling. Lights flickered above, casting most of the platform into shadow. Three starats moved around the crates at the far end of the platform, close to the tracks.

There was one human amongst the starats. She crouched low, facing away from the newcomers. All Rhys could see of her was her blonde, slightly curled hair. A cold shiver ran down his body, starting at the tip of his ears and sinking all the way to his toes. His body numbed.

"It can't be," Rhys choked. His mind screamed at his eyes. They were lying to him. He could not be seeing that particular human. She was a mirage. A ghost.

The human turned around at the sound of Rhys's voice. It was her. He had not seen her for fifteen years, because that had been when she had died. Her shuttle had been shot down.

"Alistair, what a pleasure," the human said brightly. She didn't even look at Rhys.

Alistair bowed his head. "Essie. We have some starats to see you. They came from Pluto. They're the ones who sent the message about the subspace weapons."

The human looked at Rhys for the first time. Her brown eyes were achingly familiar. She held out her hand towards Rhys, with no trace of recognition on her face. "Welcome to Green Park. You can call me Essie."

Rhys didn't move. He couldn't. He was completely frozen with fear and confusion. She was dead. There was no way she could be standing here in front of him.

"Rhys, are you alright?" Elijah said quietly, nudging his elbow into the frozen starat's side.

The human frowned slightly. "Rhys? I knew a…"

"Stephanie," Rhys croaked. "Stephanie MacArthur. How are you here?"

Silence met Rhys's words. The human stepped back. Her face went completely white. None of the starats spoke. Rhys's hand shook as he fumbled through his pocket.

The human spoke first. "No one has used that name in over a decade. Few here know it," she said. Her voice trembled, and tears had come to her eyes. "How do you know me?"

Rhys couldn't loosen his throat enough to answer. He simply reached out with his hand and pressed something into the human's. She stared down at her hand, partially clenched into a fist. She unfurled her fingers and stared at the wedding ring Rhys had placed there. Her breath hitched in her throat.

"How…?" the human asked. She stared at the ring, then slowly looked up to the starat. "Rhys?"

Rhys held a hand to his muzzle. His fur felt damp. "It's me," he said, his voice sounding so small to his ears. "You've barely changed at all."

"You have," Stephanie said. She laughed nervously. "The stories… the rumours. I didn't know if they were true. I didn't think they were possible. How…?"

Rhys took a trembling step forward. She dropped to her knees. He couldn't hold himself back any longer. He ran forward and embraced her. She wrapped her arms around him, and together they both laughed and cried at the same time. The terror at hearing her voice faded into nothing. The confusion could wait a few moments longer. All that mattered now was joy. Absolute, pure joy.

Kalisha's voice broke through. "Alright. What the fuck just happened?"

Rhys reluctantly moved away from Stephanie's embrace. He turned around to face the other starats. "Elijah. Kalisha. This is Stephanie. She was my fiancé before she died in a shuttle crash fifteen years ago."

"She's doing remarkably well for being dead for fifteen years," Kalisha said dryly.

"I think we both have a very long story to tell," Stephanie said. Her voice had not changed in the many years since he had last seen her. But for a few lines on her face, she looked almost as though she had simply skipped the previous fifteen years. Nearly two decades of life she should not have had.

"I think that's putting it quite mildly," Rhys replied. He managed to smile, but it was a nervous one. The initial joy was wearing off, instead replaced by worry and confusion. Panic was also building in his chest. He was scared to know Stephanie's story, to know why she had lived for fifteen years and never tried to get in contact with Rhys. With her fiancé.

Stephanie rose to her feet. "Gordon. Can you finish up in here, please?"

One of the starats who had been helping Stephanie before the interruption nodded his head. He stared at Rhys. "Right you are, Essie."

Stephanie cleared her throat. Most of the emotion left her voice, leaving her sounding like a leader; in command and calculated. "Alistair, do you mind helping? I'll take these three up to my office if you need me for anything," she said. Her shoulders hunched slightly, but otherwise she showed no sign of the emotion that had been in her voice moments earlier.

Feeling immensely confused about everything, Rhys followed Stephanie back up towards the concourse. Elijah and Kalisha came with him. He was glad of their company. They were his grounding in real life, while Stephanie still felt like an illusion; a remnant of his old life come back to haunt him. She couldn't be real. She couldn't be.

***

Stephanie made coffee. She still knew exactly how Rhys liked his.

No one spoke. The three starats had all sat down in chairs that had been crudely modified for tails with holes cut out the back. Rhys stared at his lap, unsure just what to say.

The small office appeared to also be where Stephanie lived. A desk took up most of the space, with the wooden frame of a bed leaned up against the wall. Much of the remaining wall space was taken up with cupboards, all built together from battered fragments of wood. Little looked new, or even used in the purpose it had been constructed for. Everything was cobbled together. Only the small stove and kettle looked to have always been such.

The four coffees were all in mismatched cups. Stephanie handed them out, then sat on the edge of the desk. There were no more chairs for her to sit on. She held her steaming cup of coffee in both hands. "So. Story. Should I go first, or should you?"

"I wasn't meant to be dead for fifteen years," Rhys said. His voice shook still, and he struggled not to keep an accusation out of his tone. The fact still remained though, that she had been alive for so long without telling him. "I think you should go first."

Stephanie took a deep breath to compose herself. "Well. I didn't die on the shuttle. That much is obvious. Everything had seemed normal leaving Shanghai, until I started to speak to a starat. I had what we call an understanding. I saw her as a person, not as an animal."

Rhys shivered. He closed his eyes. The dream he had seen on Pluto flashed through his mind. "Rina."

"Yes," Stephanie said warily. "Have you met her already?"

"No," Rhys said slowly. He wasn't sure how to keep going without sounding completely crazy. "I dreamed about her. About you. I saw the missiles hit the shuttle."

Stephanie stared at Rhys. "You can do it too? The strange powers?"

Rhys flicked his ear. He laughed. Of course Stephanie would know all about that. Rina and Arnav had told her on the shuttle. "I could. Before... well, I'll get to that later."

"I still can though," Kalisha said, demonstrating her powers by pulling a spoon towards her and stirring her coffee, all without touching the cutlery. She grinned, but the usual look of shock didn't come from Stephanie. The human merely nodded and gripped a little tighter around her cup of coffee, as though fearing Kalisha might try and take it from her.

"Rina saved me. I didn't know how she did it at first. I don't think she knew too much about it either," Stephanie explained. Her foot tapped in mid-air as she frowned down at her drink. "All three of us survived that fall. Rina. Me. Arnav. We landed in Tibet, and we knew right then that we could never come back to imperial society. The Vatican tried to kill Arnav and Rina. If the church knew someone had survived that crash, then they would not stop hunting us. We had to remain dead."

Rhys draped his tail across his lap. Stephanie had chosen the lives of two starats over her own. Over the life she had been sharing with Rhys. But it wasn't just them. Rhys bowed his head. Had the Vatican learned she had survived, then she would have been killed too. It wouldn't have just been the starats. Stephanie would have been a loose end that needed to be tied off.

"How did you survive?" Rhys asked.

"The fall? Rina's powers. She slowed us down and lessened the impact. Still hurt us, though. We were injured, but we managed to make it to a nearby village," Stephanie explained. She paused to sip at her coffee. "We stayed there a couple of weeks to recover and work out what to do. We couldn't come back to the main cities. We had to stay rural. Stay isolated. The Vatican and Empire don't have the reach they would like in some of the smaller regions, so it gave us the chance to remain safe. We stayed in Tibet for a year before moving on.

"From Tibet, we travelled west, slowly moving through the Middle East and towards northern Africa. We didn't have a destination in mind. We just stayed low, out of sight. I'm not proud to admit we stole what we needed, but we always made sure it was from those who could afford the loss."

Stephanie paused. She looked across to Rhys, a nervous grin on her face. "I wanted to send a message to you. I wanted you to know I was still alive, but I didn't dare risk it. I couldn't. I always checked in on you when I could. I followed your progress. You seemed to move on quickly."

Rhys laughed and shook his head. "I moved on because I had to. It took me years before I stopped thinking about you every day. If I knew you were still alive..." Rhys hesitated a moment. What would he have done? He struggled to remember the raw anguish of losing

Stephanie. That had been a different life, almost literally. "I would have abandoned everything to find you again."

"And that's why I couldn't contact you," Stephanie said. She put her coffee down on the desk and reached out to take Rhys's hand. She placed the ring back on his palm. "Will you forgive me for that, at least?"

Rhys squeezed his hand tight around the ring. "If I was still human, I might not have understood. I'd have been confused and hurt about how you could have chosen two starats over me," he said softly. He looked up to meet Stephanie in the eye. "But now, I do. I completely understand, and I forgive you for that. For my part, I'm sorry if it looked like I forgot about you so quickly. I hurt for a decade after I lost you."

"Every day was hell," Stephanie explained. She twisted another ring around her finger. "I lost everything. I had two starats for company, but I was still adjusting to them being that. Company, and not property. I slipped up a couple of times. We shouted at each other. Arnav tried to convince Rina to leave me. Thankfully they stayed. I wouldn't have known what to do if they left. We became good friends, and not just because we were all that we had."

"How did that become this?" Rhys asked, gesturing to the small, cramped office. "When did Stephanie become Essie?"

"That started to happen about ten years ago. I saved the life of a starat in Cairo, and I started to wonder what more could be done to help them," Stephanie said. She slowly drank her coffee in the brief pauses in her story. "It took about another year, but we slowly made our way back to Britannia. We started in Glasgow, but then we stumbled on the Underground and realised that it would be the perfect place to hide out, while never being far from the heart of the empire. We've been spreading through the tunnels for eight years now, slowly building and training an army of starats."

"And no one knows you're here?" Elijah asked, leaning forward in his seat.

"We've been very careful," Stephanie said. "We steal supplies when we need them, but most of what we've built our homes with have been discarded or thrown away on the surface. It's not much. It's barely comfortable, but it suffices until we're ready."

"What have you been waiting for?" Rhys asked. The tip of his tail twitched.

"I know it sounds awful," Stephanie said with a laugh, "but I think we have been waiting for you."

Rhys grimaced and pinned his ears back. His tail curled, and he nervously stroked it with one hand. "I've never been anyone special. Never more important than just another guy focused on the military. I followed orders and never questioned the authorities. You know that."

Stephanie shook her head. "You always were to me. But I get what you're saying. You may not have been special fifteen years ago, but you are now. Not one of the starats here have ever been human. You were. That makes you, and what you are capable of doing, very special."

"I don't feel special," Rhys said. He drained the last of his coffee and leaned back in his chair. "I just feel like I'm being bashed over the head with new information every day, finding out the ways the world works are all wrong. I'm just trying to survive in a new world, not to do anything great."

"I don't think any of the greats ever felt special at the time," Stephanie replied. She had a smile on her face again. A very familiar smile. When they had been together there had barely been a minute when Rhys had not seen her smiling.

Rhys rubbed his muzzle and closed his eyes for a moment. "I suppose I owe you a story now, don't I? Where do you want me to begin?"

"I was able to keep track of you for your whole career, but after Aaron defected things began to get difficult to verify, especially coming from Ceres," Stephanie said. When Rhys opened his eyes again, he could see that her smile had gone. The lines across her forehead had furrowed. She suddenly looked older, with all fifteen years of her life since Rhys had last seen her coming back.

"Ceres," Rhys said bitterly. Even the name tasted bad in his mouth now. "I guess I'd better start there then." He took a deep breath and began to recount his story.

***

Rhys had almost finished telling his long tale. Stephanie had interrupted several times, asking for clarification or further details into some aspects of his life since his transformation, mostly around what it had been like on Centaura. She had spoken of her amazement and wonder at the opportunity to visit other star systems, and her regret that she had still yet to have that opportunity. Elijah and Kalisha had occasionally added their own interruptions as well.

Cups of coffee had been refilled on two occasions by the time Rhys recounted their final departure from Ceres. That was when an interruption disturbed them. Someone had knocked at the closed door.

A starat came in. Rhys first realised he shouldn't have been surprised by that. Stephanie was the only human in the Underground. Then he realised that he recognised the starat. Her fur was a little more ragged than in his dream, but she looked more alert and confident than she had done fifteen years ago. She looked stronger, too. Rhys rose to his feet and extended his hand.

"You must be Rina," Rhys said with a smile.

Rina tentatively took his hand and nodded. "I am, yes. Forgive me, I don't believe we have been introduced."

Stephanie exhaled slowly and loudly. "This is going to sound weird to everyone. Rina. This is Rhys, my fiancé from fifteen years ago. Rhys, this is Rina. She's my wife."

"Your wife?" Rhys asked, dropping back into his chair.

"I didn't think I'd ever see you again," Stephanie said quickly. "I had to move on."

Rhys glanced across to Stephanie. There was hurt in her eyes. He inhaled sharply. "You think I…? No, I don't blame you for that. Of course you had to move on. It would have been stupid waiting for nothing. I'm happy for you," he said, speaking just as quickly. He smiled and reached out to take Rina's hand again. "You couldn't have picked someone better than Stephanie. I'm glad she has someone to share her life with."

"But you never did," Stephanie said. She shared a quick glance with Rina.

Rhys grimaced and pulled his ears back. "I might have left a little something out of my story, because I thought you might have found it weird," he said. He rested a hand on Elijah's thigh. "This is Elijah. He's my boyfriend."

"It seems we're both completely different people to who we were back then," Stephanie said with a laugh and a smile. She turned her attention to Rina. "But was there something you needed me for, dear?"

Rina nodded. She held her hands up close towards her chest, looking warily around the group of gathered starats. "Yeah, Ess. There's a message from the surface that needs your attention."

"I'll be right there," Stephanie said. She paused only to drain the last of her coffee. "Do you mind finding somewhere for these three to stay?"

"Of course," Rina replied. She leaned into an embrace from Stephanie.

The human grinned back at Rhys. "I'm so happy to have you back. We'll speak again very soon, alright?"

Rhys rose to his feet. He saluted Stephanie, who saluted back. "Go do what you need to do, Essie. We'll be here for you now."

"It's going to be just like old times," the human said. She almost bounced out of the room.

Rina kept her hand on the open door. "Shall we go get you all settled in?"

Rhys was the last to leave the small office. He glanced back into the empty room, his nose twitching as he took in the scent. Stephanie had been living there for years and he had never known she had been alive. His head hurt and his heart ached.

By the time Rhys stepped out onto the concourse, Stephanie was already disappearing around a corner. Several starats stopped and waved to her as the human hurried by. With a great effort, Rhys tore his eyes away and turned to face Rina. With tears threatening to form in his eyes, he quickly rubbed his muzzle with the back of his hand and took a deep breath.

"There's some space on the Victoria platforms," Rina said, holding out her hand for Rhys to take. She smiled nervously as her ears flicked. She looked pointedly in the direction that Stephanie had gone. "She never stopped thinking about you."

"I never stopped thinking about her, either," Rhys said, his voice tight with emotion. He forced a smile. "You are lucky to have her."

"I never thought a human would be capable of this," Rina said. She stepped back and released Rhys's hand to gesture around the concourse. Over a dozen curious starats watched on, though Rhys recognised none of them from Ceres. "I know it hurt you badly, but I can't bring myself to regret meeting Stephanie the way we did. She could change the lives of every single starat in the empire because of this movement."

"Why don't you tell us more about that?" Elijah said suddenly. He shuffled his feet nervously, scratching his claws against the tiled floor. He stared down, not quite managing to meet the eyes of anyone around him.

Rina flicked her ears back. She started to walk, waving her hand to encourage the others to follow her. Dark, faded signs still indicated the location of each of the platforms, all colour coded. "We chose Green Park because it's fairly central, and because three different lines pass through this station. Most other lines are only one or two stations away, which gives us the ability to move quickly through the city," the starat explained. She looked up towards the ceiling for a moment. "It is difficult to keep so many starats hidden beneath London, but we put in place a strict code of conduct for all starats when we started out here, and that has worked well enough even with our expanding numbers."

"How many are here?" Elijah asked. The augmented starat had straightened his back again, looking up and around once more. His ears were perked up and his eyes wide, though he did not reach for Rhys's hand like usual.

"Three years ago, there were forty of us," Rina said. Her eyes sparkled as she looked up at Elijah. "Now, there are over two thousand."

"How long can you expect to sustain this?" Elijah asked. He stared around at the darkened, dusty corners of the concourse as Rina led them to a new set of stairs. The faded sign above indicated they were going down to the northern platform for the Victoria line.

Rina curled her ears down. She put her hand on the railing to the side of the stairs. "Probably not long. If we don't have an opportunity soon, then I don't know what we'll do," she said quietly. "We might be able to spread to other stations, but the food we need is getting almost too much. We can't keep stealing it from the surface."

Kalisha snorted in laughter. "Isn't that why Rhys is here?" she said, nudging Rhys in the ribs with her elbow. "He's here to fix all the problems and work out how we're going to win."

Rhys hunched his shoulders. His ears and tail drooped as he looked away from the russet starat by his side. "I can't do that all by myself," he said quietly. He almost stumbled on the steps as they descended. Ahead of them, shadows filled the narrow tunnel going down, but there were lights beyond.

"Perhaps not," Rina said with a smile. Her tail wagged. "But there is plenty that you can do for us. Starting tomorrow, I would like you to oversee some of the training we do. This isn't just a movement, after all. We're building a militia. Every starat here is committed to fighting."

Noise filtered up from the platform below. It did not sound as busy as the first platform Rhys saw at Green Park, but he could smell and hear at least a hundred starats ahead. There seemed to be no attempt to limit the noise they made. Rhys's heart beat firmly as he thought about the prospect of training so many. He gritted his teeth and grimaced. "I'll do whatever I can to help."

Rina stepped onto the Victoria platform. Just like the others, it was little more than a narrow strip of concrete overlooking the tracks. Both platform and tracks alike were covered in boxes and small, makeshift shelters of wood and canvas. A few curious eyes looked up, but for the most part little interest was given to the newcomers. On the tracks, halfway down the length of the platform, was an open firepit that added some flicker over the top of the electric lighting.

"Looks cosy," Kalisha muttered.

Elijah rested his hand on her shoulder as he looked around, a grin on his muzzle. "It's not going to feel that much different to what we had on Pluto. It's certainly better than what I had on Charon."

Rina hopped down onto the tracks. She moved towards three of the makeshift shelters close to the yawning black maw of the tunnel leading away from the station. The boxes looked like they had been untouched for a while. There was a pile of blankets bundled up inside.

"These will be suitable for you," Rina said, putting her hands on top of the boxes. She flicked her ears back. "Should you need any extra supplies, then come and find me or Ess. We'll do what we can to get you settled in."

"We have some weapons and ammunition that we took from the armoury on Ceres," Rhys said, gesturing back to the two starats behind him. Both Elijah and Kalisha still carried those stolen supplies, though Rhys was no longer sure how big a difference those few weapons would make. Essie's Heresy already looked well supplied.

Rina quickly glanced over the stolen goods. She twitched her muzzle. "We'll have a look at that tomorrow. For now, just rest and settle in."

"Rest sounds good," Rhys said, bowing his head to the other starat, before glancing across to Elijah. He wasn't sure whether the augmented starat would insist on sharing one of the shelters with him. Though they briefly met each other's eyes, neither commented on that just yet. Rhys's claws tensed against the concrete beneath his feet.

"Arnav should be back tomorrow. We're hoping he will have information for us that will allow us to start putting together a plan, especially now with your intel," Rina said. She stepped away from the shelters. Her tail curled around her leg as she clasped her hands together in front of her body. She smiled. "All that's left for me to say is welcome, friends, to Essie's Heresy."

As Rina took her leave, Rhys slowly looked around the underground station. He could only see starats. They laughed and joked together, talking with freedom and no fear. Rhys couldn't help but smile as he watched them. The starats reminded him of those he had seen on Centaura, free from the worries of a human turning the corner and putting an end to their fun.

Of course, these starats were not free. Not yet. They were still trapped, but instead of the bonds of slavery, it was the need to live underground, out of the sunlight. It could not last for long. Rhys knew all about being trapped underground, and the thought of it happening again made his tail puff up in worry.

Wood scraped over concrete behind him. Rhys glanced back to see Kalisha dragging one of the crates around to face a second. With a flick of her hand, a blanket draped across the gap between them. Rhys twitched his nose, still finding it strange that he got none of the cinnamon scent he always associated with those powers.

The russet starat grinned as she noticed Rhys watching her. "Thought you two could do with a bit more room," she said, nudging Elijah towards Rhys.

Rhys reddened beneath his fur. He bowed his head. "Thank you," he said quietly, accepting her efforts and leaning into Elijah's dappled fur. The augmented starat tensed for a moment, before lightly touching his hand to Rhys's side.

Together, Rhys and Elijah settled down against the opening to their crude shelter. Blankets provided something soft to sit on.

"Well, we're here," Elijah said quietly. He rested his hand on Rhys's knee. "It's not quite what I thought it would be, but I'm definitely looking forward to seeing what they're capable of."

Rhys nodded. His head still spun as he thought about all he had learned already. Even learning of Stephanie's survival was more than enough to send his thoughts wild. He had not yet even thought much about what Essie's Heresy could mean to deal a blow to the empire, nor how they could use it to stop the SFU's plans for Terra.

"Tomorrow. We can think about all of that tomorrow," Rhys said with a sigh. He wasn't sure whether he was responding to Elijah, or just vocalising a response to his own thoughts.

"Tomorrow, agreed," Elijah said. He lightly pulled back on Rhys, encouraging him to lie down by his side. "Tonight, we can just rest. You especially need it. You still haven't fully recovered from Mars."

Kalisha tapped her fingers on the side of their crate and peered inside. "If you're going to be resting, just make sure you keep it quiet."

Rhys laughed as his cheeks burned. He also gave her a middle finger. He doubted Elijah had that in mind, but, as the other starat pulled down the canvas around their shelter to give them some privacy, Rhys was no longer quite sure.

In the arms of Elijah, the returned ghost of Stephanie held no sway. He was able to distract his mind from what her return meant to him, for he had someone else to pour every thought into. Someone else to get lost in. Someone else to love. He stayed quiet, but the inside of his head was a roar of emotions matched only by the thunderous beating of two hearts.

Rhys didn't get much rest, but he got everything else he could have needed.

chapter sixteen

Breakfast the following morning was little more than rice with chopped vegetables and almost negligible amounts of fried fish. It was simple and bland, but it was warm. In the tunnels of the abandoned underground, there was no sunlight to heat the air. But for the clock above the chipped sign of Green Park on the wall, Rhys would have no knowledge of the time.

Rhys had woken up in Elijah's arms, feeling rested and content. The worries of Mars were safely in the past, and even the concerns of the future felt small for as long as those furred arms were tightly wrapped around his chest. He had woken without pain plaguing his body, and though there were some shadows cast on his mind by the revelations of the previous day, he still felt a calm optimism for what was to come.

After a quick breakfast and a trip to the modified public bathrooms just off the platform, Rhys felt ready to face the day. He flexed his hands several times, tensing the muscles and feeling the tentative strength that was slowly rebuilding in them.

Rhys bumped into a familiar starat on the upper concourse, above the platforms. He was met by a squeal of delight and a tight embrace by Skye as she recognised him, before she quickly moved on to embrace Elijah. Kalisha stepped back from her hug before the Cerian starat had a chance to put her arms around her.

"I knew you'd make it back," Skye said with a grin. Her eyes gleamed in the electric light from above. "Sorry we lost you in the fight, but we had a few other distractions at the time."

Rhys pinned an ear back. "How long had you been planning that?"

Skye grinned, showing off her sharp, needle-like teeth. She rubbed her palms together. "I'd been putting down plans for years, hoping that there would be an opportunity," she said, before twisting her muzzle and lightly biting her lip. "That was a bit more of an off-the-cuff moment though. I saw an opportunity and knew we had to take it. Especially with you being there."

"I'm glad I could help," Rhys said, scratching the back of his neck. He flicked his tail as he looked around. Dozens of starats moved between the platforms, though he could see few he recognised. There was a sense of purpose to most starats, though some still walked around with a bowl or cup in their hands.

"I think you can help some more here though," Skye said. She swept her arm around the concourse. "I hear you'll be training us?"

"I believe that's the plan," Rhys said with a nod. He glanced around. "First though, I need to find Ste… Essie. I want to know what her plans are."

"I know where she is," Skye said, bouncing on her toes. "Come on, follow me."

With a flick of her wrist and tail, Skye scampered away, still bouncing with every step. Rhys glanced to Elijah and Kalisha for a moment, before following the Cerian starat. She led them down to the Jubilee platform, the same one Rhys had first seen Stephanie the previous day.

Rhys's heart still skipped a beat when he saw the human again. She was still real. She had not been a bizarre dream in which the dead returned to life. Stephanie, under the name of Essie, had really created an underground resistance against the empire. His hand squeezed a little tighter against Elijah's as they stepped onto the platform again.

Three starats surrounded Stephanie on the tracks. Rhys recognised two of the starats. Rina and Alistair were with her. The third was a male starat Rhys had never seen before, except in a dream. Arnav looked up the moment Rhys placed a foot on the platform and didn't look away. This was the other starat in Rhys's dream of Stephanie's supposed death, the one who could peer into the future. Rhys's tail swished and puffed up.

Arnav nudged against Stephanie's elbow to get her attention. The human glanced up and smiled, cutting off her quiet conversation with the other starats. She pulled herself out of the tracks and onto the platform. "It wasn't all some crazy dream," she said, her eyes wide in wonder. She grinned in response to Rhys's laughter, and he was sure she already knew he had thought the same thing.

Rina pulled herself onto the platform after the human. She looked between the four newcomers. "I'd like you to meet Arnav," she said, extending her hand towards Rhys. "He was the other starat who travelled with us. Without him, we could never have come this far."

Rhys looked over her shoulder as Arnav approached. His coppery fur gleamed brightly in the spotlights on the ceiling. His eyes seemed slightly unfocused, like he was looking at something just in front of Rhys, or just behind him. The other starat extended his hand first, gripping Rhys's hand tightly. "It is a pleasure to finally meet you, Rhys Griffiths."

"You saw me coming before I got here?" Rhys asked, his fur prickling.

Arnav snorted in laughter. "My abilities do not work that way," he said, baring his teeth in amusement. "I do not see all futures, only ones that have already sent ripples through subspace."

"I don't understand," Rhys said, curling his ears down and furrowing his brow.

"Think for a moment of a boat on the water," Arnav said, speaking slowly as he looked into Rhys's eyes. "A wave is displacement is made in the water. The same is true for every action that occurs in subspace, but instead of being pushed sideways like the boat, this ripple goes forward. Every action we take, even those in realspace, creates ripples in subspace. I can sense and interpret those ripples before realspace catches up."

Arnav pointed towards the darkness of the tracks tunnel. "I could tell you if someone were walking from out of there before any ears could hear footsteps. I can sense a missile launched towards me. I could not say if, in ten seconds, you were suddenly to punch me. An act must already have happened, or be happening, for me to witness the aftermath, even if I am not able to physically sense it."

Rhys lightly bit down on his tongue. His head hurt just trying to think of it, but he knew the same would have been true had he been learning anew about the ability to move matter through subspace. He held a hand to the side of his muzzle as he tried again to dip into that endless white, but he still could not detect even the faintest trace of cinnamon. "I think I understand," he said slowly.

"It is clear you do not," Arnav said brightly. "But you do not need to understand them. All you need to do is respect them when and if I give you an order based on my visions. Can you do that for me?"

Rhys hesitated for a second, his mouth hanging partially open, before nodding. "I can, yes."

"Good," Arnav said, lightly slapping Rhys on the back with an open palm. "I think we can get along quite nicely if that's the case. I understand my gifts are scary, but if you listen to me then I can keep you safe."

Rina cleared her throat, pulling attention back to her. "Even you can't keep us safe if we can't decipher this message," she said with a sigh. She rubbed her head, her fingers teasing through the fur between her ears.

Elijah's ears perked up. "Message? If it's a code that you can't break, may I have a look at it?"

Stephanie nodded. The human led Elijah down into the well of the tracks, where a small computer setup perched on a pile of crates. Rhys could not see what was on the screen, but he watched Elijah for a few seconds with curiosity, before turning to the other starats still around him. Only Alistair had remained in the tracks with Stephanie and Elijah.

Rhys scuffed his foot against the cracked floor. The weight of the city seemed to press down on his shoulders and the attention of the two starats who had kept Stephanie away from him for fifteen years. He breathed out slowly.

"Essie said you mentioned a group of starats from the CGP," Arnav said quietly, dragging Rhys's thoughts back to the present.

Rhys barely suppressed a growl. His hands tightened into fists. "The Starat Freedom Union, yes. We can't put all our focus into what the empire and Vatican is doing. We need to stop them as well, or any victory will be worthless."

Arnav looked Rhys in the eye again. He held the gaze for longer than Rhys was comfortable with. "If any starat has come to us from Alpha Centauri, or represents this organisation, then they have not made it known to us," the starat said softly. "We know nothing of their plans, but for what you have already told us."

"Shit," Rhys hissed. He flicked his tail and backed away a few paces from Arnav. He turned around and frowned, clasping his hands behind his back. "I wish I knew more, but I don't know what they're planning."

"We know one thing," Rina said. She placed a hand on Rhys's elbow, but he did not look back to face her. "We know they're intending on using a Denitchev drive for this, and that gives us one thing to look for."

Rhys tilted his head to the left. "What's that?" he asked, curling his ears forward.

"Shields," Arnav said simply.

Rhys looked up. Though he could see nothing but the ceiling, though many tonnes of rock and metal was the distant blue sky. There were no planetary shields surrounding Terra, nothing to cause any strong concentration of Denitchev particles, no matter how powerful the drive. The tip of Rhys's tail lifted. He should have realised that, but it had been so long since he had stood on a planet with a perfectly safe atmosphere like Terra. He ground his knuckles into his forehead.

"We've been scouring the system for any evidence of shield technology in development," Rina continued. Her hand did not leave Rhys's wrist. "We've not found anything yet, but trust us, we haven't forgotten about your warnings, because you are right. A victory over Terra would mean nothing if we were then to watch Terra be consumed by subspace."

Rhys rubbed his face, then turned around again. "I think it would be best if we didn't spread too much information about the SFU plan to the rest of the station," Rhys said slowly. He curled his tail up close to his leg as he looked down at Stephanie and Elijah. The starat frowned as he stared at the computer in front of him. Rhys glanced up again, meeting Arnav in the eye. "We don't want to spread panic about something we may not be able to control, and we certainly don't want to risk any SFU agents knowing we're aware of their plan. There could still be some here, after all."

"Let them come," Kalisha said with a growl, but anything further she had to say was interrupted by a call from Stephanie.

At once, the starats all hurried down onto the old tracks. Elijah turned to them, his tail swishing in excitement. "I think I've cracked the code," he said brightly, bouncing on his toes. "It's a new code, but it's similar to one of the old ones the Vatican used a few years ago."

"What does it say?" Arnav asked, stepping forward to peer down at the screen.

"It's a message from Cardinal Erik to Pope Adamantius," Elijah said, his eyes falling on Rhys, who had tensed at the mention of the cardinal's name.

"He's the one who chased you down, isn't he?" Stephanie asked.

Rhys bit his lip, then glanced to the human. "He's the one who ordered your shuttle to be shot down," he said with a growl. He forced himself to get control of his emotions again, and he slowly breathed out through his nose. "What does he have to say for himself now?"

"He fears the heresy is spreading too quickly for the empire to control," Elijah said slowly. His eyes flicked back to the computer every few seconds as he spoke. "He recommends the Vatican send reinforcements to help bolster the inquisitions and police forces. He speaks of a growing distrust in the emperor's ability to keep control of the planet, and he recommends that, should Emperor Neicwyk continue to refuse Vatican support, then the church can face no other option but to attack."

"They're already speaking of invasion?" Rina asked in surprise. She stared wide-eyed at the augmented starat.

Elijah nodded. He looked directly at Rhys. "Whatever you did on Mars has completely destroyed the relationship and support between Terra and Mars. It has simultaneously weakened the loyalty of Terrans towards the Vatican, but also emboldened those on Mars."

"This might be what we have been waiting for," Stephanie said. She stood tall amongst the starats around her. She tapped the clenched fist of her right hand into the palm of her left. "We may not have long before an opportunity presents itself. Rhys, I must ask you to start training as many starats as you can. They are willing fighters, but they must be taught how to survive."

"I can get right onto it," Rhys said, giving the human a smile and a mock salute. Teaching was something he could do, especially when it came to combat. His tail twitched as he looked around the small group. "What do you plan on doing?"

"If it's alright with you both, I'll keep Elijah here," Stephanie said, glancing to the starat by her side. "I want to keep track of all messages between Terra and Mars, so we're not caught off-guard by any sudden developments."

Elijah nodded before he pulled Rhys into a hug. "I'll see you soon, alright?"

Rhys smiled and leaned into the embrace for a few seconds. He pulled away from his partner. Even thinking about Elijah in that way made his heart thud loudly. "Good luck with everything here."

Arnav held his hand out. "If you come with me then, I'll take you to the rifle range," the starat said. He flicked his tail. "Skye and Alistair, you'll want to come with us as well. It's time for Captain Griffiths to show us how to really fight."

Rhys grimaced. Pressure began to weigh down on his shoulders once more. He knew that many of the starats in Essie's Heresy would never have fought before making their way to the relative freedom beneath the streets of London. If they were soon to go to battle against the might of the empire, then it would only be his teachings that would help keep them alive. All the same, Rhys knew he would not shirk from his duty. With one last look back at Elijah and Stephanie, Rhys followed the other starat. It was time to begin.

***

The Jubilee south platform ran parallel to the northern one, separated only by a narrow corridor. There was little to distinguish between them now, with the directional names only ever used for which way the trains went when the Underground had been operational. While the north platform was largely used for storage, the south had been utilised for training. There were no boxes for either storage or shelter on the southern platform, leaving an oddly clear and clean space.

Rhys paced up and down the empty platform while Arnav unlocked what used to be the public toilets. Inside was the armoury, where Essie's Heresy had stored all the weapons that they had managed to acquire. There were enough rifles to arm several thousand starats, with almost as many bullet shields. Body armour had been a tougher proposition, as it all had to be modified from those made for humans. The handful of weapons Rhys had brought from Ceres suddenly felt inadequate.

The darkness of the two tunnels on either end of the platform made Rhys's fur itch. Rubble covered the floor at the southern end; not enough to block access, but enough to make Rhys cautious any time he paced close to that end of the platform. He didn't want to stand on any sharp piece of stone and pierce his pawpads. Practice targets hung from the ceiling.

"There's no way through there," Alistair said. The Waterloo Defender sat on the edge of the platform, with his legs dangling into the well of the tracks. The more Rhys heard him speak, the more he realised the black-furred starat spoke with an accent not too dissimilar to his own.

Rhys flicked his ears and looked up, pausing his pacing. A few more starats had started to gather behind the Alistair. "What do you mean?"

Alistair pointed to the dark tunnel. "If the way was clear, we could walk directly to Waterloo through there, but the Westminster station got destroyed not long after they closed down the Underground," he explained. "That's why we had to walk the long way around."

Rhys stared into the darkness. "How many stations are like that?"

"About a dozen across the network," Alistair said. He jumped down onto the tracks and stood by Rhys's side. "I was one of the first to answer Essie's call. I escaped my old life and found my way here eight years ago. It's never felt like this before. There's so many starats who are excited about what's to come."

"It isn't going to be safe," Rhys said quietly. He didn't want the starats on the platform to hear him.

Alistair snorted with laughter. "Of course it isn't," he replied, not keeping his voice as quiet as Rhys. "There isn't a single starat here who thinks it's going to be safe. Everyone is willing to fight for freedom. That's why they came here. They refused to accept their place in life. Your job is to teach them the skills to survive."

"I'd need months for that," Rhys said, struggling to stop his tail from tucking between his legs. His ears drooped. "Everything's moving too quickly for that. We might have days at the most."

"Then you'd better teach them the important stuff," Alistair said. He slapped Rhys on the shoulder, before turning around. "Your audience is growing, and Arnav looks almost ready to begin."

Rhys took a deep breath as he turned to face the starats on the platform. There were a few hundred of them; nowhere near all that were in Essie's Heresy. Rhys planned to teach everyone the basics through a rotation system, as they could not fit every starat on the platform at once. He knew Alistair was right. He could not go into every detail, so he needed to teach the most important basics.

Amongst the crowd, Rhys could see a few familiar faces. Kalisha and Skye stood together at the edge of the platform. Mikkel and Alison were both a bit further back. Some faces he recognised from Ceres, but he could not put names to them. Arnav jumped down onto the tracks. He carried a rifle in his hands and wore a bullet shield on his wrist. He looked comfortable and proficient with both.

"Are you ready to start?" Arnav asked, holding the rifle out to Rhys.

Rhys took the weapon and lifted it above his head. Silence fell through the platform. The starat had never known an audience like this, nor a classroom. He felt strange, being below all of the starats who were to become his students, but that was a limitation of the station. He lifted his voice as loud as he could manage.

"For those of you who don't know me, my name is Captain Rhys Griffiths." He had to pause as a roar of approval met his words. Applause ran through the station, and many voices shouted their support. Rhys pinned his ears back and grinned nervously. He had not expected that, but he appreciated it nonetheless. His voice faltered slightly, but he continued to speak strongly as the clamour died down. "I cannot teach you everything I know, for there is not time. You will not become expert shooters overnight, but I can teach you how to be effective fighters. I can teach you how to reload your weapons. I can teach you how to find cover and how to use it. I can teach you how to survive."

Once again, Rhys paused. He looked around the station. Everywhere he looked, he saw determination. There was some fear, but that was a healthy response to what he said. He would have been worried if no starat showed concern for what was to come. His responsibility was making sure that as many of these starats had the skills to survive.

"Not only will I be teaching you weapon skills, but also physical ones," he continued. A few groans spread through the crowd, but Rhys did not let them build. "A soldier is fit and prepared no matter what.

We may not have time to fully strengthen you, but I still expect you to learn some exercises to keep you alert and ready."

With a growl coming into his voice, Rhys lowered his rifle. "Shall we begin?"

chapter
seventeen

For three days, Rhys got into a routine. He woke up each morning when the clock on the Victoria platform chimed six. He had breakfast and a quick meeting with Stephanie and the other leaders of the Heresy, before training the willing starat volunteers who wished to be soldiers. He quickly lost track of how many had come down to the Jubilee platform to listen to him speak, but he was sure he had to have seen every single one of the two thousand starats packed into Green Park.

There had been no significant updates from the surface, though Elijah had been able to intercept many messages between Terra and Mars. An uneasy peace had developed, with neither fleet deployed yet. Unrest had continued to spread across the planet, however. News of protests on all continents reached Essie's Heresy, but there had been no news on the SFU.

Rhys lay down in his small shelter on the Victoria tracks. Training for the day had finished, and he had taken advantage of the chance to have some relative peace. His arms ached, but not the burning agony that had plagued him since Cardinal Erik had first inflicted the Devil's Blood on him. His muscles were slowly rebuilding, with his fur gradually growing to properly cover his hands again. He was glad of the pain, for that meant he was healing.

With the canvas sheet down, the only light in Rhys's small shelter was the digital clock by his side. The electronic numbers on the face flickered occasionally, and the green glow shone harshly on the starat's eyes. Still, the clock gave him some sense of the passing of time. The chatter of starats outside was calming, keeping Rhys from worrying too much about being confined below ground. When he closed his eyes, he still saw shadows of the entity's many thousand eyes staring at him, but they were ghostly and pale.

A slight change came in the voices outside. The sound of pattering footsteps grew louder, and a few moments later the canvas sheet over Rhys's shelter was pulled to the side. Elijah poked his head in. He grinned from ear to ear. "I think it's finally happened."

"Oh?" Rhys asked, leaning forward but remaining sat down for the moment.

Elijah didn't fully come into the small shelter, though there was enough room for them both. They had enjoyed that forced proximity in the cold nights.

"Someone said something to the other. We haven't been able to see exactly what triggered this, but something has finally broken between Terra and Mars. The Martian fleet is being prepared," Elijah explained, his voice high pitched and excited, like a child who had found something wonderous in the back garden. "Essie thinks they might be preparing an attack against Terra."

Rhys yelped and jumped up to his feet, almost bashing his head against the low ceiling of the wooden shelter. "What? They're starting to move already?"

"The Terran fleet is amassing too. Ships are being recalled from more isolated outposts to return to the Star Hub," Elijah explained, still not lessening in his enthusiasm. "But that isn't even the most exciting thing."

Rhys pinned his ears flat against his head. "What else was there?"

Elijah grinned, beaming widely from ear to ear. "I intercepted another message from the Star Hub. They have a new defence system ready to deploy. One that they had been working on in secret for years. It's not been tested, but…" The starat shrugged.

"What defence?" Rhys asked. He hurriedly started to get dressed, expecting a request to see Stephanie. She had seen him without clothes on many times in the past, but he doubted she would be comfortable with that anymore. Nor the hundreds of starats outside.

Elijah cupped his hand around an imaginary globe. "A planet-wide protective shield."

"Holy shit," Rhys yelped. He stepped back, only partially dressed, and tripped over his own trousers. He fell back against the wall of the shelter, shifting the wooden structure and scraping it against the tiled floor. He took a moment to breath and recompose himself. "This is it. This is what the SFU are waiting for."

Elijah's eyes brightened. "Yep."

"We have to stop it," Rhys hissed. His tail swished. A war between Mars and Terra was nothing compared to the destruction that would happen should that shield be raised.

"We do," Elijah agreed. He held out a shirt for Rhys to wear. "Essie thinks she has an idea, but she'd like to run it by you first. She's working through some things with Arnav and Rina at the moment."

Rhys quickly slipped into the shirt on offer from Elijah. Out of habit, he slung his pistol around his waist, securing the belt into place. "Her office?"

"Nah. Too many people to squeeze into that tiny room," Elijah said. He held out his hand for Rhys to take. "She's on the Jubilee north platform."

"This is it, Elijah," Rhys said, his voice shaking slightly with the emotion that threatened to rip through him. "This is what starats have been waiting for."

Elijah grinned. "This is what we have been waiting for. You included."

"Not for as long," Rhys muttered, his ears folding in as he leaned into Elijah's side.

"Still as much a starat as the rest of us," Elijah said. He encouraged Rhys out of their shared shelter and onto the platform. The voices around them had not changed. The scent of grilled fish drifted on the air.

With growing familiarity, Rhys did not get lost as he made his way through the station. It helped that Elijah knew exactly where he was going as well, but the dark and dusty corridors were beginning to look varied to Rhys. The different platforms and their different uses were becoming more familiar to Rhys's mind, and he didn't need Elijah to nudge him in the right direction once.

Rhys's tail quivered as he ran through different scenarios in his mind. Thoughts of the planetary shield concerned him, but he was sure there was still more information to learn about it. That, above anything else, had to be the top priority. Only once Amy's plot had been stopped could they even consider the civil war brewing between Terra and Mars.

Stephanie was on the platform, using one of the crates as a makeshift table. As Rhys expected, four starats stood around her. Rina, Alistair, Arnav, and Skye crowded around the table.

Strewn across the crate was various written reports and transcripts. A holoprojector showed a technical readout of the Star Hub. Thick cabling running across the floor provided power for the projector and a pair of tablets, which were both currently switched off. The hum of a generator nearby made Rhys's ears flick in annoyance.

All eyes turned to Rhys as he approached the crate. He stood between Elijah and Alistair and placed his hands on the wood, looking over the information in front of him. Conversation had stopped as he approached. It took him a few seconds before the silence lingered, and that they were waiting for him to say something.

"A planet-wide shield is something I have seen before, on Centaura," Rhys said slowly. He sucked in his breath. "I don't think that's a coincidence. I wonder if the SFU is somehow responsible for the development of this technology, as Terra shouldn't have much reason to invest in one. It would be useless against projectiles."

"That is feasible," Stephanie said. She pushed across a piece of paper towards Rhys, upon which someone had quickly drawn a diagram of the activated shield around the planet. "We just have one problem. If we want to stop it being activated, then we need to do two things at once."

"I don't like the sound of that," Rhys muttered to himself. He pursed his lips and looked down at the diagram. He had never been given a full explanation for how the shield on Centaura had worked. The Stellar Guard had not trusted him with that information, and Rhys had found no fault with that reasoning. He wished he had been told now. It would have been useful to be able to compare the designs.

"The shield is powered by two different sources," Rina explained. She tapped her claw against the diagram, pointing to one dotted line that came from above, and then a second that originated on the planet.

Rhys moved his finger towards the upper source. "This must be on the Star Hub, right?" he asked. There was no other satellite orbiting

Terra that would be able to maintain the power necessary to fuel a planet-wide shield.

"Correct," Rina said. "The Star Hub will be outside the shield, but it has its own defences that make it almost indestructible."

"The second is in Windsor Castle," Alistair added. The black-furred starat crossed his arms in front of his chest. "We have to take down both if we want to disable the shield."

Rhys growled softly. "They're probably the two strongest guarded places in the entire system," he said, drumming his fingers against the table. His tail dipped low between his legs. "The Star Hub might be easier and taking that first might prevent air support against Windsor."

Stephanie shook her head. "We don't mean one then the other. We mean both, simultaneously."

"Fuck," Rhys said, running his hands over his face. "That's absolute madness."

"We have a few things to our advantage," Stephanie said. She looked around the group of starats surrounding her. She raised a finger for each point. "First, they're not going to be looking out for starats. Secondly, Terra is focused on Mars right now. They're not going to be keeping as close an eye on what's happening down here, unless they're in a priest's robe. Thirdly, Rhys has already planted the seed of rebellion in every starat in the system. The word goes out, and all starats down tools. Terra screeches to a halt without them, and that includes the Star Hub."

"So we time any attack with the starat strike," Skye said. She grinned and licked her lips. "Once we start, any starat we come across will join the fight. We may only start with a couple of thousand, but we'll be victorious with tens of thousands. Hundreds of thousands."

"If we can even make it close," Rhys said. He drummed his fingers against the crate. "These are two of the most heavily defended points in the system. Even starats are generally well-vetted before they're given access."

"A large scale attack likely won't work," Alistair said with a grimace. "We would get noticed too quickly. We'll have to go small, especially on Windsor. The Star Hub will have the advantage that many starats would be likely to join us once we begin, but that will not be a luxury in Windsor."

"Do we know when the Martian fleet may strike?" Rhys asked. If Terra was to deploy the planetary shield, then they would want to ensure that it was ready in time for an enemy strike.

"If their mobilisation continues at this rate, then we're looking within the next few days. Certainly in the next week," Stephanie replied. She swept her hand across the table. "We expect the shield to be raised before the Vatican make their strike."

"There's just one other complication on top of that," Rhys said. He looked around the crate. "We don't know when, or even if, the Centauran fleet arrives."

"They will be the joker in the pack," Stephanie admitted. "There isn't much we can do about them, except hope that they do not arrive too quickly. When is the soonest they could arrive?"

Rhys paused for a moment to make sure that he got the timeline right. "If they leave the same day Admiral Garter should have arrived, then we have another four or five days. So, about the same timeframe as Mars."

Alistair bared his teeth in a savage grin. "This is going to get messy."

Rhys glanced towards the starat who had not said anything during the meeting. Arnav had not said a single word since Rhys had arrived. "I know you said before that your powers mean you can't see some things, but a fleet arriving? Could you see that before it happens?"

Arnav nodded slowly. "I expect the subspace ripples should give me a few hours warning of the Centauran fleet's arrival," he said. He stared down at the table. "Other than that, I can know no more than you do."

"That's better than nothing. It could give us some warning should we need to act quickly," Rhys said. He scratched his chin. His eyes flicked back and forth as he scanned over all the information spread across the table.

Arnav glanced up at Stephanie. "I suggest splitting into two groups to attack both simultaneously. If we act quickly enough, they will struggle to scramble an effective defence to both locations. Better yet, if we control the Star Hub and Windsor, then we control Terra. Not just the shields are at stake here."

Alistair fidgeted uncomfortably. "Rhys was right. These are both the most well-guarded locations in the system. Is it even possible for two thousand starats to attack both at the same time?"

Arnav nodded. "Yes. It is possible because it is the only way." He flashed a smile. "You don't need to see the future to understand that."

"If we capture just the one," Elijah said slowly, "then the other will act quickly to crush us. We can't mistime this."

Alistair exhaled slowly, but he said nothing. Stephanie leaned to the side to listen to a whispered word from Rina. The human then nodded. "We have no choice but to make a move. Even if Rhys's information is wrong, and there is no subspace threat, this civil war gives us an unprecedented chance to make an impact. Terra is in disarray. We can't expect such a situation to arise again."

"How long do we need to prepare an assault?" Skye asked. Her tail swished eagerly, and her claws scraped against the side of the crate as though she simply couldn't contain her excitement.

"Three days, at least," Stephanie replied tersely.

"That doesn't leave a big window of opportunity," Rhys said. He glanced down over the plans again, making sure there was no information that he had missed. "If the Vatican or Centaura attacks before we're ready, we may lose our chance, and risk the SFU succeeding."

"And we still don't know for sure if the SFU have infiltrated our number," Arnav said, looking slowly around the table. "If they know we plan to attack, they might bring forward their plans to launch these subspace weapons."

Rhys pinned his ears back. He had been worried about that.

Elijah spoke up. "They won't be here still. If they were behind the development of the tech somehow, then the Denitchev bombs will be automatically linked to the activation of the shield."

All eyes turned to Elijah. "How do you know that?" Rina asked. Her eyes narrowed.

Elijah shrugged. "They wouldn't want to still be on the planet when the bombs went off. They'd be stuck in subspace with the rest of us. They'll be far away already."

"If that's true, then it makes it even more important to prevent the shield from being activated," Stephanie said. She held a hand to her chest. "I'll lead the attack on the Star Hub. Rhys, you will lead the assault on Windsor. You'll take Arnav, Elijah, and Skye with you. Rina and Alistair will come with me."

Rina swept her hand through the holographic projection of the Star Hub. "Getting up there might be the difficult part for us," she said. Her eyes flicked back and forth as she read through the diagnostics the projection gave her. She glanced up to Rhys. "I can have some readings and plans for Windsor for you to study."

"That would be appreciated, thank you," Rhys said, grateful for the offer. He couldn't think of how he could find a way into Windsor Castle, especially with a small force of armed starats. They would be shot down from a distance if they looked to be a threat.

"Whatever supplies you think you might need, we will try to provide," Stephanie added. She looked around the crate, at the starats gathered. "I understand we risk lives with this, but we have no other option. If we want freedom and respect for starats, then we must be prepared to spill blood. That blood may well be our own."

"I have already spilled blood," Skye growled. She bared her teeth and snarled. "I can spill more."

Rhys shuddered. He had seen Skye in action on Ceres. She was fearless, and he would be glad to have her by his side. He feared for any human who may try to cross her.

Stephanie met Rhys's eyes. Her lips were pursed, and her hands were tense against the surface of the crate. "There is just one more thing to discuss. We know what must be done, and I am proud that Essie's Heresy will be the one to liberate starats from their slavery." The human paused. She met the eye of Arnav and Rina in turn, then lowered her gaze. "It would not look right if a human was seen to be leading this change."

Rhys hissed softly and shook his head. "But this was your idea, wasn't it? You built this," he protested. He looked to Arnav and Rina, hoping they would come to Stephanie's defence as well, but neither starat did. They both leaned into the human but remained quiet. Rina's hand clasped Stephanie's.

The human nodded. "Yes. Without me, none of this would have happened. Essie's Heresy is mine, but I can no longer be Essie. That name is a symbol of freedom and hope for all starats, and so it must be a starat who wears that name. I have carried the name with the knowledge that I would always hand it over to a starat worthy of living up to his legacy."

Rhys bowed his head. He accepted that logic. Starats had reacted poorly to him on occasion when he had spoken about trying to change their situation. Some starats, especially those outside of Essie's Heresy would not like following a human to freedom. Especially not one who claimed the name of Essie. "Whoever you choose as Essie, I will follow them."

"I choose you, Rhys," Stephanie said.

"What?" Rhys yelped, taking a step back. His blood turned cold as he felt the eyes of everyone on him. He stammered and stumbled. "I… I can't. No… Arnav or Rina would be better. They've been down here longer with you."

"Starats look up to you, Rhys," Stephanie said. She moved away from the starats by her side. She crouched down in front of Rhys and took hold of his hands. "It's a figurehead position, mostly. A symbol they can look towards, and you are that symbol. If you take on the name Essie, then every single starat in this station will follow you to the very end."

Rhys trembled. His feet felt unsteady as he pulled away from Stephanie. He didn't want to accept this. Essie was not a name taken lightly. He was an icon for starats, the greatest sign of hope they had. What right did a former human have to that name?

"Rhys…" Elijah spoke quietly. "If there was ever a starat worthy of being named after Essie, it's you."

"He's right," Skye added. The Cerian starat stood partway between Rhys and the table. She twisted the tip of her tail in her hands. "Essie would be proud of you."

"We are all proud of you," Rina added. She inclined her head to Rhys. "We will follow you."

Rhys turned away. Tears burned at his eyes. "Fuck," he whispered. He rubbed at his muzzle.

"Will you do this?" Stephanie asked.

Rhys blinked away the tears, though his vision continued to blur. He breathed in deep and turned back to face the others. He leaned on Elijah for support. "I will, yes. If you ask it of me, then I will be Essie."

Stephanie smiled. Her eyes swum as well, though there was a little tightness around her mouth. "Good. You should record that message as well, the one you want to send out across the system."

Rhys's throat dried out, but he nodded anyway. If his face was going to be the one to bring the Centauran fleet to Sol, then he might as well also be the one to invoke a starat rebellion. Twitch would be so proud of him. "I'll do it."

"Do you know what to say?" Stephanie asked. She rested one hand on the computer as a sudden silence fell through the station.

"Now?" Rhys gasped. He ran his tongue over his sharp teeth and shivered. His clawless fingers dragged over his palm as he held both hands to his mouth.

"There's no reason to delay," Stephanie said. She did not move. No one did. All eyes remained on Rhys. Elijah's hand rested on his shoulder.

Rhys's mind worked quickly. His eyes did not stop moving as he looked around the station, taking in the gaze of every single starat. If he was to truly take on the mantle of Essie, then he would be the hope for them all; he would represent them all. That was a big weight on his shoulders, and he felt the mass of London pressing down on him. Though his throat was still dry, he nodded again. "I know what to say."

Stephanie pressed a couple of buttons, before giving Rhys a thumbs up. No one else spoke. No one even moved. Arnav's pale eyes stared at a spot just over Rhys's left shoulder.

"Starats of the empire, this is Essie," Rhys barked, projecting his voice with power and confidence. He put himself back in the mind of a captain on the bridge, something that felt almost a lifetime ago. "For too long have we let humans hold us down and keep us bound in chains. That ends now. I call for every starat to step back and stop. Accept no order from humans. Accept no demand. This is not a call to fight, a call to war. I simply ask that you stop work, every last one of you. Stay safe. Protect one another, and we will see a brighter dawn for our species. Essie calls on you."

Rhys slumped back into Elijah as the fires in his belly faded. He was acutely aware of the stares. Elijah's arm fell protectively around his chest.

"That should do nicely," Stephanie said quietly.

Rhys twisted his muzzle. "I was the person who I'm telling them to stand against," he whispered. His ears curled and he looked away from Arnav's constant gaze. "I was the human who held starats in chains."

"And so was I," Stephanie said. She swept her arm around. "And look at what we've been able to accomplish."

"Could we have done this by ourselves?" Rina asked. She shrugged. "Maybe, in time. Not here, though. Not now."

Skye nodded in agreement. She bared her teeth. "You standing up to Captain Jacques was the first domino to fall. You started this because you expected to be treated like a human. Do you still want that?"

"No," Rhys said quietly. "I want to be treated like a starat, but that does not mean I should be treated less than a human."

"Exactly," Arnav said with a growl. He still gazed above Rhys's shoulder, his pale eyes unblinking. "You are one of us, fighting as one of us. Who you were does not matter. It is only who you are, and who you will be that matters. This is why you can take on Essie's name."

Rina chuckled. "Of course you'd be the one to speak of the future."

Arnav finally turned his head. He grinned at Rina. "It does not take my gifts to know that Rhys has been, and will continue to be, the trigger for revolution."

Rhys sighed and bowed his head. "Twitch told me I would be, the very first time we spoke."

"Then look forward to when he gets to rub it in and say, 'I told you so'," Arnav said. He took a step forward and put his hand on Rhys's shoulder, next to Elijah's.

"You can't know that will happen," Rhys said, still staring down at the floor between Arnav's feet.

"I can't know, you're right," Arnav said. He gently placed a hand on Rhys's chin and encouraged him to look up. The starat placed a gentle kiss on Rhys's cheek. "It is up to you to make that future happen, Essie.. It is up to all of us."

Stephanie put her hand on Arnav and Rina. Both Skye and Alistair closed in so that all the starats present were in contact with each other, including the lone human as well. Stephanie spoke quietly. "You are Essie now, Rhys. You will lead your starats to Windsor. No one will see you as the human you once were."

Feeling safe and comforted in the close proximity to everyone, Rhys sighed again and nodded. "You're right. I can do this. We all can. For starats everywhere."

Stephanie smiled. She cupped Rhys's head in her hands for a moment, then stepped away. "I will let you all go now, but I will be in constant communication. I know the starats we have here. I know who is most capable. I will sort out who goes with who. Our time has come. Good luck, everyone. I'll speak to you soon."

Rhys was the only one who saluted Stephanie. She smiled and saluted him back.

***

Rhys frowned as he hunched over the holographic display. He was sat on the Jubilee line tracks with the projector, as it was the only place where he could find enough room to run the display. Elijah and Kalisha sat on the tracks with him, though a cluster of starats gathered on the edge of the platform to watch him. Their legs dangled over the side as they chattered to themselves, but never interrupted Rhys's musings.

For over an hour, Rhys had been browsing through the read-outs on Windsor Castle. The place was a fortress, almost as formidable as the Star Hub. Guard posts around the perimeter provided vantage points in all directions, meaning any potential threat could be spotted, day or night. There was only one gate in and out of the perimeter walls, and their foundations ran deep. Any starats who approached the gate would be questioned and checked. They wouldn't be able to sneak inside and hope the humans would be too oblivious to search for weapons. Any more than a dozen starats would rightly be treated with suspicion.

Elijah scratched at his jaw. "The castle has dungeons, doesn't it? Below surface levels?"

Rhys flicked his ears. He swiped his hand at the holographic projection, sweeping to a different view. This one showed the different levels of the sprawling inner buildings, which included four that sunk below the surface. "Yeah. No way in from the outside though."

"Are you sure about that?" Elijah asked, pointing towards a couple of features on the eastern walls of the lowest levels.

"Air circulation filters. That's not going to be much use to us," Rhys said. He tracked where the ventilation system reached the surface, but the holographic map didn't show that feature. "It has to be inside the grounds somewhere, inside the walls."

Elijah shook his head. "I don't think it is." His finger traced along the small vents towards the edge of the map. "This uses the same system the Underground used. They hooked into the same network."

Kalisha looked up. She furrowed her brow. "Are you saying…"

"We can reach the dungeons below Windsor through the Underground," Elijah said with a grin. He swiped his hand a few times and the projection changed from Windsor to a map of the ancient train network. He pointed towards one line amongst the myriad of the spider web. "We take this line here. That takes us closest to Windsor. It won't be a comfortable squeeze through the ventilation system, but it should be a way in."

"Wouldn't they have those guarded too?" Kalisha asked. She frowned as she looked down at the map.

"Not if they think these tunnels are all sealed off and inaccessible," Elijah replied. He narrowed down the focus of the projection to show just the disused tunnel close to Windsor Castle. There was no evidence of a connecting ventilation system, but that didn't deter Elijah. "This is the best way, I'm sure of it."

Rhys clicked his tongue and furrowed his brow. The tip of his muzzle twitched as his ears curled downwards. "I think it's our best shot. It will limit how quickly we can get numbers inside, but if we're smart and lucky, we should be able to get in undetected. It's also close to where we believe the shield generator is located."

"It might take us a while to walk there. We probably don't want to delay too long," Elijah said. He looked up to Rhys, who remained staring down at the hologram for a few moments longer.

"I'll speak to Stephanie and see if we can make a move sooner. We don't want to miss our opportunity," Rhys said. He clenched his fists. Fear welled up within him, but he was experienced enough not to let that show or overwhelm him. He would be able to use that fear. In combat, it would fuel him and keep him alert.

Kalisha raised her hand. "Just forgetting one thing, aren't you? Even when we get inside, this is still the elite of the elite. They're not going to be pushovers." She swept her hand around to indicate the starats perched on the edge of the platform, watching them. "You've had three days on them. They're not ready for this."

Rhys raised his brow. He bit his lower lip, then turned on his toes to face the watching starats. He flicked his tail away from his legs. "You all heard what we're planning," he called out, raising his voice to attract the attention of the entire platform. "You know the risks. You know what's at stake. Are you prepared to fight?"

A loud roar of approval echoed through the platform as every starat present shouted out their assent. They cheered and punched their fists into the air.

"Fuck yeah, Essie," one shouted. Laughter followed.

Rhys grinned back at Kalisha. He knew that the assault would take far more than just confidence and bravado, but it never hurt to have a motivated group. "I think they're as ready as they are ever going to be."

"I can only hope you're right," Kalisha replied. She lowered her eyes and didn't make any further complaints. Rhys could tell from the set of her shoulders and curled ears that she had many other things on her mind, but she kept them to herself.

Rhys flicked his tail. He leaned in close to Elijah, kissing him briefly on the cheek. "I'm going to arrange supplies with Stephanie. I'll be back soon, alright?"

"Try and get all the good stuff," Elijah said, grinning widely.

"I'll do my best."

chapter eighteen

Even despite the urgency to leave, it was still another two days below ground before Rhys's party was ready to depart. He had around nine hundred starats at his back, each armed with weapons and carrying supplies to last three days beyond the safety of Green Park. They did not expect to travel for more than a day on the march to Windsor, but the western reaches of the old Underground network were not maintained or scouted beyond Acton, close to the sprawling Heathrow spaceport. Vibrations from the spaceport were expected to have caused damage to the tunnels, which could extend the journey time.

Rhys walked ahead of the group with Arnav. They didn't speak much, except for when Arnav needed to act as the guide. The route was simple, though. The walk to Windsor was an easy one through the Underground, as the castle was on the Piccadilly line. Dozens of stations were between them and Windsor, but the way was made simple by there being no need to change to a new line. Occasional offshoots would have given a choice of route, but Rhys knew to remain on the primary track.

Once, the Underground network hadn't been confined solely to tunnels below the surface. Large parts had risen to the ground level, but sometime in the past the decision had been made to keep the tracks running solely underground. Then the network had been abandoned entirely, leaving the empty tunnels running below London.

At each station, Rhys swung his torch up to read the name, checking it off against the map he'd secured to his wrist. There were no turns to make, but Rhys still felt nervous of taking the wrong route and getting lost in the darkness.

Elijah often walked by Rhys's side, though he occasionally dropped back with Kalisha and Skye. They passed messages to and from the other starats. An initial wave of enthusiasm and excitement had faded the further they walked. In the unchanging tunnels it was difficult to maintain a constant passion for the coming events. Rhys didn't even try. They would be able to rekindle that flame when they made it to Windsor. First, they had to get there.

The tunnels were damaged in places. Walls had started to crumble from decades without maintenance, but nowhere was completely blocked, much to Rhys's relief. Rusted remains of a train lurked at one station, but it was little more than a shell of crumbling metal.

The starats didn't stop. They kept the march up for all the day, for what passed as day when there was no sunlight to see by. The only light they had came from their torches. The only sounds came from their own feet and voices, with nothing coming from the surface. That all changed a few stations after Acton, on the approach towards the massive complex that made up the Heathrow spaceport. It was one of the largest ports on Terra, stretching out across many kilometres.

The noise started with a faint rumbling in the ground, lasting for a dozen seconds before falling into silence again. The vibrations ran up Rhys's legs, starting at his feet and soon shaking his whole body. With each step, the vibrations became more severe. Dust plumed through the air as the tunnels themselves shook. Cracks had appeared in the rounded walls, but nothing appeared in danger of collapse just yet.

Rhys kept a wary eye on the darkened ceiling just in case. With every deep rumble of another shuttle launch, he could imagine the ceiling cracking that little bit more. Would there be any warning before the ceiling collapsed entirely?

"How many shuttles launch from here?" Kalisha had come back up to Rhys's side, and was staring up at the ceiling with wide eyes.

"Just under three a minute, during the day," Elijah replied, answering before Rhys could do so. He flicked his ears back. "Must be a busy day for them, as they're averaging nearly four."

"They're preparing for war," Rhys muttered quietly, almost inaudible above the vibrations through the tunnel. "A lot of personnel are going up to the Star Hub. We can only hope Stephanie and the others are able to blend in."

"Rina will keep them safe," Arnav said. He walked by Rhys's other side, his eyes constantly on the darkness ahead. His torch swept through the tunnel, glimmering off small patches of moisture that dripped down the cracked walls. "She always does."

Despite the assurance from Arnav, Rhys still felt a shiver of worry pass down his back at the thought of what was happening on the surface. Stephanie was leading a large group of starats up to the Star Hub. Rhys wasn't sure which of them had the easier task.

The vibrations through the tunnel got louder and stronger before they began to recede. For half an hour, Rhys felt like they walked directly beneath the firing engines of the shuttles. All conversations fell into silence for a short while, simply because they could hear nothing else when the regular roars pierced through the tunnels. Gradually, the sounds grew quieter again, and the endless march through the darkness continued in relative silence.

Rhys knew from the maps that there wasn't a long walk after Heathrow, but the journey was taking its toll on most of the starats. They grew weary and hungry from the long walk, and conversation never picked up again with the same brightness as before the spaceport. Nerves and fear were growing with every step closer to Windsor.

Almost an hour after leaving the worst of Heathrow behind them, the starats finally made it to Windsor. The tunnel opened into another station. Two platforms ran opposite each other, with space for two tracks between them. Torchlight shone on the crumbling walls to reveal the name Windsor etched into the faded signs.

"We're here," Rhys muttered. He pulled himself up onto the nearest platform and slowly turned on the spot, shining his torch around. There were stairwells on both platforms, at either end of the station. But for those, the only way in and out of the station was the tunnels themselves.

Elijah stood by Rhys's side. "It's getting late. Were we going to rest here, or push on?"

Rhys glanced back to the tracks. A few of the starats had taken the opportunity to get off their feet and were sat against the curved wall at the far side of the tunnel. "We'll rest here for the night. We can attack when we're rested and refreshed in the morning."

"Assuming no one from above hears us," Elijah said quietly.

Rhys flicked his tail. "Do you think that might be a risk?"

Elijah curled his ears inwards. "I haven't detected any sensors down here, but that doesn't mean there aren't any. I'm just hoping they're arrogant enough to believe these tunnels are safe."

"If there's one thing I've learned since becoming a starat, it's that humans are arrogant," Rhys replied, placing his hand on Elijah's shoulder. "They may have connected the ventilation system of Windsor to the Underground, but I doubt they'll consider it something worth guarding."

"We know they don't have patrols down here," Arnav spoke up. He stood by Elijah's side. His green eyes stared forward into the darkness, seeming to look through the shadows. His right ear flicked up. "If it pleases you to know, I have seen nothing to suggest that we are in any danger just yet. If they had already detected us, then I would likely know about it. Tomorrow, it doesn't take my gifts to know that we will all be in mortal peril."

"Encouraging," Rhys muttered, but he knew everything Arnav said was true. There was no hiding from that knowledge. Starats and humans were both going to die, and there was nothing anyone could do to stop that. He took a deep breath and glanced around the platform again. "We should find the ventilation shafts so that we're prepared for the morning."

Arnav nodded. "If it's alright with you, I'll remain behind and start organising food for everyone."

Rhys glanced up towards the stairs at the rear of the platform, then back to the starats. "We'll be back soon. Save some food for us."

Arnav smirked. He quickly saluted Rhys, before turning away and disappearing amongst the crowd. Rhys briefly caught sight of Kalisha and Skye amongst the starats, but they had both sat down and seemed unwilling to remain on their feet any longer. It would just be Elijah and himself.

No one looked up as the two starats made their way off the platform. Their torches provided the only illumination as they ascended towards the surface. A dark concourse, much like the one at Green Park, circled over the station platforms. No light shone from the surface. Dust coated the floor in a thick layer, and the smell of oil and grime filled Rhys's nose. He wrinkled his muzzle and held a hand over his face.

"We're looking for the maintenance areas," Elijah said. His muzzle was wrinkled in distaste too, but he hadn't covered his nose. "From there, we should be able to find the ventilation system easy enough."

Rhys's torch shone up to the ceiling. Deteriorated and cracked metal pipes hung down from the concrete ceiling, snaking across the concourse chamber. Small grills had once been the only holes in the pipes, providing points for air to be circulated around the underground facility. Rhys's tail tucked against his legs as his torchlight traced across the pipes. He hoped the ones that connected the Underground and Windsor Castle were better maintained.

The pipes across the ceiling all converged towards one point. Directly below where the pipes punched through the wall was a door, partially concealed by the dirt and grime that covered most of the walls. Though the door was locked, a well-placed kick from Elijah forced it open. The screech of the hinges set Rhys's fur up, and the plume of dust from inside the dark room beyond initiated a brief coughing fit.

By the time the dust cleared, Elijah had already stepped forward into the darkness. A narrow corridor snaked down to the left, descending another flight of stairs.

Rhys almost slipped on the stairs. His foot slid across a thick layer of grime and dirt, before he grabbed hold of the rusted metal bannister to the side. The bannister screeched and almost snapped off the wall at Rhys's touch, but he was able to find his balance again before continuing with more caution.

"Mind your step," Rhys said. His heart thumped away inside his chest. The last thing he wanted was a tumble down some ancient stairwell and break his neck at the bottom. He definitely didn't want the same to happen to Elijah.

Slowly, one step at a time, the two starats descended further into darkness. The faint, distant sounds of the small army of starats receded into nothing, replaced by the gentle hum and whir of machinery. A series of fans rotated, filling the otherwise total silence with the gentle whoosh of air and occasional screech of metal.

Rhys pushed open another door at the bottom of the stairs. His torch lit up a compact room with deteriorating computers around the walls. Most looked ancient, with absolutely no chance of working. One, however, looked much more recent. Small red lights lit up as

Rhys approached, his torch sweeping over the darkened screens. His tail flicked. They must occasionally send humans here to run maintenance on their ventilation systems. Though he could have accessed maintenance records on the computer, he didn't dare switch it on. That would likely flag as unexpected activity in Windsor. There were few quicker ways to get guards out to them.

Elijah's torch moved higher, towards the ceiling. Wide metal pipes were attached to the ceiling, cutting across from one wall to the other. Small grates provided places where the panelling could be pulled down, giving access to the inside of the ventilation system. Unlike the pipes in the main concourse, these appeared perfectly intact and gleamed with a brighter light than the grimy walls and ceiling.

"You mind giving me a boost up there?" Rhys asked, pointing towards the pipes.

Elijah put his torch down on the nearby desktop, before holding his hands out for Rhys to step in. He then lifted the starat up with seemingly little effort at all.

Rhys reached for the grate and pulled hard. Metal screeched and clanked, but the grate didn't fall free from the first pull. He tried again, and this time a rivet popped apart. The starat grimaced to himself and managed to force his fingers inside the small gap he had created, wiggling his hand in deeper to further pull apart the grate.

"This would have been easier if I could still use subspace," he muttered to himself. One pull with that fearsome power and he would have ripped the grate off. He shifted his feet against Elijah's hands to get a better angle to pull down. He wouldn't trade the use of his arms away, even if it allowed him to use subspace again.

"Should we get Kalisha?" Elijah asked from below.

"Nah, I got this," Rhys grunted. He pulled down hard, practically lifting himself up from Elijah's hands in the process. Once more, he tensed his elbows and pulled, putting all his weight into the movement. This time, the grate tore away from the pipe; three more rivets popping away and bouncing against the floor and disappearing into the shadows. Rhys fell back into Elijah's hands, with the other starat almost dropping him.

After tossing the grate to the side, Rhys got his elbows up against the inside of the pipe and pulled himself up. For a moment, his feet flailed in the air before he felt a gentle push up from Elijah. Inside the ventilation shaft was perfectly black, with only the sound of fans and the gentle movement of cool air on his fur to prick at his senses. The air had absolutely no scent to it at all.

Once his knees were inside the shaft, Rhys slowly turned around to face down towards the hole he had made. He reached down for Elijah to pass him the torch, finally providing some light in the darkness.

Rhys glanced in both directions. One way ended just a few metres away, a little beyond the side wall of the room below. After a quick check, Rhys saw that instead the shaft angled vertically and rose towards the surface. In the other direction, the small ventilation shaft stretched out as far as Rhys could see, with his vision only interrupted by a series of rotating fans at regular intervals. Those would need to be deactivated or removed, but Rhys had plans for that. He could see nothing else that blocked access through to Windsor Castle, which would be at the far end of the shaft. The starats would have to travel in single file, but they would be able to get through to their target, and that was the important part.

Satisfied that everything was how it should be, Rhys put the torch into his mouth before dropping down through the hole, gripping onto the edge with both hands. Elijah wasn't there to support him, but Rhys waited for just a moment before dropping down the last metre and a half to the floor.

Taking the torch back into his hands, Rhys looked around the room. Elijah had moved to the switched off computers, sweeping his hand over the dusty keyboards. The other starat glanced back, his tail held low. "After all of this, are you still interested in that date?" Elijah asked, his voice low and soft.

Rhys flicked his ears back, surprised by the question. "Of course. Why would I not be?"

Elijah didn't look back. He bowed his head and rested his hands on the terminal. "I just thought, with Stephanie still being alive, you might have… you know."

In the darkness, Rhys couldn't properly see Elijah. He appeared as little more than a black shadow. Rhys's shoulder sagged, and the light from his torch wavered as he lowered his hand. "It's been fifteen years since I last saw her. I gave up on ever seeing her again, because I truly believed she was dead. Both of us are completely different people now. Literally, for me. Even if I wanted to go back to her, she wouldn't want me. She has Rina."

"You're not even tempted?" Elijah asked. He slowly turned around, though still leaned back against the terminal behind him.

"Ten years ago, maybe I would have been," Rhys admitted with a shrug. "But after then? Not at all. Even less so now." He reached out to take hold of Elijah's hand. "What's brought this on?"

Elijah didn't answer for a few seconds. He bowed his head and smiled. "I just got worried. What would you see in me? I'm just a starat with no memory of who he really is, other than what humans told me I am. I'm an experiment that got away from its masters."

Rhys tilted his head. His left ear folded over. "Wasn't Essie an escaped experiment? The first one?"

Elijah snorted. "You think I'm like Essie? I'm not even as good as Stephanie, nor you, let alone the first starat. I'm nothing to him. You're a brave leader, which is why you can take up his name, but I can't."

"But you're important to me," Rhys said, pulling Elijah a little closer. He kissed him gently. "You've saved my life so many times already. I owe you everything. Things may not be very… conventional at the moment, but once this has all settled down, I'm willing to give it all a try."

"You mean that?" Elijah asked. His fingers squeezed tight around Rhys's.

"Of course. I'm a little rusty with the whole romance and dating thing, but I'm sure I can work out what needs to be done," Rhys replied, smirking in the darkness.

"You've still got more experience than me," Elijah said. He leaned forward and kissed Rhys back.

Rhys rested his head against Elijah's shoulder for a moment, before sighing softly. "We should report back that we found the way to Windsor."

Elijah grumbled lightly beneath his breath, a quiet growl in the back of his throat. "I suppose we must. Is this what a military life is like all the time?"

"Not quite. Normally I'm just sat on a ship being bored," Rhys admitted. He slipped his hand around Elijah's waist as they started to walk back towards the stairs.

"Do you think you'll want to go back to the military after all of this?" Elijah asked. He leaned his head sideways, his cheek resting on the top of Rhys's head.

Rhys frowned. That was a thought he had not properly entertained. For now, there was no after. There was only what lay before him and the threat of Windsor looming large. "I don't know," he said. "I don't know what else I would do."

"Plenty of time to think about it afterwards," Elijah said. He stroked his fingers through Rhys's fur. "Let's just keep each other safe until we've won."

"That sounds like a good idea. Let's do that."

***

The night passed by without any danger coming to the Underground. Conversations were muted and tension spread through the starats, though they were able to rest together and share a meal. The food was surprisingly good, being better than the rations Rhys was used to when on his ship. He had exchanged a few messages with Stephanie before he had attempted some sleep, enquiring how she had been able to carry out her preparation. Everything had gone smoothly for her, just as things had for Rhys. Now they were both in position, ready to initiate their attacks.

Rhys had not slept well, but he was able to put the poor night of sleep behind him with a much-needed coffee. He had vague recollections of bad dreams, but he couldn't recall the specifics, no matter how hard he tried. All he could remember was the sensation of dread and the quickening of his heart. They were nothing like the ultra-vivid dreams he had experienced of Stephanie and Edgar Scott.

It was a morning without sunlight. Torchlight was all Rhys had to see by as he made his final preparations. Silence was all around him. Only the occasional barked order from Arnav filled the abandoned station. Grim determination had filled the starats. Rhys looked around them, meeting their eyes when he could, and struggled not to think about how many of them were going to die. Death was inevitable in war. Rhys had conditioned himself to accept that. It didn't mean he liked the idea of leading people to their deaths.

Rhys clipped an earbud – modified for a starat's use – into his ear, giving him quick and easy connection to the voice channels he would be running with Arnav, Elijah, and Stephanie. A small wire microphone ran down his cheek, having to be twisted into a better position to account for his muzzle. He grimaced and sent a few test messages to Arnav on the far side of the station to make sure his equipment worked. Essie's Heresy had been doing good work in preparing starats beneath London, but there was only so much they could do with equipment designed for humans.

With his pistols secured at his hips, Rhys also sheathed the short knife he had been given. Most starats had their claws as weapons, but Rhys still felt vulnerable without his. A knife close to hand helped soothe those worries slightly.

A chirp in his ear warned him of an incoming communication. "How are you doing, Essie?" Stephanie asked.

Rhys's ears flicked back, still not used to being called such. "We're almost ready to move for the ventilation shafts. Are you in position?"

"We're good to go here," Stephanie replied, after only a moment of delay. "Rina's misdirection has proven an absolute charm."

Rhys looked around the dark station. A few murmured voices still spoke in conversation, but his was the loudest. He locked eyes with Arnav. He tapped his clawed foot against the concrete platform, before addressing Stephanie again. "Give us a little while longer. Once I'm in position, I'll let you know. Then we can send the broadcast."

"Just let me know when," Stephanie replied. "We're safe here for a while yet, so you've got time."

"Speak to you soon," Rhys said. He kept his hand to his ear for a few more seconds, just in case Stephanie had anything more to add, but the line remained quiet. There was nothing more to say, nothing more to plan. It was time.

Rhys rose to his feet and lifted his hand. What little conversation there was around the station died out. "Let's move out," Rhys called. Those few starats who had not already been standing got up. Fists were raised to the air, and a growing murmur of anticipation began to spread. This would have been the moment for a speech or encouraging message to share amongst his forces, but Rhys knew that one wasn't needed. Everyone knew what they were walking into. They knew what to expect and didn't need any more reminders. The time had come for action.

The sound of hundreds of starat feet filled the abandoned station. Rhys took the lead, with Kalisha and Elijah on either side of him. The long trail of starats behind them would go on for some time, forced to go two-by-two down the stairs in the maintenance corridor, and then to single file in the ventilation shafts.

A stepladder had been found during the night, preventing the need for one starat to help push others up towards the ventilation shafts. It already stood ready in the middle of the room, and Kalisha was the first to rise. She hesitated at the top, not yet slipping into the shaft. Rhys remained just below her. Elijah had moved to the terminal.

"You ready?" Rhys asked Elijah.

Elijah took a moment to connect himself up to the terminal. He tensed for a moment, then took a deep breath. "I'm ready. Deactivating sensors and alarms within the ventilation system. They'll probably notice before too long at the other end, but it should give us a little while."

"Alright, Kalisha. You go on ahead," Rhys said, turning his head to look up at the starat just above him.

"This isn't going to go wrong at all," Kalisha mumbled, her voice barely loud enough for Rhys to hear. Her words certainly didn't travel any further than him. Despite her complaints, she still clambered up the rest of the ladder and slipped inside the ventilation shaft. She crawled ahead on her hands and knees, towards the first of the rotating fans.

Rhys poked his head up into the shaft behind her. Metal screeched and the flow of air was disrupted against his fur. Bright colours flashed just in front of Kalisha, and the fan snapped back against the side wall to free the way ahead.

Kalisha's shoulders sagged, and she rested her chin on the cool metal surface beneath her.

"Are you alright?" Rhys called ahead. There would be a problem if Kalisha wasn't able to continue, as she was needed to break through the dozen other fans between them and Windsor.

Through the darkness, Rhys could barely see Kalisha's silent thumbs up. She started to move forward again, and Rhys followed right behind. Following him came the rest of the starats, making their slow way into the ventilation shaft. Rhys tried not to think too hard about the additional weight pulling down on the ancient struts. At least the ground supported the shaft for most of its length.

At a rate that seemed painfully slow to Rhys, he crawled through the ventilation shaft. The gentle movement of air diminished further as Kalisha dismantled each of the fans and pushed them to the side. There was no familiar scent of cinnamon that came with Kalisha's subspace abilities. Rhys's ears flattened. The loss of those powers still concerned him. They would have been useful, but the pain in his arms had made those abilities almost unusable at times.

The metal shaft made a lot of noise as the starats crawled through it. There was no getting around that. Claws tapped against the surface, and the weight made the metal creak and buckle. There was no indication that their presence had been discovered. Rhys could hear nothing outside the ventilation shaft.

More than ever, Rhys was put in mind of his isolation on Mars. Though sound was all around him, his vision was limited to just a narrow shaft of light, and even that was mostly obscured by Kalisha right in front of him. But for her legs, there was little he could see through the darkness.

"Left or right?" Kalisha asked, coming to a sudden halt.

Rhys only just avoided crawling into her. "Uh, left," he said, mentally bringing up the map he had studied of the ventilation network, and where in the Windsor dungeons they wanted to come out. The route was simple enough. One left turn, and they would soon come to a way out on their right.

Sure enough, Kalisha came to another stop just a few minutes later. Pale light shone against her fur from the right, and Rhys peered around her to see that there was a grate in the side of the shaft. A dusty floor stretched out on the other side, with heavy crates and boxes obscuring most of the room. The smell of dust was strong on the air, but there was no scent of humans around.

Kalisha pushed hard at the grate, shoving it backwards and ripping it away from the wall. Her subspace ability prevented it from crashing against the nearest crate or floor, but Rhys still grimaced at the sound of metal ripping apart. He half-expected to hear the boots of humans running closer, but the dungeon room remained quiet.

Kalisha crawled out and leaned against the nearest crate. Rhys followed just after her, partially crouched down with his hand on his pistol. With a gesture from his hand, he encouraged the starats following him to spill out from the ventilation shaft.

Slowly, Rhys crept further forward. The darkened room was in part of the most ancient corner of the castle. The walls were thick stone, and the ceiling was shrouded in shadow. The dusty floor had not been disturbed for a long time. There was only one exit; a wide flight of stairs led up to a closed door.

Rhys crept up the stairs and placed his ear against the wooden door. He could hear nothing from beyond, but he still grimaced any time a starat made a noise below. Every second he lingered he felt the tension rising. He wanted to be moving again, but he knew he needed to wait for all the starats to come through. They would be ready to act should their presence be discovered, but for the moment the castle above seemed oblivious to the threat in the dungeons.

Arnav came up the stairs to crouch by Rhys's side. He said nothing as he checked over his pistol, keeping one wary eye on the door. Skye followed just after him. She moved with a nervous energy, her tail and hands twitching with almost every step. She grinned with a savage smile.

Rhys held a finger to his lips, making sure that neither asked any questions. There was no need to ensure they knew the plan. They had gone over it enough times for the plan to be burned into Rhys's mind, along with the most likely backups needed. All three of them knew what, or at least who, they were waiting for.

Twenty minutes of painful waiting passed by. The hushed activity grew larger below as the starats all filtered through the ventilation system. Finally, the last starat came through, their numbers spilling out from the rendezvous point. Elijah pushed through the tightly packed crowd to find Rhys.

"Alarms triggered," Elijah whispered, speaking quietly right into Rhys's ear. "They may be sending a troop out to the station to investigate."

"Just means less here then," Rhys muttered back. He quickly sent a text message up to Stephanie to inform her that they were making their move. He got an almost instant reply.

Rhys knew what that meant. His voice had been projected through the system, telling every starat to stop work, to down their tools and throw off the chains that had been used to bind them. Rhys's voice. Essie's message. The time had come. There could be no more delays. Rhys signalled an advance. He pushed open the door and stepped outside.

The assault on Windsor Castle had begun.

chapter nineteen

Silence and stealth were critical to success. If they were discovered too soon, then a prolonged firefight would ensue, and Rhys did not have the time for that. Destroying the shield generator was critical, or he would be making Stephanie's assault on the Star Hub useless. He was also aware that his attack would be useless should Stephanie fail, but he had confidence in her.

Keeping so many starats hidden inside Windsor Castle was an impossible ask. There were cameras located all through the lower levels of the castle. It would take one security guard monitoring them to raise the alarm and their presence would be known. Rhys unholstered the pistol from his left hip and gripped the weapon tightly. He had to be prepared to use it at a moment's notice.

The dungeons of the old castle were mostly dark rooms and narrow corridors with stone walls. Winding, spiral staircases slowly rose towards the surface and the more modern parts of the castle. Stone was replaced by metal, brick, and plaster, with tiled flooring clicking beneath Rhys's feet with every step. Darkness still reigned supreme, with all the ceiling lights switched off.

Using the holographic map projected from his wrist, Rhys never once faltered with directions. He paused only to make sure the way was clear, and that his army of starats remained close to his tail.

Footsteps sounded ahead. Rhys held his hand up, calling a halt. He quickly scanned over the terrain ahead. There was no cover to hide behind. A few closed doors lined the long corridor, before it angled to the right a dozen metres ahead. That was where the footsteps came from. Two sets. Two humans. Likely a regular patrol. If they had been discovered, there would have been more of them.

Still signalling for the others to remain still, Rhys crept forward. He tried to walk on the base of his toes, keeping his claws in the air so they didn't click against the tiled floor. Pressing his back against the wall, Rhys crouched low and snuck closer to the corner.

The humans moved slowly. A quiet murmur of conversation passed between them, and their torchlights swung across the floor not far from Rhys's feet. The starat tensed and braced himself. He lifted his pistol.

As soon as the two humans stepped into view, Rhys fired. Two quick shots. One. Two. The humans didn't have time to react before they fell. Rhys's aim had been true, finding the gaps in their armour at their throats. They didn't even have time to call for help.

Rhys scampered across to the fallen bodies, making sure they were both dead. The shots had been clean. He tried not to look at their eyes. He holstered his pistol and took an automatic rifle from the dead men; high powered and with plenty of spare ammunition. The gun strained his muscles. He considered leaving it behind but changed his mind. It would be cumbersome, but useful. He grimaced to himself and looked up the stairs around the corner. He couldn't see the top, but he knew they weren't far from the ground level of the castle. That would be where the real struggle began.

"Door," Arnav called out.

Rhys didn't hesitate. He hefted his rifle up to his shoulder and squeezed the trigger. The recoil almost threw off his aim, but his grip squeezed tight around the weapon. A spray of automatic fire burst against the doorway at the top of the stairs just as it opened. Three humans fell before anyone even knew what had happened.

Shouts echoed down from above, and the patter of hundreds of starat feet came from behind. Under the cover of Rhys's suppression fire, the flood of starats began to advance.

Offence was the only form of defence. Without cover, Rhys could only keep up the assault to force back the human defenders pinned behind the doorway, where they couldn't accurately return fire. Reloading needed to be quick and smooth, with only a few seconds before Rhys needed to suppress the defenders once more.

Starats pushed open the door at the top of the stairs. Some fell back, wounded, but others forced their way through. Rhys ceased fire the moment he wasn't needed and hurried up after those who had taken point.

Bright light dazed Rhys for a moment. An alarm blared loudly, wailing as it rose and fell in pitch. Rhys's ears folded down slightly. He grimaced and gritted his pointed teeth together. He stood amongst a cluster of starats who had pushed aside the last of the human defenders. Only half a dozen humans had been at the top of the stairs. There would be many more to come.

A wide lobby opened up a couple of metres to the right of the door. Heavy oak cabinets and tables lined the side of the lobby, while a crystal chandelier hung from the cavernous ceiling. To the left was a narrow corridor. That was the way Rhys needed to go, but the garrison would come from the lobby. He didn't want humans sneaking up on their backs.

"Arnav. Set up a barricade," Rhys barked out. He pointed towards the lobby, which remained blissfully vacant of living humans for the moment. That wouldn't last long. "Keep fifty starats here and guard our backs."

"Will fifty be enough?" Arnav asked. He clicked his fingers, and two starats close to him started to haul some ornate furniture towards the corridor to block it off.

Rhys's ears folded down. "One hundred, but no more. Everyone else, with me."

Arnav quickly rounded up one hundred starats to remain behind with him. A fair chunk of their force. The rest followed Rhys as he pushed past into the corridor. He could only hope that he wouldn't need to leave too many garrison forces behind. There would still be humans to deal with closer to the shield generator. He did not want to leave himself too thin, but he knew Arnav needed the numbers as well.

Rifle in hand, Rhys prowled down the corridor, his senses all on alert. The wailing of the alarm irritated him and prevented him from properly hearing what was ahead. With the lack of cover, Rhys did not want to be caught off-guard by anyone.

The alarms silenced. The lack of noise almost deafened Rhys. Only the click of claws and the rustle of clothing reached his ears. A hushed quiet had fallen over Windsor.

A door slammed open fifty metres ahead of Rhys. A dozen humans charged out and turned.

Gunfire began with a roar. Rhys threw himself to the side, pressing his back into a doorway alcove. Some starats had not been so lucky. A dozen fell, but Rhys didn't have the luxury to see if any of the fallen had survived. Their repurposed body armour was not able to resist sustained firepower.

"Shields to the front," Rhys roared out. Not every starat had the luxury of a bullet shield on their wrist. Twenty starats quickly leaped forward, shields already prepared. They formed a protective wall in front of those without shields, half-crouching to ensure their feet were still protected. They lined up from wall-to-wall across the narrow corridor.

Rhys slipped into position behind the front row of shields, keeping his own inactive for now. He stood upright, rifle gently perched against the nearest shield for support. It took him a moment to recognise that he stood directly behind Skye.

"Keep moving forward," Rhys commanded, though there was little need for his words. The line of starats continued to move. Rhys could feel the thud of bullets striking the shields, but none of the front line shirked their duty. Return fire happened infrequently, with most coming from Rhys's powerful rifle.

A line of bullet shields faced the starats. Humans had gathered together with their own protection, but they held their ground. Rhys glanced down to his holographic map for a moment. If he was right, then the humans were just in front of the corridor they needed to reach the shield generator. They weren't moving anywhere, and their shields were too tough to penetrate. The starats had more numbers. There were several hundred of them, compared to twenty humans, but the tight confines of the corridor limited that advantage.

"Kalisha, what can you do?" Rhys called out, trying to make himself heard over the gunfire. His ears flicked and folded down from the constant burst of bullets against the shields.

Kalisha didn't respond, but her influence was immediately apparent. With a terrifying crack that was partially the snapping of bones, the humans' shields careened up into the ceiling, embedding themselves amongst the panelling.

Suddenly defenceless, the humans were quickly gunned down. Rhys's rifle lit up, inaccurately spraying bullets through human flesh, while starats either side of him picked their enemy off more accurately with pistols.

The starat shield wall broke apart as the human defence crumbled. Rhys ran forward, his eyes on the corridor ahead, before pausing by the open doors the humans had come from. He stepped over the fallen bodies, keeping his eyes raised but almost slipping on a growing pool of blood.

Gunfire pricked at Rhys's ears, from further back the way they had come from. He didn't look back. He knew he would be tempted to return and reinforce Arnav's position, but he had his own mission to complete first.

Rhys couldn't tell if more humans were coming. He couldn't hear any, but he would have liked to rely on other senses before putting his head around the doorway. The coppery scent of blood overwhelmed his nose. A dozen starats joined him. Some lingered back, waiting for orders, while others tended to the wounded. Elijah and Skye stood by Rhys's side, while Kalisha leaned against the wall a few paces away. Her ears were flat against her head, and she sucked in large, heavy breaths.

The door opened to a green park surrounded by buildings. Windsor Castle encircled the small green area completely, with vantage points for defenders coming from almost all angles. Rhys felt vulnerable just looking over the small green space, but in the centre of the open area was the target. A wide, white dish looked up to the sky, perched on top of a raised bunker and surrounded by a low wall. The bulk of the generator would be below ground, but the dish was the important part.

"Shields again," Rhys called out. He waved forwards the starats who would be needed to protect those without shields. He pointed to a few dozen who lingered towards the back of the group. "Remain in cover here and watch our rears. Shout for reinforcements if any humans come."

Grimacing as he left more of their number behind, Rhys turned his attention to the open square. Movement flashed through some of the overlooking windows opposite, but all seemed still on the ground level. He had eight hundred eager starats ready to charge. He lifted his hand in preparation to give the signal.

A low whistle gradually grew louder. That was the only warning Rhys had before the missile struck the ground just a couple of metres away. A shield was thrust in front of him, but the blast of hot air and debris lifted Rhys off his feet. Debris cracked against the shield, and he rolled back with limbs entangled with another starat.

Rhys's ears rung. He pushed himself to the side and staggered up to his feet, drawing his pistol and aiming it towards the open doors. His vision spun, but no humans were approaching. Other starats had fallen around him, slowly rising again.

"Shields, shields!" Rhys cried out. He staggered forward, fighting against the disorientation. There was not a moment to waste. Around the shield generator was a defensible location. Here was not.

At least one starat joined Rhys. A shield came up between them, sheltering them from gunfire as they stepped outside. Footsteps followed behind them, but no gunfire cracked against the shield. Not at first. A few seconds passed and Rhys's steps became surer as he led the charge across the open green.

Other starats joined them. Rhys saw them through the corner of his eyes, but he didn't look to see who was there. Shields were raised all around, protecting them from all directions. There were vantage points to fire from all angles into the open courtyard, but Rhys knew that there would be some limited cover in the middle, with the shield generator.

Rhys's head still spun, and his feet lurched from one step to the next. Were it not for the starats close to him, he might have drifted off course. Instead, his shoulders bumped up against other starats and his fingers tensed against the pistol in hand, ready to raise it at the first sign of danger.

A human rose from beyond the defensive wall. Before Rhys had the chance to aim, another starat had taken them down. At the last few metres, Rhys pushed ahead of the shields. His feet were steadier as he approached the wall, vaulting over it and expecting to find defenders on the other side. But for the unfortunate human already taken out, there was no one.

In front of the generator dish was a ramp sloping down and a door, leading towards the bunker. Rhys hissed to himself and leaned back, keeping out of direct line of fire from the garrison inside. He gestured for his starats to follow him and rebuild the shield wall. His eyes warily searched the surrounding buildings, aware that there could be humans anywhere around them. They needed to gain access to the bunker.

The bunker door was heavy metal, with no way of forcing it open by hand. Crouched down by Skye, whose shield protected Rhys for the moment, he quickly looked through what starats had come with him. He grinned. He had who he needed.

"Kalisha," he called out. "Can you break that door open?"

The russet-furred starat nodded. She stepped forward warily, staggering and swaying with each step. She closed her eyes and took a deep breath, extending her hands out in front of her chest. She grimaced, then pushed hard. The bunker door buckled but didn't break. A whimper escaped Kalisha's muzzle. She pushed again. This time, the hinges shattered, and the door was blown back and slammed against the opposite wall. Human voices cried out.

Starats advanced again, shields raised first. Rhys followed behind the first line. His pistol was ready. He bared his teeth and snarled in anger as the first armoured humans emerged from within the bunker. At a quick count, he saw twenty of them. They were outnumbered, but they had the better position and better equipment.

Gunfire cracked against the shields. Rhys flinched several times as the shields began to splinter from the force of the humans' bullets. Occasional shots were fired back, but they seemed to do no damage to the humans. The ping and crack of bullets against the shields was almost all Rhys could hear.

A stalemate threatened, and Rhys knew they didn't have the time for that. They had to break through the human defenders before reinforcements flooded the courtyard from other areas of the castle, and the nearby barracks.

"Kalisha, one more push from you," Rhys called out. He almost gagged on the smell of blood filling his nose. His ears ached from the constant sounds, and voices echoed all around him.

The humans stumbled backwards as though an invisible weight had crashed into them. The suppressive fire ceased for a couple of seconds. That was all Rhys needed. He ran beyond the line of shields, pistol raised in his left hand, and knife clenched tight in his right.

Two shots dropped one human. A line of fire seared across Rhys's thigh. He ignored it. One more step got him to the twisted remains of the door. He slashed with his knife, slicing into thick armour. The knife snagged. He jabbed in and felt blood on his hand.

Gunfire roared all around. Anything without fur was a target for Rhys. He spun quickly on the spot, yanking his blade free. His left hand swung up. He saw exposed human flesh. He fired. The human fell. Blood splattered against his fur.

Starats fought with animalistic ferocity. Tooth and claw were as effective weapons as pistols in close quarters. More and more starats flooded into the small bunker, overwhelming the human defenders.

Less than a minute passed before Rhys stood panting in the middle of the bunker with no humans left alive. Adrenaline coursed through his veins, and it took him a few moments to slowly bring down the rapid beat of his heart. He spun around on his toes and took one step forward, only to drop down on his knee as pain flared through his thigh.

"Fuck," Rhys growled, glancing down at the blood flowing down his right leg. A bullet had glanced against his thigh. He rose back to his feet and staggered towards the bunker doorway, leaning against the empty frame. He lifted his voice. "We need to secure the bunker, quickly. Make a defensible position."

Rhys scanned around the number of starats he had left, trying to ignore how much that figure had reduced. He sucked in his breath. There were too many to securely fit inside the bunker. He raised his fist. "I need a group to follow me and sweep through the castle to clear out pockets of defenders. They would have expected an attack from outside their walls. It might take them a little while to adjust to an attack from within. We can't give them that time."

"You're in no state to walk, Essie," a voice called out. Skye stepped forward. Her muzzle was stained in blood, but she looked uninjured. "I'll lead them. You keep this place secure. We can't lose control of the shield generator."

Rhys hissed, partly in pain, and partly in frustration. He knew he needed to be the one risking himself to clear away the human defence through the castle, but he also knew he would never make it a dozen steps before he couldn't walk any further. He needed his wound tended to. He nodded once. "Go. Take as many as you need but leave at least fifty uninjured here. We can fortify our position with that. Send some to reinforce Arnav as well."

Skye quickly gathered her starats Almost all the surviving starats went with her. They took most of the bullet shields. Rhys counted around one hundred starats left with him. Most had small injuries like him, but few appeared to be in imminent danger. Without the constant roar of gunfire, the square felt quiet and eerie to Rhys. He didn't expect it to last.

Rhys turned back to his defences. Starats were bringing the wounded inside the safety of the bunker, using the brief respite to tend wounds and catch their breath.

"Kalisha, can you…"

"She can't," Elijah called out.

Rhys turned around to see Elijah crouched by Kalisha's side. She had sat back against the bunker wall. She didn't appear to be hurt, but she was breathing heavily with her eyes closed. Rhys grimaced. She had over-exerted herself with subspace.

"Fuck," Rhys muttered. He limped forward to glance outside. The last of the wounded were being brought in. "We need the bunker door placed across the entry here to give us some cover. They will come to retake the generator. We must hold them off."

Half a dozen starats jumped to work, hauling the heavy door across the entrance. Rhys took the moment to look to see what supplies they had captured. The bunker appeared to be used as the control system for the shield generator, which made Rhys smile. Their job at disabling the planetary shields would be made easier with that access. Beyond a computer terminal, there was also an ammunition and weapon cabinet, complete with fresh bullet shields, but little else that could be used for defence. The fallen human bodies had already been looted for weapons and ammunition, before they were unceremoniously dumped outside.

Rhys limped to the back of the bunker and watched over the activity, before lifting his hand to his ear. He patched himself through to Stephanie, waiting for her to respond to his contact request.

She took a few seconds to open the channel. "Make it quick, Rhys."

"We've secured the shield generator this end. We're expecting a counter-strike soon," Rhys said quickly. His ears curled slightly at the sound of heavy fire coming through his headpiece. "How long do you estimate at your end?"

"We have heavy defences here. It's going to be at least half an hour," Stephanie replied. Her voice was tense.

"Shit, alright," Rhys said. His tail tucked between his legs. "Keep us updated."

The line cut out without another word. Rhys sucked his breath in. They had to hold out for half an hour. Both generators needed to be deactivated simultaneously. There was no other choice but to hold out for as long as possible.

Rhys limped forwards. The buckled door had been put horizontally against the doorway, with the remaining bullet shields strapped together and taped to the sides of the bunker. Small gaps were left to provide firing holes, but most of the open bunker door had some protection to the starats inside. Rhys was quietly impressed. There was still no movement in the courtyard yet.

"Elijah, is there any communication that you can pick up?" Rhys asked, turning again to face the starat.

Elijah placed his hand on Kalisha's shoulder and muttered something quietly to her. She opened her eyes slightly and nodded. Only then did Elijah rise to his feet. His ears flicked back and forth, constantly moving, and his eyes appeared unfocused. "Yes. They're organising a counter-response, but they estimate our numbers to be ten times what we have. They're being overly cautious, and that's giving Skye and Arnav a chance out there. The humans are spreading their numbers too thin because they think there are more threats than we can actually pose."

"Good," Rhys replied. "We can use that to our advantage. If you can keep in contact with Skye and Arnav to let them know enemy movements, that would be appreciated."

"Someone needs to see to your leg," Elijah said, looking down at Rhys's wounded thigh with a twisted muzzle.

Rhys waved his concerns away. "It's fine for now. Just a scratch. I'll be fine, I promise."

Elijah grunted to himself but didn't try to argue. He turned around to face the computer terminals, flicking through the holoscreens as he started to murmur to himself. Readouts from the inactive shield generators popped up, as well as details on the communication network through the castle. Elijah then got in contact with the other starat team leaders, guiding them on human movements. Rhys flicked his ears and turned away. His focus needed to be on the courtyard.

"I want rifles on the shield wall," Rhys ordered, speaking to the two dozen starats he still had in his command and could still fight. A dozen more tended to each other's wounds, but they were not in much of a condition to return to combat. "We have the defensible position, but the humans had it before us. It can be retaken. We must be vigilant and alert at all times. Shoot anything out there that is not a starat."

"Yes, Essie," the starats barked back. A couple saluted with a nervous grin. Others moved immediately into defensible positions.

Rhys leaned back and found a spare medical kit. He pulled out a bandage to use as a tourniquet around his injured leg, grimacing as the pain returned with his focus on the wound. He bandaged himself up as best he could, hissing softly at the pressure on the cut. He had been lucky the bullet had only glanced off him.

Before Rhys could focus on the courtyard again, Elijah called out once more. "Hey Rhys, there's a ship in orbit running a sweep on communications."

"Shit, are they planning an orbital strike?" Rhys asked, his blood running cold. There was no defence against that; not one they had control over.

Elijah's voice shook. "I don't think so. It's… it's identifying as the *Rossi*. Wasn't that stationed at Pluto?"

Rhys gasped. General Carson. Or was he here as Captain Herschel? Rhys couldn't be sure, but the former starat was potentially a lifeline. "Can you patch me through to them?"

A couple of soft beeps sounded in Rhys's ear. A familiar voice followed. "Hello? Who is this?"

"It's Rhys," the starat said, speaking quickly to stop the human from interjecting. "I want to cut right through the crap, Sam. Are you here on my side or theirs?"

There was a moment of hesitation. "Yours."

"Then I need you to dock at the Star Hub," Rhys said. He flicked his tail and swiped at his wrist-mounted communicator. "I'll put you in contact with Stephanie. She'll tell you what needs to be done to break through the defences there."

Another hesitation. "I… Rhys. Is this the right thing to be doing?"

"Yes." There was no hesitation from Rhys. "This is how we protect Terra and save it all at once."

"Alright." A third hesitation. "I've got the contact details. I'll be in touch when I can. Good luck down there, Rhys."

"Good luck up there," Rhys replied, but he didn't know whether Carson had already cut contact. There was no response from the human.

Rhys breathed out slowly. Reinforcements had come, but they were useless in Windsor. They had to go to the Star Hub. At least there wasn't an orbital strike coming.

Wiping his muzzle with the back of his blood-stained hand, Rhys limped towards the shield wall. Six starats stood either side of him, with another dozen clustered close. Most of them had minor injuries, but nothing that prevented them from standing and holding a weapon. Rhys's right leg trembled from the weight pressed down on it, but he gritted his teeth and did his best to ignore the throbbing pain.

"We won't have long to wait," Rhys said quietly, more for his benefit than that of the starats around him. He felt like they were in the eye of the storm. Gunfire still cracked all around them, but none of it was aimed at the bunker. Not just yet. They would be safe from missile fire for now. He doubted the humans would risk damaging the shield generator. Any counter-attack would have to take the bunker back with manpower.

A new sound boomed around the castle. A familiar voice crackled through loudspeakers. Cardinal Erik's savage snarl made Rhys shiver and cower.

"To the traitors and heretics thinking they can take us by force, you will be annihilated. There will not be an atom of your bodies left to remember. You cannot win. Justice and Veritas will prevail."

Rhys snarled to himself. He tightened the grip around his pistol. The voice of the cardinal reverberated through the bunker, as well as echoing through the empty courtyard. The starat glanced back to Elijah. "Do we know where he's speaking from?"

"Throne room," Elijah replied. "He's there with Emperor Neicwyk and around three hundred of the royal guard."

Rhys's tail flicked. "That's a problem for later," he said, again assuring himself. The temptation to charge after the cardinal welled within him, but he knew that such a mission would be suicide. The shield generator was all that mattered for now.

The silence outside remained oppressive. Rhys realised then what was going on, and he should have seen it sooner. He hissed quietly. The human defenders were going around the castle, sweeping up what they believed to be multiple attacking packs. Only then would they come to retake the bunker. Skye and Arnav would not be able to elude the humans for long. They needed to draw the humans out to attack the bunker.

Rhys spun on his toes. "Is there a way to broadcast a message out of here? I need to get the cardinal's attention."

Elijah's eyes widened. His mouth hung open slightly, before he nodded. He must have come to the same conclusion. "Just give me a minute and I'll get something set up."

A minute. That was plenty of time for Rhys to think of something to say. His voice had lured an invading fleet and sparked a revolution. Now it was time to commit heresy.

***

Rhys growled as he spoke into the camera, projecting his voice and image through the castle in a counter to Cardinal Erik's earlier message. He made no effort to hide the bloodstains in his fur, nor the fury in his eyes.

"You say we cannot win," Rhys snarled. He kept his voice slow and deep, resisting the urge to spit his words out quickly. "You are wrong. We have already won, you just do not know it yet. Your empire of lies shall crumble. Veritas was a fraud, just as surely as the cardinals and the emperors who spread his message. The Terran Empire ends today, and the lies of Veritas shall be forgotten. You shall be defeated by starats, the very same ones you wish to grind beneath your boot. If you want to make a futile attempt at stopping me, then you know where I am. My name is Captain Rhys Griffiths, and I act in the name of Essie, the first and greatest of all starats. In his name, I will be the starat to end this empire and to expose the lies of Veritas."

Rhys got in a two fingered salute before Elijah cut the recording. The starat grinned to himself so that he could hide the growing fear within him. He had taunted the beast. He could only hope that they were strong enough to withstand it.

A beep sounded in Rhys's ear. Skye's voice came through. "They're reorganising," she said, sounding out of breath. "Whatever your plan is, I think it's working."

Arnav chimed in a moment later. "They're going into retreat here. Expect forces to converge on your area soon."

"Understood," Rhys replied. He breathed a quiet sigh of relief. His plan had worked to that extent. He had drawn the defenders away from the more-exposed Skye and Arnav. "If you can find a defendable location that overlooks the courtyard, then do so. Otherwise get somewhere safe and wait."

"We're already on the move," Arnav replied. Skye commented a moment later to say that she was moving too. Free from constant human gunfire, they had the chance to get into a better position.

"We have movement out here." A clipped call from a starat drew Rhys's attention back to the bunker. He limped towards the door and peered out. Vision was obscured by the rising ramp towards the surface level, but Rhys could just about make out the movement of a line of heavily armoured humans advancing from the castle.

"Defensive line," Rhys called out. Starats hefted up stolen rifles, resting them against the side of the upturned door for support. Rhys crouched down amongst them, wincing as the movement twinged the cut on his leg.

The humans did not advance. They spread out into a double line in front of the bunker, guns ready to fire. The front row of humans dropped to one knee, while those behind remained standing. They were all heavily armoured, leaving no obvious points of weakness that could be exploited. These were the elite royal guard.

Rhys's tail swished as he peered around. He tapped a finger to his ear. "Arnav. Skye. The emperor may be unguarded at the moment. Might be worth testing the defences of the throne room while I have their attention."

"I'm onto it," Skye replied.

Rhys was tempted to check in on Stephanie again, but he knew not enough time had passed before Carson arrived at the Star Hub with reinforcements. He glanced down at his wrist display. He started a countdown to half an hour, when Stephanie had hoped to be in a position to deactivate the shield generator in orbit. That was how long they needed to hold out.

Rhys glanced up. Destroying the shield generator was easy enough. Surviving long enough to do so was the hard part. "What are you waiting for, you fuckers," he muttered to himself. He wished he could see more of the courtyard.

One human stepped ahead of the others, still with a helmet enclosing their face. Her voice rung out across the courtyard. "I am Commander Ellen Saville. You are surrounded. Offer your surrender and you will be taken in quickly and quietly."

Rhys laughed. He didn't know how well he could be heard, but he shouted out his response. "Weren't you listening to your cardinal, Commander Saville? There is no mercy for us. If you want our fur, you're going to have to come and get it yourself."

"We will take you, starat," Commander Saville replied. Her voice remained calm and flat, with no anger or disgust present. "We merely offer you the chance to have a merciful death."

"There will be no mercy here, commander," Rhys responded, another laugh threatening to disrupt his words. "We're both adults. I know you want to kill me. You know we have to kill you if we want to live. Let's not fuck things up with false offers of mercy."

The human stayed silent for a few seconds. "So be it."

Hell rained down on the bunker as the royal guard opened fire. The shields splintered from the first volley of gunfire, but the defences held. Just. Rhys grimaced and gestured for the starats to lower down, using the overturned blast door as cover. The bullet shields wouldn't be able to withstand much more.

In the brief lull between volleys from the royal guard, Rhys's starats returned fire. Neither rifle nor pistol fire seemed to have much effect on the humans' armour. A couple stumbled backwards, but none fell. Their reload was delayed a few moments.

Rhys ducked down as the royal guard fired again. The thud of bullets against the shields and door vibrated into Rhys's body as he huddled for cover beneath the thick metal door. One shield was ripped from the others, shredded by the sustained fire. Then silence fell again, and the call to reload drifted from outside.

Once again, the starats rose to return fire. This time, Rhys saw a couple of the humans fall. More took their place.

"Fuck, come on," Rhys muttered, dropping back down behind cover again as the royal guard took aim. They weren't risking the heavy weapons, but Rhys knew it wouldn't be long before someone in command lost patience and decided to risk the shield generator. They did not have half an hour.

Kalisha crawled across the bunker, away from the other wounded starats. She barely seemed able to move, and she slumped down against the door. "I can take half of them."

"No," Rhys retorted quickly. "You've done too much already. You'll hurt yourself."

Kalisha shrugged. "Oh. Fine then. I'll just let them all kill us."

Rhys's shoulders slumped. He thumped his fist against the repurposed door. "Don't do too much. We can deal with the ones you can't."

"I'm not going to kill myself, don't worry," Kalisha said. She hauled herself up onto her knees, peering out over the line of humans. "You just make sure those guns don't finish the job."

"I'll do my best," Rhys said. He shivered and tucked his tail close to his legs as he peered over the rim. The humans had advanced a few steps.

Kalisha sat back down and closed her eyes. For a moment Rhys wasn't sure if she was still awake, but she still breathed deeply and her hands twitched. Her right hand appeared to flick small, invisible objects towards her left hand, which clenched tighter with each movement. She shuddered and gasped. Two dozen times she flicked her right hand before she paused.

"Get ready," Kalisha said, her voice strained and small.

Another volley fire came from the royal guard. Then Kalisha clenched her fists. The gunfire ceased. Screams echoed.

Rhys quickly rose. The armour had crumpled around half of the humans, crushing the bodies inside. Those who remained unaffected had turned their attention to helping their fallen companions. It was an opportunity Rhys couldn't ignore. He rose to his feet as Kalisha slumped down.

Before the humans had a chance to recompose themselves, Rhys led the charge out of the bunker. His pistol flared as he fired, felling two humans in just as many shots. They were heavily armoured, but the visor over the eyes was still a weak point to exploit.

Every starat still capable of fighting flooded from the bunker. The royal guard quickly recovered their composure, though they did retreat a few paces at the speed of the starats' charge. It was not enough.

Rhys charged directly into the closest human. He grappled with them and sunk his knife through a gap in their armour. Blood welled from the wound. A hand grasped at the back of Rhys's neck and the starat was thrown free. He rolled to the side and fired two more shots. Another human fell.

Leaping back up to his feet, Rhys lashed out with pistol and knife. In close quarters, the humans were reluctant to open fire again. The starats had the advantage of momentum, but Rhys knew the humans would soon turn that around should the fight go on too long. He needed to take out their command.

Commander Saville was easy to find. Rhys bounced off two humans as he pushed his way through to her. He didn't give her any warning. He jumped up, wrapping his arms around her neck, trying to prise his knife into the visor of her helmet. She reacted quickly. Her hand clamped around his wrist.

Balanced precariously on the human's back, Rhys struggled to get his other hand into a good position. At such close range, he didn't trust his pistol. The commander's armour would likely deflect the bullet. He risked hurting himself as much as her.

Instead, Rhys tossed aside his pistol. His fingers found the gap between helmet and armour, and he wrenched hard. The helmet fell free, exposing the human's head. Her elbow caught Rhys in the ribs. The impact dislodged his grip, and he dropped to the ground.

"Animal," Commander Saville growled. All her focus narrowed down on the one starat. She took one step forward. Rhys took a step back, lifting his combat knife. She had no weapon other than her rifle. That was all she needed.

The commander raised her weapon. Her eyes narrowed, then widened. Then they went dull as she collapsed, a gunshot wound bleeding on her temple. She collapsed to her knees, then face-down on the grass.

Rhys's eyes flicked to the side. He saluted Elijah quickly, who stood with his right hand raised, pistol still primed. There was no time to thank him yet.

Rhys dived forward to reclaim his pistol, then returned to the fray. The royal guard were too professional to lose their morale and rout at the loss of their commander, but they had begun to retreat. Rhys quickly made a decision. There weren't enough starats to chase down the royal guard.

"Fall back to the bunker," Rhys called out. Two starats could barely walk, and they staggered back behind Rhys. "Cover the wounded."

The humans, seeing the opportunity to retreat as well, fell back towards the main castle building. A few final shots were exchanged between the retreating forces, but none hit their targets. Rhys never took his eyes from the humans, and he was the last to fall back down the ramp into the bunker.

Rhys held his hand to his ear. "Arnav. You have a dozen humans retreating back to the throne room."

"Understood, Rhys. They're still too fortified here for an assault with my numbers," Arnav replied. "From what I hear, they're waiting for reinforcements from the barracks."

"Should we return to your position?" Skye added.

"Affirm, yes. Bring any wounded too. We have supplies here to tend to injuries," Rhys said. He glanced around. There wasn't much room for everyone, but for a temporary measure it would do.

Rhys vaulted over the door and limped inside the bunker. He embraced Elijah and rested his head against the other starat's shoulder. "Thank you for watching my back."

"Told you I'd be doing that, didn't I?" Elijah said, a grin betrayed by the anxiety in his ears and eyes. "Just don't do it again in a hurry."

Rhys folded his ears. "We've still got a little bit to go. We've bought ourselves some time, but not long. If they're able to pull in reinforcements from the local barracks, then we'll be quickly overwhelmed."

"The generator is primed to overload. You just need to give the word," Elijah said. He took a couple of steps back from the bunker door and the starats keeping watch there.

"We need to wait for Stephanie," Rhys said. His hand moved up to his ear, but he hadn't heard anything further from her. He was tempted to contact her again, but he resisted the urge. His wrist still told him there was ten minutes of waiting until the half hour was up.

"How long do you think we can hole up here?" Elijah asked. He crouched down by Kalisha's side, who was still sat down with her back against the felled door with her eyes closed.

"Long enough," Rhys replied. He could only hope that was right.

With a small lull in combat, there was chance for the wounded to receive treatment. Rhys fended off all attempts to look at his leg. He limped around the bunker, finding that staying moving kept the worst of the pain away. Others needed the limited medical supplies more than he did.

Rhys didn't let his guard down, but he allowed his mind to wander slightly. With his senses still trained on the courtyard, he ran through different scenarios on what could happen next. He expected reinforcements to arrive for the human defenders. That had not been all of the royal guard, and there was another garrison nearby.

After a few minutes, the starats from the patrolling groups returned. Arnav got back first, with barely half the number of starats he had before. Most were bloodstained and carrying small wounds, but all still had the same steely look in their eyes. These were not starats that had been cowed or beaten, no matter what they had gone through.

Skye returned a couple of minutes after Arnav, still with all her number. Her starats had not been injured, but they did carry a few more heavy weapons that had been looted from fallen human opposition.

With so many starats in such a small, enclosed space, there was not much room left to move. Rhys took a few of starats out onto the generator dish. Several starats were put on guard duty, while others used their bullet shields to protect him and Elijah. The augmented starat clambered onto the base of the dish itself.

Rhys stared up at the buildings that completely surrounded the courtyard. Though the structures were modern, they had been built to look ancient. It was based on the original Windsor Castle that had once stood on the same location. Rhys wrinkled his nose and bared his teeth at the thought. So much of the empire had been built on the ruins of the old. That had never bothered him before, and he didn't know why the thought prickled at his fur so much.

Elijah tinkered with a control panel just below the dish. He muttered quietly to himself, keeping his head bowed and body low to present a smaller target. There were no humans around to exploit their potentially exposed position. Nothing moved in the windows above, and the courtyard was quiet. A couple of crows perched on a balcony and cawed to each other.

"You almost done there, Elijah?" Rhys called out. His tail swished in quick, jerky motions. His eyes flicked around from window to window, and then up to the overcast grey sky that loomed above. The gentle scent of rain was on the air, almost overwhelmed by the metallic tang of blood that had permanently affixed itself to Rhys's nose.

"Nearly," Elijah called back. His claws swiped through a holographic display that had surrounded the base of the dish, displaying a series of numbers and codes that Rhys could not make sense of from his casual glance.

Voices called across the courtyard. Rhys's ears perked up at the sound and glanced to where they came from. He could see no one, but humans certainly shouted to each other. Then gunfire broke out again. Rhys's tail tensed.

The starat leaped down from the dish, landing with a pained jolt on his injured leg. "Arnav? Skye? Did you leave anyone behind?"

"No one, no," Skye said. She approached the doorway nervously, with Arnav right behind her.

A smile twitched onto Arnav's muzzle. "I think backup may have arrived."

"We didn't call for any backup," Rhys said slowly. His fur stood on end as he stared towards the buildings, where a new battle was raging.

"No, we did not," Arnav said slowly. He stepped forward and placed his hand on Rhys's shoulder. "But Essie did send a message to all starats in the system to stop their work. Essie then led an assault on the heart of the empire. We may have told them not to fight, but they were never going to listen to us."

"Shit, they'll be slaughtered. We have to help them," Rhys said, already reaching for his gun.

Arnav pulled him back. "You stay here. You need to blow the generator. I'll take everyone else with me."

"Go then, go," Rhys said, pushing Arnav away. "I'll join you as soon as I'm able."

Arnav nodded. "Of course you will. See you soon." The starat then threw his arm into the air and bellowed in a voice Rhys hadn't thought the starat was capable of. "Everyone! To me!"

Rhys pointed to three starats who were close by. "You three, stay here with me. We defend the generator and the wounded."

Though Rhys longed to join the fight, he stepped back and watched as the flood of starats emerged from the bunker. With Arnav and Skye at their head, they poured towards the open doors of the nearest building. Towards the throne room, and the reinforcements they had not expected.

Rhys held a hand close to his ear and growled softly. He could only hope the fun wasn't over before he had chance to re-join the fray. There was a cardinal he longed to meet, especially now he had a pistol close to hand.

Elijah jumped down by Rhys's side, quickly followed by the four other starats who had been on top of the dish with him. He grinned widely. "Got them."

"What did you need?" Rhys asked. His eyes were still on the backs of the starats before the last of them disappeared into the castle.

"Codes for the outer defences. If we take the throne room, then we can fortify this place," Elijah said. He pulled Rhys close. "Just get me to the command centre, and I can keep any imperial forces out of here for as long as supplies last."

"Unless we're able to requisition supplies that are already here, that's not very long," Rhys muttered to himself. He sighed softly, then turned away. He pointed to two of the starats who had remained behind. "Keep guard here. Warn me the moment there's movement out there. Human or starat."

"Understood, Essie," one replied. He saluted, though not in any way Rhys was familiar with.

Rhys paused for a moment, about to correct the starat on how to properly salute, before smiling and shaking his head. That didn't matter anymore. He ducked inside the bunker to check up on the wounded, and to see if Kalisha had recovered. A glance down to his wrist told him that there was still another five minutes left on Stephanie's half an hour.

While the war waged on around him, Rhys had to sit and wait. His hand itched by his pistol. He would not wait for long.

***

A quiet beep sounded in Rhys's ear. A contact request came down from the Star Hub. Rhys activated the call, and moments later Stephanie's scratched face appeared in a hologram a couple of paces ahead of the starat. "We're in position," the human said.

"So are we. Give us ten seconds and we'll be ready to blow it," Rhys said, raising his voice loud enough so that Elijah would be able to hear him.

The other starat gave him a thumbs up. They had already done the work needed to overload the computer system and deactivate the generator. There was no need for actual explosives, especially as any blast could compromise the defensive location in the bunker.

"Good," Stephanie said. She grimaced and reacted to some gunfire close by to her. "We're going to try to fight our way out. Are there any teleporters active down there? That would make our retreat much easier."

"We'll see what we can do," Rhys replied. His tail curled, but he tried to keep the worry from his ears and face. "We have some resistance here, but it appears we may have received backup from local starats eager to join in on the fight. Arnav is reinforcing them at the moment."

A powerful explosion muted Stephanie's response. The hologram momentarily flickered and was drowned out by bright white light, before recovering back to its usual quality. "We're done here," Stephanie said, not continuing with her earlier, interrupted sentence. "Let us know about those teleporters, or else we'll port down to Heathrow."

"I'll keep you updated," Rhys said. His ears perked up. "Did Carson reach you? Or Herschel, if he's still using that name?"

"Yeah. He turned up at a very timely moment. We were in danger of being overrun before his arrival. Thankfully he was able to slip through the Terran fleet," Stephanie said. She glanced up again. "It seems the Martian fleet is in movement. Terra doesn't know where to defend right now."

Rhys grinned, showing off his teeth. "We're about to give them something else to think of. If we can capture the emperor, then we can force their surrender."

"Then we still have the Vatican to deal with," Stephanie commented. She grimaced and pushed her hair back behind her ears. "I've got to go. Be safe. Speak soon."

The connection between the two cut off. Rhys leaned back and exhaled slowly. He then glanced up to Elijah. "Is it done?"

Elijah stuck his thumb up again. "It's done. It will take some extensive repairs to get this operational again. When we're all done here, we can properly blow the dish."

Rhys nodded. He glanced to one of the uninjured starats. "Can I ask you to stay back here and guard the wounded. We'll be back as soon as we can."

"And if you're not?" the starat said. She pinned her ears back as she held a rifle in both hands, her shoulders straining from the effort of carrying it.

Rhys placed a hand on her shoulder. "Then we have still done what we came here to do. I ask a lot of you, but if it looks like you will be overrun, and there is no chance of our return, destroy the generator. Can you do that for me?"

The starat nodded. "I will. You can count on us."

"And you can count on us. We will come back," Rhys said. He saluted her. She saluted him back.

For a moment, Rhys's eyes slid down to Kalisha. Her eyes fluttered open. Her hand trembled as she started to lift it, before her arm dropped down again. She took in a deep breath. "I'll be fine soon, don't worry about me," she said quietly. She had an energy bar in one hand, unopened.

Rhys knew it was pointless saying anything to Kalisha. She would either be too weary to follow them, or she would ignore any commands Rhys gave for her to stay behind. He turned to Elijah. "You've got my back?"

"So long as you've got mine."

Rhys snarled. "Then let's go get these fuckers, once and for all."

chapter twenty

Rhys sprinted with Elijah just behind him. He followed the sound of fighting through the corridors, and the smell of blood on the air. If any civilians had been present in the castle, then they had all retreated to a safe location. The only bodies that Rhys almost tripped over were those of the human guardsmen and the starats they had killed.

Rhys swallowed his distaste for the death. He tightened his jaw and readied his weapon, his senses straining for any unexpected sounds. The cavernous halls of Windsor Castle provided little cover. Nowhere for Rhys and Elijah to hide, but also nowhere to spring an ambush. The way was clear.

A few straggling starats were just ahead. They had been injured, but they refused to go back for help. They pointed Rhys in the right direction and vowed to follow just behind. Rhys and Elijah had left them behind after just a few seconds.

Blood stained the carpets. Discarded weapons lay scattered across the floor. Cracks in the walls remained where bullets had struck them. Ground-based warfare had never been Rhys's experience. The brutality felt more intimate. A spaceship could open fire on another, and the carnage remained invisible to the crew and captain. On the ground, Rhys could see every stain and smear of blood. He could smell it.

The building shook. An explosion rumbled close by and dust fell from the ceiling. Chandeliers swayed and clinked against each other. A bellowed voice shouted over the diminishing rumble of the explosion. Arnav rallied the starats still.

The assault had faltered in a large, open lobby at the front of the building. Someone had forced open the wide double doors to the grounds, with one hanging on half its usual hinges. The large garden and driveway had been the site of a battle, with the gates at the bottom of a low hill having also forced open. No one was stationed inside the gunnery posts either side of the gates.

Inside the building, the starats had been able to loosely fortify the main lobby, with the efforts focused on breaking down a door through to the throne room. A dozen starats tried to beat down the doors with fist and foot, but they were heavily reinforced. Around the rest of the lobby were more starats than Rhys had started with, though many wore no armour of any kind. Their weapons were crude and simple. A few carried kitchen knives and gardening shovels. Those few with a gun had taken the weapon from a dead human.

"We've got them pinned back," Arnav called out, raising his hand to attract Rhys's attention. "Every last one of them is in there. Our new friends here dealt with the barracks down the hill, but we're expecting enemy reinforcements soon. We may need to retreat."

"Not yet we don't," Rhys said. His eyes quickly scanned the lobby. A staircase ran up the side of the wall to an overhanging balcony. He lifted his chin. "No humans upstairs?"

"Negative," Arnav replied. "We've already done a sweep."

Rhys held onto Elijah's hand. "Have you got a map in your head? Are there any other ways into the throne room from upstairs?"

"Yeah," Elijah said quickly. He shook his head. "But only to the throne balcony. There are two doors up there, one on either side. I don't know what sort of defences they'll have though."

"Alright," Rhys said, before hesitating. He glanced around the lobby again, taking in everything. He clicked his fingers. "I want the gunnery posts outside manned. We need to fend off any reinforcements. I also need some starats to come up with me to the balcony. Arnav. You keep trying to break the doors down here. Keep them distracted and their eyes on the ground."

"One problem with that," Arnav said, lifting one finger. "We tried the gun stations. We're locked out of the computers. No way we can access them."

Elijah grinned. "I have the codes. I just need to get into the central command, and I can give access to every starat here."

"Can you get that done now?" Rhys asked. He didn't want to leave Elijah behind, but he knew there was no choice. Too much needed to be done.

"Right on it, Rhys," Elijah said. He back peddled a couple of steps.

"See if you can get the teleporters active as well. We could do with Stephanie's reinforcements too," Rhys added, lifting his arm in farewell.

Elijah didn't answer. He turned and disappeared into the next room. Rhys shivered. He would need to take care of his own back until Elijah returned.

Rhys took a deep breath and took hold of Arnav's arm. "Get some starats up in those towers. Elijah will have that activated soon. If you manage to break through before me, we want the emperor alive if we can manage it. Executing him may not be the best look."

"And the cardinal?" Arnav asked, his brow raised.

Rhys's lip curled in a snarl. "I wish I could say leave him to me, but just kill that fucker if you get the chance. He can die. Doesn't matter who gets him."

"Understood. Are you taking anyone with you?" Arnav said, backing away from Rhys and gesturing to a few starats.

Rhys peered into the crowd. "Skye! You're with me."

Skye grinned widely. She scampered to his position and saluted. "We've almost got them, Essie. What else do you want from me?"

"We're going to try and flush them out or force a surrender," Rhys replied. A shiver ran down his tail as he looked into Skye's eyes. A passionate fury burned there. Blood covered her muzzle and claws. Her demeanour reminded him of the fervour he had seen in Cardinal Erik.

Arnav started to move away, before he turned and grabbed hold of Rhys's arm. His pupils dilated, and for a moment Rhys was fearful for his health. Then Arnav spoke, his voice rattling and hoarse. "There's a huge subspace disturbance coming. A fleet. Hundreds of ships. They come from Alpha Centauri. About five hours and they'll be here." He blinked and breathed in deep, his eyes returning to normal.

"Yes," Rhys hissed, grinning widely. "Now we know how long we have to hold out for. Victory is coming."

"Victory?" Arnav said, his voice still coming across shaky. "Well then. We'd better get to it."

Rhys turned to clamber up the stairs, leaving Arnav behind to carry out his side of their tasks. Each step strained at his thigh, which had gone from a sharp, stinging pain to a deeper ache. That just made it a little easier to manage.

The lobby balcony curved around most of the expansive room, giving a good view of the blood-soaked floor below, and the chandelier made of thousands of individual diamonds, crystals, and other valuable gemstones. On either side of the balcony, a corridor ran around to the side, leading towards the rooms beyond the throne room.

Wide windows lined one side of the corridor, looking out into the grounds. There was no movement outside or inside, with the only voices coming from the starats below and the humans locked inside the throne room.

Smaller windows looked inside the throne room, though Rhys couldn't see much. The small panes of glass were at head height for a human, and all he could see was the elaborate ceiling, and some patches of stonework on the balcony level that overlooked the throne room.

Rhys pushed open the first door. It slid open silently. He poked his head inside, checking the balcony. There were no humans on the narrow floor, though there was room only for a dozen starats at most. The balcony looked to have been designed to house a small group of media during speeches. He grinned to himself, then leaned back and pushed the door closed again. He looked back to the starat with him.

"We have them trapped, right where we want them," Rhys said. He checked to make sure he had enough ammunition loaded in his pistol, then tapped his belt. There wasn't much left. "We can't launch an assault from up here, but we might be able to spook them into surrender."

"What can we do up here that we can't do down there?" Skye asked, raising her brow. She followed Rhys's lead in checking her pistol. She was still almost fully loaded.

Rhys tapped his chest. "Me, mostly. They fear me. If I make demands, they might listen."

"And if they don't?" Skye asked.

Rhys flicked his ears back. "Then we might have some angry humans shooting at us."

"Sounds like a risk," Skye said. Her tail flicked up as she grinned. "I like it."

Rhys checked the bullet shield strapped to his wrist. "Is yours still intact?"

Skye answered by activating her shield. A few cracks laced across the transparent surface, but nothing that looked critical to the shield's integrity. She bared her teeth. "All good to go, Essie."

Rhys held his hand up. "Remember. We keep the emperor alive if we can. Everyone else is a viable target if they start shooting. Our main priority is to stay alive though. We stand a better chance of winning when Arnav breaks down the door."

"No shooting the emperor. Got it," Skye said. She cocked her pistol and grinned. "Let's overthrow an empire."

Rhys placed a hand on the top of Skye's pistol. "We're just going in to talk. Hopefully."

Skye scoffed. "Like they're going to let you do that. Come on. No point delaying getting shot at."

Rhys sighed and pushed the door open again. This time, he didn't try to remain silent. He slipped inside, onto the balcony and approached the bannister around the edge. He activated his bullet shield, though the protection it gave felt inadequate.

Thirty of the royal guard remained. They stood, mostly unorganised and waiting for orders, in the aisles between the rows of seats facing the throne. Another thirty soldiers stood on the other side of the room, wearing the bright, gaudy colours of the Vatican's Swiss Guard. On its raised dais was the ornate throne, upon which sat a man in a grey suit. He wore no adornments that signified him as the most powerful human to have ever existed, but Rhys recognised the short, white hair and lined face of Emperor Neicwyk. To the emperor's side was Cardinal Erik, in his usual red robes and wide-brimmed hat. He glared around the throne room, but he hadn't yet looked up. At the emperor's other side was Chancellor Roberts. The chancellor leaned on his cane as he stood in front of the throne, having a quiet conversation with the emperor. He wore a similar grey suit to the human by his side.

Rhys clapped his hands and stepped forward. "May I have your attention please."

Immediately, sixty rifles pointed in Rhys's direction. Skye adjusted her bullet shield and prepared her pistol as she stood by Rhys's side. No one fired.

Emperor Neicwyk rose from his throne. He patted down on empty air with both hands. "Stand down, stand down," he ordered the royal guard. "That's a fucking antique mural. You're not shooting it."

Cardinal Erik reddened, his face almost as crimson as his robes. His hands tightened into claw-like fists. He did not command the Swiss Guard to stand down, and the Vatican troops kept their weapons raised.

Rhys's muzzle flicked into a smile. He had an advantage. "Emperor Klaus Neicwyk. My name is Rhys Griffiths. I am here for your surrender."

"Eloquent for a starat, are you not?" Emperor Neicwyk said. He stood with his hands behind his back.

"Do not listen to this beast, sir," Cardinal Erik spat. The Martian never took his eyes off Rhys. His hand twitched by his side. Rhys could not be sure if the cardinal carried a weapon.

Emperor Neicwyk waved down the cardinal without looking back. "There will be no surrender today except your own. This rebellion will not spread beyond these walls."

Rhys smirked. "This rebellion has already spread beyond these walls. It is throughout the entire system. The Star Hub is overrun. The Martian fleet has already deployed against you. Either you will surrender to me, or you will surrender to the cardinal by your side."

"Terra is eternal. Terra will never bow its knee," Emperor Neicwyk said. His hands clasped behind his back and he looked up to the balcony for the first time. His eyes briefly met Rhys's. "That goes for you animals, and the church, should they get any ideas above their station."

Cardinal Erik dropped to one knee. The Vatican troops lowered their weapons. "I assure you, sir," he said. The emperor silenced him with a sharp gesture of his hand. The cardinal bowed his head. Even from his distant vantage point, Rhys could see the cardinal's jaw tense.

As satisfying as Rhys found it to see Erik cowed, even if just for a moment, he knew that he couldn't revel in the sensation. He placed his hands on the bannister around the edge of the balcony. "Trust me, Emperor Neicwyk. I will provide much nicer terms of surrender compared to the Centauran fleet approaching the system."

The emperor's calm visage cracked for a moment. His cheek twitched, before he slowly sat back in his throne. He drummed his fingers against the armrest and said nothing.

The chancellor tapped his cane against the stone floor and looked up. "You are the Rhys Griffiths from Ceres, are you not?"

Rhys inclined his head to the chancellor. "I am. You were one of the last people to ever see me as human."

Instead of sympathy or understanding, the chancellor's face went cold. His many lines deepened as he frowned. "Then you were the traitor we always suspected you to be. Your animal nature only loosened your loyalties further."

Rhys bared his teeth. "No, chancellor. I was not a traitor until you tried to frame me as one. If you'd have just listened to what I had to say then, we wouldn't be standing here right now. Funny how that works. You push, and I drag you down with me."

The chancellor turned away from Rhys. He addressed the emperor instead. "This creature is clearly delusional. We gain nothing from listening to it."

"Then ignore the animal," Emperor Neicwyk said irritably. He waved the chancellor aside, then snapped his fingers towards the cardinal. "Will Pope Adamantius turn his firepower on the CGP?"

"There is no CGP fleet," Cardinal Erik sneered.

Rhys turned his focus from the conversation happening below. He moved away from the edge of the balcony and took a seat on one of the chairs reserved for media. The bannister blocked off most of the view down to the throne room floor. Skye took a seat right beside him, their bullet shields still lifted to protect their bodies, should the humans below turn violent.

"They didn't really listen much," Skye said. Though Rhys didn't look to his side, he could hear the grin on her muzzle. "I still say we just blast them."

Rhys frowned. The balcony didn't offer any tactical advantage. It did allow a small group of starats entry to the throne room, but not enough to subdue the human forces below. He hissed softly in frustration. He needed a new plan. Any show of aggression would likely erode the emperor's unwillingness to open fire inside the throne room.

A frustrated scream came from the throne room floor. Cardinal Erik shouted in anger. "They are animals. We should not be giving them anything."

"They may be animals, but they have guns," Emperor Neicwyk replied, his voice still calm and even. "I merely propose…"

"I propose we slaughter them like pigs," Cardinal Erik snarled, cutting across the emperor's words.

Rhys rose back to his feet and stared down. None of the attention was on him anymore. Every last human warily watched the confrontation on the dais of the throne. The two opposing forces of guards shuffled apart a little further, dividing the room between Mars and Terra.

Footsteps pattered outside the balcony door. Though Rhys did not dare look away from the confrontation below, he thought he saw a flash of red fur in the corner of his vision.

Emperor Neicwyk steepled his hands. "You forget who you address, Cardinal. You were stationed here not to order me, but to advise me on where this spreading heresy lies."

Cardinal Erik clutched at the dangling rosary at his neck. "I can see that the rot has infected deeper than I ever knew. These are beasts to be exterminated. Take your weapons and put them to use, or I will have you branded as a heretic with them."

The emperor stood up. "Chancellor, you should retreat with me to our bunker. Commander Savi- damn it all. Penklis. You're to lead a counter-attack against the animals." He pointed up to the balcony. "Start with that one."

"Shit," Rhys swore, stepping back as all sixty weapons below lifted towards him again. Clearly the emperor had decided the loss of the antique mural was worth the defeat of the rebellion. One woman standing close to the balcony called out a command to fire. It was not a rifle she ordered. A rocket launcher. There was no chance for the shields to deflect that. They would obliterate the entire balcony just to kill him.

A burst of fire roared from the shoulder-mounted rocket launcher. Time seemed to slow to Rhys. The projectile skimmed through the air in slow motion as the humans moved a step back that took an eternity to complete.

The projectile deflected off empty air and smashed into the wall just beneath the balcony. The explosion ripped stone debris up, barraging into Rhys and sending him and Skye airborne. Out of the corner of his eye, he caught sight of another starat with russet fur, one hand extended out. Then his shoulder cracked against stone and he felt the world spinning.

The floor fell away as the balcony crumbled. Arms wrapped tightly around Rhys as he fell, with chunks of stonework debris cracking against his bullet shield, splintering it into many shards. Up became down. Senses were overwhelmed. Air moved over his fur as time snapped back to its usual flow.

He landed with a pained jolt. Pain spiked through his hips as his legs fell away from beneath him. Skye collapsed into him moments after landing, sending them both sprawled to the ground as fragments of antique stone clattered around them.

Dazed from the fall, Rhys looked up through a thick cloud of dust to see that most of the balcony had remained intact in the blast. Kalisha stood alone on the balcony, the starat little more than a russet silhouette through the haze as she leaned against the doorway. She had come just in time.

Instead of damaging the balcony like they had intended, the rocket had deflected into the sealed doors. The explosion had ripped a hole leading through to the lobby. Shadows moved on the other side. A loud roar grew.

"Defensive line!" A human voice screamed the command.

As the dust cleared, Rhys dragged himself behind some larger chunks of fallen masonry. Skye crawled beside him. He peered around the edge of his cover. All sixty humans worked together again, forming one long line to cover the emperor's retreat. Cardinal Erik stood on the throne dais alone.

None of the humans aimed towards Rhys or Skye. Their attention was on the gaping hole they had inadvertently created in the wall, breaching the only line of defence they had left.

Dozens of starats clambered through the wreckage, guns already firing. Rhys waited for their advance line to reach him, before he rose to his feet. Skye jumped up beside him.

Rhys's shattered bullet shield was only half the size it had been before, but it was still secure on his wrist. He had no time to find a replacement. Bullets thudded against it as the humans opened fire.

The human commander roared orders, her voice carrying over the constant crack of gunfire deflecting off armour and shields. Sixty humans, both Terran and Martian, began to dwindle.

Rhys snarled as he reached the humans' defensive line. The jagged edges of his shield punctured armour and flesh as easily as any blade. He rationed his limited ammunition sparingly. He fired when he needed to. Blood filled his nose. The air was thick with it.

A familiar voice echoed through the throne room. "They're animals! Slaughter them like animals!" Cardinal Erik had requisitioned a pistol from somewhere. He carried it clumsily.

Starats fell all around Rhys. They were outgunned. All they had in their favour was numbers. Rhys's ears flattened against his head as he pushed forward, ignoring the jolts in his arm as the bullet shield was struck over and over again. Numbers might not be enough. With a snarling growl, Rhys hurried forward, pushing ahead of the other starats.

Cardinal Erik did not notice Rhys until the starat's foot first stepped on the throne dais. The cardinal fired wildly. Three shots ricocheted off Rhys's shattered shield before the starat even managed to return a single shot. He missed.

"You have nothing on me, beast," the cardinal snarled. He took a step back, rising onto the topmost stair of the podium. "I have the might and blessing of Veritas on my side."

Rhys deflected another shot, keeping the shield high to protect his head. Taking another opportunity, he aimed another shot at the cardinal. His pistol clicked. Empty.

The cardinal's grin grew wider, more self-assured as Rhys threw his pistol to the side. "You can't win. Humanity prevails. Veritas prevails."

Rhys didn't bother answering. He leaped up the stairs, putting himself on level footing with the retreating cardinal. The human still towered over him, but Rhys could do nothing about that. His arm rung and vibrated from four more shots.

The cardinal kept aiming for the head. Rhys's shattered shield could not protect his torso or legs, but the cardinal showed his inexperience.

Rhys snarled as the cardinal retreated further, almost tripping down the other side of the podium behind the throne. Turning defence into attack, Rhys lashed out with the shield. The shattered edge slashed against the human's wrist. The pistol clattered against the floor. Doubt entered the eyes of the human. Blood stained his hand.

The starat punched with his left hand. Ribs cracked from the force, and Cardinal Erik stumbled back again.

Human and starat grappled. Rhys kicked out at the cardinal's legs, claws raking through the ornate robes, but not slicing through flesh. The human got his hands around Rhys's throat. Rhys slammed back against the throne. For a moment he felt dazed.

"How? Your arms?" Cardinal Erik gasped. A small trickle of blood dripped from his nose.

Rhys kicked again. This time, his claws found Erik's chest. He raked through the thick robes and sliced jagged lines through the human's flesh.

Erik screamed and struck Rhys across the muzzle. One hand was not enough to maintain a grip on the starat's throat, and Rhys rolled away.

The cardinal held one hand to his bleeding belly. He hunched over, but still lunged for Rhys before the starat had the chance to rise back to his feet.

"Animal," Cardinal Erik hissed. He reached down for Rhys.

The starat swung up with his left hand, then right. His fist caught one cheek, before the bullet shield sliced against the human's neck.

Cardinal Erik howled and stumbled back. His hand fended off the shield too late. Rhys did not waste his opportunity. He launched hard, his feet pressing into the dais and knocked Erik off his feet. Pinning the human down with a knee on his chest, Rhys allowed himself a moment to snarl at the cardinal.

"Animal, yes," he growled, before ripping through the human's throat with his teeth. He spat blood in Cardinal Erik's face. "Just like you."

The cardinal's eyes were wide. He spluttered and gurgled with no words able to make it out of his mangled throat. He convulsed beneath Rhys. His hands weakly tried to grab at the starat's face, but every time Rhys slapped them away. He didn't move until the light was gone from the cardinal's eyes, until the last breath rattled out of his torn throat.

Cardinal Erik was dead. Rhys spat in his face again, before rising to his feet to survey the scene. His bloody shield raised, ready to deflect bullets sent his way, but few seemed to care about the blood-stained starat on the throne. Only a small pocket of humans remained, mostly made up of the royal guard. Penklis cried out desperate orders, but her troops were quickly overwhelmed.

Rhys scooped up a dropped pistol, but he had no need for one. He surveyed the last resistance of the empire with impassionate eyes. One by one, the surviving humans fell.

Penklis was the last. She screamed in desperate fury. Starats swarmed around her.

Arnav struck the final blow with a triumphant roar.

Rhys sunk back onto the throne and let his pistol drop from his fingers. The battle was over. They had won.

Someone called Rhys's name. He was suddenly so weary that he could barely lift his head. Adrenaline drained from his system, and the pain in his legs and hips came to the fore. He just wanted to lie down and sleep, but he knew that they had not yet finished the job. The battle was over, but the danger had yet to pass. He slowly looked up to see Stephanie framed in the ruined doorway.

"Now that is a sight I could get used to," the human said. She stepped forward, moving amongst the fallen bodies of human and starat.

Rhys flicked his tail and wrinkled his nose, realising exactly where it was that he had sat. "Fuck off, that's not my job," he said, though he managed to force a small laugh to his lips. "There's still the current emperor to deal with. He's got a bunker he crawled into with the chancellor. Entrance must be somewhere in here."

"I'll see to it," Stephanie said. She grinned and turned to request the help of a handful of starats to discover exactly where the emperor had slipped away too. He couldn't have gone far.

Starats slowly swept through the room, tending to the wounded and mourning those who had fallen for the cause. Rhys closed his eyes and bowed his head again, listening to every whimpering groan and mournful cry. This was the cost of war. It was a cost that had not yet finished being paid. There was still more to come, but for the moment there was chance to take a deep breath and accept the sacrifices that had been made.

A hand rested on Rhys's knee. He opened his eyes again to see Elijah kneeling in front of him. He carried a roll of bandage in one hand, and gently touched his fingers through Rhys's fur with the other. "You're hurt."

"Not too badly," Rhys replied. He looked over Elijah. He could see no wounds on the augmented starat. "You got the defences under our control?"

Elijah unravelled a length of bandage and cut it with his teeth. "I did. Rina and Alistair are setting up a garrison all around the outer wall. Short of orbital bombardment, we should have the castle secured for a good while yet."

"We have to hold out for a few hours, that's all," Rhys said. He ran his hands along the armrests of the gilded chair. He had to be the first starat to ever lay hands on the ornate throne, unless some had been involved in the construction of the seat of power for the empire. "The Stellar Guard will be here then. They will be able to sweep aside the Vatican."

"Then let us hope the church doesn't launch a full assault on us first," Elijah said. He uncoupled some of Rhys's leg armour, exposing the wound in his thigh. Rhys hissed in pain as Elijah began to wrap the cut properly, covering over Rhys's earlier attempts at staunching the flow of blood.

"They will," Rhys said. He leaned back and hissed quietly, grimacing as Elijah tightened the bandage around his thigh. "Ah, fuck, that stings." He sucked his breath in and growled softly to himself. "They'll attack. Adamantius will think he's got the chance to seize total power. If he can take Windsor, he adds Terra to Martian control."

"He might be a bit pissed that his chief inquisitor was killed," Elijah said. He wrinkled his nose and grimaced. "His blood reeks on you. You're having a long shower before you even think of taking me out on that promised date."

Rhys shuddered. "I've never felt as dirty as I do now. I must look hideous."

Elijah giggled. "Like a wild animal." He held his hand out for Rhys to take, and the two starats stood up. On the dais, they higher than any over starat in the throne room. Rhys's eyes glanced up to the ruined balcony. No one was up there. Kalisha had gotten herself to safety.

Rhys rose his voice to address the whole room. "We've won the first battle, but there's more to come. Raid the medical supplies here. Get a ward set up. Then we need to fortify the gates and make sure every gunnery tower is manned."

"Right you are, Essie," Skye called out. She lifted her pistol into the air from where she stood, close to the ruined wall. "I'll start organising the defences."

"I know where the medical supplies are," Elijah said quietly. He placed his hand on Rhys's muzzle. "Will you be alright without me for a bit?"

"I'll be fine," Rhys said with a smile. "Kalisha had her eyes on my back before. I've still got everyone else to look after me."

"Back soon then," Elijah said, dropping his hand away from Rhys and descending the dais down to the blood-stained floor.

Rhys stood with his hands on his hips. He managed to disguise a dry sob as a hacking cough. There were no tears to cry, but the terror and realisation of what he had done threatened to overwhelm him. The Terran Empire lay crumbled at his feet. He turned his head to the painted artwork on the ceiling. The Centauran fleet was coming. They would grind those crumbs into dust.

He had saved Terra. He had destroyed the Terran Empire.

chapter twenty-one

"The Terran and Martian fleets have been engaged in combat for the last two hours. First shots were fired almost simultaneously to Essie's broadcast," Stephanie explained. The throne room had been cleared of bodies and the wounded. It now served as a temporary command centre for the starat conquerors. The human stood with Rina, Arnav, Rhys, and Skye. A holographic map showed the rough positions of the two fleets, about halfway between Mars and Terra. The two planets were almost at their closest points to each other, with Luna's position currently directly between the two planets. "I'm not convinced they know yet what has happened here."

"How can they not know?" Skye asked, her eyes wide in wonder. The battle was taking place almost exactly halfway between the two planets and slowly drifting towards Terra as the Martian fleet pressed the Terrans into a gradual retreat.

"They had their orders to defend Terra from any threat," Rhys explained. He furrowed his brow as he looked over the display. He wasn't sure who he wanted to win the engagement. Both would result in a siege of Windsor. "Mars became that threat. They didn't need any further orders. The chancellor was ultimately the one in charge of giving orders on the emperor's behalf. We know there's no external communication from their bunker, but the power levels below him are capable of acting without direct orders."

"So they won't need any official command to turn on us when they realise what's happened," Stephanie clarified. She tapped her hands on her chin. "I believe the current admiral of the fleet is Enkhtuya, isn't she?"

"I believe so," Rhys said. He folded his ears down. He had never had to deal with the military command above Admiral Garter, except on rare occasions. His interview with Chancellor Roberts had been one of those few cases.

"She won't hesitate to attack Windsor then," Stephanie said. She placed her hands on the table that had been dragged in from the lobby. "She would style herself as a successor to Neicwyk if she could."

"Then we had better hope the Martians win, hadn't we?" Rina said. She glanced up at Stephanie and flicked her right ear back. "Either way, we're prepared for a fight. Alistair is finishing the defences right now. I doubt they'll launch an orbital bombardment when they can't confirm if the emperor is still alive."

"Perhaps we should send out a broadcast confirming he's still alive," Rhys suggested.

Stephanie quickly shook her head. "I don't want to risk him managing to send out a coded message with any broadcast. We have him trapped and cut off right now. We keep quiet until they attack. We still have about three hours until the Centauran fleet arrives. Until then, we can't expect any more reinforcements. No help. It's just us against the might of Terra and Mars."

"We have one ship," a new voice said. General Carson strode into the room. His beard had started to grow back again but was still a shadow of its former self. "Deployed tactically, the *Rossi* might be able to delay any orbital strikes."

Rhys growled softly. "Even at half fleet strength, we're going to expect two dozen or more ships. A lone ship standing in the way would be suicide for that crew, and they might only buy us minutes. That's not worth it."

"You'll better serve us on the ground," Rina confirmed, nodding her head in the direction of the newcomer. "You did well in helping us neutralise the Star Hub, but all of our focus must now be on how we can fortify the ground. The sky is lost to us. We don't have the resources to defend up there."

"If we had been able to secure for Star Hub for ourselves..." Stephanie mused. She frowned and stared down at the table.

"It was all we could do to neutralise it," Rina said, shaking her head. "Terra is defenceless right now, but at least that means the Star Hub can't work against us."

Carson took his place at the table, standing between Rhys and Skye. "We had better hope that Bosler gets here soon, or else we're toast. There's nothing here that can withstand more than half an hour of orbital bombardment from multiple ships."

Arnav's muzzle twitched as he stared at Carson. "They'll be here when they get here," he said simply.

"Could we not evacuate?" Carson suggested.

Rhys shook his head. "There's too many wounded to move quickly," he said, shrugging. "And besides, our presence here is more symbolic than anything. If we leave, we give the victors of the battle up there an easy walk into Windsor and command of the empire again. If we wish to win with Centauran support, then we must keep hold of Windsor."

Carson scratched his chin. "Fine, I guess. I just wish there was more we can do than just hope to wait out their attack."

Rhys laughed nervously. "I would love for that too, Sam. Don't worry. None of us are happy with this. It's just all we can do. We've got some of the best defensive systems on Terra here. We can only hope they'll be enough."

Stephanie swiped at the holographic display a couple of times. The sensory map was accurate to a significant distance around Terra. It showed a barely delayed portrayal of the battle that was taking place almost halfway to Mars. Those ships were about half an hour from arriving in the skies of Terra should they all abandon the fight immediately. The battle raged fiercely, with the sensors picking up on the thousands of missiles exchanged, as well as the growing field of debris.

That was not where Stephanie's attention had fallen. Three ships had broken away from combat. All three carried Martian designations. One was the *St Peter*, the flagship of the Martian fleet and the personal ship of Pope Adamantius. The other two were personnel carriers. The battle still raged beyond them, with the Martians appearing to take the advantage.

"Shit," Rhys growled. "They think they've already won up there."

"They're moving to secure Windsor," Stephanie said. She swiped at the map projection, keeping the focus on the *St Peter*.

Rhys quickly worked out how far from Terra they were. "There's no more time for planning," he said slowly. "They'll be on the ground and ready to march in forty minutes."

Skye slapped her hand to her chest and grinned. "We shoot. We kill. We survive."

"Nice and simple. Just how I like it," Rina said. She nodded her head towards Skye. "We all know what to do. Essie's Heresy has been building to this moment for years. This is the day we throw off the shackles and live as equals in a free world. If we have to spill some more Vatican blood for it, then so be it."

"Time for Essie to lead us to one last victory," Stephanie said. She looked around the table. "For so many years I have dreamed of this moment. Let's take it before it has a chance to slip away."

Rhys growled. He lifted his clenched fist. Ever since his transformation he had fought against the responsibility of being a figurehead for change. He had never felt worthy of being the starat others looked up to. He still didn't, but that no longer mattered. To millions of starats, he was the voice and soul of Essie. Until the Centauran fleet arrived, he had to bear that weight.

"The Vatican will show no mercy," Rhys said, his voice a deep growl. "Every single human who storms this castle is our enemy. It's time to show them what a true starat is capable of."

"For Essie," Rina said, her hand grasped around Rhys's closed fist.

"Today we're all Essie," Skye added, placing her hand on Rina's.

"We will do his memory proud," Rhys said. One by one, everyone, even the two humans, around the table reached out to join hands with each other. The weight of a legacy settled on his shoulders.

Arnav nodded. "We all have. We all will."

***

Dropships streaked across the sky. Most remained out of range, but one ventured too close to Windsor. The anti-air guns plucked the military shuttle out of the sky and sent it plummeting to the ground in a dazzling plume of flame. The doomed ship landed with a terrifying explosion to the north of the castle.

The remainder of the dropships landed to the south of the castle, amongst the streets of the surrounding town, close to the ransacked military barracks. Rhys knew that the Martian personnel carriers in orbit could carry over two thousand ground troops each, if not more. This time, it was the starats who were outnumbered. Rhys was not sure if the best defence network in the Sol System would be enough.

Rhys stood alone on top of the wall over the main gates. The wind had started to pick up. It whipped against what little exposed fur that was not covered by his armour. His tail lashed from side to side as he watched the distant movement of soldiers. He checked his wrist display. A timer counted down towards Arnav's estimated time for the Centauran fleet's arrival. Just under two hours remained. He did not know how long it would take for them to sweep through the remaining Terran and Martian fleets.

The emperor and chancellor had been locked inside a bunker beneath the castle. There had only been room for a dozen inside, or else the starat army might have been able to find refuge below ground. Instead, they had no choice but to fight for their lives.

In front of the gates was a narrow gravel path in the middle of a grassy green that stretched for a couple of kilometres. Trees lined the green, providing a walkway wide enough for three dozen humans to walk shoulder to shoulder. All too soon, the Martians would be marching up the grassy clearing. For the moment, it was quiet and still.

Rhys knew the starats were in danger of being surrounded by the landing Martian forces. All they could do to help mitigate that was to spread their forces thin, taking control of the turrets and gun platforms situated around the outer walls. Should the humans breach the walls, then they would not be able to withstand the assault for much longer. Their only hope lay in the formidable defences and high walls.

"Above!" Arnav cried out. He was stationed close by, in the nearest of the gun batteries to the main gate.

At his word, the gun batteries swung into action. The automated systems lifted the massive turrets almost vertical, spinning around to open fire at several streaks of light that descended from the clearing blue sky.

Rhys watched as the missiles exploded in mid-air, intercepted by the defensive flak cannons. A ferocious display of fireworks lit up the sky, with fragments of explosive debris scattered far and wide. Rhys didn't flinch. He just narrowed his eyes and returned to his vigil. The *St Peter* was testing their defences. More would come.

The shimmer of an energy shield sprung up around the castle. Smaller in scale than the planetary shield that had been planned, Rhys had authorised its use despite his worry that Amy's SFU could still work to strip Windsor castle into subspace. The shield was necessary, though. It did nothing against projectile weapons used by the Martian forces, but it was the only way to absorb the impact of energy weapons from the *St Peter*.

Energy weapons of that scale were inefficient in atmosphere, and the flagship would not be able to keep up a sustained assault with them, but just one accurate strike would devastate the castle. They had to expect an irregular bombardment from orbit.

The shields activated. There was no flicker of white. The landscape of Britannia remained intact. Rhys exhaled, unaware he had even been holding his breath.

A quiet beep sounded in Rhys's ear. He held his hand up to the side of his face and tilted his head to the right. "I'm here."

Elijah responded. "Medical is ready. Not many here with a lot of experience, but there's enough basic knowledge to keep people alive. Are you sure you don't want me out there with you?"

Rhys shook his head, even though the call was voice only. "No. Stay there. You'll be more use helping in medical with your knowledge."

"I can't watch your back if I'm in here," Elijah protested.

"I'll do my best to stay safe," Rhys replied. He took a slow, deep breath and looked out to the amassing army. "I won't let them win."

"Promise?"

"I promise. We'll go out somewhere nice to dinner when this is over," Rhys said. He forced a smile onto his face, even as his voice was almost drowned out by the automatic fire of the anti-air turrets again. Another series of explosions ripped through the sky, sounding a little closer this time. Rhys could feel their heat a few seconds later.

"I'm holding you to that," Elijah said, his voice trembling slightly as the sound of the explosion faded. He hesitated. "I... I'll see you soon, alright?"

"See you soon," Rhys replied, before the soft beep in his ear told him the call had ended. He wasn't sure those had been what Elijah had intended as his final words in the conversation. Perhaps they could broach that topic when there wasn't a war to win.

Rhys turned his focus back to the marching army. They weren't far beyond the range of the turrets either side of the gate but redeploying those weapons would limit the effectiveness of their anti-air defences. Rhys hissed softly to himself. Windsor had powerful defences, but they weren't designed to operate without the anti-air support from the nearby barracks. If they'd had more time, they might have been able to secure the barracks. Defending on two fronts could overwhelm them, and the Martian forces almost certainly knew that.

"Arnav, we need firepower ahead," Rhys called out, knowing that the other starat would be listening out for his commands.

A few seconds later, the turrets began to move. The massive barrels pointed down the greenway, towards the formation of soldiers. Several powerful shots were fired, and moments later geysers of mud and grass were kicked up just in front of the Martian army. They did not stop advancing.

Rapid Defence Vehicles flanked the march of soldiers. Their turrets swivelled to send intercepting fire towards the heavy artillery shots from the Windsor walls. Some missiles got through the flak barrage, but the formation was relentless in its advance.

"Focus fire on the RDVs," Rhys called out. They were the bigger threat, especially when they got into closer range and could return fire on the heavy turrets.

The turret operators responded to his commands. In a dazzling explosion of orange and red, one of the vehicles burst into scorched debris. A dozen more still offered protection to the marching army. The battalions of infantry were soon close to their firing range as they slowly came to within a few hundred metres of the walls. Only then did Rhys turn away and make his way down from the gate. He was too big a target up there.

A kill box had been set up behind the gates. Over a hundred starats were in Alistair's command behind the crudely repaired structure. The gate would not withstand any assault for more than a few minutes, but Rhys hoped the formation behind it would hold back the Martian assault for long enough.

The sky lit up white. Rhys shielded his eyes and looked up. A crackling pillar of white light pierced the blue sky. It struck the energy shields surrounding the castle and dispersed in a web of electricity. A dozen missiles were intercepted by the flak cannons. Fiery explosions added to the awe-inspiring terror.

A few starats shrank back, but none broke free from their formation. Pistols and rifles were raised, with bullet shields activated. Tails swished nervously and most exposed ears were flattened down completely. A mixture of Essie's Heresy and local civilian starats stood ready to defend the castle.

Rhys stood as tall as his diminutive frame could manage. "You fight for your freedom, for the right to be equal amongst humans," he cried out, lifting his voice to compete with the roar of the turrets. "You may not all have training like they do, but you have heart and desire. We will never surrender. We fight for Essie!"

"For Essie!" the starats roared back, lifting their fists and weapons into the air. The chant spread through the entire castle, rippling out from the front lines and calling out from inside the expansive windows. The fur stood on end all down Rhys's neck and shoulders as the roar overwhelmed even that of the artillery fire. There was a savage, almost primal sound to the roar.

There was no more time to think. Instinct was all that mattered, and that meant sinking down to become the animal that humans thought starats to be. With his teeth bared, Rhys braced himself as the first strike against the battered gate almost ripped apart the welded hinges.

The turrets continued to fire. High powered missiles launched from the largest guns, while the smaller gauge turrets sprayed bullets into the air to intercept enemy missiles. They could also be used for anti-infantry, but there was no time for that. They were already in danger of being overwhelmed from the volume of fire coming from beyond the castle walls.

Smoke rose from beyond the gate. Another blast struck against the thick defences. It buckled but held. Rhys grimaced and braced himself. His pistol felt light in his hand, with a new bullet shield on his wrist.

"This is it," he muttered to himself. If the Martian forces wanted to take Windsor, then they would need to focus their entire force through the narrow gate. He would not make it easy for them.

A third explosion ripped the gate apart entirely.

Rhys braced, but the Martians did not advance. The air turned white, and for a moment Rhys feared that a subspace bomb had gone off inside Windsor. Then he recognised the burned ozone on the air and realised that another orbital strike had impacted the shields. Electricity crackled through the shield, sizzling and heating the air around it. Rhys squinted into the light.

Flames licked the highest spires of the castle as more orbital missiles were intercepted. A wave of bullets launched through the front gates. Rhys's shield thudded from a dozen impacts that pushed him back a few centimetres. He stood his ground, as did the starats around him.

Before the flames and light had a chance to clear, the humans advanced. Their rust-red armour was thick and strong, but they weren't impervious to bullets. Their shields were small, allowing them to carry a heavy rifle in both hands. They had firepower, but they weakened their defences because of it.

"Fire!" Rhys screamed, though his cry was not needed. Hundreds of starats loosed their shots, ripping into Martian armour before the humans had a chance to brace.

Wave after wave of shots were exchanged and repelled. Starats with higher power weapons were stationed in windows behind the front lines, sniping humans from the relative safety of the castle balconies. Still more came. There was an endless wave of them, pouring in through the gate and struggling to push back the starat defenders.

Crude fortifications provided small areas of cover. Furniture and broken statues from within the castle had been repurposed, giving places for a starat to retreat and reload.

Rhys never once stopped moving. Stephanie and Arnav were the main voices in his ear, keeping him informed with enemy and friendly movement around the outer walls. The turrets were able to keep most of the Martian forces at arm's length, with only a small percentage of the force capable of reaching the gates unscathed. Once there, it fell to the starats themselves to repel the enemy.

Rhys lost track of how long he fought. He retreated to safe shelter multiple times to reload. Starats were injured and killed all around him. Their blood on his armour and shield gave him the motivation to keep fighting. He could not allow the Martian attack to drain at his hope. All that mattered was the next shot, the next kill. His blood burned with white fury as adrenaline coursed through his veins. His ears flicked at every sound, drawing his attention to enemy movement before his eyes caught up.

Minute by minute, the starats held their ground against the onslaught, but there were always more humans to pour through the narrow gate. The gunfire from the wall never ceased. The only event of any regularity was the blinding bombardment of the *St Peter's* energy weapons, but the shield held firm.

Smoke choked at Rhys's throat. It tickled his nose and irritated his mouth every time he breathed in. Blood and smoke obliterated his sense of smell. His limbs ached, but if he stopped moving then he would die. He could not stop.

The tide of battle ebbed and flowed. On more than one occasion, the Martians almost broke through. Then the defenders began to push back, closer to the gate again. Humans barely made it a few paces into the inner grounds before they were forced to fortify their position, never coming close enough to get into melee range.

Rhys found himself fortified alongside Skye, whose shrieked commands had been amongst the most vocal. The Cerian starat was covered in blood, but little of it appeared to be hers. She grinned at Rhys as they both crouched behind an overturned statue of Emperor Neicwyk that had been carried out from the throne room.

Before Skye could say anything, a frantic voice came into their ears. Arnav shouted. "Incoming!"

Another blistering white beam of light cracked against the shields, but it was the explosion moments later that ripped through the castle. A missile had finally hit. A roar of fire, stone, and metal exploded outwards, sending chunks of debris hurtling through the air. Some smashed against the wall, tearing slices out of the defensive grid, while others speared through human and starat alike.

From his position, Rhys couldn't tell what part of the castle had been struck. He crouched beside Skye and held a hand to his ear. "Elijah? Are you alright?"

A small voice answered moments later. "We're fine. Didn't hit us. Windows smashed and a couple of small fires, but we're fine."

"Fuck, glad to hear," Rhys said. He glanced up over the statue to quickly scan the area. The Martian assault had been momentarily halted as a consequence of the electrified shield around the castle. The explosion had also scattered their forward line, but they were quickly reforming. Rhys switched vocal channel. "Arnav, how are your defences holding up?"

"Badly," Arnav replied immediately. Rhys could hear the crackle of flames around the other starat, as well as the occasional boom of the artillery guns, echoed moments later through the air. "One of the turrets has been compromised. We're going to take more hits like that."

"Hold them off as long as you can," Rhys replied. He gritted his teeth, knowing that task was easier said than done. He was not surprised that he got no answer back from Arnav. For a moment, Rhys was tempted to look down at his wrist. He kept his eyes raised. Counting down until the Centauran reinforcements was a distraction he didn't need. Whether they had ten minutes or an hour changed nothing. They had to keep surviving until that became impossible.

What had once been pristine lawns had turned into a churned mud field. Blood and water mingled and trickled in rivulets down towards the walls. The Martians began to retreat, and for a moment Rhys was unsure why. Then an RDV appeared in the gate, nosing its front-mounted turret into the small space.

Rhys holstered his pistol and rose to his full height. He unclipped an EMP grenade from his belt and bounced it once in his hand as he gauged the distance. The heavily armoured vehicle slowly screeched against the walls, cracking the defences as it forced its way inside. The turret began to rotate around towards Rhys's position.

The starat primed the grenade, before he lobbed it towards the RDV in a high, arcing swing. The grenade bounced once before striking the underside of the vehicle. An electromagnetic pulse blasted out, shredding the tyres and sending smoky explosions popping through the armour. The turret swung limply around to snag against the mud as it keeled over onto one side, partially blocking the gateway.

Rhys hissed in satisfaction. The wrecked RDV gave arguably more cover than the original gate had. A snarling cheer and chorus of chanting spread through the starats at the smoking sight of the ruined vehicle. "For Essie!" rung through the castle again, though this time the echoing cry sounded weary.

Rhys twitched his nose. The wrecked RDV continued to smoulder, and no more humans pushed past the vehicle. No one had evacuated the RDV. The starat took a couple of deep, panting breaths. A new smell tickled at his nose, carried on the gentle breeze. A shimmering clear fluid spilled from the back of the RDV. Oil.

The RDV had not been manned. No one intended for it to cause damage with its guns. They had sacrificed it.

"Take cover," Rhys roared, lifting his bullet shield up and dropping to his knees again. All around him, starats mimicked his movements.

Enough seconds passed for Rhys to begin to feel foolish. Then a ferocious explosion ripped through the grounds as the RDV disintegrated. Fuelled by the oil, flames spat in all directions, igniting some of the grass and trees that grew in the gardens. The blast ripped apart the gateway entirely. A large section of the wall crumbled into rubble and one of the turret towers partially collapsed.

A second explosion followed moments later as the castle was struck by another missile from the orbital bombardment. An energy beam seared down from the heavens, sending electricity crackling through the shields again. More bursts of fire followed, and the slight shimmer of the shields vanished.

"Shields down," Arnav announced grimly. "Power overload. Five minutes until reboot."

"We'd better hope the *St Peter* doesn't recharge in five minutes then," Rhys said. He glanced down to make sure his pistol was fully loaded as he braced himself for another charge to come from the Martians.

Another voice beeped into Rhys's ear. "They're flanking from the north," Stephanie warned. "We're in danger of being overrun here."

"Can everyone safely retreat back to the castle?" Rhys asked. He didn't want to fall back, as they would lose access to the outer defences and the turrets. At least the heavy guns were locked out of use for anyone but a starat.

An affirmative answer came back from Arnav, Stephanie, and Rina. By his side, Skye also nodded. Rhys sucked in his breath and hissed. Humans were starting to approach again, and this time they had a much larger area to get through. Some had to clamber over the ruined section of wall, but that just provided extra cover.

"Then retreat. Fall back," Rhys commanded. If the shields couldn't be restored, then they had lost anyway. The castle would not take a direct hit from a weapon of that strength.

Rhys took a step back. A bright flash lit up the sky. "No," he muttered, thinking the *St Peter* had fired again. "Too soon."

The beam of death did not come. Instead, the starat squinted and looked up. No weapon had fired. The flash of light faded quickly. Rhys's ear folded down, before Skye tapped him on the elbow.

"Let's go," Skye called out. A couple of thuds against Rhys's bullet shield restored his focus. He could worry about the light in the sky later.

Rhys retreated with the remainder of the defending force. He tried to provide cover for those who didn't have shields to protect themselves. A dozen fell, most coming from the remaining turrets. Arnav made it back to the castle.

Rhys and Skye were the last in. The doors closed with a resounding slam behind them, though Rhys didn't expect them to last long against the heavy firepower the Martians possessed. A broken and battered resistance of starats readied itself in the main lobby and overlooking balcony. This was the last stand of Essie's Heresy.

"Barricade the doors," Rhys called out, not letting his fears into his voice. If he was to be Essie, then that meant fighting until his last breath. He would not give up, nor would he allow anyone else to do so.

Starats scurried to carry out Rhys's commands. He helped them, dragging heavy stone statues across the floor in the hope that they would slow access to the lobby. They did not have long until the first blast shook the doors. "Get back," Rhys called, waving away the starats who were still close by. With one hand on his pistol, Rhys retreated to safety.

A beep sounded in Rhys's ear. The frantic voice of Stephanie followed. "The sensors have lost the *St Peter*. It's no longer in orbit."

"What?" Rhys yelped. He clapped a hand to his ear as he crouched into position behind a collapsed pillar. "It can't have left."

"I'm telling you Rhys, it's not there," Stephanie replied. She breathed heavily, and her rapid footsteps came through the small speaker in Rhys's ear.

Beside Rhys, Skye grinned again. "Well, at least we're not being blown up from orbit." She rested the barrel of her rifle against the fallen pillar. "Just got to worry about them out there."

"They're more than enough," Rhys replied. He growled softly and adjusted his feet, getting down on one knee. He positioned his shield to protect his head, while keeping his left hand free to continue firing. All around him, two hundred starats prepared themselves. A further one hundred were on the balcony. A few others would still be hurrying through the mazy innards of the castle, blocking off the passages behind them as they tried to funnel the Martian forces through to the main entrance.

The building shook. For a moment, Rhys thought the castle had been hit by another missile. Then he recognised the roar of dropship engines descending. He felt like swearing. Did the Vatican really need to send further reinforcements to finish them off?

"Fuckers," Rhys spat. He wrinkled his muzzle and tightened the grip on his pistol. He could hear movement outside. Heavy objects scraped against the ground. Footsteps approached then retreated. A brief silence fell. Every shuffling movement from the starats seemed a cacophony. Claws scraped against metal. Determined starats reloaded their guns. They also whispered prayers to Essie.

The doors exploded inwards with a ferocious blast of heat and air. Cracks snaked through the painted artwork on the ceiling as the entire lobby threatened to collapse. The firefight started immediately. The smoke hadn't even cleared before the first Martians stepped foot inside the castle, rifles lit up.

The starats on the balcony gunned down the first wave from above, but there was more to come. They stepped through the smoke, like wraiths emerging from the darkness.

The heavy impact of bullets against Rhys's shield numbed his arm. He barely even had a second to extend his left hand out to return fire, relying solely on the starats on the balcony to suppress fire back on the advancing humans.

"Fuck, we can't stay here," Rhys snarled. He didn't know who could still hear him. Skye didn't react. She just remained focused on the humans, squeezing the trigger on her rifle and quickly finding her aim once more.

Rhys retreated a couple of steps. His eyes frantically looked around, hoping for any obvious help or way out, but he could see nothing. Nothing but humans. Nothing but deadly weapons aimed right at him. Even beyond the Martians, through the clearing smoke, Rhys could see another wave of soldiers approaching, all clad in white armour. They looked unusually short.

Searing pain lanced through Rhys's leg. He dropped to one knee and bowed his head, keeping his bullet shield raised out of instinct alone. He hissed and whimpered, dropping his pistol to the floor.

Three loud explosions rung out just above Rhys. Starats screamed as the balcony broke apart into twisted rubble. Massive fragments of stone rained down on the lobby, with many starats trying to contort their bodies mid-air and land safely. Some managed to do so. Most did not.

Distant gunfire pricked at Rhys's ears. Too far away to be those already inside the castle, but there were no starat defenders left in the grounds. Rhys looked up. The new troops were attacking the Martians. Those who had already made it into the lobby had turned to face this new threat. The Martians turned their backs on the starats.

Rhys grabbed his pistol and slowly rose to his feet. He helped Skye rise by his side. "Centaura," Rhys whispered. He clapped his hand to his muzzle and laughed. His voice rose into a triumphant shout. "Centaura!"

Rescue had come. Rhys limped forward a few steps, lifting his shield and pistol again. The battle had turned once more. Following Rhys's lead, a group of starats charged after the humans, pinching them between starat and Centauran forces.

Sunlight broke on Rhys's blood-stained fur. Hundreds of Martian troops still fought for their lives, but they were trapped. They took no prisoner, and Rhys hitched up his bullet shield and returned to the fray.

Mud exploded up just to Rhys's right, sending him scampering apart from the remainder of the charging starats. He hissed in anger as a pair of Martians moved up, separating him entirely from his allies. He took a couple of steps back, almost slipping on the churned surface.

Holding his shield up, Rhys unloaded his pistol onto the advancing humans. Several shots hit their mark, but none proved a fatal hit. His pistol clicked. Empty. He had no time to reload. With a snarl, he threw himself forwards. He lashed out with his shield, turning the defensive utility into a weapon of its own.

The shield cracked against the visor of one of the humans. Rhys spun quickly, trying to keep out of their grip, while using his pistol as a bludgeoning weapon. He dented the armour of one, causing the human to stagger back, seemingly dazed. Rhys kicked out, but only jolted his foot and ankle against their rigid armour.

A fist crashed down on Rhys's chest. Stunned and winded, Rhys stumbled back and raised his right arm, keeping the bullet shield in a protective position.

Instead, a knee came up to him, slipping beneath the shield and catching the starat on the jaw. With a pained yelp, Rhys fell backwards off his feet. He scrambled through the mud, trying to keep away from the humans. Two rifles aimed for his head.

A low whine increased in intensity. A beam of focused light burst from the right, striking one Martian with explosive force. Rhys shielded his eyes from the intense ray, which cut off a moment later. The human stumbled and fell without a sound. His companion swung his rifle around to the side, but a second whine preceded another blast from the ray.

Rhys blinked away the bright afterimages in his eyes to see his saviour was a starat. He was clad in combat armour that covered most of his body, but leaving his left leg exposed. A gleaming, cybernetic leg with claws as sharp as any blade. In his hands was a boxy type of pistol Rhys had never seen before, with a deep red glow coming from within the elongated muzzle.

"We're not done yet, Captain," a familiar voice said. The starat lifted his visor for a moment. William grinned from within.

Rhys could have hugged the starat right there, but he held himself back. William was right, there was still a war to win. He simply saluted the starat and grabbed his pistol from where it had fallen. He quickly reloaded. His wounds ached, but confidence and adrenaline gave him the willpower to continue.

With his back to William for protection, the two starats made their way to the bulk of combat. Some Martians tried to retreat, fleeing over the walls. Rhys ignored them. They were no threat.

"To your right," William called.

Rhys glanced across, lifting his shield and pistol. Two shots and the Martian fell. "Two more," Rhys said. His eyes tracked the two red-armoured Martians. Any structure the attackers had previously held had evaporated with the Centauran assault. There were only small bands of Martian troops, slowly being pushed back towards the ruined gates. Two shots thudded against Rhys's shield, but it held firm.

William's pistol whined again. A blast of fierce light struck one of the Martians, who fell in an instant.

"Shit, I need one of those," Rhys said, his eyes wide. He opened fire with his pistol, bringing down the second Martian. His weapon felt weak in comparison to the destructive energy beam William carried.

"Special issue," William replied. Though Rhys could not see his face, he could hear the smile in William's voice.

One by one, the remaining soldiers began to surrender. Most lifted their hands, dropping their weapons down to their feet. Of the thousands who had stormed the castle, only a few dozen remained. The Vatican forces had surrendered. The battle for Windsor Castle was over. The starats had won.

Rhys leaned against William for support as weariness overwhelmed him. He panted for breath as he held his hand to his ear. "How are we all doing?"

"Hurt, but alive," Stephanie quickly replied. "Rina's here too."

"Same here," Arnav confirmed.

"And me," Skye added. Rhys could see her, still close to the ruined gates. She was being tended to by a Centauran starat for a wound on her foot. Alistair crouched close to her, his black fur visible as he removed his helmet.

Elijah was the last to check in. "I'm fine here. I'm coming out to you as soon as I can. There's nothing more I can do in medical without extra supplies."

Rhys exhaled slowly. So many had fallen. So many lives had been lost. He bowed his head and allowed a brief swelling of emotion at the thought. They had sacrificed their lives to better those for starats across the empire. Rhys would not allow that victory to go in vain.

"Seems like you've been busy," William said. The other starat unclipped his helmet and attached it to his belt. His ears perked up as he holstered his pistol as well.

Rhys stared around the ruined grounds. Bodies lay everywhere. Rubble smoked amongst the muddy ground, and small fires were being put out. Voices shouted as starats searched for friends and companions amongst the fallen. The Martians who had surrendered were silent as they were bound.

"Just the usual," Rhys whispered. He wasn't sure what else to say. The weight of everything crashed down on top of him, pushing him to his knees. He couldn't stop the tears coming to his eyes. A mixture of a laugh and sob came to his mouth as he looked up at William. "Still think I'm the same oblivious human you thought I was?"

William's ears pinned down. He crouched by Rhys's side. "That's what I called you, when you first came down to see me." The starat sighed and rested his hand on Rhys's thigh. "Please tell me you didn't do all of this just to prove me wrong."

Rhys smiled softly. "In a way, I did," he said quietly. He was distracted by movement ahead. Some of the Vatican troops were being led away, with more Centaurans coming from their shuttles at the far end of the green.

"You're a fucking idiot, you know that?" William said with a laugh. He nudged Rhys on the shoulder, pushing him over into the mud. He shook his head and chuckled. "Tearing down an empire, just for me."

Rhys stuck his tongue out. "There was some selfish motivation as well," he said with a grin. "I did it for me. And for Twitch and Richard. For every starat."

A shadow passed across William's eyes. Rhys didn't press for a reason, but William turned away. His voice cracked. "Well, if you need to hear it from me, then you are not an oblivious human."

"Thank you," Rhys said, getting to his feet again. The weight of his actions still crushed his shoulders, but William's words did mean a lot to him. It had been a while since he believed himself to still be the ignorant human he once was, but he appreciated William telling him so. After all, William had been the one to suffer more than most because of Rhys's old obliviousness.

Another starat called Rhys's name. Elijah sprinted out from the smouldering castle. He quickly closed the gap between them. Rhys stepped away from William and almost leaped into the embrace from Elijah, whose arms wrapped tightly around him. Elijah pressed his muzzle against Rhys's, and the two kissed passionately, happy to see each other again. The fear that Rhys had been carrying that he may never see Elijah again was finally able to disperse on the wind.

An amused chuckle reminded them of the other starat standing next to them. William grinned, with little trace of the pain in his eyes lingering. "You know Twitch is going to absolutely love this, right?"

"He's here?" Rhys asked. He leaned into Elijah, his tail wagging.

William pointed to the smoky sky. "He's with the fleet-admiral, but I'm sure it won't be long before he comes down."

"It sounds like there's a lot of stories to tell," Rhys said. His eyes drifted upwards. If the Centauran fleet had amassed above Terra, then he could see no evidence of it. Nor was there any sign of the *St Peter*.

"There's a lot that happened on Centaura, and I want to know what happened here as well," William said, with some of his sorrow coming back to his voice.

"We'll have time to talk soon. But first, we should help clear up this mess."

There was still a crumbling empire to finish destroying.

chapter twenty-two

"It's over."

Skye was the latest starat to sit on the throne. She draped her body across it, her feet dangling over the side of the ornate arm rest. She held her head in her hands and gazed up to the mural on the ceiling, paying no attention to the activity around the throne room.

"At what cost?" Rhys asked. He did not expect an answer. He merely vocalised his thoughts as he stared across the room. The secret bunker had been opened, and the emperor and chancellor pulled out from their hidden refuge. Under heavy guard, Fleet-Admiral Bosler was in conversation with them both. Some words occasionally drifted across the throne room to the dais, but Rhys intentionally turned his ears away. That was a conversation he wanted no part of.

Skye snorted. "At the price of our freedom."

Rhys pinned his ears back. He looked up to the starat on the throne from where he sat, on the bottom step of the dais. The throne room had been cleared out of the dead and the rubble, but the smell of blood still tickled at the back of his nose. A few other starats from Essie's Heresy were sat around him, with the Centauran forces doing most of the clean-up work. While the grounds around Windsor were quiet for now, Rhys could not imagine it would stay that way for long.

"There will still be people fighting," Elijah said, putting words to Rhys's concerns. "They won't accept what's happened here."

Skye waved her hand. "That's for them to deal with," she said, gesturing to the fleet-admiral and her entourage of guards. "We've done our part."

For that much, at least, Rhys could agree with. The Centauran fleet-admiral had not yet spoken to Rhys, but she had given him a brief, curt nod before she had initiated her conversation with the deposed emperor. He knew there would be a lot of uprisings and protests across the planet, and indeed across the system, which would take a lot of force to quell. Rhys wanted no part of that. He had no desire to aim a weapon in the direction of a civilian.

"Stephanie seems keen to keep up the work," Elijah said. His hand rested on Rhys's as he sat on the floor just by his side. His ear perked up. "Is she Essie again, or is that still you?"

Rhys shook his head and spread his hands. "I don't think anyone is now. Or maybe all of us are. He is a memory and an inspiration, but now?" He shrugged and looked around the room. Few paid much attention to the small group of starats clustered around the throne dais. "He will always be the first free starat, but now he doesn't have to be the only one."

"Shame, the name suits you," Elijah said, smirking.

Rhys replied with a roll of his eyes. He slowly rose to his feet, ignoring the ache in his legs and the pain in his ankle. Raised voices came from the side of the room as the emperor was led away with the chancellor amongst two dozen armed guards. The emperor walked with his head high, while the chancellor was hunched and leaned heavily on a cane.

The fleet-admiral remained in the throne room. She approached the dais with her hands clasped behind her back. She still wore her battle armour, with her helmet and pistol secured at her hip. "Well, Captain Griffiths. I must say, I had lost all hope of seeing you again."

Rhys inclined his head to the human. "I had my doubts as well," he said, unsure if she expected him to salute her. He kept his hand by his side. "I trust Amy's treachery was discovered on Centaura?"

"We had some great help from Twitch," Fleet-Admiral Bosler said. She held her hand out towards the door. "We are about to begin our negotiations for the terms of surrender with Emperor Neicwyk. Would you care to join us?"

Rhys's ears flattened against his head. His tail tucked between his legs. "Does it have to be me, Fleet-Admiral? I am no diplomat, nor am I a politician."

"We would prefer someone from the empire to represent the starats," Fleet-Admiral Bosler said. Deep lines spread across her forehead as she frowned. "This cannot simply be humans discussing terms."

Claws pattered against the ornate stone dais. "I could do it," Skye said brightly. She stood by Rhys's side, bouncing on her toes.

Another starat approached from the other side. Alistair lifted his hand. "I, too, would like to find starats their new place in this world. I would like to join these discussions."

"I can vouch for them both," Rhys said, flicking an ear as he glanced across to the other starats. He was glad that someone else had volunteered for it, for he had no interest in sitting in on a never-ending argument with little hope of resolution. He could not imagine Emperor Neicwyk would concede much, even despite his position of utter defeat.

Fleet-Admiral hesitated. She opened her mouth to speak, before closing it again. She then shrugged. "Alright. I guess there isn't really going to be any starat who will be able to speak for you all. Might as well be you two."

"Yes," Skye said, pumping her fist in the air. She grinned widely as she started to follow the human. She turned around and walked backwards, facing the starats around the throne. "Don't worry, I'll make sure that old creep doesn't get anything from us."

"He'll learn to respect starats," Alistair added. He beamed widely.

Rhys watched the starats leave with the fleet-admiral, before turning to face the others. "I'm going to have a little walk around the grounds to see if there's anything small that needs doing," he said. He forced a smile to his muzzle, but he knew it wasn't work that he needed to do.

Lifting his hand to stop Elijah from getting to his feet, Rhys quickly turned and started to follow the fleet-admiral. While they both turned right to go deeper inside the chaotic castle, Rhys made his way directly to the muddy grounds. Too many thoughts plagued his mind, too many distractions pulled at his senses. He needed somewhere quiet.

No one stopped Rhys as he made his way out of the ruined gates. Centauran aircraft patrolled overhead, with foot soldiers marching around the perimeter. No Terran forces would be able to get close to

Windsor Castle without the Stellar Guard of Centaura knowing about it. Even beyond the protective walls of the castle, Rhys knew he could feel safe. He trudged away from the noise, keeping his eyes low but ears perked.

Clouds had come across the sky again, blotting out the darkening sky and the sunset. Rain was expected to come soon, but it was Britannia. Rain was always expected to come soon.

There were footprints in the mud as Rhys moved away from the path down the long green. In the shadows of the small forest to the side, the starat found who had made them. He did not turn away. Stephanie was perhaps the only person he wanted to be near for the moment, though guilt did bother the back of his mind as he thought of Elijah.

Stephanie lifted her hand as Rhys approached. "I suppose I should have expected you to be out here as well," she said quietly. Away from the castle, there were fewer noises to distract them. Wind lightly brushed through the trees, and somewhere in the distance, voices shouted. They came from the surrounding suburbs. They were too distant and faint for Rhys to make out what was being shouted.

"I needed some time to think," Rhys said, curling his tail around his leg as he crouched down a few metres away from the human. He slowly sunk back to sit down, resting his head against a tree trunk with his tail swept to the side. A couple of leaves drifted down to land on his fur, but he did not brush them away.

"We've just been through a lot," Stephanie said. She shuffled across the ground to sit a little closer, but still out of arm's reach. She had a couple of scratches on her face, but any blood had already been cleaned up. "We cut the head off the empire and handed over Windsor Castle to the CGP. That's going to be difficult to come to terms with for a while."

Rhys sighed and closed his eyes. He rubbed his hands either side of his muzzle. The short, coarse fur on his hands tickled at his nose. "That's not what is bothering me, though. Well, it is. But not as much as… It's silly."

"You know you can tell me anything," Stephanie said. Her voice was soft and gentle. With his eyes closed, Rhys could almost ignore the fifteen years that had passed since he had said goodbye to her at the Shanghai airport. The feeling of his tail against the bark of the tree behind him gave a permanent reminder of all that had changed since then.

Rhys sucked in his breath. He lowered his hands to twist his fingers through his tail. His ears both flattened to his head. "I haven't let myself get close to anyone since, well, you," the starat admitted. He stared down at his tail and hands. "I'm scared of messing things up with Elijah."

Stephanie's arm settled around Rhys's shoulder. He leaned his head into her. "You just brought down the empire, almost by yourself, and you're scared of falling in love?"

"I told you it was silly," Rhys said, curling up as he leaned against Stephanie's body. He sighed softly as her hand lightly stroked through his fur.

"He's good for you. And you're good for him," Stephanie said quietly. She kissed Rhys between his ears, but she did not let the contact linger for too long.

Rhys had so many conflicted thoughts in his head. Even sitting next to Stephanie and listening to her voice brought back so many memories. He could be comfortable with her again, and some part of his heart ached for those days to return, but he also knew that could never happen. Too much had passed, too many years had gone by. Both of them were different people now, even if Rhys forgot all about his transformation.

"I was a nervous mess when we started dating," Rhys said with a grimace. He pulled his tail free from his hands and thumped it amongst the dry leaves on the ground. "I know I'll be just the same again."

"It worked out well the first time," Stephanie said. She removed her arm from around Rhys's shoulders. She reached out to take his hand. "Just be yourself and I know you two will be happy together."

Rhys spread his arms wide. "I feel like I'm stilling learning who I am, especially after all of this," he said, his ears flicking back. He grimaced. "But I'll try. I'm just scared. It's been over fifteen years since I've done anything like this."

"Perhaps you need something to distract you," Stephanie said. She helped Rhys up to his feet and gestured to the castle. A couple of starats came out from the main gate. "How about the throne? It looked like it suited you."

Rhys snorted with laughter. "Not a chance of that. I can lead a ship. Maybe even a fleet. But a whole system? That one isn't for me."

"Then what do you think you will do?" Stephanie asked. She and Rhys took a couple of steps away from the trees, back towards the castle.

"I don't know yet," Rhys admitted. He had put no thought into what he might do. Everything had been focused on the next step, of surviving one day longer. "I've only ever known the military, but if Centaura has won this war, then who is there left to fight?"

"You'll work it out," Stephanie said. She looked up to the cloud-covered sky. No stars shone through, but they were still there, beyond the clouds and the light pollution of the nearby city.

"How many do you think you'll go and see?" Rhys asked, looking up to the sky with Stephanie.

The human laughed. "I've still got to catch up to you. Then, who knows?"

"Who knows indeed," Rhys replied with a sigh. Perhaps now that Terra had been broken free of the shackles that had been placed on it, there could be a new, more optimistic future for the humans and starats that lived there. His attention came back down to Windsor. The two starats who had come out from the castle gate continued to get closer. They looked familiar. A shiver ran down into his tail.

Rhys broke away from Stephanie. He ran as quickly as his tired, weary legs could manage. One of the other starats matched his movements. Rhys and Twitch barrelled into each other, falling to the ground as they embraced. Joy burst in Rhys's heart.

"I knew you would be alright, Captain Rhys," Twitch crowed. He nuzzled into Rhys's shoulder, arms wrapped tightly around the other starat.

"I'm so sorry I didn't come back," Rhys said, struggling to hold back the tears. "I should have been there for you, but I wasn't."

Twitch didn't let Rhys go. He kept his arms tight around the other starat, head resting on Rhys's shoulder. His body shook as well as Rhys's. Both let go of the tears in their eyes. "It's alright, I know it wasn't your fault."

"And you can walk again," Rhys said, choking back on the guilt that threatened to come up with the tears. He managed to look down at Twitch's legs, which looked utterly perfect. Like Rhys's arms, there was no trace of the Devil's Blood left in them.

This time, Twitch did loosen his grip on Rhys. He sat up and stretched out his legs, wiggling his toes. "With a little help. Look at what I can do," the starat said, beaming widely. He pressed on his thighs, just below the cut of his shorts. To Rhys's surprise, a small panel opened, revealing with electronics within.

Rhys looked up into Twitch's eyes just in time to see the shadow there. It was gone in an instant, so quickly that Rhys wasn't sure it had even been there. He swallowed, trying to wet his suddenly dry throat. "They couldn't be healed, could they?"

Twitch shook his head. He looked down at Rhys's hands, and his eyes lit up brightly again. "But yours were," he said, lightly brushing his fingers over Rhys's forearms.

Two shadows stood over the starats. Rhys glanced up. Stephanie had caught up with them again. David also stood over them, and the larger starat held out his hand to help Rhys and Twitch up off the ground. He pulled Rhys into an embrace as well, less forceful than Twitch's, but still firm enough.

Twitch gasped and giggled as he looked up to Stephanie. "Have you got a human, Captain Rhys?"

Rhys groaned, while Stephanie laughed.

"We haven't been together for a long time," Stephanie said. She then tensed slightly as Twitch approached. "You look identical."

"Twitch, this is Stephanie," Rhys said quickly. "Stephanie, this is Twitch. He's my…" Rhys floundered to find the right word.

"He's my clone," Twitch said brightly. He swished his tail and giggled to himself, before his head tilted to one side. "Not for a long time? You used to be together?"

"We were engaged, a long time ago," Rhys admitted. He curled his tail up over his legs. "I thought she was dead all this time, and now I find out she had been secretly leading a starat rebellion right here on Terra."

Twitch grinned widely. "You sure do know how to pick them," he said, before holding out his hand. "But come on. There's a lot of people who aren't quite convinced you're still alive either. We've just finished getting everyone down from the ships."

"I should leave you to that," Stephanie said, taking her arms from around Rhys's chest.

Rhys shook his head at the same time Twitch did. "Absolutely not," Rhys said firmly. "You can come with us too. Once they learn what you've been doing here, these starats are going to love you."

"I didn't do much. It was all Rina and Arnav, mostly," Stephanie said with a shake of her head, her cheeks reddening slightly.

Rhys giggled and raised his brow. "Trust me. They're not going to accept that excuse. They never did with me."

Stephanie sighed softly and allowed herself to be led away. She put her hand around Rhys's shoulders and walked alongside him, back towards the castle. Twitch bounced ahead of them, almost skipping with every step. His synthetic legs moved smoothly and gracefully. They were perfectly natural in their gait. Had he not seen the electronics beneath the fur, Rhys would never have known they were cybernetic. A touch of sorrow came to Rhys's ears as he looked at them. He had not been quick enough to save Twitch's legs from Cardinal Erik, but that human could do no more harm to starats.

Twitch squeaked in delight as he babbled on, leaning into David for support. "There's so much we need to tell you, Captain Rhys! You weren't there, so we were trying to do what we could to fight all the bad people. There was Amy to stop, but also the president. He tried to blow up the planet too, and I was the only one who could stop him. And then there was Snow too with her freaky, scary magic. I had to stop her there too. And then... oh. There's some sad things too."

Rhys's ears pinned back. He wasn't sure he wanted to know what had put the sudden sorrow into Twitch's eyes, or the dullness into his voice. All the emotion seemed drained out of him, and the other starat no longer bounced with each step. His tail hung low.

"What happened?" Rhys asked. His throat felt dry.

"Not everyone made it," Twitch said. His shoulders slumped and he turned around. He stopped walking. His muzzle twisted. "Amy killed Leandro, and Richard died in an attack. There was nothing we could do for them."

"Fuck," Rhys growled. He bowed his head. "I'm sorry she turned on you. I wish I could have gotten a warning back to you when I realised what she was doing with Snow. What happened to them?"

Twitch's tongue flicked out to lick his muzzle. "Amy survived. The Stellar Guard captured her. I killed Snow myself," he said with a whimper. He stared down at the ground as David's arm tightened around him. "I had to kill people. I hated it. But her? I suppose she deserved it."

"I hope you never have to do anything like that again," Rhys said. He did not like the look in Twitch's eyes, though that quickly faded as his usual bright smile returned.

"I sure hope so too, Captain Rhys," Twitch replied. A shadow remained in his eyes that hadn't been there before, but he started to walk again with a swish in his tail. "But come on. Everyone's waiting for you."

***

While large parts of Windsor had been destroyed almost beyond repair in the bombardment from the *St Peter*, enough of the castle still stood to act as a base of operations for the occupying Stellar Guard. Work had already begun to start repairing some of the least damaged regions, though Rhys could tell that a lot of work would be needed to restore the old building.

The occupying force had converted one of the many halls into a temporary dormitory, with supplies carried through from the Centauran shuttles that had landed just beyond the castle walls. Starat and human mingled together, with many of the Terran starats in conversation with their brethren from across the stars.

A cluster of familiar faces waited for Rhys. He saw them a moment before they saw him. He hurried forward to the group of starats and two humans. Aaron and Carson were the humans present, while William, Nick, and Steph sat with them. They all rose to their feet.

"Told you he was alive," William said, grinning as he puffed out his chest. "Saved his life from a couple of Vatican soldiers."

"We never said you were wrong," Steph retorted, the diminutive starat shoving William in the ribs.

Rhys hurried forward and embraced Steph, leaving Twitch and David behind. He then turned to Aaron and embraced his oldest friend, but he hesitated when he turned to Nick. The black-furred starat held his hand out. Rhys took it, then pulled him into an embrace. Nick's hand hovered above Rhys's back for a moment, before resting against him.

When they parted, Nick still didn't quite meet Rhys's eye. "I, uh. I suppose I should give you a second chance."

"It's all I ever wanted," Rhys replied. He took a step back and smiled, looking around the small group of friends he had missed. He was painfully aware of the two who were missing, of those who had not survived whatever had befallen Centaura. His breath caught in his throat for a moment, and he bowed his head. He would never hear another story from Leandro, and he would never get the chance to fully make things up with Richard.

Aaron's attention had moved from Rhys. He stared at Stephanie as she came into the room, and his face had gone completely white. Like he had seen a ghost. Just as Rhys had thought he had done.

"How is this possible?" Aaron whispered. "It can't really be you, right?"

Rhys flicked his ears back and extended a hand towards Stephanie. "Everyone, this is my former fiancé, Stephanie. I had thought she was dead, but it turns out she was here all along, leading a starat rebellion. Were it not for her, we would not have had this victory today."

"I think we've all got a lot of stories to tell each other," Aaron said. He took a couple of steps forward, before giving Stephanie a hug. Twitch squeaked and rubbed his hands together in glee, bouncing from one foot to the other.

Amongst the movement all around the temporary dormitory, Rhys caught sight of the one other starat he desperately wanted to see. Aware that the eyes of his reunited friends were on him, Rhys waved Elijah over. The augmented starat smiled nervously as he approached, his tail tucked low.

Before Elijah could say anything, Rhys wrapped the starat up in his arms and kissed him on the muzzle, not caring about the attention they were getting. "I'm sorry for running off before. I just needed time to clear my head about a few things."

"It's alright, I understand," Elijah said. He returned the kiss and smirked. "You aren't able to have as many thoughts at once. Takes a little longer to get everything through your head."

Rhys stuck his tongue out, but he was quickly distracted by an excited squeal just behind him. Twitch bounded up and pulled both Rhys and Elijah into a hug. "You didn't get a human, you got a starat!" he crowed in delight.

Rhys turned around and grinned bashfully. He leaned into Elijah's side. "Everyone, this is Elijah. He's the reason why I'm still alive, and I love him for that."

There were so many questions all at once. Rhys pinned his ears back, feeling like he was on Ceres, trying to answer questions from the starats when he was still new to his body. He didn't know where to start, but Elijah spoke up for him.

"I think we all owe each other stories," Elijah said, squeezing his arm protectively around Rhys. "But we've had a pretty hectic day, and I think there's a group of starats preparing some fish. We should get something to eat, and then we can catch up on what everyone has been doing."

Rhys nodded, grateful for the intervention. He flicked his tail close, between his legs. "And I'd love a shower as well. My fur is a mess."

Twitch giggled and pinched a couple of fingers over his nose. "I mean, I wasn't going to say anything…"

Rhys gave Twitch the middle finger and grinned. "I missed you too."

***

Rhys had to wait a short while, but the showers in the Windsor barracks and private rooms had all been opened for use by those who needed them. He washed away the blood and mud that had caked to his fur, relieved to finally feel clean again. Towelling himself dry was the usual irritation, but he felt much better when he got out of the showers. Food was another wait, and it was largely military rations with only a tiny portion of the promised fish, but Rhys didn't mind that at all. He cared about the company.

Twitch told the story of what had happened on Centaura first. He was not the skilled storyteller Leandro had been, but he had the encouragement of his companions to keep speaking, even when he stumbled over a bad memory or difficult time. He relied on interjections from David or Aaron when he got details wrong, but Rhys gradually began to get a good picture of how close Amy had been to completing her plans on Centaura.

Then it was Stephanie's turn. Mostly for the starats' benefit, she started her story fifteen years earlier, when she had still been engaged to Rhys. She introduced Rina and Arnav, even though the two weren't present, before jumping forward to her time as Essie, leading a rebellion right below the streets of London. Twitch had gazed on in awe at her, until finally it came to Rhys's turn.

Rhys stumbled as much as Twitch, and he leaned on Elijah to help sift through some of the things he still found confusing. From Pluto to Ceres, and then to Mars his story went. William's eyes had lit up when Rhys recounted the story on the summit of Olympus Mons, but he didn't offer up any interruptions. No one could resist the moment when Rhys recounted how he had killed Cardinal Erik in the throne room. Loud cheers interrupted the other starats and humans through the temporary dormitory. Only Twitch remained silent. His shoulders sagged and his eyes closed as he leaned into David's embrace.

William thumped his tail against the floor. He sat back against the wall while his fingers idly rubbed over the metallic gleam of his cybernetic leg. "I never thought I'd live to see days like this," he said softly. He smiled as he looked towards Rhys. "I utterly despised you for so long. When you were human, I think you deserved that hate. Now, though? You helped make all of this possible."

"I just did what I had to," Rhys replied. He bowed his head and tucked his tail between his legs. His ears both curled down as the fur on the back of his neck prickled up. "I don't think I did anything special. Any starat would have done the same."

"You still did it, though," Steph said. The diminutive starat sat next to Stephanie. The two namesakes had shared a few conversations with each other already. They had seemed to take quite a liking to one another. "Sure, you had help. You had the advantage of being human once, and enough people still cared about you. Doesn't mean you didn't do all those things."

"You've helped starats everywhere," David added. His dark ears were perked upright as he smiled brightly. "You've made our lives so much better from the moment we met you. We'll always be in your debt."

"I'm just glad I could help," Rhys said. He leaned back and hugged his arms over his legs. "Though I won't lie, it has been exhausting. I'm looking forward to just lying down in my bed and doing nothing at all."

"With Elijah?" Twitch added with a wink.

Rhys blushed and snapped his mouth closed. His ears felt warm. Elijah's arms were tight around his chest. They didn't quite meet each other's gaze. "Perhaps."

Twitch giggled to himself. He stuck out the tip of his tongue. "Thought so."

Rhys flicked his ears and floundered for a change in conversation. "You didn't mention what happened to Admiral Garter. Did he come back with you?"

"He did," Aaron said with a nod. "But not directly with us. He went with some of the fleet to help control the belt and surrounding regions. I'm sure he'll get in contact with you as soon as he's able."

"It feels like Sol is going to be a very different place when this is all done," Nick said. The black-furred starat leaned forward. He still had some of his military-rationed meal left uneaten, but he didn't seem too eager to finish it. Rhys didn't blame him. The meals were uninspiring and mostly tasteless.

"It's going to feel free," William whispered.

"We'll never forget the blood that had to be spilled to make it so," Rhys added.

Twitch raised his fist. "For Leandro."

William lifted his fist too. "For Richard."

Rhys didn't hesitate in raising his arm. "For the memory of Essie."

"For us all."

chapter twenty-three

Two weeks had passed since the capture of Windsor by the Stellar Guard when Rhys finally made it home. He stood in front of his house in the outskirts of Cardiff like he was in a dream. For two weeks he had helped with the changing of the guard in Windsor, but he had not wanted to be involved in the installation of a new leader.

For generations, a succession of emperors had ruled Terra. A new president would soon be elected, changing how Terra governed itself as it moved to a more Centauran style. Resistance was expected, but the Stellar Guard was helping to maintain control through the system. Without the authority of Emperor Neicwyk or Pope Adamantius, there were few leaders for the empire to turn to.

None of that mattered to Rhys right now. He trusted those, like Aaron Lee, who had stayed back in Windsor to ensure that they would lose none of what they had fought for. Starats across the empire were being freed. Soon, they would be completely equal with humanity. Rhys was no longer needed as Essie.

"It's been a long time since I've been here."

Rhys turned at the voice. He smiled at Stephanie, who remained on the pavement with Rina and Arnav. She leaned on the brick wall.

"You're welcome any time," Rhys said. He held out his hand to the human, the ghost from his past who had become quite real again. He managed a smile. "Let's not make it fifteen years this time."

"I'll do my best," Stephanie said with a laugh. She took Rhys's hand in her own and held it for a second, before turning away. She held her hand up and waved. "I'll see you soon, Rhys."

Rhys did not move away as he kept his hand raised. Stephanie started to walk away with Rina and Arnav, but she was not leaving his life this time. Rhys could never have expected going fifteen years without her when he had said goodbye at Shanghai, but this was different to that. Even so, he could not prevent the occasional tear leaking into his fur as she turned the corner with one last wave.

The gate closed with a rusted screech, though Rhys had not touched it. He glanced back. Kalisha stood in the open door of his home. "Come on," the russet starat said, holding out her hand. "You're going to make Elijah jealous if you keep fawning after her."

Rhys rolled his eyes and stuck up his middle finger. "You're a bigger tease than Twitch," he grumbled, but he wiped his eyes with the back of his hand anyway.

"You're always so receptive to it," Kalisha said with a smirk. She closed the door behind them.

The inside of the house was crowded. Five starats packed into the small kitchen, which soon became seven with Rhys and Kalisha. The windows were all open, as not even the scent of seven starats could fully overwhelm the grime and dust that choked at Rhys's nose.

"It's not as nice as your one on Centaura," Twitch said with a flick of his nose. He grimaced as he opened one of the cupboards. "Bleh, that's gross."

Rhys laughed. He could never have imagined welcoming starats into his home, let alone his life. He couldn't believe how many friends he had missed out on before his transformation, simply because he had refused to see starats as equals. Now, as one of them, his life was so much better. He smiled at Elijah warmly, but it was not just the augmented starat.

"You're all welcome to stay here as long as you like," Rhys said, standing in the middle of the kitchen with the others all around him. He slowly turned to face them all. Twitch and David. Steph and William. Kalisha. Elijah.

"Go and take him to dinner," Twitch said, surprising Rhys. He hadn't realised how long his gaze had lingered on Elijah.

Rhys blinked, his cheeks turning red beneath his fur. "But we have so much to do here," he said, sweeping his hand around the kitchen. He dreaded to think about the dust in the carpet, or the cobwebs in the corners by the ceiling.

"Go," David said with a laugh. "We'll be just fine here."

Though he wanted to protest and argue, Rhys extended his hand to Elijah. His heart felt like it swelled, both at the contact from the other starat, but also from the love he felt for the friends around him. "I know a really good restaurant down by the waterfront," he said in a small voice, trying his utmost not to stammer and stumble like a love-drunk teenager.

"We'll be back later," Elijah said, taking hold of Rhys's hand.

Twitch giggled. "Bring him home by ten."

Raucous laughter filled the kitchen. Rhys couldn't help but join in, but he also extended his middle finger to Twitch. That only made the starats laugh louder. He was so glad to have them back, but this was going to be a time with just himself and Elijah. Not even the ghosts of the past would stop him from enjoying his date night.

Leaving the other starats behind, Rhys and Elijah walked alone. They were two free starats without a care in the world except for each other.

***

For nearly a week, Rhys just enjoyed the ability to rest and do little. He showed his visitors the sights around Barry and Cardiff as the summer sun lit up the city. Rhys knew things could never last, but he wanted to enjoy every second of it for as long as he could. The future was still coming, and there were going to be many hard decisions to make. Some had to be made very soon. Rhys wasn't looking forward to those.

The time came quicker than anyone wanted. The starats caught a shuttle up to the Star Hub. Tears were shed between them before they departed the surface, and most of their emotions had been shared by the time they left Terra. Conversation had returned to normal on the journey, and Twitch's enthusiastic excitement spread through the rest of them again. Rhys leaned against Twitch for most of the journey, supplanting David from his usual place. No one complained, especially not Twitch.

The Star Hub gleamed as it always did. Rhys felt a little numb as he walked through the shining corridors. Outside the many windows he could see the bulk of the Centauran fleet, preparing to depart to Proxima Centauri. Their pacification efforts were no longer required in full. A garrison was going to remain behind to ensure the peace remained, and that a democratic government was installed to replace the ousted emperor, but most Centaurans would be going home.

Twitch caught sight of the ships outside, noticing Rhys's distraction. "Are you sure?" he asked.

Rhys nodded. "Yeah. It won't be for forever, but right now, I just can't."

"I understand, I think," Twitch replied. His hand squeezed tight around Rhys's. "This is your home. I never really had one of those, but Centaura is where I started to feel safe."

"And that's why you should go back. You'll be happy there, I know it. You'll do great things," Rhys said. He pulled Twitch into an embrace, partly because he wanted to give Twitch the comfort, but also because it forced him to move and look away from the gathered fleet.

"I'm going to miss you, though," Twitch replied. He wriggled free of Rhys's embrace after a few moments and began to walk again, but he kept his hand tightly in Rhys's.

"And I'm going to miss you," Rhys replied. He looked ahead, where most of the other starats were excitedly talking to each other. "My life has been changed so much since I met you."

Twitch stuck his tongue out. "Well, you're much more attractive now. Plus you've got a hot boyfriend."

Rhys laughed and flattened his ears against his head. "Not exactly what I was thinking of, but I suppose you're right."

"Oh, right. The leading a revolution thing?" Twitch said, nodding vigorously. "I guess that counts too."

"You once told me that I would change things, just for being a starat," Rhys said softly. They approached one of the main lobbies in the Star Hub, where hundreds of humans and starats had gathered. Almost all of them were part of the Stellar Guard, ready to return home. "I never realised just how true that would be."

Twitch giggled. "Rhys Griffiths, destroyer of empires," the starat said, sweeping his hand around to the side. "What are you going to destroy next?"

Rhys didn't think his ears could pin lower. His tail tucked. "With any luck, nothing. Perhaps the forest of weeds in my garden."

Twitch stuck his tongue out. "I suppose that could be fun too. But you've got your whole life ahead of you. That can't be all you want to do."

"I suppose I could go back into the military," Rhys said with a shrug. "If I'm lucky they might even give me my old rank back. But other than that, well I'm a bit too old to realistically think about a new career."

Twitch came to a halt. He turned around and placed his hands on Rhys's shoulders. "Too old? Rhys, I'm not yet twenty-one."

Rhys's ears perked up. "You are? Somehow, I always thought you were older than that," he said with a frown.

Twitch didn't say anything. He smirked and giggled, waiting for Rhys to say something else expectantly. Rhys grew a little nervous, unsure just what he was missing. His tail tucked close, and his ears slowly drooped again.

Twitch slapped his forehead. "You're a smart starat, Captain Rhys. You can work this out. If I'm twenty, and you have an exact copy of my body, then…" The starat trailed off, rotating his hand around to encourage Rhys to continue the sentence.

Everything clicked into place. "Holy shit. I'm twenty?"

"There we go, you got it," Twitch giggled. He grinned widely and slid his arm around Rhys's shoulder to start walking side-by-side with him again. "You're twenty again, with what? An extra thirty years of experience?"

"Twenty-three," Rhys grumbled. He jabbed a finger against Twitch's chest. "I'm not that old. Wasn't that old. This is all confusing."

"Ah, close enough," Twitch said, giggling a little as he pushed Rhys's hand away. "Either way, you don't have to do the same thing all over again. You can do whatever you like."

Rhys pinned his ears back and took a deep breath. The revelation of his body's younger age surprised him, but also brought new possibilities whirling around in the forefront of his mind. He felt almost paralysed with options. "I… I don't know. I'll have to think about it."

A flicker of sorrow and pain passed across Twitch's eyes, before it was hidden away again. "Well… so long as whatever you do means you can come and visit, I'll be happy."

"I will, I promise. I'll send messages and I'll visit whenever I can," Rhys promised. He pulled the other starat into another embrace, resting his forehead against Twitch's. "You will always be an important part of my life."

"I should hope so. I'm pretty spectacular," Twitch said with a grin. He bounded back away from Rhys, scampering across the packed lobby towards David and the other starats.

Rhys sighed to himself and smiled, hurrying after Twitch. David, William, and Steph all stood waiting for him, with Elijah hanging back a few steps.

A call went out across the PA systems, announcing that boarding had begun. The time had come so quickly, and Rhys no longer knew what to say. They had already said most of their goodbyes on the surface, but the final one seemed so difficult.

"You've all helped me be a much better person," Rhys said hesitantly. He held his hands out, but before he could react, he heard footsteps approaching from behind. A starat's hand slapped on his shoulder, and he turned around to see Aaron and Nick.

"On that same shit again, Rhys?" Nick asked. He held his hand out for Rhys to shake. "Forget who you were. Embrace who you are now."

Rhys flicked his ears back. His tail swished as he shuffled his feet. He nodded once and sighed. "I suppose you're right. But I can still thank starats like you for making sure I truly became that better person."

"I'll let you have that one," Nick said, sticking the tip of his tongue out.

Rhys turned to look up at Aaron. "You're going back to Centaura too?"

"I am, yes," the human replied. "Might not be permanent. There's talk of a Terra/Centaura liaison office being established with me and Carson as part of the team, so I might be travelling between the two systems a lot."

"Well, I hope to get plenty of visits from you," Rhys said. He shook Aaron's hand firmly, before turning his attention back to the starats.

There was nothing for anyone to say. There was no need for words, but Rhys closed the distance between them and just embraced them all. Four starats circled around Rhys, hugging him tightly. He felt their close presence and enjoyed every last moment of it. Soon, the unimaginable distance of space between Sol and Proxima Centauri would separate them, but Rhys knew that they would always be together in other ways. It was a parting, but it would not be forever.

Rhys's cheeks weren't the only ones that were wet when the embrace reluctantly ended. "I'm going to miss you all."

"We're going to miss you too, Rhys," Twitch replied.

"You stay safe," Steph said. She held onto Rhys's hand for a moment. "And we'll see you again sometime soon. We'll look after your house on Centaura."

"You look after Elijah. He's a good starat for you," David said with a smile.

"Me look after him? That would make a change," Rhys replied. He grinned and glanced back at Elijah. "He's the one who looks after me."

"We should go," William said, glancing over his shoulder. He offered his hand to Rhys one last time. "Like Nick said, forget who you were as a human. You're no longer that captain who didn't care about the starats on his crew. Richard would be proud of you, and I am too."

Rhys bowed his head. "Thank you," he said, his voice thick as he struggled to speak through a lump in his throat. "That means a lot to me."

"You were a lousy human, but you're a wonderful starat," William said. His eyes sparkled with more than just tears, and his muzzle was pulled up into a grin.

"I'll do my best," Rhys said. He took a couple of steps back, giving room to a few other humans who were trying to get to the airlock doors. Nick and Aaron both moved to stand with the other departing starats, leaving Rhys alone with Elijah. He leaned into the larger starat, resting his head against Elijah's shoulder. He lifted his hand in farewell as, one by one, the starats began to move towards the airlocks.

Nick and Aaron were the first to leave. The human who had started the whole chain of events with his defection and the childhood friend Rhys had forgotten all about. Steph and William followed just after, leaving Twitch and David as the last two to go through the airlock.

Twitch hesitated. He turned around to face Rhys one last time. He lifted his hand, but instead of waving goodbye he saluted Rhys. With a laugh, Rhys saluted Twitch back.

"Hah!" Twitch giggled. He stuck his tongue out. "Knew you couldn't resist. Goodbye, Captain Rhys. Until next time!"

Then he was gone. Twitch turned and scampered inside the airlock, with David by his side. They were quickly lost in the crowd, but Rhys didn't move until the airlock doors had hissed closed. Only then did he allow himself to turn away and drop his arm. For all the noise and activity still around him inside the packed lobby, Rhys felt a crushing sense of loneliness on his shoulders. One that lasted only for a few seconds, when he felt Elijah's arm shift around him.

"Are you alright?" Elijah asked. His hand gently ruffled through the fur on the back of his neck.

"I'll be fine, yeah," Rhys replied. He took a deep breath and wiped the sides of his muzzle with the back of his hand. "How about... how about we go and get some dinner? At that restaurant overlooking the bay that you like?"

Elijah smiled. "That sounds great." His arm squeezed around Rhys's shoulder. He tilted his head back towards the airlock doors as they slowly started to amble away. "I know you love them all, but you'll always have my love too."

The ring Rhys had once given to Stephanie burned a hole in his pocket. His ears curled as they heated up, a blush burning across his face. The question he wanted to ask at the restaurant almost spilled out of his mouth early. He snapped his jaw closed and swallowed the question back.

"I've been a lot of things recently," Rhys said slowly, taking care with his words so he didn't say anything he didn't want to say yet. "I've been a human, a traitor, a heretic. I've been through so much, but in love? That's something I didn't expect to happen again. It's going to be a whole new adventure with you."

"I can't wait to see where it takes us," Elijah said. He paused for a moment to kiss Rhys.

Rhys couldn't believe his luck. He had fought so hard, but now that struggle was over. Terra shone below the Star Hub. A whole new world had been created from the ashes of the Terran Interplanetary Empire. TIE was no more. The Vatican on Mars had crumbled into almost nothing. Everything had changed. Just like Terra, Rhys felt like he was stepping into a fresh new dawn. A new life was waiting for him.

He had been reborn.

J.F.R. Coates